THE TALISMAN

Also by John Godey

THE TALISMAN

by
John Godey

G. P. Putnam's Sons
New York

Copyright © 1976 by John Godey

SBN: 399-11696-6

Library of Congress Cataloging in Publication Data

Godey, John, 1912-
   The talisman.

   I. Title.
PZ4.G57544Tal3 [PS3557.028] 811'.5'4   75-44148

PRINTED IN THE UNITED STATES OF AMERICA

For J.M.F. (1886–1975)

All the characters in this book are fictional. I wish to stress this particularly where characters occupy real and sometimes distinctive positions. I have utilized these positions—some of which used to be known as offices of public trust—for the purposes of the novel and cast them with characters strictly of my own invention. In short, the positions are actual, the characters in them are not, and any resemblance to real people—past, present, or future—is a coincidence.

J. G.

Part I

1

The sentinel stepped out on his left heel, rocked forward to the toe, and with eccentric speed paced along the black strip heel and toe, heel and toe, toward the southern limit of the post. A glint of sunlight curled around the end of his bayonet.

A child's voice tolled off the steps. ". . . sixteen, seventeen, *eighteen!* I counted eighteen, Mother."

Booth, watching the boy's eager bright face turned upward for approbation, stifled an impulse to correct him. The boy's mother beamed and patted his head.

The sentinel halted, stamped his right foot, and executed an exaggeratedly precise left face that turned him toward the marble sarcophagus, a gleaming white bulk just above him; beyond, past the flat sweep of the plaza, the amphitheater reared up, a towering ellipse surrounded by a marble colonnade. Between the sarcophagus and the amphitheater, set flush in the gray granite of the plaza and barely visible from where Booth stood, were the three slabs of white Vermont marble that capped the graves of the Unknowns of World War II, Korea, and Vietnam. The sentinel froze. A small brown bird, perched at the forward edge of the sarcophagus, tilted its head and stared at him.

Booth became aware that the boy was looking up at him with that steady unabashed innocence peculiar to small children and dogs. He met the boy's gaze for a moment, and the boy ducked his head and smiled.

He returned the smile and said, "Twenty-one steps, sonny. You must have missed a few."

The child buried his face in his mother's skirt. The mother scrutinized Booth for a moment, then moved away a few paces.

Booth glanced at his watch and felt a twinge of uneasiness.

The sentinel executed another smart left face, stamped sharply to complete the turn, and then, in an elaborately stylized maneuver of slaps and holds, shifted his rifle from right to left shoulder arms. *In respect for the entombed heroes, the guard bears his rifle on the shoulder away from the graves.* Booth could recite the tourist guidebook from memory. A few shutters clicked, a movie camera whirred. Facing the north end of the post, the sentinel froze in a twenty-one-second pause.

His uneasiness deepening, Booth swept his eyes casually over the onlookers pressing against the chain that separated them from the sentinel. The crowd was unusually large for this time of year, although it was nothing like the mobs that had tumbled out of the Tourmobile buses when he had first begun coming to the tomb site in the summer. Except for a scattering of preschool-age children here and there, most were adults, many of them wearing plastic name tags that identified them as members of the Nonferrous Metal Workers Union. Obviously they were delegates to a convention who were using their spare time to see the capital sights, which, inevitably, included Arlington National Cemetery and the Tomb of the Unknowns.

Booth looked at his watch again. Ten minutes past the hour. He made another sweep of the crowd, no longer concerned with faking detachment now, urged on by anxiety, a dull palpable pressure squeezing up from his ribs against his heart.

Where is Manero?

He turned front and watched the sentinel rock forward and begin his brisk heel-and-toe strut along the rubber mat. A voice to his left and slightly behind him said, "My father fell at St.-Mihiel."

She moved forward into his view, a woman in her early sixties with a serene face and clear forthright blue eyes. Automatically sympathy trembled on his lips: *Sorry. I'm terribly sor-*

ry. But St.-Mihiel was sixty years ago, a trifle late for condolences.

"He was buried where he fell, well, not *exactly,* not in no-man's-land, but in the American Cemetery near St. Mihiel. He was disinterred in 1921—not he alone, you understand, there were three others—and he was selected and returned home on Admiral Dewey's old flagship, the *Olympia.*" Her voice was conversational, an unobtrusive, pleasantly modulated voice that paused briefly, then softened a shade toward being confidential. "And they placed him there"—a neat ecru glove edged in black pointed upward unemphatically at the sarcophagus—"interred him there with great pomp and panoply. Though the sarcophagus was not put up until somewhat later."

He looked at her more closely. Her hair was gray, painstakingly but not elegantly coiffed; her face was plain, redeemed by a lovely smile. A schoolteacher children would like, even cherish. Or a minister's wife, temperately involved in good works?

"I was a small girl when he died. I was born in 1912, and St.-Mihiel was 1918. . . . " The sentinel thumped, and she turned and looked at him for a moment. "So you see I was six when he made the supreme sacrifice, and only nine in 1921, when they brought him here."

What has happened to Manero? Her smile was fixed on him sweetly, soliciting his attention.

"I was here for the interment, don't you know. November eleventh, 1921. Everyone was here. President Harding, Mr. Coolidge, General Blackjack Pershing, Marshal Foch. We came from Waterloo by train, day coach, and because my mother could only afford a single ticket, she held me in her lap."

Waterloo, and by day coach. There goes her credibility, he thought dryly. Her father was Napoleon, and she's the dauphin in drag.

"Waterloo, Iowa, of course."

Of course. He owed her an apology. She entertained no claims to being the dauphin. Now her story had foundation.

"For the past twenty years I've been coming here alone to visit his grave on his birthday. Today he would have been eighty-four. It's strange, isn't it, only eighty-four, considering how remote that war seems. Eighty-four. That's not so terribly old in these days of increased longevity, do you think?"

"Oh, no, certainly not."

"He had blue eyes and fair hair. I'm said to favor him, though my hair"—she touched her head lightly with her gloved hand—"it's all gray now. Perhaps his is, too, or even white. They say that the hair continues to grow after death. Still, it's foolish of me to think of him as white-haired, since he was in his early twenties when he died."

Someone was watching him. He wrenched his gaze away from the mesmerizing blue of the woman's eyes. The crowd was faced to the front, focused on the marching sentinel. Backs of heads, averted profiles. A blue-uniformed security guard lounged against a sawhorse, bored. He checked the crowd again, and this time he found someone looking at him—a young man in a wine-colored leather jacket open on an orange shirt, with a wild head of blond hair falling over his eyes in silky bangs like a sheep dog's.

"Would you like to know how I know it's him?"

The young man was staring at him with an odd mixture of challenge and indifference. But it wasn't Manero. Manero was dark and wore his black hair short and cropped close to the head. Doc had described him as looking like "a Renaissance dog robber." Caro, after studying a photograph, had said that he reminded her of "an easy-living Florentine monk with a taste for French wines and an occasional pretty housemaid or handsome young seminarian, whichever was closer to hand."

The woman's touch was on his sleeve, feathery, uninsistent. "Shall I tell you how I know it's my father?"

He nodded his head politely.

"My mother told me so." She placed her hand on her breast. "She knew it *here*. With certainty. She knew it in her heart."

She lifted her face to him, and if there had been the least

suspicion of triumph in it, he could have moved away. But he saw only earnestness and modesty in the unaltered plainness of her features. So he stood there helplessly as her pleasant commonsense voice continued.

"She simply *knew*. Standing here in 1926, she *knew* whom all those dignitaries were paying homage to. She cried just a little, not out of sorrow but pride. She passed away twenty years ago."

He started to search the crowd again, but her voice drew him back.

"She went before her time, poor soul. Medically sound in every organ. She died of . . . but surely you can guess?"

He shook his head. She would not want him to preempt her secret, and he could not bring himself to do so.

"Of a broken heart," she said matter-of-factly. The blue eyes examined his face and the voice lowered, taking him into her confidence. "The Unknown Soldier of World War One is Corporal Thomas T. Worley, of Waterloo, Iowa. It was *Soldier* then, you know, before they changed it to *Warrior*. He would have been eighty-four years old on this day."

He could no longer bear looking at that honest sensible face. He turned away with a gesture that was part embarrassment, part benediction, then tried to arrest it in midair. His hands, with no place to go, lit on the lapels of his topcoat. His finger brushed the stiff ripples of the tiny American flag pinned to the coat, then closed over it in despair. He was wearing it on the left lapel.

Abruptly he backed out of the crowd, apologizing profusely when he jogged the elbow of a man with a camera to his eye. A murmur rose in the crowd as the relief commander sauntered down the path from the temporary guard barracks at the left of the amphitheater. Booth walked back to the grassy plot between the twin walkways leading out to the road, fumbling at the pin of the metal flag. As much in anger as clumsiness, he pulled the pin away from the left lapel, tearing a few threads.

He remembered—botching the pinning of the flag on his right lapel, dropping it twice before succeeding—that he had made a fuss over not wearing the pin on the traditional left-

hand side. It had struck him as being too standardly con-
spiratorial, like an infantile game the CIA might play. Bùt in
the end, because there had to be some means of assuring his
identification for Manero, and wearing a carnation wasn't
any less objectionable, he had agreed and, of course, had put
the pin on the left lapel. He grimaced, less for his stupidity
than for what it signified in terms of unconscious childish defiance.

And now what? Undoubtedly Manero had shown up,
probably on time, at that, and left when he was unable to find
a man fitting his description and wearing a miniature flag
pinned to his right lapel. Manero would not hang around;
from everything Doc had said about him, he was a man who
kept his own risks at a minimum. Fuck-up, Booth said to
himself bitterly, damn obstinate fuck-up. Maybe Manero
would return. He had no alternative but to hope so. Otherwise they would have to—pretentious word—abort.

He walked back to the crowd, which was pressed up
against the chain now in anticipation of the changing-of-the-
guard ceremony. Off to one side he saw the daughter of the
Unknown of World War I. She was speaking to a young
woman holding an infant in her arms, unemphatic, plausible, her plain features lit up, transformed by her smile. Poor
creature, he thought. Poor creature? But at least she must
know her right lapel from her left.

Cameras were clicking and whirring as the relief commander, at the south end of the post, began his elaborate rit-
ualistic inspection of the newly arrived relief guard. It was
the white-glove inspection to end all white-glove inspections.
He snatched the rifle from the rigidly braced sentinel and
twirled it from position to position with sharp slapping
sounds. His movements were deft and theatrical, made for
show. He brought the piece to his eyes, tilted it to catch the
reflection of any stray mote of dust, whirled it into a new position by tossing it up and catching it in midair like a juggler,
rubbed his white glove briskly over the surface, then held the
hand up and snapped his head around to examine it with
deep suspicion. The crowd ate it up, as well it might. Al-

though Booth had seen it himself dozens of times in the past months, he still found it an intriguing performance.

Somebody is watching me. But when he swept his eyes slowly from left to right and then back again, he saw nothing. Everyone seemed absorbed in the inspection.

The relief commander had tossed the rifle back to the new guard and now faced him squarely, examining him from head to toe with slow deliberation. One of these days, Booth thought, an overzealous commander would run his gloved finger up the guard's nostril to be sure it was passably clear of snot. The notion made him smile, and it occurred to him that it was one of the very few he had allowed himself in the past several months. Well, if he had missed Manero by his own stupidity, it might be the last for many more.

The relief commander stood behind the guard, inspecting the back of his neck—not for dirt, God forbid, but to make sure that it was appropriately clean-shaven. Booth knew the sentinels razored their necks daily and, according to scuttlebutt, pumiced their shoulder patches to make sure that no single filament of the material stood up. The commander's eyes traveled painstakingly down the guard's stiff blue-clad back, checked the gold belt and the hang of the tunic's short skirt. Satisfied at last, he barked an order: "*Shoulder* HARMS!" Ranging himself alongside the guard, he shouted, "*Forrrd* HARCH!" and strode with the new guard to the exact midway point on the black stripping. "*Halt!*" Both men stopped. "*Right* FACE!" The sentinel turned to the crowd, and the commander marched to the north limit of the post, where the old guard, frozen, awaited him.

"Dr. Mastermind, I presume?"

The whisper came from just behind him. Booth stiffened. He watched the old guard and the commander march briskly in step to join the new guard.

"Lapelwise, you got things straightened out finally, right?"

The voice was soft and mocking. Booth turned his head a fraction and caught a glimpse of a shaggy mass of blond hair, a grinning mouth, and smooth plump olive cheeks. He faced front again. The commander stood between the two sentinels. All three were braced, eyes fixed above the heads of the crowd.

The voice said, "You could play the shell game with those soldiers. Shuffle them up and you would never tell one from the other."

In one form or another, visitors to the tomb rarely failed to comment on the alikeness of the sentinels. In fact, as Booth had learned, they were screened as scrupulously for uniformity as frozen fruits and vegetables were. Their height was specified (six one to six three), and beyond that there was some physiological yardstick that measured them for the set of the mouth (no pendulous lips here), the size and shape of the nose (straight, unfleshy), the absence of facial blemishes, the prominence of the cheekbones, and the athletic flatness of the cheeks. Small, darkly tinted sunglasses concealed any possible variation in the color of their eyes.

"You just know that boys like those never jerked off or missed chapel."

Without turning, Booth said, "Who are you?"

"Why, I am Mahster Sergeant Adrian, christened Attilio, known as Al, Manero, all present and accounted for. Sir."

The relief commander began his set speech to the spectators. "Ladies and gentlemen, may I have your attention, please. I am Sergeant Butterworth, Third United States Infantry, the Old Guard, commander of the first relief, Tomb of the Unknowns. We request that everyone remain standing at attention during the changing of the guard and maintain silence. Military personnel in uniform will salute at the command 'Present arms.' Thank you."

"It talks," Manero said.

Following the salute, the retiring guard marched off to the left. The sergeant joined him, checked the breech of his rifle (for what—contraband?), ordered, "*Porrt* HARMS!" and then, "*Fawll* HOUT!" The guard started up the path to the barracks. The sergeant watched the relief guard complete a heel smash and a turn, then went up the path after the off-duty guard. The barracks door opened, and both men disappeared inside.

The crowd dispersed, streaming down the walkways to the

road, where the Tourmobile bus would pick them up and take them on to the old Custis-Lee Mansion.

"I saw you earlier," Booth said to Manero. And then, with a touch of indignation, "Nobody told me about the hair. It's a wig, I suppose."

"Hairpiece, we call it." Manero lifted the blond shock to show his neatly cropped black hair. His eyes were brown, elongated, clever. "The very best Saran. Forty dollars and you only have to wash it every two weeks."

Booth said coldly, "Why didn't you tell us you were going to disguise yourself?"

"What disguise? It's Class A uniform for off the post. No hair, no chicks." The eyes narrowed. "Anybody was in disguise, it was you. Wearing that flag on the wrong lapel. Terrific. It could have fooled anybody."

"All right," Booth said.

"I watched you for thirty minutes." Manero swiveled his neck and rolled his eyes, mimicking furtiveness. "Look, Ma, I'm a conspirator."

She came up from behind Manero, her gloved hand extended. "I wanted to say good-bye to you, sir. I enjoyed our talk."

Her grip was firm. She released Booth's hand, bestowed her lovely smile, then went down the walkway to the road. Home to Waterloo for another year, until the next birthday of Thomas T. Worley, Unknown Soldier of World War I.

"Who's the little lady?"

Manero's smile was insinuating, and Booth fought down an urge to defend the woman. Instead he shrugged and said, "Poor thing. She's slightly demented."

"*She's* demented?-But *you're* okay?"

It was at the very least an arguable point, Booth thought, but inadmissible to oneself as well as to strangers. He said, "Am I going to have trouble with you?"

"You can have it if you want it," Manero said.

Booth shook his head. "No, I can't afford any."

Manero's watchfulness eased. "All right," he said mildly. "Relax. You're all tensed up." His smile, its cunning diluted, offered truce. He tilted his head toward the sentinel, pacing off his post before a handful of spectators. "Six years at Fort Belvoir, and would you believe it, I've never been near this place."

"I've never been to the Statue of Liberty," Booth said, and felt that he was completing a ritual *pas de deux* of peace. "Let's get away from here."

Manero pointed upward. "Which one is it?"

He meant the slabs. "The one at the left," Booth said. "At the right is Korea, and in the center, behind the sarcophagus, Vietnam."

"I saw them plant the Nam vet in '76 on the TV. Big fucking extravaganza."

"Let's take a walk," Booth said.

"Why not the Nam one?" Manero asked. He smiled and answered his own question. "Because it could be a spade, and nobody would give a shit. Right?"

"I've got the money," Booth said.

"Betcher ass, you have," Manero said. He looked at Booth with curiosity. "Was War Two your war?"

"I was in it, if that's what you mean."

"That's what I mean. I didn't think you started it or anything like that."

"Then why ask?"

"Jesus, you're touchy. I'm just trying to place your age. Does that make you touchy, too?"

"I'm fifty-one," Booth said. "I was seventeen years old, right out of high school and into the army."

"My father's fifty-one," Manero said. "But he never associated with a lot of kids twenty years younger than him, and he sure wouldn't be thinking of doing anything like you're doing."

Booth shrugged. The sentinel stamped his foot resoundingly. Booth remembered the chatty security guard who had told him that the heavy shoes had shock-absorbing cleats built into them and that "the general likes to hear heels click."

He turned away. Manero fell in beside him, and they started toward the walkways.

"Will we have the truck?"

"Certainly," Manero said. "The money makes it official. One M-two-ninety-two expansible van truck, two and a half tons, seventeen-foot body, mounted on the M-forty-six chassis."

"Okay," Booth said. He realized he had been holding his breath.

"So now you're all set to go raise hell. Your driver knows what to do?"

"Yes."

"This kind of crime—you know what's going to happen to you if you get caught? I'll tell you: boiled in oil."

Two young girls came up the walkway toward them. When they drew abreast, Manero lifted his absurd wig and tipped it politely. The girls looked startled, then burst into pealing laughter as they hurried on toward the marching sentinel.

Manero crossed the road to the rotunda and Booth followed. They circled the fountain and walked to the balustrade. Below, the land fell away sharply, and Washington lay spread out in the distance. Overhead a 747 climbed up the sky.

"The envelope, please," Manero said.

Booth took the brown envelope from the inner breast pocket of his topcoat and handed it to Manero. It was bound around with a fat rubber band. Manero weighed it pleasurably in his hand and then slipped it into one of the pockets of his leather jacket.

"Five thousand," Booth said. "That's correct, isn't it?"

"You kill me," Manero said. "Your tone. 'That's correct, isn't it?' Talking down your nose, like you're the big fucking aristocrat dealing with somebody in trade. Well, all I'm doing is turning a dishonest little dollar. Compared with that, what you're doing—"

"Keep your voice down," Booth said, looking over his shoulder at the road.

"You think I need five thousand all this bad? I mean, I'm a hustler, but I got some principles, I draw the line. I'll be frank with you. If it wasn't for Doc, for that crazy *cugin'* of mine, I wouldn't have touched it."

"Calm down," Booth said.

21

"I got this fucking Sicilian thing about family. Doc's father and my father were brothers, they loved each other. . . ." Manero squinted upward, where the plane was disappearing. "So in a way *I'm* a bleeding heart, too."

"I appreciate what you're doing," Booth said.

Manero's earnestness dissolved. He looked at Booth mockingly. "But just because I've got family sentiment, I don't lose my head. I oblige my *cugin'*, but I take the cash, too. You, you're one hundred percent bleeding heart, right?"

Booth said nothing. Over Manero's shoulder he caught a glimpse of the Washington Monument, a slender gleaming spire against the blue sky.

"You self-righteous fuckers burn my ass. You know why? Because you go around trying to fix up the world. But the world can't be fixed up. No way, no way. Leave it alone, Chrissake."

"I'll think about it," Booth said. "Did you see the new burial grounds?"

"You think it might turn me on?" Manero patted his bulging pocket. "This is what turns me on."

"We have to pass by it, anyway."

"I hate walking," Manero said. "Nobody walks—that's the motor-pool motto."

As they came out of the rotunda to the road, a Tourmobile bus rumbled by. It pulled in at the mall and unloaded a fresh group of tourists. Many of them wore the name tags identifying them as members of the Nonferrous Metal Workers Union. Some of the men carried their coats over their arms. The sun was high and brilliant, and it warmed up the autumn air to a deceptive summertime softness.

They went on in silence. Manero began to sweat. He walked with his head down, grunting, his pace labored and awkward. Suddenly he stopped and put his hand on Booth's sleeve.

"You hear shots? Rifle fire."

"Carbines. Three shots. There's a burial. Listen."

The soft air brought the sound of taps to them in snatches, sweetly sad and elusive. The long sustained final note died away. They started walking again.

"That's how they plant them?" Manero asked. "With volleys and sad music? A hero's burial." He was silent for a moment, panting. "I wonder where he fought."

"Or *if* he fought. It might have been a spouse or child or some Congressman with a wartime light colonelcy, a big desk in Washington, and a uniform tailored by Brooks Brothers. He might never have seen an army camp, much less a battlefield.

"They let fucking Congressmen in? Then they damn well don't bury Manero here."

"Don't worry. By the time you're ready there won't be any more room. Not here or in any of the other national cemeteries."

"What do you know?" Manero looked shaken.

"They're running out of room for the dead. There are about a hundred of these cemeteries throughout the country, and a third of them are already filled to capacity. In some of them they're burying eligible people—spouses and minor children—vertically."

"Vertically?" Manero was shocked again. "Does that mean what I think it means? Standing up?"

Booth smiled. "No. In tiers, one on top of another."

Manero seemed relieved. "Well, as long as they're together, right?"

"Arlington is taking over about two hundred acres of the south post of Fort Myer. That'll last until about 1984, barring a brushfire war or two, and then they'll be fresh out of burial ground here."

A black sedan approached them from behind and swung out wide to pass them. The car was marked U.S. ARMY, CEMETERY SECURITY FORCE. Two blue-uniformed men sat in the front seat, relaxed. The car disappeared around a turn.

"What do those jokers do?" Manero said.

"They patrol the cemetery."

"At night, too?"

Booth nodded. "All night."

"What happens if they spot you? Don't tell me." He sighted an imaginary gun. "*Ratatatat.* Shoot the ears off them. Right?"

"We're not going to shoot anybody," Booth said.

"With Asbury around? He'd shoot his own mother just to hear the bang."

"No shooting. That includes Asbury."

"You got a clear understanding, right? No shooting. Those cops in those cars got the same understanding?"

Yes, it was a unilateral understanding, Booth thought. If there was shooting, they would be sitting ducks.

"It's one thing, you know." Manero said, "when you can shoot back. That's why wars are tolerable. *Some* wars. That old war of yours was an okay war, wasn't it? I mean, as wars go."

To their right lay a gently sloping burial ground with hundreds of general-issue tombstones. The stillness was pervasive; the Georgia marble of the tombstones appeared pristine and unweathered in the sunlight. "A lovely place for the dead to rest," Booth had once heard a woman on a Tourmobile bus say. "They must be so happy."

"A triumph of military organization," he said. "From whatever angle you look at them, whatever row you follow, any line or any diagonal, they're perfectly lined up like soldiers on parade."

Manero gave the burial ground a brief uninterested glance. "What was your rank? Were you a combat soldier?"

"I was a combat soldier." He paused self-consciously. "By the time I was mustered out I was a major. Infantry."

"Infantry," Manero said. "Dog's work. Stupid. You have to make the army work for you. If you use your brains, it's an easy hustle. I got rackets going for myself all over the place. Mostly I run a car-rental business with the army's vehicles. I'm the Hertz of Fort Belvoir. I'm making lots of money, building up my capital, and I'm learning all about how power operates. Another couple of years and I'll get out and make it work for me on the outside. How much farther, Chrissake? My arches are breaking down."

"Not much farther. Did Doc tell you we're going to weld some of our machinery to the floor and roof of the truck? We'll remove it later, but there will be scars."

Manero shrugged. "One way or another, that truck is going to be identified."

24

"I wouldn't want you boiled in oil."

"Manero?" He tapped his heaving chest. "Don't worry about Manero. Worry about yourself. Doc swears by you. He told me your whole history, and what stands out is that you're a good man. But you never won anything in your life. You're a loser. All through your whole life you're a loser, and that means only one thing—you *want* to be a loser."

"Look," Booth said, "I don't really give a damn what you think about me."

Manero's eyes narrowed shrewdly. "Wrong. That's your trouble, you *do* give a damn. Me? The only opinion of myself that I respect is my own. If my mind worked like yours, I'd kill myself."

They turned a bend in the road and a riffle of wind tugged at Manero's wig. He put his hand on his head to anchor it.

"That's it, just ahead," Booth said.

The grounds comprised three acres, fronting the road and running back on an irregular upward slope. Dozens of shade trees had been spared so that, Booth thought, it, too, would be a lovely place for the dead to lie. But at this point it resembled any other construction site in an early phase. It was a clutter of turned-up earth, boulders disturbed from a thousand-year rest, uprooted trees, piles of rubble, trenches, holes, and a crisscrossing series of ruts and goudges. Strewn about randomly was a clutter of machines, vehicles, and implements—bulldozers, backhoes, dump trucks, army trucks, several trailers serving as headquarters for the various contractors. Here and there signs were planted on poles in the soft earth. CUDONE BROTHERS, GENERAL CONTRACTING. VITELLI AND SONS, LANDSCAPING. The largest, in red and green lettering, and bearing the familiar castellated insignia, stated that the project was under the jurisdiction of the Army Corps of Engineers.

"That's where you're going to be tomorrow night?" Manero said.

A group of men in hard hats were working near the road, bare to the waist, sunburned, muscular.

"Yes," Booth said. "Up above, as far away from the road as possible." It would be an agonizing wait, but there was no al-

25

ternative. The only way to be in the cemetery before it opened in the morning was to go in the night before.

"About fifteen hours? I'd flip if I had to sit in a truck for fifteen hours. Or anyplace else. I don't care how scintillating the company is. Not to mention having to pee. You better put a potty in the truck."

Cardboard boxes, lined up neatly on the verge of the road, contained mulch, bone meal, tree bark and—Manero, seeing them, said, "Holy Christ!"—box after box of GI headstones, their rounded ends up, standing erect on their own weight.

They moved on. Manero was silent until the road leveled and he could catch his breath. Then he said, "I'll tell you something, Booth—it's too crazy."

Booth had to steel himself to keep from looking back at the site.

"What I mean by that: things that are a *little* crazy sometimes work. But things that are *too* crazy, they never work. One little item gets screwed up, and that screws up everything else, and it all falls apart and you've got some kind of massacre."

"It will work," Booth said.

"You know," Manero said, "one way or another, you're going to throw the entire fucking country into an uproar."

"Yes," Booth said. "That's the idea."

In the parking lot, a short distance from the Visitors Center, Manero led the way to his car, a low-slung fire-engine-red Alfa-Romeo convertible with the top down.

"My sweetheart," he said, running his hand over the fender. "I wish I could tell you how I promoted it. . . ." He cocked a black curving eyebrow. "Want me to drop you off someplace?"

"Thanks, no." Booth shook his head. He had had his fill of Manero. "I'm not leaving yet." He watched Manero climb into the car and settle himself behind the wheel. "I want to thank you, whatever your motivation."

Manero turned the ignition key and the car started with a roar. He gunned the motor, then let it ease down to a soft purr. He listened to it appreciatively. "Beautiful." He clutched, slid his floor stick into low, then shifted back to neutral again. He squinted upward. "So tell me, what's *your* motivation? I mean, leveling all the way, not what you tell yourself, but the deep-down truth."

Feeling outsize, Booth looked down at the ridiculously low car and said nothing. What would Manero know of any truths but his own?

"I know why Doc, for instance, is doing it," Manero said. "He was in Nam, he hated it, the war, the reasons for it, the killing, the shit, everything connected with it. He still does. Fucking Sicilians, right? They never quit. Maybe some of the others, like Asbury, it's the excitement. I know why *I'm* doing it—a little bit for my cousin, a little bit for five grand. But you. You weren't anyplace near Nam, your war was three wars ago. I know why you *think* you're doing it or *think* you think you're doing it, but what's the deep-down underneath reason?"

"It's a matter of conscience." But the answer was a declination of Manero's invitation to search his soul and he knew it, and so must Manero. "It's that simple."

Manero looked up at him for a moment, then swept his blond shaggy wig off his head and tossed it on the seat beside him. "It blows off when I got the top down." He put his hand on the gearshift knob. "Well, best of luck."

Booth nodded. Then, because the gesture seemed ungracious, or as if to recapture some intimacy that had never really existed between them, he said, "I'll remember you to Doc and Asbury."

"Asbury is an asshole," Manero said. "You'll find out. *Contact.*"

The car leaped away with a roar. Booth watched it speed toward the exit, a red streak punctuated by Manero's sleek black head. The car made a squealing turn and disappeared. Slowly Booth began to walk to the Visitors Center. He had been on his feet all day. He felt very tired.

2

After Manero's alien self-serving assertiveness, the Parmentiers were like a return to the old homestead. Although they had never met, they were to recognize each other at first sight as congeners. Here his motives were not questioned but honored.

The Parmentiers lived ten minutes from the center of Alexandria, on a backwater country road. Booth noted with satisfaction that he had not seen a single car since entering it. A mile or so farther on, the taxi stopped with a certain tentativeness before a large weathered house behind a labyrinthine tangle of denuded forsythia bushes. An oversized mailbox with PARMENTIER painted on it in shiny red nail polish stood atop a post beside the road.

"This is the place." Booth got out and paid the driver.

The house was a thing of afterthoughts, of unexpected additions built on helter-skelter, as if on impulse. It needed paint badly, and the gutters were twisted and in places rusted through. The barn was off to the right and set back deeper than the house on a rutted path curving off from the packed dirt driveway. The barn was large, and it would serve well, Booth thought, if only it held up for forty-eight hours and didn't simply subside from natural causes.

While he was trying to guess which part of the house was its entrance, he heard voices and walked toward them to the rear of the house. There, where the land dipped, and beyond a series of patches that appeared to be vegetable gardens, he saw a tall bearded man chopping wood, grunting as he swung an ax with tremendous force and no great accura-

cy. Closer to the house, wearing a man's mackinaw and a friv-
olous pink tam on a lustrous fall of ash-blond hair that
reached halfway down her back, a pale young woman was
chattering to a child who was grubbing at the earth with a
tiny hand. Bent forward effortlessly, doubled on himself, the
child suddenly raised his hand. A thin squirming worm tried
to escape through his fingers.

The woman clapped her hands in applause and said, "But
don't hurt it, Jamie."

The child smiled and tried to put the worm in his mouth.

The woman said quietly, "No, I don't think so. It would
hurt the worm, wouldn't it?"

The worm writhed out of the child's chubby fingers and
fell to the ground. The child's smile vanished. The bearded
man discovered Booth. The child, regarding his empty
hand, squealed with anger.

"Bruce Parmentier? I'm Ken Booth."

Parmentier dropped his ax and strode forward eagerly, his
hand extended. His smile was boyish, a bright glow in the
forbiddingness of his huge black beard. The girl was watching them gravely.

"Steph, this is Ken Booth. Stephanie, my wife. And the little one is Jamie."

The woman got to her feet and put out her hand. She was
fragile, tired-looking. She had beautiful teeth.

"It's so nice to know you, Mr. Booth." A warm and courte-
ous voice, its modulation not acquired, Booth thought, but
inbred. Her father—he risked a trifling speculation—was a
corporation lawyer worth at least two million.

Jamie, unable to find his worm, was red-faced, grunting
with frustration.

"Are you hungry?" Parmentier said. "Have you had
lunch?"

Stephanie scooped up the baby and they all entered the
house through a screen door that led directly into a large
cluttered kitchen. Booth and Parmentier sat down at a round
kitchen table covered with worn discolored linoleum scarred
here and there by ancient knife wounds.

Stephanie, holding Jamie on her hip, brought vegetables,

beach plum jelly in a mason jar, a giant loaf of whole wheat bread. He didn't need to be told that the bread was home-made and of all natural ingredients, that the outsize carrots, peppers, tomatoes, and grotesquely misshapen radishes came from their own garden, unfed by chemical nutrients.

He ate hungrily and they watched him with approval. He apologized to them for his appetite and, to himself, for a cer-tain snideness that had crept into his thoughts when he had categorized the ecology of their table.

Parmentier, his large, weather-cracked hands folded on the table, said earnestly, "We're delighted to have you here." He smiled. "You know, in our little underground world you're a sort of celebrity."

His mouth full, Booth protested. He welcomed the diver-sion when Stephanie poured coffee for him. She had put Ja-mie down on the linoleum floor, where he was crawling in pursuit of something else that moved.

Still holding the pot, she said, "We do admire you," and Booth thought: Five years ago she might have used the same words, with the same artless simplicity and lack of preten-sion, to the jockey who had ridden her father's horse. Re-move the mackinaw and the funny hat, dress her in the ap-propriate gown and add a touch of pink to her lips, and she would be ideal in the role of a girl being presented at the Court of St. James'.

Parmentier picked up on her statement. "We do, you know. Not so much because you've seen the inside of a jail or been slugged with a nightstick—we've all had the same ex-perience—but because you didn't *have* to, you *opted* for it, whereas we . . . it was *natural*." He stopped and looked helplessly at Stephanie.

Smiling, Booth came to his rescue. "You're trying to avoid saying that I'm an old man in a young man's game. Or that fighting injustice is an inherited trait of the young but an ac-quired one of the old."

"You made sacrifices we didn't have to make. You changed your life."

"So did you."

"Yes, but we were younger, and we experienced the war, so that our indignation was firsthand. Oh, Christ, I'm messing it up."

Stephanie walked calmly to Jamie and bent over him. She fished in his mouth and extracted something alive. Jamie howled. She picked him up, tucked him under her arm, and went out of the room.

Parmentier followed her with his eyes, then said in a subdued voice, "I told Stephanie about it. I don't know whether I was supposed to or not, but we tell each other everything. Do you mind?"

Booth spread his hands. "Well, you've already told her."

"She thinks it's magnificent."

"It's a criminal act. I hope she realizes that."

"Don't talk to me about crime. I spent three miserable years living with it. . . ."

At Yale he had been an editor of the *Law Review*. The doors of Park Avenue offices had been wide open to him. His father, like Stephanie's, was a partner in a distinguished law firm. He had chosen instead the nitty-gritty of work as public prosecutor of a small town in New Jersey. But he had had no vocation for it. In fact, he had been horrified by his brief, which charged him with trying to send to prison social outcasts, misfits, the criminally insane. The problem was that he kept looking behind their transgressions, which were frequently ugly, vicious, mindless, to the poverty and brutality of their lives, their social handicaps, the system that doomed them from birth because they were black or foreign or the spawn of poor white families. X-ray vision, a fatal affliction. So he had quit a step ahead of being fired for having the worst prosecutory track record in the state and opened his own office to defend the very people he had formerly prosecuted.

"But you know what happened? The same people that beat the rap when I was prosecuting them were going to jail when I defended them!"

Well, no, that was a little joke. He worked like a dog for his clients, usually without pay, and a fair proportion of them

were adjudged innocent. But—and this, finally, caused him to give up the law in despair—as often as not, it was the guilty who went free, the innocent who were punished.

"Given that the advocacy—mine—was as competent and dedicated for both, for those I knew were innocent and those I knew were guilty, the fault must be with the law. My conscience started troubling me again—as much for the guilty I helped free as the innocent I saw sent to jail."

So, one fine day he had let his beard grow out, given away all of his J. Press suits and Brooks Brothers shirts and ties, looked for a place in Maryland but settled for this one instead, and moved in with Stephanie. They earned enough to live on by selling their vegetables (could there be a market, Booth wondered, for radishes that looked like giant carbuncles?), by reading proof for a law journal (Parmentier), and selling occasional articles to an architectural magazine (Stephanie, who was a qualified architect).

"We're happy," Parmentier said. "Our life is free of, well, crap."

But Manero was happy, too, Booth thought, and his life was not free of crap, but founded on it. The bluebird of happiness was a most adaptable bird! He looked at his watch, and Parmentier was at once apologetic.

"Here I am mouthing off, wasting your time. . . ."

Parmentier insisted on taking him out to the barn without further delay. He tugged the huge doors open after removing a two-by-four from wooden hasps. Filaments of cobweb floated down, and spiders, dislodged from their broken nests, moved sluggishly for cover. The barn was cavernous, and it stank of decades of offal, animal bodies, rotted vegetation, and age. The molding floor was littered with old artifacts: harnesses, a rotting saddle, broken ladders, an antique harrow, milking pails, feeding troughs, remnants of stanchions.

Parmentier was looking at him with anxiety, as though he were on trial.

Booth said, "Well, we'll have to run two trucks in here and shut the doors after they're in. . . ."

"All this junk? Don't worry about it. I'll shift it all to the back of the barn. There'll be enough room for a dozen trucks."

"Can you manage it by yourself?" Some of it appeared rusted into the ground, annealed to the earth it had once mastered.

"I won't be doing it alone. Stephanie will help." He smiled and said with pride, "She may not look it, but Stephanie is very strong."

Looking deep into the ancient shadows of the barn, Booth said, "There's considerable risk, you know."

"Nothing like the rest of you will be taking."

"If things go wrong, Stephanie could be cited as an accessory. And where will that leave Jamie?"

"Jamie is an accessory, too." Parmentier's white teeth shone through the thicket of his beard. Then, more soberly, he said, "If we don't take risks for what we believe in, we don't take risks for *anything*. And that means we don't *believe* in anything. And what is life without belief?"

If he had fed juries such homilies when he was public prosecutor or, for that matter, counsel for the defense, it was little wonder that he had not won many cases, Booth thought, and at once reproved himself. Parmentier meant what he said and was not squeamish about saying it, however pious it might sound.

Booth said, "There's not much risk involved with the Drivurself—it's a common enough vehicle—but the Engineers van . . . and we'll be running it in in broad daylight and then out again an hour or so later."

"It's a mostly black neighborhood, and very few outsiders ever come through it. There's not much traffic at any time. You saw that yourself, didn't you?"

Booth nodded. "If it's spotted and somebody reports having seen it later on. . . ." He became aware that Stephanie had slipped into the barn.

Parmentier said, "We understand about the risks. And compared to the chances the rest of you will be taking. . . . Steph?"

The Talisman

"It's perfectly all right," Stephanie said. "We don't mind." She smiled and her pale face became illuminated, almost mischievous.

"When you clean up in here," Booth said, "keep in mind that we'll want some extra space to stack the furniture." He looked into the gloomy depths of the barn. "Is there any kind of light in here?" But he knew the answer before Parmentier shook his head. "We'll bring some kerosene lanterns along with us. Do you have many visitors?"

"Almost none. We've invited our neighbors to come visit us, but . . . I don't know, they just won't mingle."

Babes in the woods, Booth thought. They didn't perceive that their black neighbors, far from being pleased by the idea of a white man breaking the code by moving in, would be suspicious, resentful, even contemptuous of it.

"Well, that eliminates that problem." Booth paused. "That's all, except that when it's done, well, you're going to hear a great deal about villainy, depravity, moral obloquy. We're going to be denounced from one end of the world to the other. There won't be a single voice raised on our behalf."

Parmentier and Stephanie were half smiling at each other, and Booth realized they were mildly embarrassed for his inability to accept that they were consciously committed and prepared for much worse consequences than merely being condemned by people whose views they scorned anyway.

He said, "All right. Thank you."

They both laughed and then, successively, embraced him. He felt the tender pressure of the girl's breasts. Parmentier scraped his face with the roughness of his beard and hugged him.

Over Booth's protests, Parmentier insisted on driving him back to his hotel. He sat alongside Parmentier in the front seat of a dilapidated pickup truck, incongruous in his tweed topcoat, striped tie, and near-crew haircut as they rattled through the antiseptic boulevards of Washington's Northwest. As they approached the hotel, he recalled the bedrock

34

chastity of the Parmentiers' style of living and felt impelled to apologize for the elegance, however temporary, of his own.

"It was the only place that had a room available, other-wise—"

"Look," Parmentier said earnestly, "you *deserve* the best."

Directing him into the circular drive, Booth thought, I could tell him I liked to fuck turtles, and he would rationalize it into something admirable. The doorman's face froze at the sight of the pickup truck, but he bit the bullet and came forward to open the door.

"See you tomorrow," Booth said.

"Tomorrow."

The pickup roared away. The doorman, still game, ran ahead and started the revolving door for him. Booth went through the bustling lobby and rode up in the elevator to his room. He lay down on the bed and started to reach for the phone, but inertia weighed his arm down and he never made it. His eyes closed with exhaustion.

In the adjoining seat on the plane, Manero challenged him, his ancient Renaissance eyes slanting mockingly. "So tell me about your motivation. I mean the deep-down, *deep-down* truth."

Manero was extraordinarily clever. Devoid of guilt or pity himself, he characterized those traits as weaknesses. Tone deaf himself, he could draw music from the conscience of others. Cheap, phony hustler, why didn't he just throw him out of the goddamn plane?

"Not what you *believe* you believe, but the real deep-down inside of you, under the hide of you." Manero was singing his words.

"Bastard, I told you why: a matter of conscience."

"No good. Too easy."

"Moral indignation, a sense of justice, even, yes, yes, love of my country, of its sad corrupted people."

"Selfless, right? Well, that's the greatest selfishness of all."

"Venality is thinking that everybody is as venal as your-self."

"Don't throw your cheap aphorisms at me. Instead, get to the underneath. Draw up a bill of particulars. I'll help you. One: attempt to recover your lost youth. Two: sneaking affection for the army, when you took pleasure in your skill at killing people."

"Shut your ugly mouth! I hated war, hated the tyranny of the army, most of all hated killing!"

"All retroactive. When you were doing it, you loved it."

"Manero, you're a fucking liar. There is no bill of particulars."

"And above all, vanity."

Booth raged silently until the plane landed. He found a taxi and went home. He pushed the bedroom door open, and it creaked silently. The contrariety puzzled him, and he paused a second on the threshold before entering the room. Caro lay naked on the bed, her legs spread apart, writhing, with a boy on top of her, handsome as a statue, his rump rising and falling, graceful, rhythmic. Caro lifted her head, craning over the boy's plunging shoulder, and said reproachfully, "It's the last word in inconsiderateness to arrive in the middle of someone's fucking me."

He retreated to the living room, but Caro was there before him, her flesh soft and dusky in the subdued light.

"Remember," she said, no longer reproachful but saddened, as if by a predictable betrayal, "you promised me you would understand."

"I haven't forgotten. I did say I would understand if you found somebody attractive and wanted. . . ." His voice trailed off.

"Well, then?"

"I don't want you to *want* to!"

She said gently, "No matter how fast you run, you can't overtake a generation."

Item one in the bill of particulars: Recapture lost youth. He heard Manero laugh.

Pleading silently, he followed her back to the bedroom, where the boy was still propped up on his elbows. She slid beneath him into position.

* * *

36

He opened his eyes and lay still for a moment to adapt to being awake, then roused himself to look at his watch. It was six o'clock, and he had promised Caro he would call no later than five. He went into the bathroom and threw cold water on his face, then gargled, as if to wash away the aftertaste of his dream.

He gave the operator his number. Still foggy, when the ringing began he braced himself. If a man answers, hang up. Christ, it was only a silly dream! Caro answered.

"Caro?"

"Yes. Is it all right?"

"I'm sorry about being late."

"Is it all right?"

He saw her at the phone, a cigarette in her mouth, her head tilted, the gray eyes squinted against the smoke. She was wearing the faded blue jumper, a perfect backdrop to the tawniness of her skin.

He said, "It's all right. It's fine. Everything is arranged. Will you call them and tell them so?"

"Yes. As soon as we're finished." She coughed, turned her head away from the phone.

"Caro?"

"Yes?"

He thought of Stephanie Parmentier, of her delicate breasts pressed in innocence against his body, and his emotion overflowed, merged with his feelings for Caro. But he couldn't bring himself to speak of them. The dream haunted him like a guilt.

"Ken? Is there anything else?"

"Yes." He paused. "You ought to cut down on your smoking."

"I know. But this isn't the best time for it, is it?"

He attempted a laugh that failed badly. "I guess one of us should say something memorable."

"Ken?"

"Yes."

"Be careful, please."

"Yes, all right." He looked through the window of his room at the jutting wall of a courtyard. A portion of the red brick was stained by a scaly white exzema. "Do you remember when I first called you from this hotel, after I had met Bateman? Well, I think it's the same room."

"It seems a long time ago."

"Two months, that's all."

"Well, it seems a long time ago." She was silent, and with nothing to say to fill the gap, he listened to the hum of the wires. "I'd better start calling them, Ken."

"Yes. I'll see you Wednesday night, Caro."

"Okay."

She hung up.

He held the phone, reluctant to break the connection with her. But it occurred to him that with the circuit unbroken, she wouldn't be able to use the phone. He hung up.

3

Asbury awoke, as he had bidden himself to do, at five. He stirred and brushed against Caro's softness. She lay on her back, covered to the top of her nose. He propped himself on an elbow, peering down at her through the predawn grayness, then started to draw the blanket down. Still asleep, in a protective reflex, whether against the chill of the room or in some virginal atavism, she clutched the blanket. He yanked it through her fingers and uncovered her breasts. She opened her eyes and stared at him blankly.

He flipped the blanket off her body and rolled over on top of her. He said, "One for the road, baby."

Her eyes opened wide, offended, but he had already begun to part her thighs with a cleaving palm, and her defense crumbled. She closed her eyes, sighing, and raised her body to receive him. Her arms encircled his neck, her legs lifted, and her heels nested in the sockets of his hips.

When they were finished, she withdrew immediately to her privacy, although she was still pinned beneath him. For a moment, with malice, he pressed down on her and heard her grunt with discomfort before, pushing upward, he vaulted clear of her body and the bed in a single athletic spring.

She drew the blanket up under her chin and rolled away. He went into the bathroom, where he used what he hoped was Booth's toothbrush. He grimaced at his short blond hair and patted cold water on the nape of his shorn neck. He hated the plucked look, although he couldn't deny that long hair would have been a giveaway. And it did restore the natural toughness of appearance that the old Prince Val hairdo had tempered. He went back to the bedroom.

He was pulling on his socks, still naked, when he noticed the photograph on the bed table. He put on his Levi's and shirt, then took the picture in its metal-lined frame to the window. He tilted the blind and held the photograph at an angle to direct the light across its glossy surface. The likeness was unmistakably of Booth, thirty-odd years younger, his features barely formed, the jawline tender, wearing an army uniform with a bar on each shoulder.

Smiling, Asbury went back to the bed. He nudged Caro's shoulder. "What kind of an asshole would keep something like this beside his own bed?"

She opened her eyes and focused on the picture. "Put it back."

"That's no answer." She pulled the blanket over her head and he raised his voice. "I'll *tell* you why. Because that crappy war was the high point of his life. That's why he thought this whole deal up—to relive the bold brave days of his youth."

Her voice muffled by the blanket, she said, "Oh, shut up."

"To prove he isn't over the hill. To compensate for what he can't perform in bed. He's a jerk."

She opened her eyes. "He's not a jerk, and he's not bad in bed, either. Just because I let you sleep with me is no reason to draw dumb conclusions."

"*Let* me sleep with you. You're so goddamn horny you'd let a banana fuck you."

"You *are* a banana." She retreated beneath the blanket again. Asbury stared at her for a moment, then shrugged. He put on his combat boots and sheepskin jacket and went out.

It was growing light and the weather promised to be clear. The West Village streets, an hour or two before the hard usage of the day began, seemed fresh and expectant. Asbury's shaved nape felt the bite of the wind, and he turned his sheepskin collar up. He found a cruising taxi on Eighth Street and gave the driver the address of the Drivurself office uptown.

The clerk at Drivurself was heavy-lidded and bored. He

found the reservation card for the medium panel truck quickly enough, but dawdled over the forms.

Asbury fidgeted. "Look, if you don't mind, I've got a long way to go and I'd like to get started."

"Take it easy," the clerk said, "you'll live longer."

Asbury bent far over the counter toward the clerk. "Don't give me any fucking advice. Just fill out that form and keep your fucking mouth shut."

They were alone in the office. The clerk assessed the flushed face an inch from his own, and the threat of the long rangy body, and said nothing. He lowered his head to his work. Asbury held his position, knowing that his closeness was a continuing menace.

Carefully masking his resentment, the clerk put the form on the counter. "Sign here and here, Mr. Hart."

The driver's license belonged to a vet who had learned to mainline in Nam and had recently flipped out disastrously. He was upstate in a laughing academy and a strong candidate for prefrontal lobotomy. His name was Tom Hart and his signature was ideal for forging: it was short, and it was a large childish script. Asbury had practiced it an hour a day over the past week, and he signed it now with confidence. The clerk, intimidated, barely compared it with the signature on the license. He handed Asbury a duplicate of the form and returned the license.

"It's all ready for you, sir," the clerk said. He pointed to a painted steel door leading to the garage. "Right through there." The clerk turned on a weak smile. "Lovely day for driving."

Asbury recognized with a thrill of pleasure that the clerk was now thoroughly cowed. Too bad he hadn't been able to achieve the same effect with the girl. Maybe he should have smashed that stupid picture. Over her head. He pushed open the door to the garage. A shiny green panel truck was waiting, its motor running. A black kid in dungarees and a T-shirt held the door for him.

"One of the new ones," the kid said. "Less than two hundred miles on it."

"So?"

"I picked it out special. If I wanted, I could have given you one of the old crates."

Asbury paused, halfway into the truck. "What's the going rate?"

"I don't specify. Whatever you feel it's worth."

"I feel it's worth zip, nothing." Asbury said. "Any comments?"

The kid looked at him for an instant, his face stolid, then turned away. Asbury laughed, swung up into the truck, and shot out through the garage opening into the quiet street. As he headed east a golden sun flooded through the windshield into the cab.

The flooring of the house, Eddie Raphael was fond of saying, had the give of a trampoline, and in normal circumstances he would have heard Paula moving about overhead. But his first awareness of her came when she spoke to him from the cellar stairs.

She said, "Jason is awake. He's crying."

The tarp was stiff, and in trying to mold it to the shape of the vacuum pump, he had cut his finger superficially. But it continued to bleed stubbornly.

"You're hurt," Paula said.

"Tell Jason to go back to sleep," Raphael said. "Don't let him come down here."

She checked behind her to make sure she had shut the cellar door. "I warned him he wasn't to come down. He'll obey *that* much, but I can't get him to stop crying. It's very atypical of him."

Raphael grunted, tugging at a slipknot in the nylon cord he had thrown around the tarp. He braced his foot against the tarp for leverage. His shoe left a dusty imprint on the canvas.

Paula said, "He's aware that something extraordinary is going on." She paused and added almost bitterly, "Is that so surprising?"

"Just tell him I'll be back *soon*."

"Do you think that will satisfy *Jason? He* says you're *never* coming back."

Raphael frowned at the ungainliness of his package. "Tell him I'll be back tomorrow."

"Eddie! We don't lie to each other, and we've never lied to Jason, either."

"You already *have*, by telling him I was going away on a business trip."

"Could I have *possibly* told him the truth? Was there any conceivable way of doing that?"

She came all the way down the stairs. She was barefoot and in her nightgown. Her face was blotchy; her eyes were ringed from lack of sleep. It troubled him that she should look so unattractive all because of him. He took her in his arms. She clung to him tightly.

"Eddie, I don't want you to go." She was half sobbing.

She pressed herself against him, and he knew she was trying to arouse him. He tried to disengage himself. She clung.

"Paula, for God's sake, go upstairs and take care of Jason."

"You've already done more than your share with all this." She gestured at the cluttered cellar floor. "It isn't fair that you should have to go, too."

"I *don't* have to, Paula. I *chose* to."

She was struggling to reach him with her questing body, and he was holding her off at arm's length.

He said, "You told me you accepted my going."

"That was when it was just an idea. I approved of the idea, I don't approve of. . . . Oh, Eddie, I don't approve of your *dying.*"

She broke his hold and writhed against him, and he felt himself begin to erect. He pushed her off again. "Stop it, Paula." He turned his wrist to look at his watch. "Asbury should be here any minute, and I'm not finished yet. Go upstairs and try to keep Jason busy."

"He's crying. Don't you understand? He won't tolerate my trying to keep him busy."

"Then go up and stop his crying."

He pulled away from her and gave his attention to the vacuum-head frame, which was lying in the center of another tarp. It would have been a very simple matter to construct if it hadn't been for the reinforcement struts, coming up out of the frame itself and forming an arch. But, given the weight they would be working against, he had had to take precautions to make certain the frame wouldn't buckle.

"Even if it does work," Paula said from behind him, "even if the whole thing does come off, they're never going to stop searching for you, no matter if it's years, decades. How can we exist like that?"

"That's nonsense. Once it's all over, we'll be in the clear."

"You'll all go down in history as the most unfeeling monsters of all time. You know that, don't you?"

"Only the people whose opinion we don't care about will feel that way. You believe in what we're doing, don't you?"

"Of course I do, but. . . ." Her voice became a wail, and he knew that soon the tears would come. "But I don't want you to be hurt, in any sense."

"Nobody's going to get hurt." He folded a stiff section of the tarp over the frame, then sidled to another corner, keeping his back to her. "No dying. Nobody hurt."

He wished he believed it was true. He wished she believed it. And he wished Jason believed it, although he knew that Jason somehow sensed everything, although he had been told nothing. Jason, he was prepared to admit, would have been burned for a witch in any other age than this. And perhaps in this one, too.

"He's here," Paula said. "I heard a car door slam."

Asbury was already knocking at the curtained door that led to the outside. Raphael let him in. Even wheeling a dolly, Asbury's arrogance and recklessness of bearing were in no way ameliorated. Before he shut the door, Raphael caught a glimpse of a green truck in the driveway.

Asbury looked around him with his hands on his hips. "God damn it, you were supposed to have all this shit wrapped up by the time I got here."

"Don't call it shit," Paula said. "If it weren't for what you call shit in your ignorance—"

"Paula," Raphael said, "go upstairs to Jason."

"You're going to come up and say good-bye to us before you go, aren't you?"

"Of course. I'll have the rest of this packed in about ten minutes." He saw her expression and knew she was aware that he was appeasing Asbury, not her. At the same time, he realized that Asbury was ogling her near nakedness. "Go upstairs, Paula."

"And we'll be up to say good-bye," Asbury said, smiling.

She started up the basement steps. Her nightgown was caught in the cleft of her buttocks, and Asbury was watching her openly.

"How about lending a hand?" Raphael said.

Asbury ignored him until Paula went through the door and shut it behind her.

Doc stood at the window and watched the green Drivurself pull up below and double-park. Asbury and Raphael got out; Asbury opened the rear of the truck and took out a dolly and started to hump it up the curb. Raphael gestured vigorously. Asbury dropped the dolly and went back and locked the doors of the truck.

Doc grinned. Typical Asbury. A good man in a fight, but not a genius for details. It occurred to him that outside of himself he had never met anyone who liked Asbury, not even other Movement people; or anyone, except himself, who wasn't afraid of Asbury. But *he* wasn't afraid of Asbury because he wasn't afraid of *anybody*. That unusual trait, an army psychiatrist had once told him, was compensation for being a sawed-off runt. Actually, he was five seven and a fraction, which wasn't all that runty, though it was more than half a foot smaller than Asbury.

Asbury was a shit, but he couldn't help liking him, mainly because he didn't dislike anybody, either. *That*, the psychiatrist had said, was a seriously disturbing factor; it wasn't healthy to like everybody.

"So you'd like to cure me, make me a normal human being who hates people?"

"That's an unfair way to put it, but I would like to work with you."

"Fuck off," Doc had said. "I'm no fucking white mouse."

45

The psychiatrist, who was by rank a major, had taken offense, but, because he was a psychiatrist before he was a major, had subordinated umbrage to curiosity.

"You're not afraid of me?"

"Shit, no."

"Not that I would do it," the psychiatrist said, "but I could put your ass in a sling for talking to an officer like that. Doesn't that concern you?"

"Why should it concern me? Like you said, you wouldn't do it."

"But you didn't know that until I said so myself."

Grinning, Doc said, "I knew it from the second I walked in. I said to myself, this character is a soft touch, have a little enlisted-man fun with him."

The psychiatrist said, "Why are you hostile to me?"

Doc was astonished. "Hostile? Christ, Major, I *like* you."

The major asked again if Doc would "work" with him.

"Okay," Doc said, "I'll do it on one condition."

"Yes?"

"The condition is that before each session you have to suck my joint."

"You go too far," the major said, then turned suspicious. "You're doing this deliberately. Why? What motivates you to do it?"

"Testing your reactions to stress. I'm trying to find out what makes *you* tick."

That had actually made the major laugh, and they had shaken hands and parted friends.

Before he left, Doc said, "Anytime you get swollen feet or a bullet wound or like that, come see me and I'll take good care of you. Professional courtesy."

The major laughed again and said, "You're a clown."

"Shrewd diagnosis, Major."

But it wasn't. He *played* the clown, which was different from being one. He was really a very serious person. Well, tell the truth, maybe not very, but sort of.

He opened the door, and Asbury wheeled the dolly in, followed by Raphael. He shook hands with them.

46

The Talisman

"The last time I was up this early," Doc said, "was up
around Pleiku. A dawn assault. They turned me out of bed
and sent me running over to the aid station. They were already bringing guys in, and inside of two minutes, with night
shit still in the corners of my eyes, I was up to my ass in
blood. Later on they walked a Cong in—he couldn't have
been over thirteen—"

"We're running a little late," Asbury said. "Otherwise we'd
love to hear your war stories."

"—and to make a long story short," Doc said, "some Ma-
rine who had had his ear shot off tried to choke him to
death."

Raphael said, "What happened?"

"We're running late," Asbury said.

"He had a bulldog grip on the Cong's neck and wouldn't
let go. Finally a doctor jabbed him in the ass with a scalpel
and he let go."

Asbury was pointing at the row of cardboard cartons
ranged along the living-room wall. "This is the matériel?"

"I haven't heard that word in quite some time," Doc said,
"and I haven't missed it, either. Yes, that's the matériel. Uniforms, caps, cotteridge belts, webbing, and et cetera. We're
all noncoms except for Booth. He's going to be a big light colonel."

"Shit," Asbury said.

"You can be a six-striper. I got one of those. In the long
carton, marked WEEDING RAKES, four M-sixteens, one forty-
five automatic. In the soup carton, dynamite, fuse, and per-
cussion caps."

"Where's the ammo?" Asbury said.

"Ammo?" Raphael frowned. "We agreed that there
wouldn't be any ammo. Booth says their rifles aren't loaded."

"Booth *says*. But if he's wrong? You and Booth can carry
empty guns. Not me."

"In the big Mother's Gefilte Fish carton," Doc said, "fifty
magazines. One thousand live rounds. If you shoot straight,
you can kill a thousand guys."

Raphael said, "We agreed that the guns were for a show

47

of force, but that we wouldn't use them. We agreed, Doc."

"You're bleeding," Doc said. "Let me have a look at that finger."

Raphael put his hand behind his back. "Leave the ammo behind. I don't want to have anything to do with it."

Asbury lifted the Mother's Gefilte Fish carton and placed it on the dolly. "I'm willing to die for a cause, but not because I've got an empty rifle. I'm a fighter, not a martyr."

"It's a righteous war," Doc said. "Just like Booth's righteous war. Maybe more so."

"I don't want to see anybody killed."

"Shut your eyes and you won't see it," Asbury said. He bent over the carton containing the rifles. "Grab an end."

After a moment, gloomily, Raphael pitched in. When the dolly was loaded, they trundled it out to the self-service elevator and down to the street level. They returned to the apartment and gathered up a bed, two bed tables, a standing lamp, a sling chair, and a rug. They worked quickly and efficiently, and when everything was stowed away in the truck, Asbury shut and locked the rear doors.

"That's the beauty of Jackson Heights," Doc said. "It's always dead, night and day."

He went upstairs and returned carrying a medical bag.

Asbury said, "Why didn't you tell me about that before I shut the doors?"

"Because my *materia medica* doesn't ride in the back of a truck with the common freight. It sits up front with me." He patted the bag. "Disposable syringes. Very hygienic. One to a customer. Fast-acting barbiturate. Alcohol. Absorbent cotton. Band-Aids. . . ."

"Get in," Asbury said. "We're going back to Booth's place and load up the furniture, and then we're on our way."

"Back?" Doc said. "What do you mean by *back?*"

Asbury smiled. He climbed into the front seat of the truck. From the curbside, Doc and Raphael got in. Asbury started up the truck and pulled away.

"You know something?" Doc said. "You're a cocksucker, Asbury."

* * *

They were finished a few minutes before eight. The last piece of furniture was loaded, the dolly was lifted into the rear of the truck, and Asbury locked the doors. Caro shook hands with each of them and wished them luck. Doc and Raphael got into the front of the truck. Asbury lingered.

"You want me to give Booth any special message for you?" He smiled innocently.

"Tell him I'll see him tomorrow."

"You'll see me tomorrow, too."

"Forget it."

She moved away from him to the front of the truck. A sanitation truck came down the street and flushed the curb with water. It splashed her ankles. Doc smiled down at her and made a V-for-Victory sign. Asbury climbed in behind the wheel. As the truck moved off, all three faces turned toward her. They looked young and very straight in their new short haircuts. It was hard to get used to. Before the truck turned at the corner Doc stuck his hand out of the window and waved. Caro turned and went upstairs.

Except for the old spinet and a vast ugly sideboard Booth had inherited from his mother, the living room was now bare. In what she construed as childish malice, Asbury had taken the bed away, with the straight-faced explanation that "we need it to be plausible." The bed tables remained, surrealistically flanking nothing. Something else was missing. She frowned at the bed tables. Booth's picture in uniform. It was gone.

Anger rose and subsided in an instant. Getting mad at Asbury was like hating a typhoon because it sometimes hurt people. A typhoon had no moral knowledge of its destructiveness, and neither did Asbury. And wasn't it this reckless and amoral quality, the opposite of Booth's almost Calvinist preoccupation with guilt and pity, that was his attraction? He was a natural sin, and that made him an exciting bed partner. Her loins stirred with memory, and for the first time she felt a twinge of guilt. Furious—at Asbury for being what he was (never mind typhoons, he was a shit!), at herself for a bourgeois reaction she thought she had sloughed off years ago—she went into the kitchen and began to clean up, working swiftly, almost vengefully, as though to purge herself of unclean thoughts.

When there was nothing left to do, no more rage to vent on menial tasks, she took the portable typewriter from the closet and sat down with it on the living-room floor. She pulled on a pair of thin rubber gloves and removed the lid from the machine. She took out the typed sheets of notepaper from the clip that held them to the underside of the lid and placed them on the floor beside her. She addressed two of the remaining envelopes from the dime-store package, inserted one copy of the letter in each, sealed them and put stamps on them. Then she clipped the envelopes under the lid and covered the typewriter.

There had been, as with almost everything at every turn, a great deal of argument about the letter. In the end, it had been boiled down from almost two pages to a few sentences. By the same process of streamlining, the original number of newspapers to which the letters would be sent had been cut from two dozen to seven: three in New York, two in Washington, two in Boston. She would mail the Boston letters tomorrow. Booth would attend to the Washington and New York letters. The eighth letter—or the first—which they had taken to referring to as the master letter, although it was different from the others—would be left at the cemetery.

The machine itself was very old, with at least two dozen distinctive lesions that would make its work recognizable even to an untrained eye. Booth had construed that as an advantage. "If crank letters come in to the newspapers, as they probably will, there'll be no problem identifying ours with the master letter. As for the machine itself, it'll end up with everything else on the floor of the bay." Even if it was eventually recovered, Caro knew, there was no hazard. She had bought it for cash over ten years ago at a flea-market sale in Cambridge and there was no possible way of tracing it back to her.

She went from room to room, closing windows, making sure the faucets were not leaking, checking the pilot light on the stove—gestures which, it occurred to her, were characteristic of Booth and not of herself—and wondered if she were not doing it as a murky form of penance for last night.

At the door she took a last look around. Empty, the shabbiness of the living room became all too apparent: blackened walls where furniture had stood, indissolubly grimy flooring, the meanness of the room's dimensions. It's not much, she thought, but it's home and it's rent-controlled. If she or Booth didn't make it back, somebody would inherit a cheap apartment (*in Manhattan's legendary Village, conv. loc.*).

Her Volvo was parked three blocks away, and there was a traffic ticket on it. She removed the ticket and put the typewriter into the trunk. She headed east to the FDR Drive. From there she would cross the Triborough Bridge and take Bruckner Boulevard to the Connecticut Turnpike. Not that it really mattered, but she would make her first stop in Stamford.

The helicopter crashed time and again through the long night, and each time Dover saw the blade fall in a slow spin and slice through his left arm. But when the slant appeared out of the brush, he did nothing, just stood there in the faded pink T-shirt and rumpled shorts and and looked at the wreckage silently and dispassionately. He was the same one, Dover was positive of that. He could never mistake that three-inch-high stand of black hair, the dark eyes with a pink sty in the corner of one of them, the yellow-green stains on the legs as if he had been kneeling in one place for a long time and pressed the juice out of the grass. But he simply watched as the fountain of blood from Dover's arm pumped and pumped until it ran dry and he woke up.

But when he fell asleep again, the chopper crashed, the blade spun downward toward his upraised arm, his blood spurted, and the slant stood like a statue, with the grass stains on the wrinkled skin of his knees. . . .

He got up at six and made himself a pot of coffee. He was ready by seven, but it was far too early. He opened his valise and just to kill some time put on the khakis again. Smiling, he touched the chevrons on the sleeve. Three above and a rocker. A promotion. In the service he had been a buck sergeant. He saluted himself in the mirror, then took the khakis off and folded them back into the valise. He drank some more coffee. At eight he couldn't stand hanging around any longer, so he left his apartment and took the subway down to Penn Station.

He arrived in time to make the eight-thirty train, but his reservation was for the nine-thirty. There was no point to catching the earlier train; it would simply mean killing an hour at the other end. He sat on a bench and watched a directory board change periodically as trains arrived and departed. His train was already listed on the board: the nine-thirty Metroliner to Washington, number 342. The station kept getting busier as the trains from Long Island poured out commuters, who darted around the floor of the station like scurrying ants on a mission.

At fourteen past nine the directory board flashed a track number for train number 342, and at the same moment a loudspeaker voice, a richly accented sidewalk voice, announced that train number 342 was now boarding on track twelve. As he hurried toward the gate, he reminded himself that when he had first come up from Akron, he had felt like a foreigner with no more than a tourist acquaintance with the native lingo.

But all that had changed—as so many things in his young life had changed. But the biggest change of all—the change that made all the other changes possible—came when the slant in the pink T-shirt and the grass-stained knees had heaved the chopper blade off his arm and tied the tourniquet that had saved his life.

A slant had done that. One of theirs. A Cong.

He found a seat in the middle car of the train, stowed his valise overhead, and settled in. His eyes were heavy, but he was relaxed, no longer disturbed by his topsy-turvy dream. He found himself yawning a lot, but it was simply a tired yawn, not a fear yawn. He wasn't the least bit scared or even on edge. That was because of Booth. He had a high regard for Booth; he trusted him all the way. The operation was dangerous, but he was certain it would work and that nobody would be hurt. He was no longer uneasy about it in the moral sense, either; he didn't *care* what people would say about them.

The train started, and a voice announced over the inter-com that they were welcome to the Metroliner, that there was a bar and snack car at the rear, and that they could look for-ward to a pleasant trip. ETA Washington, three hours. The train emerged from the tunnel into a ruined industrial land-scape that soon changed to farmlands that weren't all that different from the fields he had left behind him a lifetime ago in Ohio.

He slept a little and awoke refreshed but slightly disap-pointed that he hadn't had the dream again, straightened out this time, so that the Cong with the green knees could do what he actually had done in Nam. As the train sped through the Pennsylvania countryside, his left arm began to bother him, as it did from time to time. It was no more than a mild ache and he didn't mind it; it reminded him that he was alive. Besides, it was his own fault. Before he slipped away, the Cong had indicated by gestures that he was to loosen the tourniquet at intervals. He knew that much himself, of course, from first-aid drill, but somehow, from loss of blood or shock or just the heat of the day, he had drowsed, and by the time he woke to the pain the damage had been done. Starved of blood, tendons had atrophied, and although an operation at the base hospital had been successful, he would never be without the ache for the rest of his life.

What he remembered best—*second* best; the Cong was number one—was waking up after passing out again and looking up into an upside-down face with a moving mouth that said, "Man, don't you know you're supposed to get killed when your chopper falls down?"

That was his introduction to Doc. And it was Doc who had filled him in on the fact that his life had been saved by a Cong. It was because of Doc—not only telling him about that particular Cong, but Congs in general, what they were fighting for, what the whole ugly mess was about—that his outlook had changed and his life had been reordered.

Come down to it, it was because of Doc that he was on this train going to Washington.

4

Booth woke early and fought off the temptation to get
dressed and go out to the cemetery for a final check. Check
what, for God's sake? The criminal returning to the scene *before* the crime? On that note he fell asleep again. When he
waked a second time, he dressed and walked over to a drugstore on Connecticut Avenue that served a cheap breakfast.
He bought a newspaper and went back to the hotel. The
morning passed slowly, but at last it was twelve o'clock and
time to leave.

At the cashier's desk he took note grimly of the slightly
raised eyebrows of the girl who slid his bill through the wick-
et to him. Except for tax and the phone call to Caro last
night, there were no additions to the room charge. He had
taken all his meals outside, at inexpensive coffee shops. But
he felt the room itself was indulgence enough, and so he
looked the girl squarely in the eye when he paid his bill.

He waved off a bellhop who made a pass at his valise and
hurried out a side door so that he wouldn't have to reckon
with a doorman who would expect a tip for opening a taxi
door for him. He walked a block or two along K Street and
found his own cab and opened his own door. In less than ten
minutes the cab was sweeping around the Columbus Memorial statue and into the great circular approach to Union Station, massively Roman with its three great central arches
flanked by arcades ending in pavilions.

Booth went through the door into the main waiting room,
which, he had read somewhere, was modeled after the Baths
of Diocletian. He was still ten minutes early. He asked a
trainman for the arrival track of the nine-thirty Metroliner

54

from New York and was on his way to the gate when he saw people begin to stream out of it. He put down his valise and watched, and after a minute or so he saw Dover come up the ramp.

They shook hands. Dover was excited about the train ride. "It left on time and came in a few minutes early, and they kept making announcements all the time, like a plane."

He was a child of his time, Booth thought, an airplane rider, and he had just discovered a new and exotic form of transportation. "You're going to have to get moving right away," he said.

"They sell whiskey in little bottles, like the airlines, and sandwiches. I had a drink, but I didn't eat anything."

"Well, your lunch is going to have to wait."

He took Dover's arm and hurried him along to the waiting room.

Inclined toward the faint reflection of his face on the white tile wall, Booth lingered at the urinal while two men, separately, came in and performed and went on their way. Had George Washington, had Bolivar, ever had to dawdle at a station lavatory with their cocks in their hand, pretending to be piss-shy? The image of Washington, towering, bewigged, horse-faced, made him grin, and the tile wall threw back a pale image of his teeth. Then he heard the lock of the pay stall click, and he quickly zipped himself up.

Dover came out of the stall and paused for a moment, as if for inspection. In his khakis, with his scarlet-and-white-piped Engineers cap set at an unexceptional angle on his head, he looked like a recruiting-poster soldier.

"Okay?" Dover said.

Both nodded. Better than okay—perfect. Although Dover had put his uniform aside almost four years ago, he hadn't forgotten how to wear it. In fact, all of them would pass muster. The only one who hadn't recently worn a uniform was himself. But he would get by nicely, too. The uniform made the man.

"I'm starved," Dover said. "Can't I pick up a sandwich? I can eat it on the way."

A good officer is concerned with the basic needs of his troops. "All right. Pick me up outside."

Dover nodded, and then, catching a glimpse of himself in the mirror over the row of washbasins, squared his shoulders. Booth went out of the lavatory and through the waiting room. Outside, a black cop was hassling a taxi driver. Booth walked to the end of the arcade and put his back against a pillar.

Watching Dover come toward him a few minutes later, erect and trim, hardly recognizable as the Dover he had known, it struck Booth that putting on the uniform was a form of transubstantiation; it changed the civilian to the soldier. And what about me? Booth wondered. What will happen when I put on my soldier suit? *Manero: Sneaking affection for the army.* . . .

Dover had slipped his sandwich into the pocket of his tunic. He patted it flat. "I'm ready. I'm a little nervous, but it's nothing to worry about. I was always edgy going into a firefight, but once it started. . . ." Dover's young face was cramped with earnestness.

"I'm not worried a bit." Booth listened to his own voice: confident, calming, reassuring; the Old Man bucking up the green troops. "I do less worrying about you than I do about any of the others."

"You worry about some of them?"

Wrong tack, Booth thought. "No. Not really. We're a hell of a good outfit."

He thought of asking Dover to review his instructions, but that would be betraying *his* anxiety. Dover had been a good soldier, a *very* good one before he took his wound. He would carry out orders efficiently and, after he got over his nervousness, intelligently as well.

"There's Parmentier now," he said. The pickup truck was just turning into the circular driveway. Parmentier didn't look at them as he went by and completed the circuit. "It's pretty distinctive, isn't it?"

"Sure is," Dover said, grinning.

They walked out to the street and got into the pickup truck. Booth introduced Dover and Parmentier to each oth-

er. They shook hands and Parmentier took off. They said
very little on the drive to Alexandria. Parmentier let Dover
out a block from the bus station.

"We'll be back here waiting for you. Can you find it?"

"Easy." Dover picked up his valise. "I'll take off. See you
later."

Watching him go, Booth thought, He's a baby, just like the
babies I commanded in Able Company, a baby myself. No.
Dover had done a long tour in Vietnam, and after that nobody remained a baby.

"We'll drive around a bit," Parmentier said. "I'll show you
some of the countryside."

"Fine." Suddenly Booth felt exhilarated. He said, "I think
we're going to pull it off."

Parmentier's mouth worked silently in its nest of beard before he said, "Well, yes, I should hope so."

Raphael misread Parmentier's homemade map in Alexandria, and they made two wrong turns and had to retrace
their steps. Raphael apologized—after all, if he was able to
read the most intricate blueprints, he should have been able
to decipher a simple route map—but Asbury was unforgiv-
ing.

"I drive two hundred and fifty miles without making any
mistakes, and you fuck up a simple operation like reading a
map. Some fucking scientist you are."

"I don't claim to be a scientist," Raphael said, "I'm just a—"

"If that rig of yours works like you read a map, we're all up
the fucking creek."

Anger trembled on Raphael's lips, but Asbury's barb
struck home. It was all theoretical. The premise was absolutely valid, so it should work, there was no reason for it to
fail, and yet . . . a mechanical engineer wasn't a theorist, he
was a man who created practical devices and then tested
them, and if they didn't work, he tried something else until it
did work. Well, he had tested this rig, as Asbury called it,
with improvised weights, and it worked. But in the nature of
the operation he *couldn't* test the real thing.

They found the right road and Asbury spun the Drivurself

onto it, sluing from one side of the high crown to the other.

Doc, clutching his medical bag, said, "You're going too goddamn fast."

"Fuck yourself," Asbury said. But, to Raphael's relief, he slowed down.

"Crazy sonofabitch," Doc said. "Still, there's no more real bad in you than there was in Errol Flynn." Asbury grinned.

It astounded Raphael that Doc, scrawny Doc, was the only one of them who could control Asbury, at least to the extent that he was controllable at all. He thought, There's an awful lot I haven't learned about people. He looked at the map and said, "There should be a branch-off just ahead. We take the right branch and proceed one and seven-tenths miles . . ."

Asbury slowed at the branch and checked the odometer.

". . . and we're there. Mailbox out on the road."

A car came bouncing down the road toward them. Asbury pulled to the right without slowing down. As the car went by, a dark face turned toward them.

"He looked at us," Raphael said.

"So he looked at us," Asbury said. "We're not invisible, you know. You're like a goddamn old lady."

Raphael said nothing until he spotted the mailbox. "There it is—Parmentier."

"I see the fucking thing," Asbury said, and Raphael thought, There's something wrong with a man who can be irritated by nothing.

Doc said, "Down the driveway and drive directly to the barn. Booth said the doors would be open."

Asbury bumped down the driveway and slammed the brakes on in a skidding stop. The barn doors were shut. "So much for Napoleon Booth's fucking planning."

He thumped his hand down on the horn, which blared a raucous insult to the country quiet.

"Quit it, you asshole." Doc pushed Asbury's hand away from the horn ring. "You want the whole countryside to know we're here?"

"You push me like that again," Asbury said, "and I'm going to annihilate you."

Doc smiled. "I've got a special needle for you, Asbury. The stuff they put dogs to sleep with. One of these days, while you're sleeping, I'm going to jab it into you and you're never going to wake up."

Still smiling, he climbed out of the truck and started walking toward the house. Asbury put his hand on the horn ring and pressed it. It gave out a single sharp honk.

Through the truck window Raphael saw Doc stop short as a young woman with a child in her arms appeared around the corner of the house. They smiled at each other and shook hands.

"That must be Mrs. P.," Asbury said. "Cute chick."

Raphael followed Asbury out of the truck. Doc made introductions and they shook hands. Asbury gave Stephanie Parmentier a wide white-toothed smile and said, "Hi, honey."

"You'll have to back the truck up a bit," Stephanie said. "The doors open outward."

She walked back a dozen paces and sat Jamie down on the ground. She returned and began to tug at one of the doors. Asbury went over to help, but the door swung open before he got there. He reached around her for the second door, brushing against her, smiling and speaking softly. Expressionless, she watched him pull the door open. Asbury got back into the truck, turned on his bright lights, and drove into the barn. He turned off his lights and came outside. Stephanie shut the barn doors.

"Would you boys like something to eat?"

Asbury, smiling down at her, said, "I can think of something I would very much like to eat, Mrs. P."

She looked puzzled. Doc came between her and Asbury. "Remember that needle, cocksucker?"

The muscles in Asbury's broad back tensed, and Raphael braced himself to intervene. But Doc, smiling, turned his back and walked away. Asbury muttered something, but his shoulders dropped and the tension went out of them.

Doc, kneeling beside the baby, said, "I think he's eating a worm."

Stephanie walked over without haste. "I'll take that from you, Jamie," she said, digging her fingers into his mouth.

There were a couple of civilians on the bus, but they got off at the USO center. Most of the soldiers were noncoms who, Dover assumed, had been to Washington on business; they had the look of desk soldiers, and most of them carried brief-cases.

Although Fort Belvoir contained some sensitive installations—one that had to do with computer systems and another with nuclear power—the MP's at the main gate were pretty casual about the way they checked ID cards. They barely glanced at the one Dover showed them. As the bus moved on, he sat comfortably by a window and watched the familiar standard military landmarks go by. It was a funny feeling being in uniform again and in an army camp. It was five years since he had last been in either of them, and that had been for two or three days at Fort Meade, Maryland, where he had been separated from the service. By the time the bus reached the motor pool he was thoroughly relaxed. Was anything easier than stealing an army vehicle, even without inside collusion? They were constantly being swiped, as often as not to replace one that somebody else had swiped. Paint out the serial number on the left bumper and the unit designation on the right bumper, repaint with new numbers, and you had a replacement vehicle—until somebody stole it back!

The Fort Belvoir motor pool was larger than but very similar to the pool he had worked out of before he had put in for a transfer to the choppers as a gunner. Christ, what a gung-ho young idiot he had been! He took in the layout of the pool—admin. buildings, machine shops, garage, grease pits, wash racks, and the fenced-in compound of khaki-colored vehicles. He inhaled the oil and exhaust fumes that were as nostalgic to him as the soap his mother used to bathe him in.

He found Gate C and, with his heart beating slightly faster, walked through it. A soldier fiddling with a jeep looked up at him and said, "Hi, Sarge." He nodded and went on. The encounter gave him confidence. He counted down the row of placarded spaces until he came to B-13, and there was the M-292 expansible van. He checked the stenciled number on the bumper against the one he had memorized: 2010009513. Right.

Dover was impressed by the sophistication of the M-292. Floor, sides, and roof were made of steel, it was air-conditioned and equipped with telephone, and its width could be hydraulically expanded, doubling the interior volume of the van. There were four small windows high on either side with blackout panels, and a window on each of the rear doors. They would not use the van in its expanded position or, of course, take advantage of the air conditioning or telephone. What mattered was the van's spaciousness, total enclosure, and the steel floors and ceilings for the installation of Raphael's equipment.

He climbed into the cab and sat down behind the wheel. The chain threaded through the steering wheel and the clutch pedal—the army's silly idea of how to secure a vehicle against theft—had been neatly cut through with a hacksaw. The trip ticket (form DA-2400), Booth had told him, would be taped under the dashboard. He reached down, dislodged a strip of tape, and pulled the trip ticket out. It was stamped THIS VEHICLE IS AUTHORIZED TO TRAVEL OFF POST. *Destination* was Arlington Cemetery. *Remarks:* Delivery of 30 bags of peat moss. *Dispatcher's signature:* something illegible.

Army ignition systems were keyless. You didn't even have to jump the wires. He pressed the push-button starter switch and the motor roared. He spent a minute or so checking the specifications and instructions plaques on the dash, then put the truck in gear and eased out of the parking space. He exchanged waves with the soldier working on the jeep. He drove out of the compound, and by the time he reached the main road the truck's gears and controls no longer felt strange.

At the exit sentry box the MP sergeant barely glanced at the trip ticket. He grinned up at the cab and said, "You don't want to get those nice khakis dirty, Sergeant."

It was a point that Booth hadn't thought of. But Dover said

confidently, "Don't worry about *me* getting my clothes dirty, Sergeant." He winked. "The lower orders do the hard work. You know that as well as me, Sergeant."

The sergeant laughed and winked back and waved him on.

He drove easily, and even with enjoyment, the ten or so miles back to Alexandria. He found Parmentier parked where he had said he would be. He came up behind the pickup, and Parmentier saw him in the rearview mirror and took off. Neither Booth nor Parmentier looked back to see if he was following. He kept three or four lengths behind them all the way, and in ten minutes they were pulling into Parmentier's driveway.

5

Listening to the conversation at the kitchen table, Raphael was struck by the fact that it was weeks since he had heard any serious talk. Purpose, ideals, all had been subordinated to the logistics of the operation, so that if you were an eavesdropper, you could barely have fathomed their motivation. Even now, when they *seemed* to have gotten back to ideology, it was really nothing more profound than Asbury teasing Booth.

Stephanie Parmentier had cooked a large ham derived from their own pig, fed on natural slops and glazed with pineapple. She served it with yams and homemade bread and beer. Whether it was because they were wearing battle dress—which stoked up the memory of the way they had eaten when they were actually soldiers—or simply because they were all hungry, they tore into the food with enormous appetite. Parmentier helped Stephanie serve, and they took turns holding the baby, depending on who had a free arm. They were a nice family, Raphael thought, not all that different from his own, barring that they had opted for a copped-out life whereas he preferred making his living from the Establishment. Stephanie reminded him of Paula, though she seemed calmer and not haunted by Paula's fears.

"Your metaphor," Asbury was saying. "A simple exchange of the dead for the living. Bullshit. The country is going to choose up sides purely on how dumb and sentimental they are."

Booth shrugged. "I *hope* the force of the metaphor will be borne home. But it's secondary to releasing Rowan."

The Talisman

"Suppose they tell us to screw ourselves. I mean, suppose the consensus is 'Shove it up your ass, it isn't worth anything to us.'"

"No, that won't happen."

The uniform with its silver lieutenant colonel's insignia, Raphael observed, had conferred upon Booth a new authority. His age went well with the field officer's rank, and with his fit, compact body, he looked very much like a man accustomed to leading other men into battle. He had done that once, of course, although it was a long time ago.

"Well, you *say* it won't," Asbury said. "But it's all theory. We haven't run any scientific poll, you know. Suppose they *do* tell us to stuff it. Then where are we? Then we're stuck with the fucking thing."

Booth was uncomfortable with Asbury's language, Raphael thought. He *was* of another generation. He couldn't quite accept the new freedom of expression, he didn't know that his concern for Stephanie's feelings was misplaced.

"Not a chance," Booth said. He seemed leaner than Raphael remembered him when they first met, as if, in the weeks of planning, he had worn some of himself away. "Not in this country. Maybe not in any country."

"Are you talking about the country thirty years ago or the country of Vietnam and Nixon? This country is a cesspool now, which by definition means it's full of shit."

Booth looked pained. In his way, Raphael thought, he's a patriot, he believes in his country. That was because he joined the Movement from intellectual conviction rather than pure gut reaction. That way you never quite lost the basic beliefs you were born with. The rest of us, he thought, lost them. And it wasn't just shedding a skin, it was becoming an entirely new person.

"Come back to my question," Asbury said. "Suppose they tell us they won't make the swap for Rowan. Then what do we do with our trophy?"

"Then we've failed," Booth said, "and we give it back."

"Bullshit. We blow it to hell and gone."

Asbury's teeth were clenched, the cords of his neck stood

out, and Raphael remembered what somebody had said about him: that in appearance and by inclination he was the perfect model for a pulp-magazine illustration. Stephanie was looking at him, and he felt uncomfortable. Women seemed to react to Asbury viscerally. He had surely spent last night with Booth's girl and seemed to have no doubts that he could make Stephanie, too, if there was time and the opportunity. And his own wife? Could Paula resist Asbury? In a self-punishing flash he imagined her submitting to him. Perhaps with tears of guilt, but nevertheless submitting.

Raphael said, "It's time to set up," and shoved his chair back from the table violently. The surprised reactions told him that he had spoken abruptly and loudly. He looked at his watch, knowing that the gesture was superfluous. "Dover—want to give me a hand?"

Dover got up, holding his coffee cup. Raphael told him to finish his lunch and went out to the barn. The M-292 van had been backed in. The Drivurself panel truck was farther in, with the household furniture piled beside it. Raphael lit a couple of kerosene lamps. The van was gleaming outside and scrubbed clean inside. He took the lamps into the back of the truck. He studied the van, pinpointing in his mind the positioning of the winch and the two pulleys: the winch, as far back—which was to say as far front—as possible for stability, so that the entire length of the van could act as ballast, the first pulley on the roof directly above the winch, the second just above the van doors.

When he heard Dover come into the barn, he got out of the van. "What do we do?" Dover said.

"We get all the equipment into the van, but first we weld the winch to the floor and the pulleys to the ceiling. Lend a hand and we'll get the winch inside the truck."

"This thing is a winch?"

Well, Raphael thought, Dover would be strong and willing. Muscle. Not that he himself would tolerate any independent initiative. He recognized that he was fiercely possessive about his role, but he had to be; the rest were mechanical illiterates.

With Dover he lifted the winch into the truck and carried it all the way back, just behind the cab. While he positioned it, he dispatched Dover to fetch the portable welding unit.

"It doesn't look like much," Dover said, "to lift all that weight."

Nor did a lever look like much, Raphael thought. The winch consisted simply of a drum with a pawl and ratchet, but it had an eight-thousand-pound capacity, more than ample for the work it was to do.

"How can you lift all that weight just by turning a hand crank?"

Raphael tapped the gearbox he had installed between the drum and the handle. "This reduces everything down to a forty-to-one ratio, and that makes it all possible."

"I don't get it," Dover said. "I mean I know it's going to work, but I don't *get* it."

"You don't *have* to get it," Raphael said testily, miffed not only by Dover's ignorance but by his attaching so much importance to the winch, which was the least interesting aspect of the entire operation. "Turn your back."

He put on dark goggles and started the oxyacetylene torch. Holding the torch in his right hand and the welding rod in his heavily gloved left, he laid down his bead, forward, back, and sides. The hiss and smell and spark of the torch, and the responsive flow of the steel to its heat, dissipated his irritation at once. This was his element, and he basked in it as others might in the sun or a hot bath. There were, often enough, problems in mechanical engineering that hurt the head, but the physical work was all pleasure. The only failures were the failures of planning, of concept. The hands were infallible, confident of their skill, of their symbiotic relationship to tools and materials. It was almost with a sense of deprivation that he finished welding the winch to the steel floor. But there were still the pulley brackets to be welded and the thin steel cable to be threaded through them to the winch. He had been tempted to use nylon because it was showy—what, a skinny little rope holding all that weight!— but the steel had come to hand easily and cheaply.

"You can turn around now," he said to Dover. "I want you

to hop down. Just alongside the van you'll find a pair of pulleys and a coil of cable. Hike them up here, and then bring up the step ladder."

Dover said, "You realize you just damaged army property? They're going to charge it out to you."

Raphael looked at him in surprise. He hadn't thought of Dover as being a jokester. He said, "Hop to it, will you, please?"

There wasn't all that much hurry, he just wanted to keep busy. In his absorption with the work he could push the enormity of what they were about to do out of mind.

Caro shopped in supermarkets in Stamford, New Haven, and New London. Then, with the trunk of the Volvo crammed with almost a hundred and fifty dollars' worth of food, she drove on to the Cape. She crossed the Sagamore Bridge and a half hour later arrived at the town center, such as it was.

The town's vital organs were grouped just off the highway: town hall (and weekend cinema), fire department, and police department. The fire department occupied a wing of the town hall. The police department stood slightly apart from the rest, with its own parking lot and garage. It was a compact, cheerful white Cape Cod, with a fierce painted eagle, its wings spread, over the door.

Caro turned into the parking lot and drew up beside a black cruiser lettered in gold with the name of the town and POLICE. She walked to the building and knocked at the paneled door, and a voice told her to come in.

He was standing at one side of the room, bent over a whirring teleprinter, and she recognized him even before he turned to face her.

"Why. . . ." But it took a moment for his name to come back. "Perry. How are you?"

He returned the compliment, staring at her for a tiny instant before smiling and saying, "Caroline. Be damned."

They shook hands and he flashed that fantastic smile, warm and outgoing, that had coaxed how many girls into bed with him, herself included, she could only guess at. He had filled out a little, but his hair was still golden red, worn somewhat longer now than she remembered it.

"You're looking great, Caroline."

"Thanks. You're looking great yourself."

The inevitable awkwardness, she thought, of two strangers who had nothing in common but a sort of love affair that had flamed hotly during most of one summer and then sizzled out in a very wet autumn. Still, it was more than many people had.

He was very handsome in his uniform. It wasn't the standard police blue; it had something of the color and dash of the state police uniform: tan trousers with a thick blue stripe, a modified jodhpur that ran into brown leather boots shined to a high gloss, a light blue shirt with a solid navy tie, and—it was draped over a chair—a light blue jacket matching the stripe on the trousers. There were sergeant's stripes on his shirt, and he wore a pistol in a holster.

She pointed to the stripes. "Congratulations."

He smiled and hung his head modestly. "Oh, well. . . ."

"No, really, I'm pleased."

He asked her to sit down, clearing his jacket and his hat—a spotless fawn stetson—from the chair. She sat, and he took a seat behind a desk. He was tanned and healthy-looking and, emplaced behind the desk, took on an air of authority that had been lacking seven years ago.

"Still playing football?"

She felt uncomfortable. With any of the others it would have been easy and quick. She would simply have checked in, said that she would be in residence for a few days, and that would have been enough to avert an inquiry when they made their routine patrol and saw that the house was occupied.

"It's a game for kids. I'm too old for it now."

His smile was strained, and she realized that it had been a tactless question. Perry Knorr had been the local high school football hero, the best athlete the town had ever had, and had been given a scholarship by a downstate college. It was a great opportunity for a poor boy whose education would inevitably have ended with high school, but he had messed it up somehow. Whether he had failed to make the team, or had failed scholastically, she had never known nor cared to know. Her only, and consuming, interest had been in his hard young body.

He had been twenty-one and she had been sixteen, and a month or two into that sad autumn he had married a town girl and joined the police force.

If she had opened up wounds, he concealed the hurt and said, logically enough, "What brings you to these parts this time of the year?"

She contrived a rueful look. "I had to get away from the city for a few days. Life was getting too much for me."

"Sure." He nodded sympathetically. That was another of his numbers; he was a crackerjack at sympathy. "I know just what you mean."

He might or might not. "Anyway," she said, "I thought I'd check in with the police department so that if they smelled cooking or something they wouldn't think it was intruders."

"Fine, sure, glad you did. I'll make a note."

But he didn't make a note. He was too busy eyeing her.

"It's been . . . how long, Caroline?" But then, perhaps because he might have felt he was rushing things, added, "How long since I've seen you last?"

"Couple of years ago?" she said. He had been there with his wife, who was very pretty, and a child, a toddler who had inherited his golden hair. "At the police picnic?"

"Oh, sure, right."

He didn't remember, which was okay. "How is your child?"

"Dennis? Great. There's another one now, Clarice, a year old."

"One of each, that's nice."

He accepted the inanity with a smile. "You?"

She shook her head. "None. Not married, either."

She realized even before she saw the quickening in his eye that she had said too much. He had been married long enough now to be playing around. Maybe, given that smile of his and the susceptibility of women to it, he had never stopped.

"Did you come up here alone?"

The Talisman

It was casually enough said, but now there was no doubt left in her mind. She had inadvertently given him encouragement. His phone rang. She said, as coldly as she could manage, "Yes, I've got a lot of serious thinking to do, and I want to do it alone, absolutely alone."

He excused himself and picked up the phone. He spoke chattily—something to do with a lost dog—and she heard him tell the caller to get in touch with the veterinarian, who doubled as the town dog warden. She stood up and edged toward the door. He finished his call and hung up.

"She claims her dog was stolen, and she wants me to come down and check out footprints." He smiled. "That's what most of it is like around here." He turned serious. "That and the bloody auto accidents. The boys on the next shift can play Sherlock. Footprints." He laughed.

"How many are you these days?"

"Bigger than we used to be. Three shifts of three men each, and the chief, of course. We rotate shifts every three days. . . . Would you like to see our setup?"

"I've got some food in the car that has to be put in the fridge. . . ."

"Only take a couple of minutes." He laughed. "We're not all that big."

He put his arm lightly around her waist as he guided her through the installation. He took her into the radio room, which also served as the chief's private office and the arsenal; the walls were lined with rifles, shotguns, and a few weapons she couldn't identify, all spanking clean, locked into place in racks. At the rear was the jailhouse, two small barred cells.

He ushered her back into the front office, his arm around her shoulder now, but without pressure.

She thanked him. "I enjoyed it. It's interesting, it really is." She frowned at her wristwatch. "I've got to run."

"It's good seeing you again, Caroline." His inflection was guarded, but it was a line thrown out, subtly baited.

"Good to see you, too, Perry."

She smiled, carefully, not too infectiously, and went out to her car. As she began to pull out of the parking lot, he appeared in the doorway and waved to her. She waved back—

no smile this time—and turned out on the main road. She made a quick right turn and drove a mile and a half on the winding country road that led to her parents' house, a calculatedly weathered modern construction below which, forty feet down, were the beach and the clear sparkling waters of Cape Cod Bay at high tide.

A feathery cloud of fluff, airy and pink, adhered to the baby's chin. Booth, seeing the child trying to put the fluff into his mouth, started to get up.

"It's all right," Stephanie said. She walked unhurriedly to the child and knelt beside him. "May Mother have it, Jamie?"

The baby frowned at her. The fluff was stuck on his moist lips.

"No nourishment whatsoever in that, darling," Stephanie said. Her hand moved swiftly and the fluff disappeared. The baby, touching his mouth, looked bewildered. Stephanie got up.

It occurred to Booth that the child had no notion that he had been tricked, that he was being deprived of eating dirt and insects and worms by a couple of oversize authoritarians who took unfair advantage of him. So if he didn't know, why were they so tender of his sensibilities with their "May I" and "Would you please"? On the other hand, maybe they were right, observing principle with courtesy and hygiene by *force majeure*. A practical compromise.

But how practical were they, really, to have accepted the outrageous proposition that he, a member of another, supposedly more temperate generation had brought to them and, with their enthusiastic support, turned into a hard reality?

He looked at his watch, and the implacability of its invisibly moving hands gave him a pang of anxiety. Without saying anything, he went out through the slattern kitchen door, around the house, and into the barn. He stood silently in a shadow and watched Raphael at work. Dover stood by, looking helpless. Booth understood how he felt. Raphael was proprietary about his contraptions and scornful of the layman's ignorance of them. Booth sometimes had the uneasy

71

The Talisman

feeling that Raphael cared more about his machinery than the Movement.

Dover made him out, peering through the shadows, and straightened up, braced, in automatic reflex to the light colonel's pips. Then he smiled at himself uneasily and attempted a joke. "Sir. Come to do an inspection?"

He was still gung ho, Booth thought, although he had switched allegiances, converted by a battlefield miracle or, at least, what he took to be a miracle. But the miracle was a phony, man-made. The little man with the grass-stained knees who had put a tourniquet on Dover's arm was not a Cong but a medic in an ARVN Ranger Battalion. Doc had been aware of it (not that he could tell one slant fron another, either; the ARVN medic had told him about Dover) and simply combined a talent for irony with zeal as a recruiter for the Movement by solemnly confirming Dover's belief that his life had been saved by the enemy. Although Doc was reasonably sure Dover's conversion was solid enough at this point to withstand a revelation of the truth, he had sworn Booth to secrecy. As he put it, he revered the truth, but less as an absolute than as a convenience.

The packed earth of the barn floor was stacked with rifles, uniforms, a box containing explosives. Farther back, near the Drivurself, were piles of furniture. He looked inside the van. Raphael was standing with his hands on his hips, wearing a look of almost melancholy concentration.

"Something wrong?" Booth said. The floor of the van seemed disorderly, with gear strewn around haphazardly, or so it appeared to him.

Raphael frowned. "Why should there be anything wrong?"

"No reason," Booth said. "Mind if I come up?"

Raphael held out his hand. Booth braced the sole of his army boot against the edge of the truck, and Raphael hiked him up. The steel pulleys were welded solidly to the roof. A slender cable ran through them to the winch, anchored just behind the cab. It appeared shipshape enough. But the vacuum pump, the electric motor, the mesh hose, and the vacuum head and frame looked like a jumble.

Raphael, reading him, said, "Never mind what it looks like. It's all hooked up and ready to go. Except for the connection to the van engine, naturally." Raphael touched his toe to the hose that joined the pump to the ungainly frame. "All I have to do is link that line up to the battery and we're ready to pump."

"This gizmo isn't attached." Booth pointed to a series of ropes like a four-bodied snake with hooks at each end.

"Of course not," Raphael said. "We attach it only after we drop the vacuum head and the slab. Then we hook this— what you call gizmo—up to the winch."

"And it attaches in a matter of seconds?" Booth said.

"Seconds. Exactly. And it attaches to the casket handles in seconds, too, provided all of you aren't all thumbs."

Booth nodded. Raphael's testiness was probably as necessary to him as the egotism of the surgeon was necessary to the confident butchering of flesh. Below, Dover was peering into the van.

Dover said, pointing vaguely, "I don't understand how a vacuum—"

"You don't have to understand," Raphael said. "All you have to do is follow instructions."

Tell him he sounded like a fascist or even a technocrat, Booth thought, and he would try to kick my ass. Raphael's feistiness was disturbing; he was normally the most equable of all of them.

He said quietly, "Eddie, if there's nothing more to do, go take a break. We'll be moving out in a little over an hour from now."

Raphael said, "I need the time. You want it to work, don't you?"

Christ, Booth thought, he isn't *sure*, we're going to be risking our lives on a supposition.

Raphael met his eyes, reading him. "Are *you* sure? You've planned this thing out for months, but are you absolutely one hundred percent sure that it's going to work, that nothing unforeseen can happen, that you didn't miscalculate, that some invisible factor isn't going to screw up everything?

Well, if you're sure, so am I."

Yes, Booth thought, Raphael was right. All you could do was try to eliminate chance and error to the best of your ability, and that was what he had done. That was what Raphael would have done.

He said, "Well, yes, Eddie, *I'm* sure, but only because I'm perfect."

Booth smiled broadly to underline his joke, but even so it took Raphael a while to catch up to it and respond with a smile of his own. It was a warm pleasant smile, and Booth realized that this was the first time he had ever seen it.

Almost shyly, Raphael said, "Would you like to check me out?"

Booth nodded. Below, Dover was shifting awkwardly from foot to foot, looking bored and uncomfortable. Booth said to him, "No need for you to hang around, Bobby. Take a smoke break."

Dover looked at him in surprise. "I don't smoke."

"Well, then, a piss break. You piss, I hope."

Dover smiled. "I could use some more coffee. Okay, Colonel?"

"Colonel," Raphael said after Dover left. "That kid doesn't realize that the army was the happiest time of his life. It makes you think, doesn't it?"

Booth knelt beside Raphael. "Go ahead, Eddie."

Raphael placed one hand on the electric motor, the other on the vacuum pump. Both were painted green, the coating chipped and scuffed from usage.

"Check me," Raphael said. "The pump hooked up to the motor." His hands moved as he talked, touching, patting, caressing. "The pump and motor are keyed to this coupling." He patted something. "Give it a yank, please."

Booth tugged at the linkage, cold metal insensitive to his touch. "Check," he said solemnly.

"So," Raphael said, "when we turn on the motor, the pump starts working immediately. Hose connected to the pump. Check me?"

The vacuum hose was some twelve or fifteen feet long, rubber encased in steel mesh, flexible so that it could be

The Talisman

looped or twisted. It lay coiled on the floor like a fat, well-fed, benevolent snake.

"A-okay," Booth said.

He was being tested, he thought, rather than the equipment. Raphael was instructing him, and whether he expected him to understand fully or not, he did expect him to pay attention. Among other things, Raphael was a pedant.

"The other end of the hose is attached to the frame and chamber. Thus, once we're in position on the slab, we suck out the air and create our vacuum."

"Yes," Booth said.

"Here"—a decisive tap with a stiff finger—"a sleeve-welded metal pipe, airtight, and hose properly attached with base clamp. Here—a vacuum gauge welded into the chamber. It's a form of pressure gauge that registers inches of mercury. When the needle indicates twenty-eight inches of mercury, we know that we have a viable vacuum. Not a perfect vacuum, of course; there's no such thing as a perfect vacuum."

Booth thought of the imperfections of his *viable* little group, of the lesions of character that might leak out into disaster, of the imperfections of his own motives, which Manero, who knew better than most that there was no such thing as perfection, had challenged. . . .

He looked doubtfully at the unprepossessing little electric motor. The vacuum pump seemed even less substantial, perhaps twenty pounds' worth all told. Could the motor be counted on to activate the pump, the pump to vacate the air, the vacuum chamber to adhere, the frame to support the massive deadweight of the slab?

". . . transformer," Raphael was saying. "Input and output wires. Hooked up to the truck engine. Check? The electric motor runs on one hundred and ten volts; the truck battery is only twelve. Hence a transformer to step up the battery voltage to one-ten."

"Check," Booth said.

"I'm going to start the machinery," Raphael said, "a dry run. You want to see it?"

"No," Booth said, and tasted fear in his voice. "I only want to see it once. In the cemetery." He stood up and brushed his hands. "The frame and the chamber. Will you test those, too?"

"No practical way of doing it."

"Then how can you know if they'll stand up?"

"If the underlying principles are right and the construction is sound, they'll stand up. We'll know tomorrow morning for sure, won't we?"

It was a casual way to put the question of ultimate success or failure, and Booth did not answer it. He jumped down from the truck. Raphael called out to him.

"Yes?"

"Asbury got Doc to bring live ammunition for the M-sixteens. He means to use it. I mean, Asbury means to load his rifle with it."

Booth went over to the pile of uniforms and rifles. He pulled back a tarpaulin and there they were, neatly stacked, fifty clips of twenty rounds each, shiny and lethal.

"I don't like the idea of it," Raphael said.

Booth went back to the house. When he entered through the kitchen door, Asbury jumped to his feet and shouted, "*Ten*-HUT!" Dover and Doc rose, too, and braced to attention. Asbury snapped a mock palm-forward British salute. Dover and Doc threw the standard American salute.

Instinctively Booth started to return the salute and managed to check it only at the last instant.

He said, "Asbury, can you come outside for a moment, please?"

Asbury clowned. "Are you calling me out, suh?"

Booth turned and walked out, leaving a heavy silence behind him. A moment later Asbury came out and walked over. They stood on the dried-out matted grass facing each other. They were roughly the same size, but Asbury contrived to seem to be looking down from a superior height. It was a trick of the eyes, Booth supposed. Asbury never stopped trying.

"*Oui, mon colonel?*" Asbury was smiling, relaxed in a hip-shot pose. "I am a troublemaker, *hein*, with the pretty Madame Parmentier?"

The approach threw Booth off-balance. He said with surprise, "I hope not."

"Routine," Asbury said. "Give me a half hour alone with her and I'd have her on her back."

"It's about the ammo," Booth said.

"What ammo?" Asbury's eyes were guileless.

Booth said, "Don't play games. I saw it, under the tarp. A thousand rounds of M-sixteen ammo."

"Doc told you. I'll kill that little bastard."

"Nobody told me. I discovered it by accident."

"Bullshit. If it wasn't Doc, it was Raphael. They both knew."

"That isn't the point," Booth said wearily. "The ammo is the point. We agreed there wouldn't be any."

"*You* agreed."

They had all agreed, including Asbury. After a heated discussion Booth had called for a show of hands, and Asbury and Doc had gone along with the vote. But they obviously had never intended to abide by it.

Squinting into the sun at Asbury's handsome face, Booth said, "There will be no live ammo, Asbury."

"There will be live ammo in *this* soldier's piece, *mon colonel*." He dropped the mockery and said, "Get it straight, my friend. I won't face six armed men with an empty gun."

"Their rifles aren't loaded."

"Maybe and maybe not. But they do have bayonets."

"They won't try anything against what they'll assume are loaded rifles."

"They'll assume right, because mine *is* going to be loaded. Otherwise, Colonel, you can go in without me."

It canceled out the entire argument, and Asbury knew it. Without him, without any one of them, it couldn't be done. And so, not even hoping to convince himself, he said, "I don't want anybody hurt, them or us."

It was a full retreat in the face of Asbury's ultimatum, and Asbury knew it. "I won't shoot unless I have to. But if I have to, I'll shoot to kill. Isn't that what they taught us in the army?"

Beyond Asbury's sloping shoulder, Booth saw Raphael turn the corner of the house, walking with his head down, abstracted.

Asbury swiveled his head. "Ah, here comes the mad scientist."

He turned and watched Raphael approach. When Raphael was a few paces away, Asbury called his name softly and stepped forward a pace. Raphael's head lifted slowly, in response to his name, and that brought it into the right position to take Asbury's fist flush on the mouth.

6

At the top of the Parmentiers' driveway Booth ordered Dover to turn off his motor, then rolled down his window and listened intently for the sound of a car in the country stillness. After a moment he drew his head in and told Dover to go on. With its heavy tires throwing gravel, the big van pulled onto the blacktop.

Asbury sat between Dover and Booth in the cab; Raphael and Doc were in the expansible body of the van. Asbury was slumped in his seat with his long legs braced against the dashboard, his knees up against his chest. His handsome profile was rigid, the jawline hard.

They met no cars on the Parmentiers' road. After that, particularly near the center of Alexandria, traffic became heavier. But an army truck carrying an officer and two noncoms was commonplace in the capital area, and they would scarcely be noticed. Nevertheless, Booth breathed easier when they edged into the speeding traffic flow of the Capital Beltway, which headed west at that point before turning north. There were more direct routes they might have taken, but on the Beltway they were safely anonymous. The van handled smoothly; the large body barely swayed. Recalling the hard-sprung trucks of his own army days, Booth wondered if some humane general had issued orders for comfort or if it had simply come about through Detroit's dedication to luxury, even for working vehicles. In either case, Doc and Raphael would be grateful.

He shook his head, remembering the look on Raphael's face when Asbury had hit him. Neither fear nor anger, but reproach. Raphael believed in order—at least, the order of *things*—and perhaps felt that men should be like things, governed by meticulous rules of behavior which were as immutable as the great formulas of science.

At the moment of impact—the inimitably ugly sound of a fist striking vulnerable flesh—Booth had been convinced that everything was finished, all the hopes and planning done in by a sudden spasm of mean temper. Asbury, enraged, his face muscles establishing vectors of violence, lean-hipped, his fist swinging at the end of the arc of his arm, was an apotheosis of a poster hero. All it needed was an artist cheating with speed lines to make it a perfect pulp illustration.

Raphael staggered back, his mouth bloodied, and Asbury shouted, "You fucking informer, you fucking old lady!"

Booth had reacted by instinct, by reflex. He had come up behind Asbury, thrown his arms around his waist, and whirled him away from Raphael in a kind of grotesque partnered dance. Asbury resisted, planting his feet and throwing his elbows, but Booth clung to him, pitting his strength against Asbury's and winning. When Asbury kicked backward at his ankle, he shoved with full force and sent him spinning away. Asbury checked his momentum, turned and charged, already swinging his fist in a long-armed blow. Booth stepped inside the punch, and Asbury's fist went over his shoulder. He pushed Asbury off, rammed into him with his shoulder, and knocked him down.

Asbury landed on his butt, skidding, and a puff of dust came up under him from the sere grass. Screaming, "Motherfucker, I'm going to kill you," he scrambled to his feet and came on in a rush, head down. Booth waited for him, no longer detached but eager, wanting to hurt him. Still, he held back from hitting him, which he might have done, and instead, sidestepping, looped his arm around Asbury's neck and bulldogged him, whipping him down in a jarring fall.

The others were pouring out of the door, but he paid no attention to them. He bent over Asbury, furious, and shouted, "Behave yourself, you miserable sonofabitch, or I'll put you in a goddamn hospital!"

Someone grabbed him from behind and pulled him away.

Then there was a whirl of shouts, questions, explanations, accusations, himself silent, the adrenaline subsiding, leaving him trembling and remorseful and yet, at the same time, pleased, even purified at having acted savagely and efficiently. The first coherent voice to emerge from the hubbub was Doc's. Reaching up to Raphael's height, swabbing his mouth with a handkerchief, he turned to Asbury, laughing, and said, "Fuckface, you hit the wrong guy. It was me who snitched about the ammo. When I'm through here, I'll put a splint on your dumb ass."

After that, somehow, the tension eased, perhaps because they were all eager for relief from it, and everything turned into a form of rueful comedy. Himself standing there quietly, torn between pride and guilt. Raphael, who could neither tell a lie nor suffer hearing one, denouncing Doc's confession as false, and Doc stuffing his handkerchief into Raphael's bloody mouth to gag him. Dover looking on the verge of tears at the sight of all these people he admired behaving like children. The Parmentiers laboring to maintain their cool, pretending that nothing had happened. And, a final slapstick note, little Jamie plucking a fistful of cashmere from his mother's sweater and trying to locate his gaping mouth with it.

It threatened briefly to turn serious again when Asbury scrambled to his feet and screamed at Doc, "You little wop bastard!"

Doc, smiling, pulled a shiny scalpel out of his pocket. "One step farther, and I'll make a tenor out of you."

Unexpectedly Raphael threw his head back and bared his bloodstained teeth in a raucous laugh. Surprise at his laughter stopped everything dead. Doc, clowning, jumped back from Raphael as if in terror. Jamie, alarmed at the sound, began to cry. Doc shook his head at Asbury in mock despair.

"Asbury, you're one crazy cocksucker."

It was a shrewd choice of adjectives, feeding Asbury's sense of himself as an untameable maverick, and he broke into a smile that made him boyish and appealing. Suddenly everyone was shaking hands in a saturnalia of mutual forgiveness, camaraderie, and sheepishness: Asbury and Ra-

The Talisman

phael. Doc and Asbury. Dover, pathetic in his relief. The Parmentiers, now that the crisis was over, had turned solemn and weepy, and Booth thought, they're too angelic for this world, they can't accept that belonging to the Movement didn't automatically confer sainthood, that a shit with a deep belief in the same things they believed in was still a shit. . . . He stirred himself and went around shaking hands, too, and then, very coolly, he was ordering everyone into the barn.

"We're taking off. Let's move lively, gentlemen."

Asbury, looking straight ahead through the windshield, said, "I'm not that easy to knock down. You caught me off-balance. Otherwise I would have put you squarely on your ass."

"Yes," Booth said, "I know."

Asbury looked frustrated. He hadn't expected agreement and in fact hadn't wanted it. Glancing sidelong at his sullen, baffled face, Booth regretted that having knocked Asbury down, he couldn't have capitalized on his new position of strength by putting his foot down about the live ammo. But it wouldn't have worked. Asbury would simply have walked out on them. And so he had said nothing, and the live rounds had been packed into the van with the rest of their gear. He could only hope that nobody would give Asbury the provocation to use it.

The bombardment began suddenly, with a flat dull *crump* that made the house shake. Caro went outside to the porch. There were two planes overhead. They made a wide circle over the water, then came in low and dropped their bombs. The first missed, sending up a spray of water; the second struck the ship near the stern, and a powdery spume rose up from the deck. The thump came echoing in a moment later. The planes were already spiraling up.

The *James Longstreet* lay dead ahead, about a mile over the waters. The navy had towed it there years ago to serve as a target ship, and it had endured and survived innumerable batterings from the planes that came in once or twice a day

82

and bombed it with simulated high explosives. It never moved. It sat passively, impregnably, suffering assault after assault, and it never sank.

She watched the planes make another pass—two near misses—and then skim upward and head home to their base, leaving the sky serene and untenanted. She went back into the house and filled ice-cube trays. Then she made up the bed under the patchwork quilt in the smallest of the bedrooms facing the water. It was the room and the bed she had slept in ever since her parents had built the house. A half dozen years ago she had stopped coming during the season and came, on occasion, only in the autumn, after everyone had left.

Fin de saison.

The room, the entire house, would need to be swept of the sand that had seeped in since her parents had left. But not now. She poured herself a small tot of whiskey and went out onto the porch to wait for the sunset. Already the sun was dropping slowly but perceptibly toward the waiting curve of the water. The air was cold and brittle, and the huge sun was white, icy bright, in a pale blue and pink sky. Against the chill she was wearing the red sweater with the roll collar that she had first worn as a teenager. It kept her warm with its thick old wool and its memories of a simpler time.

On its high bluff, the house overlooked the grand sweeping semicircle of the bay. The front yard led to the edge of the steep, perennially crumbling slope, which they constantly dressed with brush to halt erosion, although each year a bit more slid down toward the beach. Except at the edge of the land the beach was barely visible, so that from the house at high tide only water could be seen, and it was easy to think of the house as a boat riding the waters.

The other houses on the street were boarded up for the winter, as they always were by mid-October at the latest, and the surrounding silence was complete except for the purl of the water and the screams of the gulls. The tide was out now, and you would have to walk a quarter of a mile before the water came as high as your hips. A convention of gulls was clustered on the drained sand, several hundred of them.

From time to time one would take off, on some scent or impulse the others did not know, flapping strongly until it reached a thermal, where it used its wings with the greatest economy, soaring and dipping gracefully.

The sun had come down to the horizon, and its color had deepened toward red. The water trapped in the troughs of sand by the receding tide glittered like a fractured jewel. The peacefulness of the moment was almost palpable (as a child Caro had imagined its texture to be something like lamb's wool). It was the best time of the year on the Cape. *Fin de saison.* The French phrase seemed to catch it perfectly—its sadness and its solace, the melancholy of a year slowly dying toward its end.

Tomorrow would be different. Tomorrow they would all arrive, bringing reality with them.

Half the sun was gone, bisected by the horizon. Its color had deepened to magenta, and the sky was streaked yellow and black and bloody red. Just before the sun disappeared, a single plane came out of the sky and dived toward the target ship without dropping a bomb. Then it circled away and she thought it was gone, but it reappeared in an unexpected quarter of the sky and dived down again and strafed the ship. The flashes were a series of bright streaks, followed an instant later by a stutter of sound. For some reason it was disquieting and forboding, and suddenly Caro felt the cold. She got up and went inside the house. The plane went on home without firing again.

With the Arlington Memorial Bridge (*"symbolic link between the North and the South"*) at their back, they headed toward the glassed-in guard box at the entrance to the cemetery. The time was four thirty-five. A stream of cars was coming out on the opposite side of the road. They were the only vehicle entering.

Booth said to Dover, "He may ask to see the trip ticket. Have the papers ready."

But when they paused at the box, the guard merely nodded and said, "Good afternoon, Colonel."

They rolled on into the cemetery grounds.

Asbury said, "Rank has its privileges, Dover. Shiteating guard sees three of us but greets only the big light colonel. It's a good afternoon for sergeants, too, isn't it, Dover?"

I should have some sort of apocalyptic *this is it* feeling, Booth thought, but I've been living with it so long and intensely that the event itself—or its beginning, at least—seems like an anticlimax.

"The uniform makes the man," Asbury said. "He's a phony colonel, but the guard can't see that, can he, Dover?"

"Well," Dover said, "we're phony sergeants, aren't we?"

"Oh, Christ." Asbury slid far down on the seat, his knees up in a long V, his cap tilting forward over his eyes.

"Sit up, Asbury," Booth said.

Asbury gave him a slow smile. "Is that an order, Colonel?"

"We're pretending to be soldiers," Booth said patiently. "Sergeants don't slouch when there's an officer sitting next to them."

"Well, since you put it so logically and it's not an order. . . ." Asbury took his time, but finally straightened up.

Dover said, "Which way?"

"It's immaterial," Booth said, "as long as you keep moving. We're killing fifteen minutes, that's all."

The McClellan Gate was off to the left, quaintly formed of red stone, the original entrance to the cemetery, now isolated and without function. How many times in the past months had he walked past them, Booth wondered, how many times had he read the inscriptions on each side at the top of the arch? Enough to memorize them. On the near side: *On Fames* (damn that missing apostrophe!) *Eternal Camping Ground Their Silent Tents Are Spread/And Glory Guards with Solemn Round the Bivouac of the Dead.* On the opposite side: *Rest on Embalmed and Sainted Dead Dear as the Blood Ye Gave/ No Impious Footsteps Here Shall Tread the Herbage of Your Grave.*

Wrong, Booth thought, the impious footsteps are here.

Dover said, "Can we go by it? The tomb, I mean. Outside of pictures, I've never seen it."

In the operational sense, it didn't matter that he hadn't seen it. He would know what to do; he had been rehearsed in detail. "We'll pass by it eventually," Booth said. "Keep on as you're going, past the Visitors Center."

"It's dumb and risky," Asbury said, "tooling around the roads for fifteen minutes. We should have come in just five minutes before closing."

It was another one of the minor points they had debated. Entering five minutes before closing time minimized the risk of being seen by a cruising security car, but it might have given the guard at the box reason to remember them. On balance, it had seemed a better bet to arrive fifteen or twenty minutes before closing and take their chances with the security guards. There had been no substantive disagreement. Asbury, in his present mood, was just prepared to bitch about everything.

One of the black security cruisers was standing by at the parking lot to see that the few cars that still remained pulled out before the gates closed. The van moved on past the Visitors Center, which was mostly a staging area for the Tourmobile buses. A shuttle bus was waiting there to transport passengers back across the Potomac to the Lincoln Memorial.

Dover said, "I had no idea this place was so beautiful."

Booth nodded. It was prettier in the summer, with the foliage in bloom, but the bare trees with their black branches scribbled against the somber sky created a more appropriate beauty of their own.

Asbury said, "The dead wouldn't change it for the world."

Dover, pointing, said, "What's that thing sticking up over there?"

"It's the Netherlands Carillon, a gift from good Queen Juliana. Right near there the first military burial took place, in 1864. Private William C. Christman, a Union soldier." An ancient casualty, perhaps with a minié ball rusting in the cage of his skeleton.

"Terrific," Asbury said.

"Company G, Sixty-seventh Pennsylvania Infantry," Booth said.

Booth recalled a Tourmobile spieler mentioning that he made ten or twelve trips a day in the summer season. They had their patter memorized, including jokes and gee-whiz statistics. And I've heard it so often, Booth thought, I can do the number myself.

"On your right," he said, consciously mimicking the flat cadence of the spielers, "is the grave of Medgar Evans. If you look up, you can see Arlington House in the distance, highest point in the cemetery, formerly the Custis-Lee Mansion, once occupied by Robert E. Lee, Bobby, and remind me someday to tell you the story of how the U.S. government screwed Mrs. Lee out of the property. The bronze man sitting on the bronze horse is Field Marshal Sir John Dill. Over there on the right, Quartermasters Hill and Chaplains Hill. On the left, that big area of graves, World War Two dead. *My* war."

"Oh, Christ," Asbury muttered.

"No, it's interesting," Dover said. "What's this thing called?"

"MacArthur Circle, named for Dugout Doug and his father, Arthur MacArthur. The only father and son ever to be awarded the Medal of Honor." They swung through the circle and straightened out again. "Over there is the Serpens Memorial. The *Serpens* was an ammunition ship that blew up in 1943 or thereabouts. Biggest mass burial in the cemetery. I forget exactly how many."

"My God," Dover said. "Good Christ, look at *that*."

They were approaching the Field of the Dead, row upon row of GI headstones stretching out like a field of rigid truncated wheat—more than eleven thousand repatriated casualties of World War I who had been disinterred from their military graves in Europe.

"Tell him what it is," Asbury said.

"Dead soldiers," Booth said. "In a little while you'll be able to see the Rough Riders Monument."

"The *what?*" Dover said.

"More dead soldiers."

"We should have an intercom to the back of the van," Asbury said. "I hate to think of Doc and Raphael missing all this."

On their left was a sanctuary that would be kept forever wild, no matter how many corpses clamored for admission to the dwindling burial ground. In the summer, when Booth had first seen it, it had been lush and green and dappled. Now it was a tangle of interlaced branches rising from a carpet of yellow and tan leaves. The Custis-Lee Mansion towered above on the right.

"From the front of the mansion," Booth said, "there's a fine view of Washington spread out down below. Pierre L'Enfant is buried there, the man who designed the city."

Asbury groaned.

Booth ignored him and returned to his monotone narrative. It was helping to relieve his tension. And, he was certain, Dover's. "South of the mansion there's a granite sarcophagus over a vault that contains two thousand unknowns of the Civil War."

"Two thousand?" Dover was shaking his head. "All unknown?"

"There were eighty thousand unknowns in War Two and about eight thousand in the Korean War. I don't know about Nam. All told, in military cemeteries throughout the country, about one in ten are unknowns."

"What's that?" Dover pointed, and the van swerved over the crown of the road.

"Keep the fucking truck on the road," Asbury said.

Dover corrected, apologizing.

"Over there," Booth said blandly, "we have the Confederate Monument, erected in 1914, courtesy of the Daughters of the Confederacy."

Sir Moses Ezekial was the sculptor of the monument, and his weary bones, uprooted from their grave in Italy, lay at the base of the monument. Much wandering, Booth thought, from his ancestral home in the Sinai desert. The monument was topped by a heroic figure of a woman, Grecian of nose, handsome of hip, head crowned with olive leaves. She faced to the south and she held a laurel wreath in her left hand, a plowshare and pruning hook in her right. Around her, arranged in concentric circles, lay the Confederate troops who had died in the Washington area.

"Where's the Kennedy grave?" Dover said.

"You won't be able to see it from the road," Booth said.

"It's a little way ahead and above us. Keep on going. We're almost to the tombs. You'll see a rotunda on your right. It's directly opposite, but you won't be able to get more than a glimpse. Don't stop, don't slow down. It's three minutes of five."

Asbury said calmly, "There's a security car coming toward us."

"Making a final round before the gate closes to check on stragglers," Booth said. "He'll assume we're on our way out."

As the cruiser passed them, one of the guards lifted a languid hand over his half-open window and waved to them. Dover waved back. He grinned, pleased with himself.

"The construction site is about a quarter of a mile ahead, on your right," Booth said. "Go slow. The workmen quit at four thirty, and they usually clear out fast. But we'll make sure they're gone. If it's clear, I'll show you where to turn in."

The van moved smoothly along the gently curving road. Dover looked tense and serious. Asbury looked bored.

"That's it, just ahead," Booth said. "Slow down and run close to the verge of the road. Slow. . . ."

In the interior of the van, working in the dim light diffused through the glass partition behind the cab, Doc removed the wet handkerchief from Raphael's battered lips. The last of the ice cubes had melted away.

"Leave it alone," Raphael said, holding onto the handkerchief.

"Don't be testy with your doctor," Doc said. "Let go, please."

Raphael allowed him to peer at his uncovered mouth. Gently Doc touched the lower lip.

"That pulpy lip flesh puffs up fast," Doc said, "but it heals good, too."

He felt naked without the handkerchief, Raphael thought, as if a secret shame had been exposed. He took the handkerchief back and covered his mouth.

"It stopped bleeding," Doc said. "Don't lick it or move it any more than you have to. Does it hurt?"

Raphael shook his head. "Swollen, but no pain."

"I haven't lost a patient with a fat lip yet. Relax."

"It shouldn't have happened," Raphael said flatly.

"You've just defined life. Life is things happening that shouldn't happen. I should have packed along more ice cubes."

"I wonder what's going on out there," Raphael said.

Doc shrugged. "I guess we'll be pulling in soon."

"I've thought about it," Raphael said. "And I'm more angry at myself than at Asbury. For not hitting him back. Don't you think so?"

"You should have kicked the living shit out of him."

"I don't do the right thing instinctively. I should have hit him back by instinct, by reflex. Whether or not I'm capable of kicking the shit out of him."

"Asbury isn't as good as he thinks he is. You were coming toward him, no defense, and he had a clear shot, and all he could do was mess up your lip a little."

"Isn't that enough?"

"Somebody who could really hit would have knocked a couple of your teeth out."

Raphael parted his lips slightly and touched his teeth. They seemed firm enough. "Why didn't I hit him back? What's wrong with me?"

"Not my field of competence," Doc said. "I only heal flesh."

They were silent, their backs and bottoms picking up the sway of the van as it took the mild curves of the road. Then Raphael said, "You do have a vocation for healing. Did you ever consider becoming a doctor?"

"Too much work."

"What *do* you do? I mean, your regular—"

"I haven't got any regular. When things get too rough, I work as a detail man for a drug company. Otherwise I just deal a little."

"Deal? You mean drugs?"

"In a small-time way, just to keep body and soul together."

Raphael sat for a moment in shocked silence. Then, almost fearfully, he said, "What does Asbury do?"

"Asbury lives off welfare and women."

"Christ!"

"Christ!" Doc mocked his tone. "You think we're freaks? Well, you're freakier than we are. How long have we known each other? In all that time, until now, you've never been curious about what we do. That's what I call freaky."

Raphael said, "I'm deficient in relating to people. I'm aware of it."

"So you happen to dig machinery more than you dig people. Everybody has got his own problems. I like you anyway. Christ, I even like Asbury. I would like a scorpion or a polar bear if it met me halfway. I like everybody, that's *my* problem. Relax."

The van slowed and made a sharp turn to the right. It bumped jerkily, the wheels thumped out of sync, and then the floor tilted sharply.

"We're there," Doc said calmly.

They braced themselves as the van careened wildly on a rough upward pitch. Suddenly, still slanted sharply, perched on a tilted sideward angle, it came to a stop. The motor switched off.

"Well," Doc said, "here's where we spend the night." He sighed. "Fifteen fucking hours."

The rear doors of the van opened, and Dover jumped in, followed by Asbury. Booth came last, and he quickly drew the doors shut and locked them.

7

Sitting in the back of the van, and with that clarity of vision that darkness sometimes engenders, Booth reflected, not without irony, that the idea for the operation, which had originated with a certified lunatic, had been watered by despair and germinated in desperation. It was a study in the growth of an abnormality in which doubts were not only dismissed but obliterated.

When the idea had first been broached, it had struck him as being utterly repulsive, utterly ridiculous, wildly impossible. But as obstacle after obstacle was overcome, his early emotions disappeared without a trace.

With the exception of Caro, he had not told anybody about Bateman, and so he himself was accepted as the author of the original idea. Later, although it would have done no harm to reveal Bateman's role, neither would it have served any useful purpose, and so he continued to hold it secret. Anyway, by then Bateman was dead.

He had spoken to Bateman only once. It was in Washington, after a demonstration in front of the White House that had been a dismal failure. No more than a dozen had turned out for the demo, and of that number three or four were teenagers, postpuberty radicals testing causes en route to inventing one of their own. Even the signs they carried were tatty, frayed from use in previous demos: FREE FRANCIS ROWAN, LAST CASUALTY OF THE UGLY WAR. LEGACY OF A NATION'S SHAME—LIBERTY FOR ROWAN.

And, of course, Rowan's famous statement from the wit-

ness box: I DO NOT RECANT, I DO NOT REPENT, I DO NOT SHIFT
AN INCH FROM MY BELIEFS.

There was no press coverage. In fact, as they told one
another with mordant gallows humor, even the FBI dis-
dained to take their pictures. After a while they stopped
shouting slogans and simply shuffled along in sullen dispirit-
ed silence.

To make matters worse, they were upstaged by another
demonstration a few yards farther along Pennsylvania Avenue. The other group, more than three hundred strong,
were the Friends of the Apple Growers of New York State. A
week earlier the President, in an uncharacteristically un-
guarded moment, had been heard to say, when offered an
apple, that he didn't like apples because eating them caused
him to break out in a cold sweat. He had since tried to re-
tract, denying that he had said he disliked apples, praising
them as the healthiest food on earth, featured in the Bible,
stopping short only of claiming that he *enjoyed* breaking out
in a cold sweat.

Nevertheless, the Friends of the Apple Growers of New
York State came down to picket him. Wearing old-fashioned
straw boaters, apple-red trousers and skirts, healthy and joy-
ful, they formed a long tireless picket line, chanting their
theme over and over again "An apple a day keeps a President
in office." They offered apples to passersby, overflowed into
Lafayette Park across the street, were irredeemably good-
natured. And the media turned out for them, including two
of the three major networks.

Asbury had picked a fight with one of the apple demonstrators, but they restrained him. Soon afterwards they called
it quits. Most of them went to a bar on Rhode Island Avenue,
where the fashionable Northwest began to slide off into black
territory. The postmortems were noisy, equally divided between hopelessness and fierce declarations of bigger and better efforts to come. After a while Booth wandered off. The
others would recover before long—they were young, resili-
ent—but his own mood of dejection seemed incurable.

He had walked aimlessly through the nearly empty streets

of Sunday Washington. Finally, more because of tiredness than any real desire for a drink, he stopped in at the bar of one of the city's famous old downtown hotels, still shabbily elegant and surviving on its past glories. Bateman came in as he was ordering his drink and sat down next to him. Booth recognized him as having been at the demo briefly.

There was nothing unusual about Bateman. He was of medium height, spoke softly with a slight speech impediment, and was less than averagely intense, in terms of the temperament of most Movement people. He was clean, almost excessively neat, and, although long-haired and tieless, not the least out of place in the hush of the hotel bar.

"The demo was a flop," Bateman said, "because it was psychologically inappropriate. We were trying to remind people of precisely what they've been struggling to forget for ten years. They tried forgetting the war in Vietnam while we were still heavily engaged in fighting it. When we pulled our troops out, it became easier. When the North walked into Saigon, it became still easier. Why do you think unconditional amnesty took so long? Because the country didn't want to be reminded of something they were pretending never existed. So, here we are saying that it did exist, that there was one more detail to clean up. Francis Rowan? Who's Francis Rowan? They've forgotten who Francis Rowan is, like they've forgotten who Dan Berrigan is. Or, if they remember at all, probably get the two of them mixed up."

Booth said, "The country is anesthetized. Up until recently there was always a stubborn streak of idealism flickering under the self-interest. The politicians helped kill that streak, sometimes by example, sometimes, as with Nixon, not only by example but deliberately, as a modus vivendi, by appealing to the worst in the American character. It used to be a country that cared about injustice, but not any longer."

Bateman said, "If you can see all that, why can't you see that trying to win over public opinion is impossible?"

"I don't agree that it's impossible. We did it once before, in the war. We actually managed to turn public opinion against our involvement."

"Yes, because apple-pie-and-mom lovers were dying out in the boondocks. Who's dying now?"

It was an inarguable point, and Booth knew it. But to accept it was to accept defeat, to go out of business.

"Insead of wooing public opinion," Bateman said, "you should be trying to alienate it."

"We're doing a pretty good job of that right now."

Bateman ignored his smile. "Appeal to the *authentic* American character. Apple pie and mom is bullshit. Violence, death, and terror—that's what the American citizen longs for out in the boondocks of his fantasy life."

Booth ordered a second round of drinks.

"The point is this," Bateman said. He no longer looked calm, but Booth set it down to the effect of the booze. "They'll never *give* us Rowan. We have to *take* him."

So, for all of Bateman's mildness, he was in sympathy with the Young Turks in the Movement, the adventurists. Storm the prison and remove Rowan by force. Bomb this or that. Kidnap a prominent citizen or his wife or child. Dump LSD in the reservoirs.

Bateman put half his drink down in a single gulp. "I know the answer," he said. "Blackmail. Extortion. *Wrest* Rowan from their slimy grasp." He leaned forward, his eyes gleaming. "You're beginning to look uncomfortable. You're afraid to face it. After today's fiasco that's all that's left."

Booth picked up his drink, determined to finish it quickly and get out, but Bateman had already signaled for another round.

"I'm twenty-six years old," Bateman said. "You're probably twice my age, but I've already seen more horror than you."

"It's possible." The reference to his age nettled him.

"Do you know where I was during the war in Nam?" Bateman was becoming flushed.

"War is hell," Booth said. "I've heard about it."

"I wasn't *in* the war, I was someplace worse." Bateman paused and then said, with an air of triumph, "I was in a laughing academy. Not a private sanatorium. A state asylum. You know what they're like?"

Booth squirmed on his stool. He said nothing, but waited uncomfortably for Bateman to continue.

"I'm twenty-six years old," Bateman said, "and all told I've spent seven years in asylums. That's one-quarter of my life."

"I'm sorry," Booth said.

"Breakdowns, depressions, a touch of the old skitz." Bateman laughed. "Nothing serious."

"I'm sorry," Booth said again.

"I don't make a secret of it. I have neither shame nor scruples about talking about it."

Or about inflicting it on strangers, Booth thought. Maybe it would serve him right if I told him *my* life story.

"You must understand," Bateman said conversationally, "that when I'm not skitzy or in a depression trough, I'm perfectly lucid and sometimes brilliant."

He might have been talking about his cold symptoms. He was unquestionably lucid—too *damn* lucid—Booth thought, and yet everything he said sounded tainted now.

"I have to run," Booth said.

"It's okay," Bateman said. "I'm accustomed to having people duck out on me."

He knows the way to my heart, Booth thought. "I'm not ducking out, I'm getting a ride back to New York." Bateman's smile was sadder than tears would have been. "I'll finish my drink. . . ."

"What I was talking about before . . . You think I meant violence, bombing, that kind of shit?" He shook his head, and his pathetic smile turned secret. "It's old-fashioned, unimaginative. And it lacks a theme, what I call metaphor." He put his finger alongside his nose in a parody of slyness. "Barter the dead for the living. Metaphor, right?"

Booth shook his head. "I don't follow you."

"You'll see. Do you mind if I have another one of these?"

Booth thought of warning him off, but shrugged instead. He wasn't the boy's keeper, wasn't his father. But Bateman seemed to forget the drink himself.

"Talisman," Bateman said.

"What?" Booth wondered if he had been inattentive.

"Barter the dead for the living, that's the metaphor. But not any old dead. That's where the talisman comes in."

Maybe his lucidity came and went, Booth thought. He said, "I don't understand."

"The problem is to compel the government to release Rowan." Bateman was deliberate, almost pedantic. "In order to accomplish that, we must convince the government that by doing what *we* want it to do, it will also be doing what the *country* wants it to do."

"That worked well enough with getting out of the war. But we can hardly rally that kind of support for releasing Francis Rowan."

"Not directly. That's the whole point." He ticked his first two fingers. "One, metaphor. Two, talisman."

"Yes." Booth said. "You said that already. But I don't know what it means."

"And three"—Bateman ticked a third finger—"don't be afraid to offend."

"Oh, we've offended, all right."

"Only in a standard, limited way. When I say offend, I mean get down low, as low and nasty and disgusting as it's possible to be. I mean offend the whole fucking world." He cocked his brow challengingly. "Let me ask you something. If I could tell you a sure way to spring Rowan, but one that would make you the number-one shit of all time in the eyes of the world, would you do it?"

"Look," Booth said, "I'm not about to rape one of the President's daughters or anything like that."

"You didn't answer my question."

"How can I? I don't know what you've got in mind."

"It's wild," Bateman said matter-of-factly. "But I didn't get it staring at the padded wall in the nuthouse. I got it right here in Washington."

That was nuthouse enough, Booth thought, but kept the notion to himself.

"I was down here in seventy-six," Bateman said, "for the big Bicentennial bash. I went out to Arlington Cemetery and watched them bury the Unknown of the Vietnam War. Some show. Patriotic sentiment, sanctimony rampant, and tears, more fucking tears; I thought I would be washed away in the tears. Okay?"

"Okay," Booth said impatiently.

"And so I got the idea," Bateman said. "Snatch the remains of the Unknown Soldier and threaten to destroy them unless the government agrees to release Francis Rowan."

There was a sudden lull in the undertone of conversation in the bar, as though, Booth thought, Bateman had been overheard and everyone was as stunned and startled as he was himself. But the hush was a coincidence, one of those inexplicable pauses that sometimes overtook everyone in a crowd at the same moment. No one was stunned, no one had overheard.

"Now you understand," Bateman said, still conversationally. "The metaphor—barter the dead for the living. The talisman—the absolutely perfect icon of the American spirit of patriotism."

When the first shock passed, Booth wasn't certain whether to be angry or to laugh. Instead he interposed a rational objection, and it wasn't until much later that he understood that by doing so he was acknowledging that Bateman's proposition was, if not viable, at least not beyond the boundaries of possibility.

He said, "You know, this isn't 1918. People aren't taken in by patriotic nonsense anymore."

"Maybe *you* aren't, and maybe the people you *know* aren't. But out there. . . ." Bateman made a broad gesture and knocked his glass over. It broke, and his drink spilled onto the bar. "Out there it's still 1918."

"I don't believe it. The country has matured, it's more skeptical and can't be manipulated by jingoism. Granted, patriotism gets a lot of lip service, but with the possible exception of the South, it isn't real. Even if it was, it would be neutralized by their feelings about Rowan."

Bateman heard him out with a patient sweet smile. "Thank you for making my point for me. Count up the people who hate Francis Rowan and you'll know exactly how many people would want to save the holy bones of the Unknown."

Booth regarded Bateman's tolerant smile and said angrily, "Well, whatever else its virtues might be, it takes the prize for repulsiveness."

"Thanks again," Bateman said. "If *you're* revolted, think of how the rest of the populace will feel, and start reconsidering your argument. Anyway, my own feeling is that a dead Asiatic baby on the end of a soldier's bayonet is a lot more revolting."

The hotel bar was filling up; the buzz of conversation was becoming louder and more animated. Booth said, "How in hell did you ever think of such a crazy idea?"

"Easy. I'm crazy." Bateman picked up a shard of broken glass and placed an edge gently against his wrist. "That and one other thing: I care more about Rowan, and I'm willing to risk more than you are."

He pressed the glass slowly but with increasing pressure against his wrist. Booth reached over and took the glass from his fingers. Bateman didn't move his wrist. The skin was unbroken, but a red line showed where he had been applying pressure.

"Come on," Booth said roughly. "Don't pull that stuff."

"Don't worry. Nobody who's serious about suicide ever tries it in a crowd."

Booth was shaken. "Well, I'm glad you don't want to."

"I didn't say I didn't. All I said was that if I did, I wouldn't do it where I could be stopped."

Booth got up. He put some money on the bar. "Look, are you sure you're all right?"

"I'm not your responsibility, but thanks for the kind thought." Bateman raised his hand and signaled to the bartender. "Broken glass here. Would you mind taking it away? And I'll have another of the same."

Booth hesitated. "About, well. . . ." He lowered his voice. "About the talisman. You haven't figured out a way of doing it, have you?"

"I didn't try."

"I see."

"You see? Maybe it's impossible, I don't know." He stared at Booth. "On the other hand, do you know that it *can't* be done?"

Booth shook his hand. It was dry and, while not quite limp, oddly unassertive.

"I wouldn't touch the Nam Unknown," Bateman said. "By statistical probability he's a black man. But aside from that, Nam is still too controversial, and you'd just muddy up the whole idea with extraneous emotions."

"Good luck," Booth said.

"Good luck to you, too."

Bateman's smile, like his grip, was dry and unassertive. Booth turned and made his way out of the bar to the street.

He had been lucky to get the room. A cancellation came in at the very moment the clerk was informing him that the hotel was full up. He registered, waved off the bellman who tried to grab his briefcase—it contained leaflets but passed as luggage—and went up to his room. He shucked his coat, stretched out on the bed, and phoned Caro. She answered, distantly, but then her voice quickened. He told her he was calling from Washington.

"Is everything all right?"

"I'm fine," Booth said. "Has there been anything on the demonstration?" But he already knew the answer.

There was an interval before she spoke, as if she had first shaken her head. "Not yet. How did it go?"

"It was awful. A bare dozen of us showed up, no interest from spectators, no coverage, even the cops were bored. It was an absolute waste of time."

"Don't say that." Her voice was sharp. He guessed that apart from asserting the strength of her own beliefs in their cause, she was trying to head him off from feeling sorry for himself. He took the hint.

"Look, Caro, I'm calling from a hotel. I'm staying over in Washington tonight."

"Oh?"

His ex-wife's instantaneous reaction would have been suspicion of his involvement with a woman. Caro's response merely invited him to explain his change of plan if he wished to.

He said, "You don't mind, do you?"

"Of course not." Then, after a pause, she surprised him. "You don't have a clean shirt."

In the old days, at the height of the antiwar demonstrations, he had packed along an extra shirt in case the one he was wearing became bloodied. The good old days. He smiled sadly. "I should be back tomorrow afternoon."

"All right."

He was silent and then, longing for her, said, "It's such a depressing little room."

"Yes, well . . . it's only for one night, isn't it?"

So much for demonstrativeness. And yet he hadn't really said anything that brimmed over with warmth and love himself, had he? The size of a hotel room! Couldn't a man who was lonely and missed his girl come out and say so?

He said, "We're running up a bill. See you tomorrow."

He got up and went out into the dark streets. He found an all-night drugstore, where he bought a safety razor and an inexpensive shirt. In the morning he shaved, put on his new shirt, and checked out of the hotel. He cut across Lafayette Park, facing the north lawn of the White House, the scene of yesterday's debacle. He crossed Pennsylvania Avenue at the corner and walked down East Executive Avenue. The White House loomed up behind the high fence and the carefully tended banks of shrubbery. Already there was a long line of sightseers queued up for an official tour of the White House. As he passed the various security booths leading into the grounds, the guards glanced at him casually. One said "Good morning" in a soft southern voice, and, taken by surprise, he answered with a stiff nod. No fraternizing with the enemy.

At the Ellipse a girl in a tourist-information pavilion pointed out the Tourmobile stop across the street. A bus had just pulled in. He sprinted across the street and joined a milling crowd of tourists. But there was room for him. At the height of the summer season two or even three buses were hitched together to handle the mobs.

The spieler was bored, but showed a trace of animation as

they approached the Lincoln Memorial, perhaps because she was black and Lincoln was still an acceptable hero in the black consciousness.

"You will notice that the great pillars of this most popular of all D.C. monuments—there are thirty-six of these pillars, one for each state of the Union in Lincoln's time—appear to be evenly spaced. But if they were evenly spaced, they would give the appearance of bulging. Therefore they are unequally spaced to make them *look* equal. This is an architectural thing. The statue of Lincoln is nineteen feet high. Those of you who wish to visit Arlington National Cemetery must get off here for the shuttle bus."

In the men's room at the Visitors Center in the cemetery, he had to wait five minutes because the urinals were monopolized by a large group of Filipino pilgrims. Filipino pilgrims! He relieved himself and went out to join the inevitable long line waiting for the bus that made the rounds of the cemetery. He sat in it stolidly, listening to the voice of the spieler (a cheerful one), and got off dutifully at the Kennedy gravesite, then went on to the Tomb of the Unknowns.

As he went up the walkway for the first time and saw the massive sarcophagus of the World War I Unknown, with its marching sentinel, he knew at once that Bateman's idea, however beguiling it might have sounded, was patently impossible to carry out. From the rear rank of a crowd that was five deep he watched the changing of the guard, then took the bus on to Arlington House, where Lee had paced his rose garden in the night and at last decided to place his sword at the service of Virginia.

Returning to the Visitors Center, he was torn between embarrassment and a nagging and irrational sense of loss. He boarded the shuttle bus for the return to Washington, but a moment before it started, he got off. Slowly at first, and then more rapidly, he walked the half mile back to the tomb.

He reached home after midnight. Caro was asleep. He undressed and went into the living room. Through the window

102

the Village street was still and empty. He sat in one chair, then another, then stood at the window again. Eventually he swallowed two aspirins, which was as close to taking pills as he ever came. He went back to the bedroom. Settling himself in bed, he accidentally jostled Caro's shoulder. She awoke, or perhaps had not been asleep, and turned into his arms. He was aroused at once and they made love, preliminaries unnecessary, urgent, wordless, and exhausting.

In the morning, when he awoke, she was sitting over her coffee. She told him that there had been several phone calls for him the day before, one, aggrieved, from the man who was to have driven him home from Washington.

"I owe him an apology," Booth said. "Instead of meeting him I was sitting in a bar absorbing wisdom from a lunatic."

"Was the demo as bad as everyone says? Morale is rock bottom."

The demo seemed an irrelevancy, something that had happened a long time ago. "His name is Bateman, he has seven years of state asylums under his belt, and, Caro, he wants us to snatch the Unknown Soldier and hold him as ransom for Francis Rowan's freedom."

She discounted the mockery of his tone. "But that's what you stayed over in Washington for."

Her mind was like a chess player's; it searched beyond the immediate move to its underlying purpose. He waited for her to ridicule the idea, but she said nothing.

"How do we know it can't be done? That's a direct quote from Bateman."

It was a feeble attempt at the light touch, and her mind had already rejected it as irrelevant. She said, "Is it possible?"

"It's a criminal, vicious, revolting idea."

She said flatly, "Is it possible?"

"You don't seem the least bit shocked or indignant." She made a little gesture of impatience. He went on. "I was a very good platoon lieutenant and company commander because I had an instinctive tactical mind."

"Would they give up Rowan for it?"

It occurred to him that the conversation was disjointed,

not a dialogue but a series of tangential monologues. He said, "The whole idea is a sick childish fantasy. I'm too old to be even discussing it. Too sane, too."

"Maybe there's been too *much* sanity. Maybe that's why Rowan is still in prison. I'm afraid he's going to rot there."

Yes, he would rot there. That's what it came down to. He said, "I suppose it wouldn't hurt to talk to somebody about it."

"You could talk to *me* about it."

He found himself quoting Bateman at frequent intervals.

Booth was fully aware that if he wanted to be dissuaded, or even sought neutral counsel, Asbury was not the first candidate for the job but the last. As for Caro, in the end she had come back to her insistent theme: Is it possible? Can it be done? He was disappointed at her lack of enthusiasm, even though her failure to laugh at the outlandishness of the idea or to be horrified by it was a form of endorsement. He knew that Asbury, the adventurist, would not be hobbled by practical considerations. And that was what he wanted: an unquestioningly favorable response that he could turn into a commitment for himself.

The presiding element of Broome Street was dust. It combined with oxygen to make up the basic component of the atmosphere. The street itself was narrow, crowded by small aged buildings crowding against one another as if for moral support. Both sides of the street were lined with trucks manned by muscular drivers and their helpers, wearing sweat-yellowed T-shirts, smoking incessantly, and conducting ordinary conversations in hoarse bellows to compete with the roar of the city.

The Committee for Justice and Human Reparations—they had retained their original name as one after another of their objectives came to pass: withdrawal of American troops from Vietnam, ending the war, unconditional amnesty—shared a storefront office with an express company which consisted of two nearly identical squat and hairy men who seemed to spend most of their time screaming on the telephone. An eight-foot-high partition of composition board that fell four feet short of the mottled metal ceiling separated the halves. One of the express-company men—Booth could never be sure which—had lost a son in Vietnam, and he allowed the committee to use the office without charge. In the beginning, conscious of the gap in the partition, they had conducted their business in whispers, until they realized that the express-company men were totally without interest in them.

One of the expressmen stood in the common doorway. Booth nodded to him, and the expressman looked back at him blankly; he never seemed to recognize any of them except generically. Booth went on into the committee office. Doc was there, with a couple of teenage hangers-on. Booth waved a greeting and leaned against the partition to listen to Doc, who was discussing Sunday's demo: ". . . beating a dead fucking dog . . . disaster of a war is a dead letter and all everybody wants to do is forget it ever happened. . . ."

Looking around the office, Booth thought, It's as tacky and tired and defeated as we are. The walls were brown chipped plaster, the painted window gave them privacy but nearly eliminated natural light, so that the cluster of three small-wattage bulbs in the ceiling burned day and night. The furniture was hand-me-down and begrimed, the rotted board flooring sprung underfoot. And everything was grayed down by dust seeping in from the street.

The picture of Francis Rowan, a grainy blowup from a photo taken at the time of his arrest, was badly faded and barely discernible under its patina of dust. But the handsome face, with its glowing martyr's eyes set deep in the bone, was instantly recognizable.

". . . fucking dynamite," one of the teenagers was saying. "We oughtta blast the shit out of something."

The teenager's face was earnest, its unformed features half hidden by hair. Booth stopped listening. They were pitiable: a cynical Nam veteran, a pair of teenagers, a middle-aged partisan who had adopted a cause for reasons he might not even truly understand.

He turned away abruptly. Doc's voice called after him, but he ignored it. He brushed by the expressman and went out.

He walked for a block or two, weaving from sidewalk to gutter to bypass the drawn-up trucks and their shouting crews, until he found a coffee shop with a telephone. He shut the door of the booth against the odors of fry cooking and the swell of voices and dialed Asbury's number.

"Ken Booth. I want to talk something over with you."

He heard Asbury yawn. "Okay, but what's to talk over? It was a fucking downer."

"It isn't about the demo. Something else."

"When you didn't show up for the ride home, we figured you had had it and gone and done the Dutch act."

"Are you free now?"

"Matter of fact. . . ." Asbury paused for another yawn. "One guy did do it. Out the fucking window. Christ."

Booth felt a nauseating wave of despair, futility, loss. "Who was it?"

"I don't think you knew him. He came down for the demo on Sunday. Character named Harvey Bateman?"

He was to think of his answer, later, as a declaration of intent. "No, I didn't know him."

"He dived out the window of his shrink's office."

"How'd you learn about it?"

"This morning's paper. I knew him slightly. A fucking nut."

Fucking nut—Bateman's epitaph. He remembered Bateman's neatness, his speech impediment. He shut his eyes to obliterate the memory. "Can we meet someplace?"

"Come on up here, if you want to. Give me a half hour to get rid of a bimbo and then come up. Okay?"

In the background he heard a girl's voice protesting.

He bought a *Times* at the first newsstand he came to and leafed through the paper until he found the story. It was short, three column inches of type, too brief, he thought, for a man who had packed seven years of asylums into his life. "Harvey Bateman, 26, plunged to his death. . . ." Halfway through a session with his analyst he had excused himself to go to the bathroom. He had climbed up on the toilet seat, wriggled his way through the small bathroom window, and sailed down to the Park Avenue pavement fifteen stories below.

Exit, flying, the author of the plan to snatch the remains of the Unknown Soldier. Booth threw the paper into a receptacle and walked on.

Asbury's shack-up was a Hispanic girl, unpretty except for large lustrous black eyes. She was sitting on the edge of a classically rumpled bed in the corner of the studio apartment when Asbury let him in. He was wearing a blue terry-cloth robe. The girl was naked.

"Sorry," Asbury said. "She begged for an encore in such a convincing way that I was helpless to refuse. You want a crack at her? Hey, big tits, you ball my friend—okay?"

"Fawk you," the girl said tonelessly.

"She knows only two phrases in English," Asbury said. "When she's mad, fawk *you,* and when she's passionate, *fawk* me, *fawk* me."

"I no like you," the girl said. She snatched up a bra from the floor and shrugged her breasts into it. Booth walked to the window and looked out at the street and a truncated view of Washington Square South. Behind him Asbury was ragging the girl, and she was responding sullenly. He watched a young man wander down the street, staggering, zonked out. He lurched against a car, slid along it, draped himself over the hood, and seemed to go to sleep. Suddenly he got to his feet, stared around wildly, and then zigzagged down the street.

"She wants to say good-bye to you," Asbury said. Booth turned to see the girl, fully dressed, wearing red checked pants and hugging an imitation fur jacket to her throat.

"Fawk you," the girl said to Booth. Asbury opened the door for her. "Fawk you."

"And fuck you, too, senorita." Asbury pushed the girl out of the door and shut it. "I'm God's gift to women, right, Booth?" His smile turned sly. "You're like the senorita, right? You no like me."

It was a mistake to think that people who were insensitive

about others were necessarily insensitive about themselves. Booth shrugged. "I've got something important to talk to you about."

Asbury studied him and chose to accept his words as a retreat. "Okay. What's on your mind?"

They moved to a table next to the kitchenette and sat down.

"As you know," Booth said, "I've always been opposed to dramatics, to violence. But after the demonstration on Sunday I've been wondering. . . ." He trailed off. Asbury's tapping fingers had increased their tempo. He had about thirty seconds of patience left. "Well, I've changed my mind."

"Yes? Well?" Asbury seemed unimpressed. "So what do we do—burn down the Justice Department? Tunnel into the prison?"

"Snatch one of the Unknown Soldiers," Booth said, "and hold the remains until they turn Rowan loose."

Asbury's fingers froze over the table, stiff and tense, and his mouth fell open in surprise. But he was a quick study. In the next instant he was on his feet, his eyes gleaming, reaching across the table and pumping Booth's hand.

"Man, you're a fucking genius! Let's do it!"

Booth grinned back stiffly. Their most reckless man approved. It was the reaction he had counted on and, in fact, courted. And yet he felt no elation. The plan that had been originated by a lunatic had now been underwritten by a wild man. He recognized a fatal momentum that he would do nothing to attempt to stop.

8

The building was a long low structure on the south post of Fort Myer. Booth drove past it to a sign that read SOUTH POST VISITORS PARKING LOT. A handsome, hard-eyed WAC corporal stepped out of a guard box and held up her hand. He explained his business to her and she waved him in. He parked the car and then walked back to the building. A passing soldier in paint-smeared fatigues directed him to Lieutenant Jamison's office.

Lieutenant Jamison stood up as he entered. He was a young man with a baby face who stood about six three and must have weighed two hundred and twenty-five pounds. His cheeks were pink, and he looked eminently fit.

"Good morning, Lieutenant. I'm Arthur Holder."

"Delighted to see you, Dr. Holder. Good morning, sir."

"Please," Booth said. "I never use the title. Not professor, either."

It was a line he had invented and practiced before his arrival, a touch of verisimilitude that he hoped would prop up his performance. He was not really much of an actor or a liar.

"Certainly, sir," Jamison said agreeably. "Won't you sit down, sir?"

The office was a small cubbyhole, and the desk was ship-shape. Although it was crowded with papers and brochures, it seemed neat and organized. Jamison took his seat behind the desk.

"Sir, I believe you told me over the telephone that you wished to write an article about the Old Guard?"

He had driven down to Washington early in the morning in a car he had borrowed from Asbury and made half a dozen phone calls. He had been shunted respectfully (it was standard army practice to address civilians as "sir") from one office to another until, finally, he had been put onto Jamison.

"Not an article, a book." Was he being tested? Did this apple-cheeked shavetail, who from his physical condition might be better used in the field than behind a desk, somehow suspect him? Nonsense! Nevertheless, he took pains to keep his story straight. "And not on the Old Guard exclusively, as I mentioned on the phone, but on special infantry units in general."

Lieutenant Jamison nodded. "As you doubtless know, the Third Infantry is the oldest active infantry unit in the United States Army."

"Established by a resolve in Congress in 1784," Booth said. He had boned up on the unit in the library. He smiled. "It's my business to know about such things."

Jamison looked disconcerted. "Well, then, there isn't much I can tell you, sir."

He was upset because it would be difficult for him now to go into his spiel. "All I have is book knowledge, Lieutenant. What I'd like is a firsthand look at the activities of the men of the Old Guard. I've seen the firing parties at Arlington and of course the sentinels at the tomb, but only as a spectator."

"Have you seen the changing of the guard?"

"Yes, and I'm very impressed. It compares favorably with the changing of the guard at Buckingham Palace."

Jamison flushed with pleasure, and Booth thought, It bothers me to make a fool of this pleasant and perhaps not too bright young man.

Jamison picked up a brochure entitled "The Old Guard" —black lettering on a chaste white ground—and offered it across the desk. "Perhaps you would wish a copy of this, sir?" Booth took the brochure. "Would you like an escorted visit to the tombs?" Booth nodded. "As I told you on the phone. . . ." He looked apologetic. "But first I must clear it with General Dammerling. It's just a formality."

While Jamison phoned, Booth leafed through the brochure. TODAY A DUAL MISSION: official ceremonial unit, also responsible for defense of the nation's capital. THE PRESIDENT'S OWN: ceremonial functions for the White House (had these been the soldiers Nixon had dressed up in buskins?). Pictures of guard with Coolidge, wearing ten-gallon hat above the face of a skinflint small-town banker; Lyndon Johnson standing up straight in his own version of a military bearing; John Kennedy, slim, detached. A MUSICAL HERITAGE: the Fife and Drum Corps, in unragged Continentals, at the annual Easter Egg Roll on the White House lawn. THE LAST HORSEMEN: a flag-draped casket on a caisson, drawn by three pairs of white horses, with Third Infantry soldiers mounted. A SECOND MISSION: the Third Infantry in tactical drill, practicing to defend the city of Washington. . . .

Lieutenant Jamison hung up the phone. "General Dammerling will see us now, sir."

Dammerling was a buck general, recently promoted, to judge from the shininess of his silver star. He sat in a large and well-appointed office on an upper floor, and his questioning was sharp. What is your university? Who is your publisher? What precisely is the theme of the book? What part does the Third Infantry play in the book?

"The Tomb of the Unknowns is a shrine, sir, the sanctified repository for four heroes who gave up their lives for their country and were borne here from foreign shores and laid to rest in high honor among their comrades of all wars from the very first."

General Dammerling spoke feelingly and Booth listened with foreboding. Was he going to be stopped cold here?

"We of the Old Guard accept our mission of protecting the tombs as a privileged trust. We are dedicated to safeguarding the peaceful slumber of our dead comrades-in-arms, to whom we are bound by the invisible skein that ties all warriors together."

Well, Booth thought, I'm a part of that skein, too. Haven't I, too, spilled my blood for my country? The general was about his own age, and judging by his battle ribbons, which

he wore in colorful tiers along with the blue combat infantryman's badge, they had fought in some of the same places.
And, he thought wryly, on the same side.

"It is our firm policy," the general said, "to oppose com-
mercialization of this resting place of the honored dead."

"Well," Booth said, "my books never sell more than a few
thousand copies, so you couldn't really call them commercial."

The joke fell flat. Or simply didn't register. The general
was off again in full cry. Lieutenant Jamison's eyes were
blinking in dazzlement, although he must have heard the
same spiel many times before. Booth was certain that it *was* a
spiel, that no matter what his auspices (unless from a higher
military authority), the general would have delivered it.

"The honored dead must rest in peace, secure from desecration. I regard any such desecration as a viler crime than
murder. At least the potential victim of a murder has an opportunity to defend himself."

Try murdering *me*, the general's fierceness seemed to be
implying, and I'll show you a trick or two.

Booth waited, but the general, staring across the desk, his
aggressively clean-shaven jaw jutted, appeared to have
finished. Perhaps he was waiting for a response, granting the
prisoner at the bar the opportunity of pleading on his own
behalf. Jamison was still blinking deferentially.

"I share your beliefs, General," Booth said. He paused,
and then went on grimly. "I'm entitled to wear a few of the
same ribbons I see on your chest, including the Combat Infantry Badge. There are a number of *my* old comrades lying
out there in that cemetery, too. I have no intention of dese-
crating their memories."

"I see." The general looked thoughtful. "What was your
rank?"

The utter idiocy of the question took Booth aback for a
moment. "My rank? I finished up as a major. I ran a rifle
company."

Something flickered in the general's eyes, and Booth
thought, with a savage joy, I outranked him; when it counted, I outranked the sonofabitch.

The general stood up behind his desk. He had the air of a man who had made a command decision. "I hardly think we need fear any indiscretions from a man like you, Major. Lieutenant Jamison will escort you to the tombs and offer any help you may require."

Jamison stopped blinking, braced, and said, "Very good, sir."

The general came around the desk and extended his hand. Booth shook it, secretly torn between rage and wild laughter.

They stood behind the crowd of spectators watching the sentinel pace, stomp, turn, shift his rifle, freeze.

"Twenty-one paces," Lieutenant Jamison said, "and a twenty-one-second freeze. Twenty-one, as you know, sir, is the number symbolic of the twenty-one-gun salute, the honor reserved to the nation's highest and bravest."

Booth scribbled a note on the back of the brochure.

"In summer, at the height of the tourist season, the guard is changed every half hour. Out of season his tour is an hour, and at night, after the cemetery is closed to visitors, it's two hours. At night they're a *leetle* less perfectionist in the drill." He stopped and reconsidered. "But so little that it isn't visible to the naked eye."

Booth wrote, "Not visible to the naked eye."

Jamison said, "That's really off the record, sir."

"Sure." Booth drew a line through the note.

"Thank you, sir. As you doubtless know, the tomb sentinels consist of three reliefs, each of which is on twenty-four hours and off forty-eight, rotating through three hundred and sixty-five days a year. Incidentally, you can identify the relief by the number of times the sentinel racks the bolt of his rifle. Once if he's a member of the first relief, twice if he's second relief, and so on. Of course, the relief commander announces which relief it is, but still, knowing about racking the bolt is a sort of inside bit."

"What hours does the relief go?"

"Oh six hundred to oh six hundred. Actually, though, the last tour of the retiring relief runs from oh five hundred to oh seven hundred. This gives the old relief and the new time to get out of each other's way. So there's a sort of overlapping, you might say."

Booth wrote, "0600–0600, hour overlap," and tilted the brochure so that Jamison could read it.

"How many men comprise a relief?"

"It varies between five and six, plus the relief commander. And there's a sergeant of the guard, who is in charge of all three reliefs."

Booth watched the sentinel do his stylized shifting of his rifle from right to left shoulder arms. "The rifle is the M-fourteen?"

"Yes, it's the standard M-fourteen, but with the stock revised to make it lighter to carry."

"When I did guard duty in basic training, way back when," Booth said, "I carried an M-one. Some nine or ten pounds, if I remember correctly. Of course the rifle was empty, no ammo."

"The sentinels' piece is empty, too."

"I see. Is that off the record, Lieutenant?"

Jamison looked stymied. "I don't know. Never been asked that before."

"Let's make it off the record," Booth said.

"I'm sure you've noticed the uniformity of the sentinels? In a little while, when the guard changes, you'll see three of them together, and it's hard to tell them apart one from the other. That's uniformity."

Booth wrote, "That's uniformity."

"They're all very slim, as you can see. That's a requirement. If we had our way, we'd like all three reliefs to be exactly the same height. Say six two, for instance. But we realize that would be prejudicial to men of other heights who wanted to be sentinels. So, at this time, the reliefs vary from six foot even to six three. Second relief is six foot even, first is six three, and the other is six two."

"No six one?"

"Not at the present time." Jamison seemed relieved that Booth didn't make a note. "However, that's just the way it happened to work out, not prejudice. No prejudice of any kind in today's army."

Booth made a note: "No prejd in army."

To the left, at the top of the winding path, the barracks door opened and the relief commander appeared. He sauntered slowly down the path. Jamison looked at his watch.

"Six minutes to the hour. In exactly two minutes, carrying his rifle at port, the new guard will come down and join him. Do you know why the relief commander is so casual at this point?"

Booth shook his head.

"So as to keep the spectators loose. So that when the changing of the guard begins, they're reverent and mature, but not uptight."

They watched the change in silence, except when Jamison whispered, "Two racks of the bolt—see? Second relief."

When the change was completed, Jamison invited Booth to visit the barracks. They started up the path, and Jamison explained that the present quarters were improvised. The permanent barracks were situated under the amphitheater.

"I imagine the men spend most of their off-hours sleeping?" Booth said. "I'm sure *that* hasn't changed since the old army."

"Very little sleeping," Jamison said. "They have too much to do."

Booth wrote, "No slpng," and said, "Such as what?"

"Caring for their equipment, their uniforms, their personal hygiene, policing the barracks. That inspection the relief commander gives them down there? It's for real. And he checks them out *before* they leave the barracks, too."

If Booth had hoped to find the men of the second relief swilling beer, reading dirty books, or screaming raucous army jokes at one another, he was disappointed. They were almost exactly as advertised: shaving, running patches through their rifles, brushing their tunics, polishing leather and brass. . . . The relief commander was watching a movie on a color television set, but he was sitting erect, practically at attention.

115

As they entered, a sentinel shouted, *"Ten*-HUT!" and they were all up and braced in a split second, chest out, butt in, chin up.

"At ease." They loosened up at Jamison's command, but they didn't sit down, nor did he invite them to. "Major Holder is writing an article on the Old Guard. I'm sure that if he has any questions, you will be glad to answer them."

The men's eyes, bright and clear, snapped to Booth and then front again.

"They're yours, Major Holder."

"Please sit down, gentlemen," Booth said.

In a body, as if by the numbers, they all sat. Their faces were composed, attentive, alert. Their hair was cut so short that the scalp showed through. One of the men, who had been holding a cigarette, stubbed it out in an ashtray, then jumped up and went out, taking the ashtray with him.

Jamison said, "When an ashtray is used, it is immediately emptied and washed out."

The room was not greatly different from the dayrooms Booth remembered, except that it was infinitely neater and cleaner than any he had ever seen, and, of course, it was carpeted. Sofas, comfortable armchairs, lamps, end tables, the television set—in effect, a large living room.

"Corporal Simmons, would you care to take Major Holder through the barracks?"

Simmons jumped to his feet. "Would you be so good as to follow me, sir?"

He was not the first visitor, Booth thought as he followed Simmons. There was a patter for this, too:

"Beds, sir. . . ." Five army cots, with the blankets drawn so tightly that the proverbial coin would probably have bounced to the ceiling. "Monday is our big cleanup day, sir. We GI the whole barracks. But we spend a lot of time *every* day keeping our home in order. Baseboards here, sir, are repainted every ten days. Carpet is swept several times a day. . . . These are our kitchen facilities. However, we don't do much cooking, as a field kitchen is brought in with chow three times a day from the fort's consolidated mess hall. Also, a driver makes two runs a day to the PX. . . .

116

"The log, sir. Here we enter such events as the raising and lowering of the flag, the opening and closing of the cemetery, transfers in and transfers out, unusual incidents, et cetera. . . ."

Quite suddenly Booth felt disgusted by his imposture. Simmons, with his grave courtesy, his carefully controlled facial muscles, his shaved head and plucked neck, struck him as pathetically vulnerable. He was not the enemy. He was simply a boy who believed sincerely in his sworn duty to guard four unfleshed corpses. In his sense of mission, Booth thought, he is not so different from me.

"Would there be anything else, Major?" Simmons seemed to have sensed the lag in his attention.

"Thank you very much. I think that does it."

They went back to the main room, and Booth suddenly thought, Men sitting in easy chairs, in sofas, can't get up quickly. And in that rather obvious insight about half of the plan came together.

The other half came later, after Lieutenant Jamison had driven him back to the south post and he had reclaimed his car and driven to Arlington Cemetery. Instead of taking the bus he had decided to walk to the tombs. Partway there he paused in the road to watch the civilian workers who were toiling up a hillside cutting out a new gravesite. A few of the workmen—they were mostly young, red-tan under their hard hats—looked at him without interest. He walked on, suddenly exhilarated.

The two halves came together in a beautifully fitted join as he was driving northward through the tunnel under Chesapeake Bay. Except that he didn't know if any of it could be made to work.

He reached home at nine o'clock, exhausted by the drive. Asbury was there.

"I need the car tonight," Asbury said, "so I thought I'd come down here. Save time."

He was sprawled in a chair, a drink in his hand. Caro was sunk into the sofa, looking sullen.

"Your old lady was kind enough to give me a drink," Asbury said. He held his glass up, as if offering it as evidence. *We weren't making it, your honor. How could we be if I'm sitting here and she's sitting there and I got a goddamn drink in my hand? What am I—a one-handed lover?*

Booth went out to the kitchen. There was a tray of ice half melted on the sink drain. He spilled off the water and dumped some ice in a glass and poured whiskey over it. Nothing happened, he told himself. At least not yet. Maybe it would have, in another ten minutes, but I walked in too soon. What we have here is guilt and tension; no orgasms have taken place, no release.

He went back to the living room. His whiskey tasted terrible; gall was a poor mixer. He looked at Caroline. She had not stirred; her expression had not changed. Asbury's legs were extended, his combat boots stretched across the rug.

"So?" Asbury said. "What went?"

Booth took the car keys and tossed them across the room. Asbury caught them showily, snapping his hand over them like a man plucking a fly out of the air.

"Well?" Asbury frowned.

"I'll have a better idea after I talk to Eddie Raphael."

"Raphael?" Asbury was irritated, or simulating irritation, it didn't matter which. "What the hell has that bourgeois asshole got to do with it? What kind of deal can it be if it has to be checked out with Raphael?"

"Can I freshen your drink?" Booth said.

"No, you can't freshen my drink. I want to know why you have to consult Raphael. Why don't you consult somebody who's going to risk his ass? Like me."

Booth got up and went to the kitchen to fix himself another drink. When he returned, Asbury was standing, his legs braced apart. Jungle Jim prepared for a showdown. Booth sloshed the ice gently in his glass.

"Well, Mr. Booth," Asbury said, "you can go fuck yourself. I'm out."

Booth glanced sidelong at Caro and thought, I can't afford to lose Asbury. Not because he's indispensable, but because I'd be losing him for the wrong reasons. He said mildly, "I'm

not trying to hold out on you. But before I find out some
technical information from Raphael—"

"He'll queer it," Asbury said. "Raphael is a mouse, a sell-
out. I won't work with Raphael."

"You won't have to. He's going to be our, well, technical
adviser."

"And I'm what—a field hand?"

Booth sighed. "All right. Sit down."

Asbury took his hipshot pose. "Look, don't fucking *tolerate*
me."

Caro spoke for the first time. "The air is so goddamn full
of macho I can't breathe." She got up and walked out of the
room, and presently the bedroom door slammed.

Asbury said, "What's eating *her* ass?"

The same thing that's eating mine, Booth thought, and
said, "Sit down, and I'll fill you in."

"You could have said that five minutes ago."

"Yes," Booth said. "It's been a long day."

Asbury accepted it as an apology. "I'll take that drink
now."

Booth took his glass. The shut bedroom door was a reproach. He went back to the living room. Asbury was seated.

"Here's how I think we can do it. . . ."

In Raphael's subsurface playroom adjoining his work-
room, they sat on imitation-leather chairs with a huge butch-
er-block coffee table between them. There were blue-white-
yellow café curtains on the windows, which were set high on
one wall. There was a television set, a bridge table holding
the components of a hi-fi set and, on the fake beams, the
speakers of a stereo system painted blushing pink to match
the color of the ceiling. A small plastic ball and bat, a toy
hook and ladder, a dump truck, a chessboard with plastic
men, and a "computer game" were piled in a corner.

Raphael said, "I know it's damp and sticky down here, but
I'm trying to put in central air conditioning."

"It's not bad," Booth said.

"I've ordered the components, but they take forever to

119

come. I didn't say I wouldn't help. What I've been saying is that it's wildly desperate and, well, outrageous."

Booth took the postcard out of his pocket. He had bought it in a drugstore in Washington. The photographer had stood near the amphitheater, facing east, and shot the changing of the guard at an oblique angle past the heads of a few spectators. The relief commander was facing the camera; the old and new guards had their backs to it. Beyond the black strip of rubber mat the slabs of the crypts were clearly delineated in the floor of the plaza. Past the sarcophagus, a white block from the rear view, the photograph shot down the steps to the lawn between the walkways and thence out to the rotunda across the road and a postcard-blue sky.

Booth said, "That's how it's done normally, when they're not doing work on the amphitheater." He handed the card to Raphael. "What you have to do is picture the black rubber mat on the steps below the sarcophagus, the changing of the guard there, too, of course, and the spectators down at the foot of the steps behind a chain."

Raphael suddenly palmed the card as the cellar door opened. Paula Raphael came down the steps with a tray holding coffee and cups and slices of cake. She was trailed by a little boy with blond hair and serious brown eyes.

"This is Jason," Paula Raphael said. "This is Mr. Booth, darling."

The boy came to Booth's side and said, "I'm four years, eight months, nine days, four hours, and nine months old."

"And nine months?" Booth smiled. "How much does that add up to?"

"Five years, five months, nine days, and four hours."

"Now, Jason, please." Paula frowned at him.

"Well, he asked me," the boy said. "I didn't add it up until he asked me."

Raphael said, "It's a family disagreement. Jason maintains that his age should be counted from conception on, so that he's his actual age plus nine months."

"Whether I was alive or not by legal interpretation, I certainly existed during the nine months of gestation. So, therefore, I am my legal age plus nine months. Do you agree?"

Booth was not used to children, and certainly not to children like Jason Raphael. His own son, who was now twenty-three, and from whom he received an antiseptic letter two or three times a year, had been a rollicking little boy with no suspicion of precocity. He looked at Raphael for help.

"Well," Raphael said unsmilingly, "the question remains unresolved, so we compromise. That's why Jason states his legal age and adds the nine months on at the end. There's honor enough for all of us that way."

"Except at nursery school," Jason said. "Two boys kicked me in the behind for giving my age that way. There's no honor in that."

Booth started to laugh, but the boy was not joking. "Well, Jason, I've never given this particular problem any serious thought. I'd like a little time, and I might have an opinion before I leave."

"That's fair enough," the boy said.

"Come, Jason," Paula said. "Let's let Daddy and Mr. Booth do their business."

The boy followed after her but paused at the top of the steps and said, "Will you really give it serious thought?"

"I'll certainly try." When the boy and his mother had left, Booth said, "He's an extraordinary child."

"Yes." Raphael looked broodingly at the closed door. "Well, that's another problem." He brought the postcard out and studied it. "I presume the sarcophagus is marble?"

"It's Vermont marble, and it weighs fifty tons."

"Well, you can forget about it, unless you plan to use a huge charge of dynamite." He looked up in alarm. "I hope you don't—"

"No. We're not thinking of the sarcophagus at all, but one of the other three."

Raphael studied the photograph. "Are those slabs marble too?"

Booth nodded. "The World War Two, Korean War, and Vietnam War Unknowns are buried in concrete crypts under those marble slabs. We want to break through one of the slabs so that we can lift the casket out. Can we crack it with a jackhammer?"

121

"I don't know too much about marble, but from observation I know it's breakable. A jackhammer is awfully noisy."

Booth nodded. "We would have to create some sort of diversion. Would the jackhammer do the job?"

"How thick is the marble?"

"About six inches."

Raphael studied the postcard. "I imagine a good jackhammer would crack it up. I don't know how long it would take. You could experiment. Buy a piece of marble and rent a jackhammer. . . ."

"How long it takes is critical."

Raphael continued to study the postcard. "It wouldn't surprise me if you could use vacuum suction. It's practically silent, and you could probably lift the slab without even breaking it."

"What's vacuum suction?"

"They use it to handle steel plates or big sheets of plywood. Did you ever see films of a steel mill in operation? They lower a vacuum head from a hoist, pump the air out, create a suction, and up it goes. When they want to drop the sheet, they simply kill the vacuum."

"We're not equipped like a steel mill," Booth said. "Let's come back to the jackhammer."

"It's not nearly as good."

"Yes," Booth said, "but we have to be practical. We can't set up any elaborate machinery and we have limited funds."

"It wouldn't cost more than a few hundred dollars." Raphael suddenly looked interested. He picked up a pencil and a pad. "Do you know how the slab is fastened to the crypt?"

"No idea. It doesn't matter, if we're going to break it up."

"Probably grout—sand and cement—if it's fastened at all. With all that weight, it won't move, so why bother? How big is the slab?"

"Ten feet long by five wide."

Raphael was making notes on the pad in a spidery hand. "You'll need a vacuum pump, an electric motor, some nylon or steel cable, a hoist of some kind, and the vacuum head and a frame to attach it to. The vacuum head and frame represent the only real problems. How much can you afford to spend?"

"We have some money, but we're not a factory. All that machinery. . . ."

"I could probably pick up a good secondhand pump and motor for about a hundred dollars apiece down on Canal Street. We'll want a winch, and a gear box to reduce the ratio, so that we can crank the casket up by hand. Then there'll be odds and ends—couplings, hose, a pressure gauge. . . ."

"You're going a little too fast for me, Eddie."

"The motor and the pump weigh around twenty-five or thirty pounds each. The winch and some pulleys. . . . Everything is small except the vacuum chamber and the frame that holds it. They have to be made to order. They would probably cost as much as a thousand dollars if you got them from a commercial house. On the other hand, if we made them ourselves"—he scribbled some notations on his pad— "maybe four or five hundred."

Booth said, "I think you've lost me."

"Do I have to begin with basics?" Raphael sighed with elaborate patience. "A pump. You must know that a pump is a device that's used to move fluid from one place to another— for example, to pump water out of a flooded cellar. In our case the fluid is air, and the pump will take the air between the surface of the slab and a vacuum chamber and evacuate it, thus creating a vacuum. It gets rid of all atmospheric pressure. But surely you know all that."

"I still don't see how that flimsy equipment can lift up a heavy slab of marble."

Raphael turned in his seat and placed his pad on his knee so that Booth could see it as he wrote. "Given—a slab ten feet by five feet. Okay. That's fifty square feet. A hundred and forty-four square inches to the square foot. Multiply that by fifty and you get seventy-two hundred square inches. Then we multiply by fourteen, the number of pounds per lifting power per inch—actually it's fourteen point seven—and we get one hundred thousand and eighty, the number of pounds that can be lifted by suction. That's fifty tons, which is a good deal more than the slab weighs. And it's *not* flimsy equipment, it's just simple and inexpensive."

"Don't be offended. You said there would be no noise?"

"*Practically* none. The hum of an electric motor, the truck engine running, maybe a slight tearing sound when the marble separates from the grout. . . ."

"And it works?"

"Give me a vacuum and a chamber that fits," Raphael said solemnly, "and I'll move the world. In the formula I gave you, shave off an inch. Forty-nine square feet instead of fifty, to allow for a margin around the edges of the slab to make sure the seal doesn't leak."

"How long will all this take to do?"

Raphael shrugged. "A half minute to pump the vacuum, another thirty seconds to lift the slab and drop it, maybe a couple of minutes to wrestle the coffin up and manhandle it into the truck. Say six or seven minutes all told?"

Booth contained his excitement. Raphael was drawing a sketch on the pad, his head bent, his forehead wrinkled in absorption. Of all of them, Booth reflected, Raphael most closely resembled the veterans of World War II—the war over, he had reentered the mainstream: career, house and mortgage, shrink for his wife and child. . . . True, he retained an interest in the Movement struggle, but mostly as a moral commitment. It would diminish as time went on, as he prospered, as his obligations multiplied, and before long it would disappear.

"The electric motor," Raphael said, "would work off the truck engine. We'll need a transformer. . . ."

It would be simple to manipulate Raphael from technician to participant, mostly by allowing him to enmesh himself through his fascination with his own machinery. Or he could stop him short by a word or an attitude. It was as clear-cut as that—he held Raphael's immediate fate, perhaps his future, in his hands.

He said, "It sounds good. Will you help us?"

Raphael agreed. He would buy all the required gear, make the chamber and frame himself, to save some five hundred dollars (but really, Booth knew, because his interest was piqued and his ego involved), and teach them how to use it. "But it stops right there as far as you're concerned. You won't take part in the actual operation."

But he knew that in time Raphael would come in all the way, and he would make no effort to prevent it. And thus, Booth thought, I have broken through a moral barrier—I'm no longer just a man who is willing to sacrifice himself for a cause, but to sacrifice others as well. At one bound, I have joined the company of saints, martyrs, and villains.

Raphael was seeing him out when he suddenly remembered his promise to the boy.

"What shall I tell Jason?"

Raphael looked shocked. "Tell him what you think. Be honest with him."

Upstairs, in the living room, the boy ran over. "Did you come to a decision?"

"I'm sorry, Jason. I think it's incorrect to count the nine months before birth."

The boy seemed on the verge of contending the point, but his mother gestured sharply and, crestfallen, he merely said, "Did you consider it? Is that your considered opinion?"

"You mustn't question Mr. Booth's integrity," Paula said.

"It's my considered opinion," Booth said.

No less than the father, he thought, he could manipulate the son and prepare him for the hard realities of life.

In one of his infrequent moments of detachment, Booth characterized himself with some humor as "author (from an idea by the late Harvey Bateman), director, impresario, actor, angel, and casting director."

He had become an accumulator of information, people, and artifacts, and the chief, and only, contributor of money. His ex-wife's remarriage five years before and his son's coming of age had relieved him of financial pressure, and now he was able to live in modest comfort on his inheritance from his mother. To be sure, she would have disapproved of the use to which he was putting her money. But ten years ago she had disapproved of his throwing up his job—and tenure!—at Alfred to join the Movement. For that matter, she had disapproved of his joining the army, of his marrying Janine, and of his divorcing Janine. In her lifetime she had rarely approved of him. Nevertheless, she had loved him in her Calvinist fashion, had remembered him in her will, and died as undemonstratively and with as little sentience as she had lived.

If there was any of his mother in him, he was hard-pressed to discern it. Even less could he see himself in his father, a dim conventional soul who had practiced law in a dusty way and died without leaving a single vivid memory of himself. But Booth was wise enough or modest enough to perceive that he wasn't *sui generis* and that he undoubtedly carried his parents' genes; he just didn't consider the point important enough to pursue to a conclusion.

He also knew that he was not the first man to be blessed— or damned—by sudden waking from a lifelong sleep, or, as the modern parlance had it, breaking out. For a man who had turned forty, he had been a premature antiwar militant, far ahead of his generation in seeing—as only the "kids" did at the start—that the Vietnam War was an abomination.

He had always felt, regarding his "conversion," that it was somehow inseparably entwined with the fervor that he had held about "his" war, the "good" war. He had believed in himself, both as to morality—"what we're fighting for"—and as to his responsibility to the men he led. Afterward, something had been missing. He had married, begat a child, gone to college, found a job as an economics instructor at a college. At thirty-eight he became an associate professor and, if he had kept his nose clean and published now and then, would have gone on to a full professorship.

A decent life, but one that left him dissatisfied. He was a man to whom comfort was uncomfortable. After divorcing his wife, he found that little had changed, although his expectations had been high. His life still seemed to lack focus, passion. What he sought, although he was as yet unable to articulate it as such, was his own moral equivalent for war, something that would bring out the best in him. He found it in fighting against war.

He could not remember now, nor had he ever been able to

pinpoint precisely, the moment when he had converted to an antiwar stance intellectually. But he did know when it became a visceral commitment because he had the scars to prove it. He had joined a small group of faculty members, all very young, all sectarian radicals—neither of which he was—in support of the student antiwar movement. He attended rallies and demonstrations, always in the rear, on the periphery, and contributed money, but his convictions were still intellectual. It changed dramatically, one sunny afternoon, when the town police charged a sit-in on the steps of the college president's house. The sharp crack of a hardwood nightstick on the bone of a skull, the flow of blood, had triggered something forgotten in his past—anger, pity, the excitement of battle—and he had charged into the fray. He had taken a blow on the head himself and seen, with a sort of grim exhilaration, the color of his own blood.

The men you bled with were your "company." He moved from the periphery of commitment to the center. He was aware that he was estranging himself from his own generation, a courageous thing for him to do, though he never thought about it much in that light. Eventually his peers straggled up to his position, but by then he had moved on, and they were never to catch up with him.

He had recognized himself belatedly as that puzzling breed of men—reformers, do-gooders, servants to the underdog, bleeding hearts—who found peace through militancy. He had discovered his métier.

Doc was the essential, almost indispensable, recruit. He was dedicated, nerveless, and a hustler. More than any of the others, he had kept up his army contacts, and he was known and trusted in army camps—by "liberated" soldiers—from Fort Dix to as far south as Fort Myer. On his visits to the camps he would proselytize on behalf of the Movement while conducting his business, which was the dealing of pills and pot. He operated on a small scale and sporadically, just enough, as he put it, "to ward off a steady job and to accommodate my friends and admirers."

Doc did not disappoint him. He listened with a small appreciative grin and, when Booth was finished, said only, "I'm in." Then he ticked off the items on Booth's laundry list of matériel requirements with "no sweat" or "gotcha" or "no problem." He numbered among his confidants supply sergeants, armorers, medics, company clerks—a gamut of men who would steal anything in an army camp and pass it on at a modest price.

He had anticipated that Doc would come up with an effective way of sedating the sentinels, but his help with the procurement of an Army Corps of Engineers van was an unexpected windfall.

"Attilio Manero," Doc said. "My cousin. He's a big-shot sergeant in the motor pool at Belvoir."

"Is he in the Movement?"

"He's in the Al Manero movement. He's corrupt to a fault and never allows politics to interfere with business."

"Can we trust him?"

"If he takes the money, he'll deliver. He's an honest crook."

"I mean afterward—he won't sell us out?"

"He believes in two things—money and family. He's my *cugino*. He'll keep the faith."

"He'll take the risk?"

Doc smiled. "There won't be much risk—not for him. He'll see to that before he makes a move. I'll phone him tonight."

After Doc had recommended Dover to drive the van, all that remained was a safehouse to hole up in, and Caro volunteered her parents' place on the Cape.

The cast was complete, the props were obtainable, the script was written. Minor changes could be dealt with in rehearsal.

Booth had been in prison once, but only for a few hours. At the height of the antiwar demonstrations he had been swept up in an indiscriminate haul with several dozen others, including a famous activist writer. It had not been a pleasant experience, but the grimness had been relieved by a sense of community with the other protesters and purified by anger

and laughter, not to mention an exhilarating virtuoso performance by the novelist.

Now, in Lewisburg, with an endless series of gates closing
behind him, he recognized that his experience had been
amateur; this was the real thing. He was searched with
efficient professionalism before being taken to a small bare
room with two slat-backed chairs facing each other across a
wide wooden table. Francis Rowan sat in one of the chairs.
The guard, who had instructed him not to shake hands, and
to keep his hands on the table and in clear view at all times,
remained in the room.

"Hi, Roger." Rowan smiled at the guard, who made no response, but sat down on a chair against the wall. "Good
morning, dear friend." Rowan smiled broadly at Booth and
said, "I'm not allowed to rise. Consider this my warm and
loving greeting." He placed his fingers together in the East-
ern *namaste* and bowed his head.

Booth sat down facing him. The table was ten feet across,
and even if both of them extended their hands, they would
not touch. Still, he obeyed the guard and kept his hands folded at the edge of the table.

"I'm glad to see you looking well," Booth said. He had
heard Rowan speak many times and marched behind him,
but had never met him face to face. He felt awkward, not so
much awed by him as dislocated: the distant shadow turned
into present flesh.

"I'm feeling quite well." The remarkable orator's voice was
almost uncomfortably vibrant at close quarters. "With the exception of my digestion." He turned to the guard. "Will you
bear me out on the quality of the food in this place, Roger?"

The guard's brow raised and lowered neutrally.

"It is almost a hundred percent starch," Rowan said, "and
badly cooked starch at that." His frown turned quickly into a
self-deprecatory smile. "It may seem to you to be a petty
complaint, but here inside we are removed from great
causes, and those that remain *become* great ones."

"Yes," Booth said uncertainly. "I think I understand."

"We are in process of forming a committee to deal with the

warden on the question. Our first meeting is scheduled for next week. The warden is not an entirely unreasonable man"—he winked at the impassive guard —"and I have reason to expect that we can negotiate an improvement. Then, perhaps, I will manage to lose my unsightly paunch. Vanity, yes, vanity does not abandon us at the prison gates."

In fact, Booth thought, he looked marvelously well. His shoulders were square and broad in the blue-gray prison twill, open at the collar to show the strong corded neck. His face, smoothly tanned, was unlined, confident, open and even extroverted, with only the eyes—set deep into the bone structure, an intense blue-gray (almost a match for the color of his shirt)—indicating the man of deep and passionate conviction. They were the slightly disquieting eyes of the martyr.

With the sense that his timing had somehow, inexplicably, gone awry, Booth said, "I bring you greetings from those of us who are dedicated to the cause of your liberation, as well as from thousands of others who sympathize deeply."

"Thank you. It's good to know that one is not forgotten. Yet I'm not so concerned for my own freedom as a fact—as you see, prison has not broken me—as I am for my freedom as a rallying cry for all we have fought for and, some of us, suffered for."

"Yes," Booth said, "I think we understand that."

"Not," Rowan said with a smile, "not that I would mind getting out of this place as a personal matter also."

He threw his head back in a roaring laugh. The guard yawned behind his hand.

· "I can't tell you how pleased I am that you look so well," Booth said, and thought: What do I mean—that martyrs should properly look at least a little haunted? "You have a tennis player's tan."

"I'm out all day with the construction gang. They offered me a job in the library, but I volunteered instead for the road gang. If I rejected such special privilege on the outside, I certainly couldn't accept it here in prison."

Booth glanced at the guard. He was yawning again, but his eyes were alert. There would be no way of telling Rowan about their plans. Not that he had intended to go beyond the merest hint that something was afoot.

He said cautiously, "I do want you to know that we have not abandoned our efforts on your behalf. We are trying."

"I love you all profoundly and abidingly," Rowan said. "And if you carry any message back, it must be this: that no man can ask for more blessing than to have good and generous and loving friends."

Booth realized with a sense of despair that there was somewhere a break in the connection. Rowan was a star and Booth a supernumerary. Despite the brooding quality of those zealot's eyes, Rowan seemed more the cheerful preacher than the martyr.

He said hesitantly, "Actually, I have come specifically to tell you"—he glanced at the guard, who had neither moved nor changed his expression—"that we're starting a new, shall I call it, campaign."

Rowan smiled benignly, and Booth thought, I'm not making it, I'm not putting anything across. He tried another tack.

"We believe that this new campaign will result in your freedom. We want you to know"—he slowed his voice down and said with emphasis—"you will be free, and in the very near future." His voice echoed falsely like the voice of a ham actor.

"I know the difficult task you are pursuing against indifference, callousness." A hard glitter lit up Rowan's eyes, and now, Booth thought, he looked the martyr. "People must not be allowed to forget. They must never be allowed to forget."

But they had already forgotten, Booth thought, it was their genius that they *could* forget.

"If I brood," Rowan said, "it is because here in prison I can do so little of what I wish to do. If I have transgressed, it was in the service of my conscience that I did so. Do not worry on my behalf. I am healthy, I am not abused or mistreated, I have the esteem of my fellows. In the matter of the odious chow. . . ." His smile was broad, his teeth brilliantly white and perfect against his tanned skin. "It is a nullity against all the genuine suffering of the world, and it is trifling of me even to mention it."

The guard's chair legs scraped. "Time's up."

And everything unsaid, Booth thought. Dismally he stared across the table at Rowan's wide cheerful smile, and realized suddenly that his teeth were capped.

9

Now, after ten hours of immurement, the van had become their world, a world shrunk down to a dark interior of men and machinery, shapes that were barely distinguishable from one another except that the men occasionally moved. The air that seeped in through the minimally opened rear door of the van kept them alive, but its freshness became tainted almost at once by the smell of grease and oil, of body odors, of baloney sandwiches, of the contents of the oil drum, which was tolerable when it was capped but overwhelmed them with its stink each time someone lifted the lid.

Booth had promised himself not to look at his watch again until he had reckoned that a full hour had gone by. But when he pulled his sleeve up to uncover the luminous watch dial, it was three minutes past three. Seventeen minutes had elapsed. Had the watch run down? He resisted the urge to shake his left wrist, to jog the watch into motion again. Instead he bent low over the watch and saw the sweep second hand ticking its measured pace around its orbit.

"My friends stink worse than death." The voice was Doc's, coming languidly out of the darkness. "So can you imagine how bad my enemies would smell?"

Someone snored.

"Asbury faking it." Doc laughed softly. "Showing he has nerves of steel and can sleep like a baby on the eve of battle."

Booth heard a grunt as a humped shadow rose, moved, paused, moved again, paused. He knew it was Raphael, checking his gear as he had done half a dozen times before.

What could he tell in the dark? What could have changed? But, of course, it must be Raphael's way of fortifying himself against the drag of time. The shadow moved, paused, muttered, then went back to the front end of the truck and subsided.

"What time is it?" Dover's voice, thin and plaintive. "I wish it was this time tomorrow."

Only the least self-conscious of them, Booth thought, would have dared articulate what the rest would at worst dare only to think.

"This time tomorrow, jerk, you could be dead." Asbury's voice.

"I told you he was faking," Doc said.

"What?" Asbury's voice rose truculently. "Faking *what?*"

"Let's keep it down." Raphael's voice, nervous. "I mean, it's okay to talk quietly, but—"

"Those phony snores," Doc said. "Don't you know you can't fool a doctor?"

"Dr. Asshole." Asbury yawned audibly. "I've got a joint in my pocket. It would help some if I could breathe in a couple of refreshing lungfuls. How about it, Colonel?"

"No," Booth said.

"No," Asbury mimicked. "The quiet voice of command. No, says the colonel."

"Horse's ass," Doc said. "The glow would show ten miles away in this darkness."

"Want a drag, Dr. Caligari?" Asbury's voice became teasing. "Think of it, lovely grass, pulling down into the lungs, filling up the old capillaries. . . ."

"Go back and fake you're sleeping again," Doc said. "Dover. Dover?"

"Yes?"

"You're like the kid in a war movie. Clean-cut, innocent, tugging at the heartstrings. . . . You listening to me, Dover?"

Asbury said, "Or in the prison pictures he's the new kid who gets buggered by the whole cellblock."

"What I want you to do, Dover, I want you to stop being that kid in the war movies."

"I don't know what you mean, Doc."

"I mean stop saying things like you wish it was this time to-morrow; just go to sleep."

"I'm too nervous to sleep."

"Keyed up is the word. Right, Mr. Asbury?"

"Fuck yourself. Now you won't get a drag of the joint the colonel won't let me burn."

Booth got up stiffly, staggering against the tilt of the truck. He steadied himself and edged back to the slit of open door. His view was a narrow oblique one down the hill toward the road. In the starlight he could make out the bulk of other trucks, of a trailer, a backhoe, mounds of earth.

The night was utterly still; the dead slept in tranquillity, secure beneath their bulwark of tamped earth. He thought of the remains that would be uprooted a few hours from now: some twangy boy from a Border State, perhaps, who had killed his dozen Nazis, aiming with uncanny accuracy by Kentucky windage until some other bullet or, more likely, shell or grenade had stopped his simple heart. . . .

"Argh!"

He realized that in disgust with his sentimentality he had spoken aloud. He pressed his face against the slit in the door and welcomed the breeze on his burning face.

Doc lifted his head from the black medical bag (pillow and spiritual comforter) at the sound of someone prying open the lid of the makeshift latrine, cursing its stubbornness. The lid came free, and immediately the van was permeated by the sickly sweet odor of excrement. Peering through the darkness, Doc recognized Asbury, holding the lid like a buckler against the stink.

"Asbury," Doc said, "this is the third time that you're shitting."

Asbury's voice, querulous: "What are you, a shit counter?"

"I keep a close watch on the health of the troops," Doc said. "Your shitting soldier is a jittery soldier."

"Bullshit."

"Right," Doc said. "You know why the bull shits in the bullring? Because he's scared of dying."

135

"Keep that up," Asbury said, "and I'll pick you up and stick you in it headfirst."

Doc laughed. He heard the susurrus of Asbury's pants sliding down his legs, followed by a staccato clatter, like a tattoo on a snare drum. Doc laughed again, joined this time by Dover and Raphael.

"Christ!" Asbury said.

"We're supposed to be under silence discipline," Doc said. "Asbury, you just blew it."

Dover guffawed. From the rear of the truck Booth said in a sharp whisper, "Keep it down!"

"Asbury," Doc said, "your shit smells scared."

Asbury groaned, then said, "You don't shut up, I'll put a bullet through your fucking head!"

"Well, hurry up and shoot before I die of shit smell."

"I told you to keep the noise down," Booth said.

Doc lay down, adjusting his head to a hollow in the soft leather of his medical bag. He wouldn't damage anything. The syringes and cotton and alcohol were carefully stowed away on one side of the bag. He liked the idea of disposable syringes. Protected his patients from infection. Nothing to worry about, men—needlepoint sharp and sterile and in like a breeze, no pain, no smart, and next thing you know. . . . Fear not, gentlemen, you are being ministered to by the finest needle inserter in the continental United States. Everybody comes to Doc. . . .

EVERYBODY COMES TO DOC
NO-PAIN, NO-STING, NO-FAINT SHOTS
ADMINISTERED

He smiled, remembering the sign he had glued to the wall of his station in the Reception Center dispensary. Every word of it true, too. While his fellow medics were stabbing quivering young flesh with routine incompetence, he would be edging his point in with the utmost finesse, whether he was siphoning blood out of reluctant veins or shooting in the good stuff of antityphus or antitetanus.

"Move on, soldier, let the poor sonofabitches behind you move up."

The clenched eyes opening and gazing in astonishment at the bared arm and: "You mean it's over?"

Exiting at the end of the long rectangular building, they would see the unlucky slobs who had been stuck by one of his brutal colleagues, heads between their legs, pale and trembling, their arms ecchymotic. In time, word got around, and knowledgeable inductees would shift places in the line, trying to get him instead of one of the others.

He was, Doc thought, and no question about it, a respecter of persons.

In a way, it occurred to him, he had liked the army or, at least, his function in it. It had given him the opportunity to be a medic, and that was what he loved. When he went to Nam, he began to like the army a lot less, because it was the army, after all, that prosecuted the war, but by way of compensation he liked his work even more as his duties shifted from treating foot blisters to helping with appalling wounds.

He had never felt a conflict of interest between his hatred for the war and his zeal for his job. He could oppose one and dedicate himself to the other with equal energy.

In a manner of speaking—if you wanted to stretch a point—he had carried that same equipoise over into civilian life. He still disliked the Establishment, but nevertheless brought solace to its wounded (in spirit) by supplying what it pleased him to think of as medication. He dealt the uplift of pills, the consolation of grass, occasionally the anodyne of cocaine. Smackheads were out; the occasional lid of heroin that came his way he would flush down the toilet.

He had organized his life to his own taste. Not enough work to make him uneasy, not enough money to corrupt him. And how many other dealers could make the claim that they fucked their main supplier? He smiled comfortably in the darkness, thinking of Agnes O'Reilly, and presently a lazy, unassertive erection took shape.

Until he had met her and—no point being modest about it—swept her off her feet, Agnes had been sexually inhibited, which was to say that she fucked with a sense of guilt rather than pleasure. Hence, she would perform only in the missionary position and would scarcely move, as though to suggest that she submitted rather than participated. But under his tutelage she had gradually learned to execute interesting variations and, what's more, to enjoy them. He shared the rent for her cozy apartment in Jackson Heights and also had the use of her car when it pleased him.

Given that she was the nurse in charge of the drugs cabinet for her floor in the hospital, together with her devotion to him, it was the most natural thing in the world for her to supply him with steady, modest amounts of Demerol, amphetamines, and other pills—nothing to incite suspicion. She was still uneasy about it, but he had instituted a Pavlovian system of reward. Each time she made a delivery of contraband, he rewarded her by doing something she liked very much in bed.

Asbury broke in on his reflection. "Somebody Chrissake find me the toilet paper."

"Ah, Asbury," Doc said, "make sure you wipe off the edge of the can."

"Fuck yourself."

"You want to leave assprints? That's the latest wrinkle in crime detection. They can read assholes like fingerprints."

Booth cut across Asbury's response, his voice urgent. "Quiet!" Then, in a tense whisper: "A car just stopped down below on the road. Not a sound."

The interior of the van became hushed. Doc rose on his elbows. By straining he could see Booth flattened against the door, his eye to the opening.

"They're getting out of the car." Booth seemed calm now. "Two of them. They must be security guards. One of them is coming up the hill."

Asbury's whisper was furious. "Where is that fucking M-sixteen?"

"Quiet," Booth whispered. "Quiet."

The flashlight moved erratically as the man holding it moved upward in what appeared to be a random course over the broken ground. Once, when he headed off to his left, he came squarely in the headlights of the car below, and Booth could see that he was wearing the blue uniform of a security guard. His movements seemed without plan, although he continued on a generally upward path in the direction of the van. At times he paused and played his light from side to side over the bulk of a bulldozer, a backhoe, a conical pile of gravel, or a dislodged boulder.

Behind him, in the van, Booth could hear the faint sound of muted breathing. The security man broke his pattern to go slightly downhill. The beam of his light focused on the door of a construction trailer and moved in on it. A hand and then an arm came out of the darkness behind the light, and fingers tugged at the hasp of a padlock. The ring of the padlock dropping back when the fingers released it was startlingly loud. The light swung in an arc and started uphill again.

Booth had already begun to push the door shut when he realized that even the sound of closing it, far less locking it, would give them away. The light darted away and flicked over a machine, then suddenly swept back uphill and blinded him. He ducked away from the impact and flattened against the wall of the van. He judged that the light and the man behind it, illuminated by the backglow, were no more than ten or fifteen feet distant from the van.

The light remained in steady focus on the van for what seemed a very long time, then began an antic purposeless movement that puzzled Booth. There was a sudden flare behind the light, and a few seconds later Booth smelled cigarette smoke. The guard had apparently put the light between his knees or under his arm to free his hands. He saw a puff of smoke billow out into the light and then rise into the darkness.

The man was not moving. His cigarette glowed, lighting up his face—a strong chin, a dark skin, lips that seemed set in contemplation. Then the flash flickered upward, cut a sweeping arc, and turned away. Booth let out his breath and followed the erratic descent of the flash as the man picked his way down the hill. When he reached the road, the flashlight flicked off. A moment later Booth heard a car door slam. He followed the red brilliance of the car lights as they moved smoothly down the road and disappeared. The color lingered brightly on his retina as he turned away from the door.

"All clear," he said softly.

The release of pent-up breath was like a great sigh. Doc said, "That dude lucked out, not seeing us. Asbury was going to shoot the ass off him."

Raphael's voice was shaky. "Too close, too close for comfort."

"Asbury is disappointed," Doc said. "Now God owes him a corpse."

Asbury said nothing. His breathing was loud and ragged in the stillness.

Raphael couldn't keep his hands off his gear. Even sitting, he would reach out in the darkness to caress the plumpness of the electric motor, tug on the tautness of a cable, probe a joint for firmness.

In the jittery period when they had been in imminent peril of being discovered by the security guard, his concern had not been for himself or any of the others (or even his wife and son), but only for his equipment. No sense deluding himself, he was a machine freak, helplessly entangled in a lifelong infatuation with the creation and operation of devices that would do things more efficiently than they had been done before.

He was not here because of his devotion to the Movement—though he subscribed to it—but because, having designed the machinery for a disinterment, he could not have borne not seeing it operate. Or, to tell the truth, operating it himself.

He was not an ivory-tower scientist, he was a pragmatist, a journeyman, and such people reaped their rewards not from theories but from practice.

And so he had become an active participant in the operation, concocting a lie in his eagerness. "It's a very delicately balanced mechanism," he had told Booth. "I could teach you or somebody else how to run it, and it might succeed if everything went off perfectly. But one variation from the norm, one minor malfunction, and you'd be lost." He had left Booth no choice but to give in.

He reached out his hand and fondled the cold metal belly of the electric motor.

Dover looked on in horror as the lid of the Unknown's casket slowly creaked open and a creature of slime and melting bones rose up. He didn't let the dream go any further; he waked himself up. He understood what lay behind the dream: He had never quite overcome his uneasiness at violating a grave. But he had kept his feelings secret except once, when he spoke about them to Doc.

"Bobby," Doc had said, "it pains me to tell you that you still have one foot in the straight world. The dead don't feel anything. Dead people are shit."

"Don't say that!"

"Do you have strong emotions about shit? Would you care if somebody took a pile of shit on a shovel and moved it elsewhere? Stop worrying about shit and start worrying about the sufferings of the living."

"Still," he had said stubbornly, "it's a desecration, and it bothers me."

"The real desecration was their death," Doc said. "Besides, they've been dug up before, they're used to it."

Dover protested. "But that wasn't desecration. How could they bring them home if they didn't dig them up?"

"Why did they have to dig them up? Why not leave them where they lay, in fucking Flanders Field or Bastogne or An Loc or wherever? I'll tell you why—so they could make a fucking pageant out of it for the politicians."

"The politicans horned in on it, but the Unknowns, well, they were buried with the highest honors, weren't they?"

"Listen. Back in nineteen-fifty-something they buried the War Two and Korean Unknowns at the same time. Before they lowered the coffins into the crypts, they took the flags off the caskets and gave one of them to Eisenhower and one to his Vice President, Richard Nixon. How would you like to have had your guts ripped out at Inchon, say, and then have them give your flag to Nixon? There's your fucking highest honors for you."

Dover shifted his position against the wall of the van, and his foot nudged somebody's leg. He apologized.

"Don't disturb your seniors," Doc said.

"Did I wake you up?"

"Worse. You busted up an erotic dream."

"I'm sorry."

"Now I have to start the preliminaries again and I may never end up in the same place. Lie down and go back to sleep."

Dover let his head down, but he didn't shut his eyes. Unlike Doc, he knew he would have no trouble picking up the fragments of his dream.

Asbury's bowels were still roiled, but he would sooner have shit his pants than use the can again. Doc's humor, if that's what he called it, curdled his goddamn milk. Sooner or later he would go around and around with Doc and beat some humility into him. As for the loose bowels, forget it. He might get a little uptight waiting around, but once the action began he was dynamite.

He slid his hand inside his pocket and fingered the joint, neatly wrapped in silver foil to keep the grains from scattering. A couple of solid drags would settle his stomach down. But much as he hated to admit it, Doc was right. The flare of a match would show for a mile in the darkness. On the other hand, it was beginning to get light. Another fifteen or twenty minutes and showing a light wouldn't matter.

For no particular reason that he could think of, he said aloud, "Doc, you're a cunt. You're pure cunt."

Raphael said in surprise, "What?"

"You're one, too," Asbury said.

The night was over. Pale light filtered through the crack in the door, and above, a cloud lined in a soft edge of pink moved slowly in the sky. The interior of the van was light enough for Booth to distinguish men from machines.

He put his eye to the door slit and looked down the hill to the road. In approximately forty minutes a security car would pass by on its last round before heading for the cemetery gate, where it would stand by as the civilian workers and the first visitors of the day were admitted. As soon as it went by or, to be exact, a minute afterward, they would begin the operation.

Overhead the pink-edged cloud was no longer visible; somewhere out of sight, in a rearrangement of the sky, another cloud had blocked out the sun. A bird fluttered down to land on a heap of upturned earth. It pecked at something, turned full circle, pecked again, paused to listen, and flew off, beating a path above the truck and out of his line of sight.

He thought of Caro. Would she be awake, taking coffee at the window that overlooked the calm sweeping semicircle of Cape Cod Bay? Or was she still asleep, frowning in protest against the hungry gulls circling the water and squawking their anxieties?

By choice he placed her in bed, an arm outside the quilt, pale tan set against the pale blue of her short sleeve. The top buttons of her pajamas were undone and a breast had tumbled out, lying like a plump tawny bird against the whiteness of the sheet. His loins warmed. Shaking his head to reprove himself, he moved out of the bedroom, out of the house, to a gull's-eye view, wheeling in a wide hunting arc directly over the roof. He came up the road in a car and saw the house at the end of its row, with a dune to its right, as he had for the first (and only) time, almost exactly a year ago. He had known Caro for two weeks then, and although they were already lovers, this was their honeymoon. It was their best time. But before it was over, the relationship had already begun to slide subtly downhill. It had lasted out the year, but it would not survive much longer. It was petering out, the way things did. The breakup would be more painful for him than for Caro. At his age he couldn't stand anything ending. Endings were a prefiguration of the final end.

Caro finished her coffee and lit a cigarette. He smelled the sweet aroma of pot. But Caro didn't smoke pot. He picked his way quickly back into the truck. The roach end was glowing, and behind it Asbury's cheeks hollowed as he sucked in deeply.

"Put that thing out."

Asbury smiled up at him. "I think your age is showing. You think this stuff is injurious to the health, right, like jerking off?"

There was some truth to it, Booth thought. He had tried grass on a few occasions without liking it and with a persistent sense of sinning. In his youth nobody smoked pot except decadent jazz musicians.

He said, "We're going into action soon, and I'd like you to be alert. After it's over you can smoke up all you want."

"You're kidding," Asbury said. "Ninety percent of us fought Nam on grass and hash and pills and ferchrissake smack. You think grave robbing is tougher work than shooting slants?"

"Don't call them that." Dover's voice, indignant.

"Asbury," Booth said quietly, "put that thing out."

"And if I don't?"

"If you don't, I'll put it out for you, you sonofabitch."

He had already started forward, his fists clenched, when Doc, moving with astonishing speed, neatly plucked the roach from Asbury's fingers. Asbury lunged, but Doc fended him off.

"You're hogging it," Doc said. "Share it around—right?"

Asbury's scowl faded. He smiled upward at Booth and said, "Right."

Doc brought his fingers together at the end of the roach and snuffed it out.

"God damn you!" Asbury rolled toward Doc, who made the roach disappear.

"Dummy. . . ." Doc showed his empty hands. "If we use it up now, we won't have anything for a victory smoke later."

"You sonofabitch, you're playing his game."

"Me? Your friendly neighborhood dealer?"

"We don't call them slants."

It was Dover again, his voice dogged, pursuing an irrelevant theme that he alone was attuned to. But he created a diversion. Asbury turned on him.

"When you popped at them out of that flying machine of yours, what did you call them?"

"That was before I knew better."

"It has nothing to do with their nationality," Doc said. "We just happen to call everything we try to kill slants—cops, deer, pedestrians. Right, Asbury?"

"Anything dead, too," Asbury said. His anger seemed to have dissipated. "That stiff we're going to dig up? A slant."

"Asbury's right," Doc said. "Listen to Asbury, Dover, and get straightened out."

"I don't like it, either," Raphael said.

Asbury turned to Raphael, smiling. "The master mechanic don't like it? Well, I'll tell you, mechanic, your machinery is a slant, too."

Doc laughed, then looked up at Booth and winked. Booth turned away and went back to the door. Another crisis was averted, and no thanks to him. He had let his anger get out of hand, and only Doc's coolness had prevented a blowup.

He heard the motor in the distance and looked at his watch. Twenty-five to eight. The security car was running a few minutes ahead of schedule.

"Dover. Come back here, please." Dover came up behind him. "Wait."

He kept his eye pressed to the door, listening to the sound of the motor coming nearer. Dover was breathing heavily. His gaze went down the slope without seeing it, focusing on the road.

When the car appeared, a black sedan with two figures in uniform in the front seat, Dover's breathing quickened. The sedan glided smoothly along the road and passed from view. Booth pushed the door open.

He stepped back and said to Dover, "Okay. Let's move on out."

Dover jumped down, pushed the door back, and then ran around to the front of the van. Booth shut the door. The mo-

tor started up, and in another moment the van began its jolt-
ing descent down the slope to the road.

Bracing himself, Booth turned inward. Asbury was sitting
in a crouch, cradling his M-16 in his arms. Doc was holding
his medical bag in his lap. Raphael was trying to embrace as
much of his gear as possible to keep it from rolling around.
The van tilted down, then up, nauseatingly, and leveled off.
They were on the road.

"Over the top," Doc said softly.

10

They were crouched at the rear of the van, Asbury and Raphael carrying M-16s, his own .45 strapped around his waist in a shiny new holster, Doc armed—it was the proper word—with his black medical bag. It reminded him of landings he had made in LST's, except that no one was shooting at them. The van stopped, and if Dover had followed his instructions, it would be short of the mall and the walkways, so that it would not be visible to the sentinels.

Booth shoved the van doors open and jumped down to the road. The others followed. The van moved forward slowly, past the opening, with Asbury, Doc, and Raphael trotting along on its far side. When it was past the opening leading up to the tombs, they ran out from behind the van and headed upward into the undergrowth to the left of the mall. Paralleling them, Booth started climbing on the right. The pitch was gentle here and would not become steep until the point where the steps began. In the summer the foliage would have provided good cover. Now they would have to time their upward movement to the sentinel, climbing alternately to each other when he was faced away from them in his freeze.

Lying flat on the slope, Booth saw the van back up to the opening. It would be visible to the sentinel, but there would be no reason for him to question the familiar presence of an Army Corps of Engineers vehicle. Booth shifted his position and watched Asbury move upward in long-legged strides, followed less picturesquely by Raphael and Doc.

The sentinel was facing the tomb now and they could

move simultaneously for twenty-one seconds. Crouched, Booth climbed upward, not hurrying, avoiding fallen branches that might snap and give him away. Three more spurts and he would be in position. The others, heading for the barracks, had a greater distance to cover.

When he hit the ground next, he was almost exactly parallel with the sentinel. The rubber strip was placed on the steps ten feet below the sarcophagus. Prone, Booth studied the measured tread of the sentinel as he came toward him, rocking heel and toe, heel and toe, his young face impassive.

Pressed close to the earth, he inhaled the smell of rank vegetation. It reminded him of his army training and, later, combat itself. It was a condition of war that you were safest when you were closest to the earth. When the sentinel turned away, Booth climbed again. The incline was steep, and he scrabbled forward on hands and knees, digging hard with his legs for leverage. When he went to cover, he was on a line slightly below the sarcophagus, gleaming in the pale sunlight.

Far to his left he saw the other three rise and make a run for the path that led up to the barracks. If someone came out of the barracks, they would be in plain view. But it was still five minutes before the relief commander was due to leave the barracks. They cut sharply off the path and huddled together against the wall of the barracks. They were above the normal sightline of the sentinel, and if he looked up and to the side, he might see them. But he would look straight ahead.

The sentinel came toward him, and now Booth was above him. He had a long serious face under the shadowing peak of his cap, his lips compressed and determined, his skin tanned by exposure to the autumnal sun. He came to a halt, stomping, facing almost exactly where Booth had lain before his last dash uphill. Across to the left Booth saw the others, led by Asbury, turn the corner of the barracks. They went quickly up the wooden steps. Asbury opened the barracks door and all three went inside. The door shut.

The sentinel had completed his freeze facing the tombs. He turned left, reshouldered his rifle, stomped, and then paced off toward the south end of his post. Booth humped up on all fours, straightened, and sprinted at an angle that brought him onto the steps. He reached the sarcophagus and slid down with his back against it.

His heart was pounding and he was winded. He heard the sentinel stomp before turning. As he reached for the automatic in his holster, he noticed that his uniform was flecked with bits of dead leaf and twigs.

A senator or congressman or something, visiting the tombs, had once asked him what he thought about while he was marching his post. "Sir," he had said, "we're too busy to think. A tombs sentinel must be physically and mentally alert at all times. This duty requires much concentration and stamina."

"You just turn off your mind?"

"It isn't turned off at all, sir. It's zeroed in on the components of the drill."

Remembering the incident, Spec Four William Burgess smiled inwardly. Later, in the barracks, Tommy Shaw, his best buddy on the second relief, had played senator. "Tell me, soldier, what do you do if you get a hard-on while you're walking your post?" Tommy had answered the question himself. "Sir, next time you get a hard-on, try stomping your foot the way we do, and see if that don't shrivel it right up."

Now, rocking heel and toe from the north to the south boundary of the post, Spec Four Burgess reflected that he had told the senator about fifty percent of a lie. It was true that when you first started as a sentinel you didn't think of anything but execution, partially because you weren't all that sure of yourself and partially because you were still being observed and were nervous about fouling up. But as time went on, it became automatic and you really didn't have to think about what you were doing. So you had to be a robot not to think about *something.*

Freezing in the twenty-one-second pause, he didn't count off the seconds as he had when he was a rookie sentinel. You simply developed such a precise time sense that you were infallible. But you weren't an automaton. You achieved perfection through training and repetition, but you were *human*. They took that for granted in England. In a film, he had seen people walking down Whitehall Street, right past the Queen's Household Guard sitting on his horse, without gawking at him. On the other hand, in the same film, he had seen tourists—a lot of them American—doing everything possible to make the guard lose his composure, even going so far as to touch his horse or his leg. It made you wonder that the guard didn't sometimes lash out with his saber and cut off a few heads.

The sentinels felt that way themselves sometimes. Fortunately, unlike the English guards, they were allowed to speak out when necessary. If the crowd became unruly, a sentinel would face them and say, "The spectators must maintain a respectful and dignified attitude during the changing of the guard, which is a solemn and serious ceremony." It always worked; they would clam up.

He unfroze, faced about, stomped, and froze again.

Sometimes it wasn't that easy. Once—it was during his second or third week as a sentinel—a dog had dashed out of the crowd and begun snapping at his heels as he marched. Although there were special spiels designed to handle most situations, none of them covered unruly dogs, and he had simply reacted instinctively and shouted, "Halt!" That had gotten a big laugh from the crowd and from his buddies, too, when he got back to the barracks.

Still, it didn't equal the reaction of another new sentinel who, taunted by a drunk who tailed him around the post, raised the butt of his rifle and yelled in desperation, "You don't get the hell out of here I'm going to bash the shit out of you." The next day he was transferred out.

No question—being a tomb sentinel was a demanding job, but nobody twisted your arm to become one. It was entirely voluntary, and the closest the Third Infantry came to a recruitment program was to show a film on the Old Guard in basic training. He had become interested through the film and followed up on it. He went to see the sergeant of the guard and was told to start practicing the routines of the sentinels on his own, after hours. Eventually, when he had convinced the sergeant of the guard that he was serious, he was taken to see the colonel for an interview. The colonel had tried to discourage him. As he learned later, that was standard procedure, to, as the colonel put it, "weed out all but those young men of most unimpeachable character who sincerely wish to dedicate themselves selflessly to guarding the nation's honored dead." If he persisted, the colonel said, he would be painstakingly investigated as far back as his elementary school records.

He had passed muster and, after serving on firing parties at funerals, was assigned to an intensive two-week training period, eight hours a day of practicing the sentinel drill. Next he was assigned to an Honor Guard Company. This was followed by additional training supervised by veteran sentinels, and at last he was ready for his first tour—this same tour, in fact, 0700–0800, before the cemetery opened. He was carefully observed and given critiques and suggestions. Then came the written test, covering about three hundred problems to do with guarding the tombs. One hundred questions were asked, and you could miss only five in order to pass. He boned up endlessly, and it paid off—he had gotten ninety-eight right out of the hundred. Next he had gone up before the board—composed of sergeants and sentinels—for an oral examination. And finally, an interview with the colonel, which ended with the colonel coming out from behind his desk and shaking his hand. He had made it.

His time sense told him that it was about ten minutes of eight. In five or six minutes the relief commander would come out of the barracks, and the first tour of the second relief would be over. Well, he was ready for relief. He had had a long session the night before with his girlfriend, and he was beat. In fact, he had had only two hours of sleep before making it out to the cemetery by 0600.

He swung away from the sarcophagus, reshouldered arms, and paced off toward the north post. He executed his right face, stomped, and froze.

"Don't move."

He knew that the cold pressure on the back of his neck was the muzzle of a gun. The voice was close to his ear, and he felt a tickle of moist breath.

"Do exactly as I say, soldier, or I'll blow your head off."

The slender plucked young neck seemed pathetically vulnerable, as fragile as a bird's. Booth said, "Don't move—I warn you—or I'll kill you on the spot." The harshness of his voice grated on the morning air.

He reached over the boy's shoulder and grabbed the rifle just below the bayonet stud. He pulled it free and tossed it away behind him. As it clattered down the steps, the boy winced. Dropping a rifle was the first sin in the lexicon of an infantryman.

"Start walking up the steps toward the sarcophagus. Don't turn around."

From below, Booth heard the sound of the van's motor. The van started climbing the steps, bucking and bouncing. This would be the noisiest part of the entire operation, but the powerful growl of the engine was low-pitched and would be blanketed by the folds of the terrain.

"Keep going," he said to the boy. He followed closely behind him, maintaining the pressure of the gun on his neck. When they reached the plaza, he said, "To the right, march."

He had snapped the order out, but still he was not prepared for the precision of the boy's execution, and for an instant the .45 lost contact with the boy's neck. He closed the gap hurriedly, and the boy hunched his shoulders to cushion the impact. The truck was bumping crazily up the steps, and Dover, visible through the windshield, was bouncing in the seat, fighting the wheel. The boy turned his head to look at the truck, and his pace faltered.

"Never mind," Booth said. "Keep moving."

He pushed the boy behind the sarcophagus. Dover shot by them onto the gray granite of the plaza. The gears clashed as he reversed, then filled until he was parallel to the sarcophagus, his wheels straddling the crypt slabs. He pulled ahead so that the rear of the van cleared the slab over the crypt of the World War II Unknown.

The boy was in a half crouch between the sarcophagus and the looming van. For the first time they were facing each other. Suddenly the boy straightened up, his hands down at his sides along the red stripe of his pants. He's seen my pips, Booth thought, and is bracing by reflex.

He said, "Sit down with your back against the sarcophagus."

The boy stared at him in bewilderment.

"Do as I say," Booth said sharply, and gestured with the .45.

Whether in reaction to the menace of the automatic or to the lieutenant colonel's silver leaves, the boy obeyed. He put his back to the sarcophagus and slid down it tentatively.

"Stretch your legs out," Booth said.

His uncertainty resolved by the order, the boy did as he was told. He trusts me, Booth thought, or at least he trusts my authority, the way those other boys did, over thirty years ago.

Dover dropped down from the high cab to the granite flooring and started running around to the rear of the van. His footsteps faltered but didn't stop at the sound of the shot. Booth winced.

The sentinel turned toward the barracks, then looked up questioningly. "It's all right," Booth said. "A blank cartridge."

The rifle shot had been unmistakable even though its sharpness had been muffled by the barracks walls and the wind blowing against it. The odds were good that the sound would not carry to the cemetery entrance. *But it carried to me.*

Asbury has fired, he thought, and I can't pretend to be outraged or even surprised. Although I wouldn't admit it then, that shot was inevitable from the moment back at the Parmentiers' when I wouldn't risk Asbury's walking out; maybe, even, as long ago as when I first enlisted Asbury, knowing his temperament, knowing my own. And if that is the case, whose finger pulled the trigger?

He called out harshly to Dover, "Move it, Bobby."

As in the army, you carried on. Tomorrow you might lose the war, but today you fought on. He heard the doors of the van opening. Dover was functioning. Another one who trusts me, he thought.

The sentinel was sitting stiffly, almost at attention, his legs stretched out in front of him, the stripe on his pants barely wrinkled. "Permission to speak, sir?"

Booth curbed his astonishment and, because the boy's trust and belief locked him into *his* role, nodded his head.

"Is it games, sir?"

The remark about the blank, of course; the boy had put two and two together.

"War games. You're Red Force, sir?" The boy's eyes were checking out his uniform, searching for the bit of red cloth that would identify him as a member of the mock enemy forces. "Wasn't there an attack like this mounted against Washington a few years ago, sir? Red Force raided the Third Infantry's. . . ."

But the boy's voice petered out, and Booth thought: He isn't doubting the idea of Red Force, he's simply minding his manners; other ranks didn't question officers of field grade.

"Sorry, sir."

Booth made a gesture forgiving him and looked at his watch. Eight minutes to eight. In a minute or two the three in the barracks should be appearing.

He said to the boy, "Take off your tunic and roll up your right sleeve."

"Sir?"

"Do as you're told, tunic off, shirt sleeve rolled. By the numbers!"

"Yes, sir. Can I stand up, sir?"

Booth shook his head. "Remain seated. You can manage."

Dover came around trailing the wires that led from the electric motor and would be hooked into the van's battery. He paused, his brows raised, and mouthed the word "shot?"

"We'll find out," Booth said. "Carry on."

Dover went by. Booth looked at the boy. His tunic was already off his shoulders, bunched between his back and the marble of the sarcophagus. Off to his right, in the direction of the barracks, Booth heard the slam of a door.

"Hurry up," he said to the sentinel.

"Sir." The boy was trying to pull the tunic out from behind his back. "If I could stand up. . . ."

"No. Roll up your shirt sleeve."

He saw Asbury coming up over the rise, his rifle held aloft in one hand, running in long-legged strides. It was an Asbury moment, Booth thought, the dramatic appearance, the paradigm of a magazine illustration. Raphael appeared behind him and, an instant later, Doc.

Asbury, his teeth gleaming, veered off toward the van, followed by Raphael. Doc, laboring, came straight toward them.

"Red Force troops," the boy said.

"Yes," Booth said.

Doc dropped to his knees beside the boy. His black bag was open, and he was rummaging in it. The boy's eyes showed a new apprehension as Doc took out a syringe.

"Sir?"

"It's all right," Booth said.

Doc began to scrub at the boy's forearm with an alcohol swab, and the boy shrank away. Doc caught his arm in a firm grip. "Relax, soldier, you won't feel a thing."

The boy looked up at Booth. "Sir?"

"New form of biological warfare," Booth said. "It's all right. We're not using the real thing."

"Right," Doc said. "Dry run."

Using his left hand, Doc twisted the boy's rolled-up sleeve into a tight torsion and tucked in an edge to hold the pressure.

"Improvised tourniquet," he said. "Saves time." He tapped the raised vein in the boy's forearm. "Ever see a lovelier antecubital fossa?"

With his teeth, he nipped the plastic cap off the point of the syringe and quickly slid it into the vein. He undid the boy's sleeve and then injected the contents of the syringe. The boy was looking up at Booth, who nodded reassuringly. Doc slipped the needle out of the vein, pressed his cotton wad to the puncture for a moment, and then took it away. The boy's eyes closed, and he slumped.

"Bull's-eye," Doc said. Gently he draped the boy's tunic around his shoulders. "Don't want him to catch cold."

Booth watched him close his bag. "I heard a shot."

"Asbury. He shot the relief commander."

"And?" Booth's heart was pounding.

Doc shrugged. "In for a dollar."

Doc stood up, and together they ran around to the rear of the van.

The moment after Asbury fired, Raphael had turned his back to the relief commander, but not soon enough to obliterate the sight of a pallid face and a red spurt of blood from the chest. Now, as he followed Asbury and Doc out of the barracks, the colors merged in a pink frothy afterimage. He had concentrated on Doc, watching him move along the line of bare arms: tourniquet, wipe of alcohol, sliding in the needle, emptying the syringe, pressure on the puncture hole . . . and one by one the sentinels shutting their eyes and keeling over, like toy soldiers tipped by the hand of a capricious child.

He labored upward toward the tombs, his breath whistling, his heart pounding. The sight of the van calmed him; he began to think of the job. He reached for Asbury's outstretched hand and hiked himself into the van. Dover was standing beside the slab.

Raphael looked back. "There's a pebble on the edge of the slab," he said. "It might break the seal of the vacuum. Get rid of it." He turned to Asbury. "Put down that rifle. You're going to need both hands."

Asbury, with routine defiance, said, "Fuck you."

But he put the rifle down and helped. Half lifting, half shoving, they edged the vacuum frame and chamber to the edge of the platform. Asbury jumped down, and with him and Dover pulling and Raphael pushing from the truck, they eased it to the ground. Meanwhile, Raphael checked the connections: the steel-meshed hose in the vacuum head; the electric-motor wires running around to the van's engine; the steel chain through the eyehole in the top of the frame passing back through the overhead pulleys to the winch in the depths of the van. . . .

He watched Asbury and Dover wrestle the frame over the

slab. He jumped down, got on his hands and knees, and, shouting instructions, maneuvered the rubber gasket rimming the chamber so that it was centered precisely on the slab with an indented margin of an inch on all four sides.

"All right, that's it." As he straightened up, Booth and Doc came around from behind the sarcophagus. He yelled to Dover, "Are the wheels chocked?" Dover nodded. "Okay, get into the cab. When I yell, move the truck forward."

Dover went around to the cab, and Raphael jumped back into the van. Booth was looking up, his face pale and strained.

"Okay," Raphael said. He was getting more relaxed by the minute. "I'm going to start the pump going."

He pressed the button of the electric motor and heard it hum. There was a whooshing sound from the pump. He let it run for thirty seconds by the sweep hand of his watch and then turned the electric motor off. The vacuum seal should be sufficient. No need to check the mercury gauge. He was very sure of himself now.

He called out, "Stand clear. I'm going to lift."

He ran back to the front of the van, and took the handle of the winch. He gave it a single full turn (at a gear-box ratio of 40 to 1, it took about two seconds to complete a full turn) and heard a sudden shout from outside. He ran to the back of the van. The slab had lifted a fraction of an inch. Easy. It must simply have been grouted. He smiled and went back to the winch. Given the weight of the slab, it would take about fifteen turns, or thirty seconds, to lift the slab a foot off the ground. That would be enough.

He forgot to count the turns, but stopped when he heard Booth yell, "High enough."

He pounded on the partition between him and the cab and saw Dover's head turn. He shouted, "Move forward. About five feet, then stop."

The van edged ahead, laboring under the weight of the slab dangling from its rear end. Raphael ran back and looked out. The slab was swaying back and forth ponderously, a foot above the granite floor. Doc, Booth, and Asbury were staring down into the open crypt.

Raphael ran back into the truck and opened the relief valve, killing the vacuum. He heard the crash as the slab dropped free onto the plaza floor.

He skipped back to the rear and shouted, "Disconnect the frame."

Booth and Asbury undid the frame from the eye hook and tumbled it off to one side. In its place they attached the improvised lifting device with the four dangling hooks. When he was satisfied that it was done properly, he waved them away and shouted to Dover. He braced himself against the side of the van as Dover backed up until his wheels reached the chocks. The dangling hooks were now centered over the open crypt.

He lingered to watch Booth and Doc slide down into the crypt, with their feet resting on the lid of the casket. Asbury maneuvered the hooks into position, and Booth and Doc grabbed them and bent down to search for the handles on the casket. He went back to the winch, grasped the crank handle, and waited. When he heard a shout from outside and saw Doc and Booth climbing out of the crypt, he began to turn the handle.

This would be the longest part of the disinterment operation. If he had gauged the weight of the lead-lined bronze coffin correctly, it would take about eighty or ninety turns of the winch handle, almost three minutes, to raise the casket six feet to ground level, and then another two minutes to bring it up to the height of the van floor.

He didn't bother to count the turns. There were too many, and, besides, he would be able to see the casket himself as it emerged from the crypt.

"She's coming up! Christ, she's coming up! Raphael, you're a fucking genius!"

Asbury's voice, a shade short of being hysterical. The unscientific mind, Raphael thought, astonished that a few basic laws of mechanics worked. Still, he felt a thrill of elation himself: no slips between the drawing board and the field. But he didn't allow it to slow him down; he turned steadily on the winch handle.

Another shout outside, this time several voices at once.

The top of the casket had reached ground level. He continued to turn, and the casket inched its way upwards. It was covered with verdigris—the crypt wasn't airtight—the greenish hue combining with the red-brown of natural bronze to edge the color toward black. There was a sprinkling of powdered grout on the lid.

Asbury, Doc, and Booth were all in front of the crypt now, pushing back on the coffin to keep it from wedging against the lip of the crypt. They were struggling against the massive weight of the casket, bent almost double, their feet braced for purchase. The bottom of the casket was now almost up to ground level.

"Keep pushing when it comes up," Raphael yelled, "so it doesn't swing under the truck."

When the casket cleared the crypt, it threatened to overwhelm them. But they dug in and held and kept control of it.

When it reached the level of the van platform, Raphael screamed at them. They jumped out of the way and the casket's natural momentum swung it forward and it thumped heavily onto the van floor. The van tilted backward.

"Push!" Raphael screamed.

He grabbed at one of the hooks as all three ran behind the casket and heaved. It ground with agonizing slowness into the van and the wheels settled.

"Push!"

The entire casket was now inside. As Booth, Asbury, and Doc hopped in, he jumped out of the way. The casket came forward with comparative speed now, squealing as it slid over the floor. When it was a few feet from the partition, Raphael screamed, "Enough! Stop!"

Doc collapsed across the casket. Booth and Asbury straightened up, trembling.

Raphael shouted, "The frame. Get it inside." Although it was unlikely that any of the materials could be traced back to them, they had decided to eliminate all possible clues.

They all jumped out again. Booth went back to the crypt, took the letter in its white envelope from his pocket, and dropped it into the crypt. Then he returned and helped Doc and Asbury wrestle the frame into the van.

Booth, his face red, pouring sweat, looked at his watch. "Four minutes of eight. Fine."

Doc, gasping for breath, said, "Congratulations, we're successful ghouls."

Raphael looked at the casket and felt a sudden chill. His part of the operation was finished now, and he felt at the same time bereft and frightened.

"Your uniform is dirty," Doc said to Booth.

There was a sprinkling of powdered grout on the shoulders and breast of Booth's uniform. He brushed it clean. Then he walked unhurriedly to the rear of the truck. He's got his composure back now, Raphael thought, and is setting a good example to settle the troops down.

Booth eased down from the rear of the van. Smiling, he said, "Okay, we're moving out. Make yourselves comfortable."

The last thing Raphael saw before Booth shut the van doors was the marble slab. A chunk had broken off in an irregular pattern at one corner.

The nose of the van was tilted sharply forward, and the vehicle heaved crazily on its springs. Booth, bracing himself against the motion with his legs and both hands, said to Dover, "Slow down, or you'll kill them all back there."

"Yes, sir," Dover said. He pumped his brake and the wheels skidded, but the violence of the motion eased.

"We've got plenty of time. I'd like you to get us to the gate at about five minutes past eight."

"Yes, sir."

Dover was regressing, Booth thought, putting his faith, as he had once done so unquestioningly, in the hands of his superior officer. With a sudden pang, he remembered the trust in the face of the sentinel.

It was a relief to reach the bottom of the steps. Dover speeded up slightly, perhaps unconsciously, and ran over the chain he had burst before climbing up the steps. He took the left of the two walkways, braked at the short flight of steps leading out to the road, and eased down them. Ahead, through the tilted windshield, Booth saw the rotunda and,

below it, the distant spread of Washington. A plane was circling slowly in the sky, winking brightly as it caught the sunlight.

Dover pulled out into the road. Booth took a last look up
the steps to the shrine. The amphitheater loomed up, serene
and massive. Below, the sarcophagus gleamed handsomely.
From here nothing they had done was visible except that for
the first time since 1937, when the twenty-four-hour guard
had been instituted, there was no sentry pacing the black
mat.

"Head toward the gate," Booth said. "Slowly and smoothly.
Naturally."

Dover nodded. His face was flushed, but he handled the
wheel competently, easing gently around the curves in the
road. Then the Visitors Center came in view. A Tourmobile
bus was standing out front, waiting for the first sightseers to
arrive for the cemetery tour. It would be at least a half hour
before it reached the tombs.

A few cars were beginning to enter the cemetery parking
lot. To the right was the south post of Fort Myer and the long
low building where he had spoken to General Dammerling.
Well, the general would have something substantive to
scream about this morning. In the distance a seemingly endless row of headstones climbed up a gentle hill into the sun.
The entrance to the cemetery lay directly ahead of them. A
row of ten or twelve cars was moving slowly toward it. A security guard was standing in his sentry box, watching the traffic
coming in. A security car was drawn up nearby. Another was
making a turn into the cemetery grounds, presumably on the
way to making its first rounds of the new day.

Dover said, "Just sail right through?"

"No sailing," Booth said. "Go slow, ten miles or so an hour.
We're just another army truck, and they see dozens of them
every day."

"Okay," Dover said, "if you say so."

"I say so." As they came up to the sentry box, he said softly,
"Easy. Easy does it, Bobby."

The guard in the box had his back to them. There were
two guards in the security car. One of them, a young black

man, raised his hand and waved as they glided by. Booth threw him a lazy salute.

Dover expelled his breath. "We made it."

"Easiest part of the whole deal," Booth said, and, now, believed it. "Same speed, Bobby."

"Nothing," Dover said. He was looking at the rearview mirror. "They're just sitting there."

"It's going to be another little while before anybody discovers what happened, and with all the confusion, maybe hours before they learn that an Army Engineers truck left at a few minutes after eight."

They moved on against a small stream of traffic heading toward the cemetery. This was the Avenue of Heroes, with its huge rotunda and empty niches where busts were to have been placed before the WPA ran out of funds. They circled toward the Memorial Bridge, guarded by its heroic statues representing Sacrifice and Valor. Ahead was the omnipresent white shaft of the Washington Monument. They crossed the bridge.

"All right," Booth said. "Now we're in the District, and they'll have to extradite us if they want us back."

Dover looked at him uncertainly. It was a poor joke, Booth thought, but it was an expression of his relief.

As if to make amends, he sharpened his tone. "All right. Now over to the Key Bridge and back into Virginia."

If eventually some unexpected witness remembered seeing the van, he would report that it had crossed into Washington, which meant that it had headed north.

"Don't rush," Booth said gently. "We're just an army truck. Nobody cares about us. Nobody even sees us. Did you ever hear of an army truck racing to get someplace?"

"Come to think of it, I don't think I ever did."

"Well," Booth said, "keep that in mind."

"Sir," Dover said.

Part II

11

A security cruiser dropped P. T. Ronsard off on the road below the tombs at ten minutes after eight. Theoretically his tour as tombs guard—which consisted mostly of answering the tourists' dumb questions—began at eight, but there was never any rush to get there since the first visitors never arrived until half past eight, sometimes even later.

He climbed the steps and headed up the walkway, head down, and so it wasn't until he reached the grassy space where he would take up his post that he saw the broken chain. His surprise turned to shock when, looking upward, he realized that there was no sentinel pacing the mat in front of the sarcophagus.

He started running up the steps, but came to an abrupt stop at the sight of the shattered marble slab lying on the plaza. He fumbled for the radio at his belt, switched it on, and then ran upward again, toward the open crypt.

He activated his radio and said, "My Gawd amighty."

A voice crackled back at him, "What? What's that you say? Speak up, man."

Ronsard turned away from the crypt and saw the sentinel crumpled at the base of the sarcophagus. He moaned.

"Speak up," the radio voice said. "What did you say?"

"Said my Gawd amighty."

The chief of cemetery security phoned the curator of the cemetery from the barracks. Waiting for the curator to come on the phone, he looked around. The scene was like a battlefield in some terrible dream: the relief commander slumped in his chair, his shirt covered with dark drying blood, the sentinels on the sofa, flopped all over one another like—the comparison was unwholesome but he couldn't suppress it—figures in the aftermath of some kind of sexual orgy.

The curator didn't make a sound, didn't even breathe hard as the chief laid it out for him. Which was why he had called the curator first and not General Dammerling. The general could have a breakdown on the phone or even, holding the phone with one hand, fumble his .45 out with the other and blow his brains away.

When he paused, respectfully, waiting for the curator's comment, all he heard was, "Extraordinary."

"I have taken the following steps," the chief said. "I have closed the cemetery. I am having the tour bus intercepted, and it will return to the Visitors Center and everyone on it will be asked to leave. Including the driver. All the people who arrived by car will be asked to depart. I'm conducting a search of the grounds, but I'm shorthanded."

"You think they're still on the grounds? Extraordinary."

Extraordinary again, the chief thought, by which the curator means to say that it isn't his baby and that because he isn't checked out to handle crimes, he'll fade out of the picture and leave the baby to me.

"Extraordinary," the curator said for the third time. "Who would do anything as weird as this?"

I'm not paid for psychiatric work, the chief thought, and said, "Sir, would you mind phoning General Dammerling and telling him?"

"You're sure just the one man is dead?"

"The others are breathing. Their sleeves are rolled up, so I assume they've been drugged."

"I didn't mean to imply that one death is insignificant, you understand."

"Look, sir," the chief said, "I have to be in about four or five places at the same time. If you would please call the general and ask him to bring about twenty men and a couple of doctors?"

"Very well. I'll call the . . . general at once."

The chief was sure that the curator's pause was taken up by a grimace. Well, better him than me, he thought. "Very good, sir," the chief said. Better his eardrum gets perforated than mine.

Al Manero told his Spec Four to hold the fort and went around to the mess hall. He sat near the kitchen munching doughnuts with his coffee and swapping army wisdom with the mess sergeant. When he heard someone bound up the steps, he made a guess: It's the Spec Four. But he was wrong. It was Robinson.

Robinson flopped down beside him. "Sarge, the fucking thing is missing out."

"What fucking thing?"

"The expansible. The M-two-ninety-two I'm supposed to rotate the tires on." Robinson's dark face was shiny with sweat. "My van, it ain't there."

Manero sighed. The mess sergeant glowered at Robinson out of long habit of glowering at lower ranks.

"Believe me," Robinson said. "The fucker ain't there, it's missing out."

Manero sighed again. "Robinson, do I assign people vehicles that aren't there?"

"Never did," Robinson said. "Till now. Now you did it."

"Let's see your work order." Manero rolled his eyes at the mess sergeant as he took the slip from Robinson. "It says here you are assigned the M-two-ninety-two in bay number B-thirteen, right?"

"Right," Robinson said. "Except there is no such truck in no such bay."

Manero handed the sheet to Robinson. "Go back there and open up your baby blues and you'll find the truck there."

"I *been* back. Also the Spec Four, Wishengrad. Nor did *he* find it, *neither*, and *he* told me to come *here*. Did you say baby *blues?*"

The mess sergeant got up. "You don't catch none of *my* people talking to they sergeant like that. I'll tell you, in the *old* army. . . ." He went back into the kitchen.

"Whut that old army shit?" Robinson said. "Robert E. Lee

army?" He watched hungrily as Manero stuffed his mouth with doughnut. "Sergeant, I swear to Gawd, that fucking truck has been fucking misplaced."

"You tell me Wishengrad couldn't find it, either?"

"Nor Wishengrad, neither."

"Okay," Manero said. He picked up his cap. "We'll go out and look for it together. And *find* it. And when we do, I'm going to have your black ass."

"Better you than that peckerwood mess sergeant."

Manero shook his head. "It sure ain't the old army. Ain't the new one, either. Close as I can tell, it's a fucking rock group."

Robinson ran ahead of him. Manero followed unhurriedly. What was the big rush, anyhow?

Watching General Dammerling as the sentinels were brought out of the barracks on stretchers, the chief of cemetery security admitted the possibility that he might have underestimated the general's capacity for feeling. As each stretcher was brought awkwardly down the barracks steps, the general acknowledged it with a word or a gesture. He rested his hand on the first, letting it trail off the blanket slowly. He stared down at the pale sleeping face of the second and murmured, "That's all right, Patterson." To the third he muttered, "Hang in there, old man"; to the fourth he said with a catch in his voice, "Sorry, Josephson." As the last stretcher emerged, carrying the dead relief commander, the general drew himself up and saluted, then ran down the path and helped lift the stretcher into an army ambulance. He saluted again as the ambulances moved off.

Although the chief of security was still technically in charge of the investigation, the FBI was on its way, and the Department of the Interior, and for all he knew the Treasury Department, the CIA, and the Pentagon. But until their arrival the general was doing a pretty good job of upstaging him.

He had stormed in with a dozen vehicles containing what seemed to be a full company of troops. The soldiers were already out scouring the grounds in vehicles and on foot, though what they were looking for the chief couldn't imagine. The general had set up a command post inside the barracks, and the chief had overheard Lieutenant Jamison telephone Fort Myer for a field kitchen. The general had also taken charge of the letter they had found in the empty crypt. The chief had been for opening it on the spot, but the general, coldly pointing out that it was addressed to the President of the United States, had dispatched it by courier to the White House.

The stomp of a boot caught the chief's attention, and he turned to watch the sentinel facing the tombs, or what was left of them. The general had routed the first relief out of the sack and brought them back with him to man the post.

The general came up beside him and, indicating the sentinel, said grimly, "He's got a full clip in that piece."

A padlock on the stable door, the chief thought. Down below, a half-dozen soldiers were plowing through the underbrush in a line abreast, heads down, like a squad policing up cigarette butts. He remembered his own army days and the squad leader's traditional cry: "Pick up anything that don't move!" Well, maybe this squad would come up with a few butts, but what else?

Lieutenant Jamison appeared over the rise. He was hatless and in his shirt sleeves. He called out, "Sir, General Gardner phoned. He says—"

The general interrupted him. "Get over here, Jamison."

The lieutenant approached, braced his muscular body, and saluted.

The general said, "You are out of uniform, Lieutenant."

The lieutenant touched his head, as if to confirm the absence of his cap. "Sorry, sir. But I thought the message was so urgent that—"

"You don't shout messages from four-star general officers," the general said. He paused to let the reprimand sink in. "Well, what is the general's message?"

"He is attending a staff meeting, sir, and his message to you is to carry on."

"Thank you. Return to the command post."

The lieutenant saluted and trotted off back to the barracks.

A racketing backfire echoed somewhere in the cemetery. Another car squealed as wheels took a turn too rapidly. Army vehicles were not engineered for silence, the chief thought; they would wake up the dead.

He said, "General, with all due respect, it's my opinion. . . ." A look at the general's face gave him pause, and he decided not to say that a lot of troops blundering around the grounds was a waste of time and would produce nothing. He softened his operative noun, too. "It's my, ah, *theory*, General, that the perpetrators have left the cemetery."

"How—in a helicopter?"

The chief was momentarily startled before realizing that the general's question was sarcasm. "I'm going back to talk to those guards at the gate again. The only way they could have gotten out with the casket was in a large vehicle through the gate."

"The Unknown must be recovered at all costs. You and your men will be held fully responsible."

The chief turned red and teetered on the verge of reminding the general that at least none of *his* men had been put to sleep or killed. Instead he merely said, "I'm going back to the gate."

"They have stolen the heart of America," the general said. "But it *will* be recovered, and they *will* be made to pay."

"Yes, sir," the chief said blandly, "and also for the way they manhandled your boys."

"They're not boys," the general said. "They're men. They're soldiers."

They sure are, the chief thought as he left, they're some fucking men, some fucking soldiers, the poor boys.

When he saw the chief's car bearing down on the gate, Marbert Morrison reviewed, as they said, his options. They were a precious few. He would either say, "Right after you talked to me I remembered something and I was gonna get back to you as soon as I could," or, "Be damn, now that you mention it, there *did* something go out!" Or, "I swear, Chief, nothing went by me except this old army truck. You don't mean to say. . . ."

Meanwhile, he hadn't had to fake being busy. Although a cordon of cars and cops had been drawn up a hundred yards away from the gate to turn away approaching visitors, he still had to handle the cars that had lined up at the gate before the roadblock had been set up. Just with the traffic alone it was messy, but also they had to be fed a story about *why* they couldn't get in. The official line was that a water main had broken, and he was tired of repeating it: "Sorry, sir, a water main has bursted and the cemetery is temporarily closed to the public." But that didn't stop them talking: "Officer, I came all the way from Ohio to see the Kennedy family," or, "I promised my aunt I would visit the grave of her son, he was killed in Korea, he was with the Marines at Inchon, General MacArthur's troops, you know," and so on.

"Okay, turn it around, sir, that's fine, plenty of room. . . ." The chief was out of his car and approaching on foot.

"Marbert. . . ." The chief was standing next to the sentry box. "Marbert, come over here."

Morrison started toward the box. Options, he thought, play it by ear, and one of the options will come to be. The chief moved back into the box and Morrison followed. Too small a place for two persons, he thought, especially when one person is the chief and the other person isn't.

"Marbert, you remember when I questioned you if any car had gone out after the cemetery opened?"

"Sure, Chief, I remember." Just blew option one, he thought.

"And you said nothing went by. Is that right?"

"Sure. Nothing did." There went option two. That reduced him to option three, which would have to be played a little slow and dumb.

"Well, Marbert," the chief said, his voice rising, "for your information, something *did* go out."

"No, sir."

"Yes. Something went out, Marbert, right past your dumb eyes with that casket in it."

"No, sir, Chief, not past *my* eyes."

"Yes, it did, Marbert." The chief was speaking now with

exaggerated patience, as if he were dealing with a child. "And I want you to remember what it was. You hear me, Marbert?"

"I *hear* you, Chief, but—"

"Good. Now that you hear me I want you to think. *Think!*"

He pretended to think, but what he was really doing was working out what the chief would say after he told him nothing had gone by except an army truck. Like: "Didn't you think that it was pretty funny for an army truck to be coming *out* a few minutes after the cemetery *opened?*" And he would say, "Hell, no, those buggers go in and out all day long." And the chief would say, "Yeah, but they don't come *out* before they go *in*."

Marbert said, "I'm thinking, Chief, but. . . ." He let his mouth fall open, and the chief looked like a bird dog on the scent, but he decided to milk it a little bit more. He shook his head and said, "Shit, that don't count."

"*What* don't count?"

"The army truck?"

The chief surprised him. He didn't holler "What army truck?" or remind him that army trucks didn't come out before they went in; he just nodded his head grimly and picked up the telephone. He rolled his eyes and said in a quiet voice, "Don't you go away, Marbert."

"No, sir," Morrison said in a puzzled voice, and gave his head a puzzled scratch. Then he looked startled and took another piece of option three. "You don't mean to say. . . ."

The chief didn't catch the performance. He was saying on the phone, "Tell the general they got it out in an army truck. . . . I don't know yet what kind of an army truck, but I'm fucking well gonna find out in the next two minutes."

He hung up the phone and turned to Morrison, who thought, Better get you some fresh options pretty fast, brother.

As Dover started to climb into the cab of the M-292, Booth said, "Put your gloves on, Bobby."

Dover flushed. They had spent ten minutes after the van was emptied washing away fingerprints, and here he was

about to touch the wheel with his bare hands. He put the
gloves on with elaborate care, drawing the fingers snug, as if
to say, Well, I may have forgotten about them for a second,
but you can see that they damn well won't fall *off*.

He inched out of the barn backward, with Booth and Parmentier guiding him. Inside, the walls of the barn seemed to
be wavering in the unsteady light of the kerosene lamps. The
doors of the Drivurself stood open, with everything strewn
around it waiting to be piled in: the furniture, Raphael's
gear, tumbled indifferently in a heap now that it had no further use, the casket. . . . Asbury and Doc were sitting on it,
passing around a roach. Raphael stood nearby, his face shad-
owed.

Outside the barn Dover backed and filled and climbed up
the driveway in low gear. Booth and Parmentier were out on
the road, back to back, looking and listening. When they
waved to him, he gunned the van's engine and swung up to
the road. He put his head out of the window to say good-bye,
but Booth waved at him furiously. As he drove off, he looked
for them in the rearview mirror, but they had already turned
into the driveway.

He was a little nervous about meeting a car, but the road
was empty and he calmed down. Booth had said it might be
hours before they realized that an army truck had been involved, and even longer before they identified it. He trusted
Booth's judgment.

Interestingly enough, there were quite a lot of army trucks
on the main road, and that gave him some confidence, too.
At one point, in fact, he met a convoy of trucks riding in for-
mation, and, oddly enough, it was an Army Engineers convoy, and two of the vehicles were M-292's identical with his
own.

He had a street map of Alexandria, but he didn't need it.
He found the shopping center, drove into the huge parking
lot, turned off the motor, and, taking his bag, left the truck.
He went across the lot to the huge discount store. The men's
room was on the third floor. It was large and clean, smelling
of disinfectant, and it was empty. He went into a booth and
changed from his uniform into his civilian clothes. No one

entered. He put his army gear in the bag and walked out carrying it.

He looked at his watch. Still a half hour to get to the bus station for the Greyhound to New York. He walked past the van on his way to the street and didn't even glance at it.

"Well, they were dazed, naturally, and intimidated by the rifles, but. . . ."

Doc paused, searching for a way to formulate his thought, tilting his head toward the distant flickering beams of the barn.

The Drivurself was packed, the casket, Raphael's rig, and the rifles and uniforms well hidden behind and beneath the stacked furniture. When Asbury and Raphael went off to the house to clean up and change clothing, Booth had intercepted Doc. Now, waiting for Doc to organize his response, it occurred to him that the relief commander had been dead for over an hour, and knowing how it had happened could not change anything, especially for the relief commander.

"Okay," Doc said, "what I'm trying to tell you is that they weren't all that scared as they were embarrassed. I mean, I think if they were standing up they would have hung their heads and scuffed their feet."

Booth nodded, remembering the sentinel's questions about war games. Maybe the others, too, in their confusion, had believed or hoped that they were being tested in some sadistic conspiracy of their superiors, and aware in that context of their failure.

"And willing to take orders," Doc said. "Fucking army mentality, you know. We could have been the goddamn Russian Army, for that matter, but *army* and giving *orders*. Orders is orders, right?"

The rear door of the Drivurself was still open, furniture piled to the very edge of the platform, not quite as neatly as Booth would have liked, but it would do.

"All except the relief commander," Doc said. "He wasn't taking orders. In fact, he was giving them."

Booth looked at his watch. "Tell me about it."

"If you're checking the time, I guess you want the short

quick version, right? Okay, we come charging in. Comman-
dos. Barking orders. Fierce faces. Waving the M-sixteens
around. Asbury is yelling, 'Freeze, you mothers, freeze!'
Beautiful. Raphael—so help me—Raphael hollers, 'Hands
up!' Hands up, for God's sake! But"—Doc paused and
looked surprised—"they handsed up. So there was only one
cliché left, and I took it. 'Reach!' Reach! And they reached.
Shows you the power of suggestion in an M-sixteen."

Don't be so funny, Booth thought, don't enjoy yourself,
the story ends in the death of an innocent.

"We made all four of the sentinels sit side by side on the
sofa. They sat at attention. Then I noticed that one of
them—he must have been the relief—was still holding his
piece. No bullets, okay, but a bayonet, so I yelled at him to
drop it. He gave me a funny look, and I thought he was going to make trouble, but he just didn't want to *drop* it. He put
it down on the carpet gently.

"Four of them on the sofa, all in a row, and the commander in a deep chair. Raphael with his piece pointed somewhere
between them. Asbury rotating the barrel from side to side,
looking wild and trigger-happy, meanwhile keeping up a line
of chatter—he'd shoot the fucking eyes out of their heads if
they made a false move, he chewed up toy rear-echelon doggies like them for breakfast. . . . Christ! John Wayne to the
life.

"Meanwhile, the commander was sitting at attention, no
expression, very cool. I ordered the ones on the sofa to roll
up their sleeves. It confused them, and they looked to the
commander. Asbury yelled, 'Roll up those fucking sleeves
like you're ordered!' He told the commander, 'You, too,
motherfucker.' The commander ignored him and snapped
at the four on the sofa, 'You will *not* roll up your sleeves.
That's an order.'

"An order. They froze where they were, sleeves half
rolled. I said something like 'Your commander is our prisoner and has no authority to give you orders. We're giving the
orders. You *will* roll those sleeves up!' I never knew whether
they would have obeyed or not. Asbury took over."

"He shot the commander?"

Doc gave him an odd look. "Not yet. He rammed the muzzle of his rifle against the commander's chest and began screaming. He looked pretty dangerous. The four on the sofa were bug-eyed. What happened next. . . ."

Doc paused. Booth saw Asbury at the barn door. He was still in his army uniform.

"It was fast," Doc said. "As best I remember, the commander slapped at the barrel of Asbury's piece and went for his sidearm. I *think* he went for his sidearm, or tried to get up, or something. So Asbury zapped him."

Asbury came around Booth and stood beside Doc. He was smiling. Doc glanced at him and went on.

"After that it was a piece of cake. The commander slumped down in the seat, lots of blood spreading on his shirt, the shot echoing. Asbury swinging around with his finger on the trigger prepared to kill *everybody*."

"Piss off," Asbury said. "I was in total control of myself."

"They finished rolling up their sleeves and held their arms out, and I just went down the line, hitting the old antecubital fossa, and they keeled over. No fuss, no muss."

Asbury's grin was a provocation. Booth ignored it. "You're sure the commander was dead?"

"Very. Right through the heart. The infallible marksman here plugged him neatly at a distance of two inches."

"What was I supposed to do?" Asbury said. "Back off a hundred yards to make it sporting?"

"I checked him," Doc said. "Instantly dead. I also checked his sidearm. Empty, like the rifles."

Asbury said angrily, "You little jerk. While he was going for his gun, was I supposed to ask him first if it was empty?"

"It was a problem," Doc said, sighing. "The commander made a hostile move. Maybe he had a loaded gun. We had to handle him. Maybe it could have been done without wasting him, but. . . ." He shrugged. "We'll never know."

Asbury, smiling again, said, "You got something to say to me, Colonel?"

Booth looked at the loaded Drivurself, bypassing the provocation of the smile, and shook his head.

"I'd like to hear you say it," Asbury said. "Out loud."

Doc intervened. "Okay, hero, you made your point. Go change your clothes."

Asbury allowed himself to be pushed toward the barn door, but he kept his smile, challenging and contemptuous. Doc shoved him out of the door and came back. Booth was rigid; his hands, at his sides, were clenched fists.

"I know," Doc said. "You'd like to punch the shit out of him. And you could do it, too. But the point is, you don't have to prove yourself. Asbury is still trying."

Booth nodded. He opened his fists. His fingers ached with tension.

"Nevertheless," Doc said, "the relief commander asked for it."

"Yes," Booth said.

"Yes," Doc mimicked him. "You feel betrayed, right? You planned it all nice and hygienic and nobody gets hurt, right?"

Whose finger pulled the trigger?

"You wanted to do it on the cheap. Well, with something like this you don't count the price. The commander tried to ruin us. Asbury prevented it. It's a war. The commander is a casualty."

He hadn't allowed himself to think of it as a war, Booth thought, because he couldn't accept the idea that there might be casualties. Doc had seen it more clearly and put the proper name to it. Doc had gotten the live ammo and, in doing so, acknowledged that they might kill somebody. Doc, who ministered lovingly to the human body, had been prepared for the dissolution of one.

"Wise up," Doc said. "We're playing for keeps."

12

For various persuasive reasons of intelligence, ambition, trickiness, arrogance, and style, Emerson Albert Griese was known by such tags as "The Domestikissinger," "Citizen Knowall," and "The Power Beyond the Throne." As a matter of taste he regarded all of these journalistic inventions as labored, but nevertheless rejoiced in them as being helpful to the Griese legend. His *real* nickname, and the one he preferred, was Eminence Griese. It had been bestowed upon him by a college classmate some twenty years ago. His special qualities had been recognized early.

His own contributions to the Griese legend were calculated and often witty. As an example, challenged on his overweening egotism by a reporter for a *Time* magazine cover story, his response had been, "My only fault is that I have none." He might have let the matter lay there, having given the reporter a newsworthy quote, but he showed his mettle by continuing: "Candor twists my arm and compels me to admit that that epigram is a crib from Pliny the Younger. You are of course familiar with his works?" Candor was the basic weapon of his armory, and he made frequent use of it in his dealings with the press, except when it was in his interests not to do so.

In point of fact—since he was *always* candid with *himself*—he understood himself to be a master of cunning and artifice. These were traits which he regarded as the *minimum* requirements for his job as first special assistant to the President. Anything less and he would have been a liability to the man and the administration he served, both of which he viewed disinterestedly as neither better nor worse, on balance, than any others he had observed in his lifetime, barring Nixon's, which he characterized as "immature."

He had been christened Emerson Albert by his father, who had fled Hungary in 1955 and risen to obscurity as a master in a second-rate New England prep school. Zoltan Griese had taught the Transcendentalists at Budapest University. He was a brilliant man and a capable teacher, but he was held back by a personality that was more Prussian than Hungarian. Despite his credentials, he always seemed to turn off college recruiters, and at last resigned himself to earning his competence and retirement pension at the prep school. The son, observing the father, perceived the value of cultivating charm. As it turned out, it was a shade beyond his best efforts; he was his father's son. And so he did the next best thing, he capitalized on his faults by exaggerating them. Would the "Venus de Milo" be half so adored if she had arms?

He had formulated his basic style at Harvard. For three rollicking undergraduate years he had harried, chivied, outwitted, and outraged his professors. In his final year he concluded that the *enfant terrible* joke had gone far enough. Without mentors to write effusive recommendations, his entry to graduate school might be imperiled despite his extraordinary grades. So he reformed and undertook to flatter his professors by pretending that he was no brighter or better informed than they were.

Certain of his enemies claimed that the "Em"—as he was known to his intimates—of his name stood for "emulation." Like William Buckley, Jr., he was a best-selling author in his twenties; and with his PhD dissertation, at that, which most fair-minded observers felt put him one up on Buckley, who had actually had to sit down and write his best seller from scratch. Like Arthur Schlesinger, he turned political activist and worked strenuously in a presidential campaign. Like Kissinger, he was foreign-born and had been drafted from the Harvard faculty for a high position in the new administration.

At the time that he joined the administration, starting out at the top of the ladder—"Next to Eminence Griese," a prominent journalist had written, "the President is the most powerful man in the United States"—he was thirty-five years old. This had established him, in his words to the *Time* reporter, as "perhaps the youngest *éminence grise* in history, and incontestably the first without a single gray hair in his head."

On this Wednesday morning, when the White House news secretary bustled into his office with an air of high urgency, he was thirty-seven years old, and before the day was over would feel thirty-eight. Glancing up from the morning's digest of news which had been prepared by the news secretary's staff, and which he always checked over before passing on to the President, Griese said, "I don't approve of people rampaging into this office. It isn't respectful. This is, after all, the historic office once occupied by Haldeman and Alexander Haig."

The news secretary came to a full stop. He was a gray-faced, gray-haired man in rumpled clothing, of a type that had become popular in recent years as an antidote to Ron Ziegler. He was an old and distinguished newpaperman who, it was said, had almost been turned down for the job because (*vide* Ziegler) he had once spent six months working in an advertising agency. What had saved him, in the opinion of many, was the coarseness and unmanageability of his hair: It was a truth teller's hairdo.

In the face of Griese's opening he had no choice but to fall back on formality. "We have a problem for the President's attention." He took an envelope from his pocket.

"Of course. But you might spare a smile for my little joke."

"Very funny," the news secretary said stolidly. "Shall I get it out?"

He fights back, Griese thought, and said, "Well, let's have your bad news."

The news secretary decided to underplay, as he should have done at the start. "It's not quite earthshaking, but, well, it's a little crazy."

"For something just a *little* crazy," Griese said, "a memo will do."

Griese's dislike of the news secretary arose from business rather than personal motives. He had learned that the news secretary was working assiduously on his memoirs and intended to leave his job in a few months and publish them immediately thereafter. Griese himself was writing nothing (a diary, after all, was merely a personal record) and would not leave until the expiration of the President's full term. At that point it would be appropriate to retire from public life. Even then it would be as much as a year and a half before his memoirs (tentative title, "A Stroll Through the Corridors of Power") appeared, if one took into account the actual writing, copy editing, changes in the galleys, binding, promotion, etc. It was galling to be beaten off the mark unfairly by a lesser book.

The news secretary realized that he had squandered any advantage he might have held at the outset by possession of special knowledge and must now make the best of the situation.

"This letter"—he fluttered the envelope—"was left behind an hour or so ago by whoever dug up the casket of the Unknown Warrior of World War Two and carted it away."

"Oh, well," Griese said, "those things do happen, don't they?" Smiling inwardly at the news secretary's look of controlled loathing, Griese thought, If they give me a foothold, will they expect that I won't climb all over them? "Those are all the facts?"

"The facts to this point," the news secretary said stiffly, "are as follows: unidentified persons, using some machinery the nature of which is as yet undetermined, pried up the slab over the crypt of the Unknown, lifted out the casket containing the remains, and made off with it. They left behind them six sentinels, five of them unconscious and one dead. This envelope was found in the bottom of the empty crypt."

Griese took the envelope, read the inscription on its front, and at once opened it, ignoring the news secretary's gasp. He read it aloud: "'The remains of the Unknown Warrior of World War Two will be destroyed unless Francis Rowan is released from Lewisburg Prison before midnight tomorrow (Thurs.). A letter containing full details was posted to you yesterday.' It is signed, 'The Ad Hoc Committee for the Release of Francis Rowan.'"

"Rowan, Chrissake," the news secretary said. "*That* asshole?"

"Ad Hoc Committee for the Release of Francis Rowan. Do you realize there's no earthly way of making an acronym out of that?"

"I don't think this is a time for irrelevancies," the news secretary said coldly. "The President should be informed at once."

"The loss of art, even a very *little* art, is never irrelevant. The President"—Griese glanced at the log of presidential appointments—"is holding a nonpartisan breakfast meeting with the leaders of the House and Senate and must not be disturbed."

"Come on, Em, those things are strictly bullshit sessions."

"Exactly. They are among the few remaining pleasures of a President. They give him the illusion for a little while that the job is worth having."

"We have to get cracking on this. It's going to be political dynamite."

"Consider me *locum tenens* for the President," Griese said calmly. "The drill is as follows: First, search for that letter. Second, arrange for Francis Rowan to be placed in solitary confinement. . . ."

"Chrissakes!"

"Do we want him speaking to newsmen?"

"No." The news secretary shook his head. "Which reminds me—we'd better put something out on this before it gets out on its own."

"Don't tell too much."

"I don't *know* too much."

Griese nodded. Before the news secretary was out of the room he was already speaking on the telephone.

They had made their good-byes in the house, so that when Parmentier signaled to them from the top of the driveway,

Raphael gunned the Drivurself up and swung out onto the road and kept going. Booth turned and saw Parmentier start down the driveway. He would wait five or ten minutes and then drive Doc and Asbury to the airport in his pickup truck.

They would all meet at the house on the Cape. It was one of their few sentimental decisions, and perhaps the only one they had arrived at without debate. They wanted to be all together to celebrate their triumph. If anything, it was less risky than dispersing and returning home, where one of them might be picked up in a hasty, indiscriminate FBI sweep. Splitting up for the trip north was simply an extra safety measure. As for the chances that the FBI would eventually get around to looking them up, that was a risk they had all accepted willingly at the outset. But, given the bureau's methodical, slow-but-sure procedure, it lay somewhere in the future, and they would worry about it when it happened.

Booth's choice of Raphael as the one to accompany him in the Drivurself had been more or less a compromise; Raphael was not the coolest of them, but on the other hand he was the most respectable-looking. Originally Caro had staked out the role for herself, arguing that it made sense, in terms of camouflage, for him to be accompanied in the furniture truck by a "wife." They had fought bitterly over it. He had contended stubbornly that it was essential for her to precede them to the Cape to open up the house, which, although it was a valid point, was not the one uppermost in his mind. His real motive was that he didn't want to expose her to the danger of being nabbed at a roadblock. In the end, over Caro's feminist suspicion that he was trying to protect her, he had prevailed.

A car came around a bend and Raphael overreacted. He pulled so far over to the right that the side of the Drivurself scraped the denuded foliage lining the road.

"It's all right," Booth said. "There's nothing to be nervous about."

"I'm not the least bit nervous," Raphael said. "Just slightly keyed up. Aren't you slightly keyed up, too?"

"I didn't mean to be critical," Booth said. He switched on the radio. A sober voice, on behalf of a bank, was urging the wildest kind of borrowing. "Yes, I'm keyed up, too."

As if reassured, Raphael relaxed visibly. "Do you think there'll be roadblocks?"

"It's possible."

"Do you think they'll make us unload the truck?"

Booth shook his head.

"But suppose they do."

"Then we'll have to do it."

Raphael's knuckles whitened as he tightened his grip on the wheel. "But then they'll discover the casket."

"Yes," Booth said.

As usual, Washington traffic was heavy. They crossed Pennsylvania Avenue in a thick clot of cars a few blocks west of the White House and slowly picked their way through the northwest area. Booth twirled the dials of the radio before settling on one station. The station didn't matter; any one of them would break into its program for this particular news flash.

They cut northeastward on Rhode Island Avenue, and presently the stony elegance of the avenue began to shade off until it became noticeably shabby. At the same time, the faces they saw on the streets became predominantly black.

Booth said, "Next mailbox you see, pull over."

Raphael found one on the next block and drew up beside it. Booth rolled down the window and after checking the front of the envelopes—one addressed to the Washington *Star*, the other to the *Post*—dropped them in the box. He returned the remaining three envelopes to his pocket.

"Odd that there's still no report on the radio," Raphael said, driving on.

"There'll be one," Booth said.

"Can you turn it up a bit?"

Booth increased the volume, and the interior of the Driv-urself trembled to the resonance of a thumping rock beat. Five minutes later, as they paused for a red light in the center of College Park, the rock music stopped abruptly. Then, after a prolonged instant of dead air, a voice said: "This just in from our newsroom. . . ."

There was another pause, and Booth visualized the announcer studying with dismay or disbelief the yellow sheet ripped from the teletype machine and thrust into his hand.

"A dispatch from the Associated Press. The Tomb of the Unknown Warrior of World War Two in Arlington National Cemetery was broken into by vandals early this morning. The cemetery has been closed to visitors, and an investigation of the circumstances of the break-in is proceeding. . . ." The announcer's voice shifted upward in tone as he abandoned the portentous news-announcing style in favor of his disc-jockey persona. "Baby, what is it with this glorious Yoo-Ess-Áy? Ripped off the grave of the Unknown Soldier? Ugh and ugh and ugh. . . ." His voice faded as he spoke off the mike. "That's all we have on this, Jerry? Yeah, that's all, up to this time. But hang on tight to us, chirren, and your favorite oasis will bring you the rest of the story as it develops. Till then, chirren, back to the Good and Plenties. . . ."

The rock group surged back stridently in mid-phrase. Booth started to lower the sound, but left it as the announcer returned.

"More on the tomb break-in: An unconfirmed report that six members of the tomb sentinels have been slain. Repeating: six soldiers have been reported slain in the grisly attack on the Tomb of the Unknown Soldier. Grisly, grisly, grisly. For further developments, stay pat where it's at."

The rock music resumed. Raphael jumped a red light.

"Don't panic," Booth said sharply. "It's coming in piecemeal and there are bound to be rumors and hearsay. They'll straighten it out."

Raphael said hopefully, "You mean it's just inefficiency?"

It was, Booth thought, the ultimate pejorative in Raphael's lexicon.

The President's unsolicited mail that Wednesday morning numbered about 5,000 pieces, an average day's haul, and assayed normal in terms of sentiment, which was to say that about sixty percent were disposed in the President's favor, forty against. Among the various enclosures were three sets of rosary beads; one cutting of a *tallith*, the Hebrew prayer shawl; a short *sura* from the Koran with a few key words underscored; one doll in the likeness of the President with a halo constructed of wire above its angelic head; another presidential doll with a large needle transfixing its heart; four letters containing human excreta; one with the cleanings from a nose; one with phlegm; one saturated in blood ("You are draining the lifeblood out of me anyway, so I thought I would spare you the trouble"); two with stiffish stains which, if subjected to chemical analysis, would undoubtedly prove to be human semen; and one, with cat hairs glued in a rectangular frame around the message, which read, "Fuck your dog Tommy Boy I hope he gets ran over," signed, "An alley cat and proud of it."

On this particular morning some dozen extra clerks had been assigned to the mailroom on the ground floor of the Executive Office Building to speed up the opening of the mail. Three special agents of the Federal Bureau of Investigation were also present. They found the letter that fitted the description of their brief less than a half hour after their arrival. They deposited it in a locked, booby-trapped attaché case and departed at once for the J. Edgar Hoover Building, where they delivered it into the hands of the director of the bureau.

In Caroline's mind, leaving the Cape was a rite of passage, a departure not from a place but a world. There were two geographical entities—the Cape was one, and the other was everywhere else.

She drove slowly over the high-arching span of the Sagamore Bridge into the other world. She had left the house immediately after hearing the first radio announcement. As she took the familiar route to Boston, she kept the car radio tuned to an all-news station, but listened to it with an odd detachment. She had spent the entire night dreaming, a succession of gruesome and illogical fantasies in which, masked and armed with a machine gun, she kept mowing down a self-renewing gallery of friends and strangers. Her emotions had been drained by her dreams.

For no particular reason she bypassed Boston and went to Cambridge instead.

As she dropped the letters addressed to the *Record* and the

Herald-American into a mailbox near Harvard Square, she remembered suddenly that it was here, at this very box, three
years ago, that she had posted a pathetic letter to her lover, a
married man who lived in Chicago and came to see her on
his frequent business trips to Boston. It had been a brave and
foolish letter, advising him that she was pregnant but not to
worry, she would have it taken care of. His reply came back
promptly, a money order for five hundred dollars. No letter,
just the money order. She had torn it up.

She reflected on the ways in which she had changed since
then. She would no longer get knocked up. She would no
longer give up ten pounds to grief. And she would certainly,
above all, cash a five-hundred-dollar money order.

She stared at the letter box for a long moment, trying to
coax back to some semblance of reality the girl who had posted her *cri de coeur* those long years ago, but the image was already fading.

She got back into the car and drove toward the Cape.

The major phoned at a bit after ten. "You listening to your
radio?"

"Yeah," Manero said.

"You hear what just came over?"

"Yeah. They say they used an expansible van."

"Well. . . ." The major laughed nervously. "Well, you better count our goddamn vans."

"I already counted them an hour ago. There's one missing.
I filed a report on it; look at your desk."

"Missing? You mean stolen?"

"Yeah," Manero said.

"Jesus sake! But it can't be. . . ."

The major trailed off. Manero let him dangle for a while.
Then he said, "It's our M-two-ninety-two."

"Christ! You *know* that? It's been identified?"

"It hasn't been identified. Didn't the guy on the radio say
they were conducting an intensive search for it?"

"Then why are you leaping to conclusions?"

"How many M-two-ninety-twos do you think were heisted
in one night?"

There was a stunned silence, and then the major said, "Manero, get your ass in here."

Manero lit a cigarette and smoked it with all deliberate slowness. He spent a full minute stubbing out the butt. Then he ambled through the admin. building corridor and entered the major's office. The major was reading the report Manero had had his Spec Four file on the missing truck.

"Don't you ever talk to me like that again," Manero said. "'Get your ass over here.' Don't ever do that again."

"Look here, Sergeant Manero. . . ." The major had the type of round face that might with effort seem sly or knowing; but anger was beyond its range. "Let's get something straight around here, Sergeant."

"Fuck off with that sergeant crap," Manero said. "Call me Al." The major made another attempt at registering anger, then folded. "Al. . . . You know what this means?"

"It means your fat ass. Chain of command. Anyway, a sergeant's not important enough for this kind of a rap. And a general's too important. A major—just right."

The major groaned. "Why did it have to be us?"

"Logistics. If you're gonna pull a weird stunt in this area, Belvoir is where you go to hist your truck." Manero reached across the major's desk for a cigarette. "Next stop Devil's Island, Freddie."

"Listen, you didn't. . . ."

"Come on," Manero said mildly. "Do I rent out trucks to people I don't know? And did I ever hold out on your cut?"

"Shhh." The major glanced around the office uneasily. "What can I do? Christ! Come up with an idea, Al."

"Don't sit here like a rabbit waiting for a pile of shit to topple over on you. Jump the gun. Call the general. Tell him you just put two and two together, and, by God, those bastards must have stolen our truck! Make like you're a fucking detective."

"But suppose it turns out not to be our truck?"

Manero shrugged. "Then you get a little reaming out for being an alarmist."

"I can't call him. I honestly can't. You know how he scares

the shit out of me. I can't even *think* of that bastard without breaking out in a sweat."

"Look, Freddie, I'm giving you my best advice. The stolen van is on the report. You have to make the connection and report it to him."

The major shuddered. "See, we're just talking about him and I'm sweating *already*. He's going to flip, Al. Christ!"

"If he gets too rough," Manero said, "you just remind him of the numerous occasions we lent him trucks *and* drivers for personal reasons like carrying a load of topsoil and moving his hippie kid's gear from college when she was tossed out, and so forth."

The major's soft pudgy hand crawled across the top of his desk toward the phone, then stopped itself and formed a loose trembling fist. "I can't do it, Al, I fucking can't do it."

Manero started to get up.

"Al . . . ." The major's voice was a high pitiful wail. "Don't go. I'll call him. Stick around, will you? Please?"

"Fuck that," Manero said, and went out.

13

The telephone rang. Griese picked it up. "Very well, send him in." He replaced the phone. "The director," he said to the news secretary. "He is heterosexual."

The news secretary stared.

"Nothing," Griese said with a wave. "I was simply trying to think of something neutral to say about him. . . . Good morning, Director."

The director of the Federal Bureau of Investigation placed his attaché case on the desk and began to turn the combination lock.

He was a fussy and—Griese sought again for a neutral descriptive—spotlessly clean man who had risen through the ranks of the bureau all the way to the top. Which meant—and after that all further characterization was superfluous—that he was an avatar of the bureaucrat.

He removed a sheet of paper from the attaché case and handed it to Griese. "This is a Xerox copy of the letter. We're running the original through our lab procedures. By midmorning we should be able to have established the kind of paper it's written on, the make and model and idiosyncrasies of the typewriter, the ribbon, fingerprints, of course. . . ."

"Yes, thank you, Director. You may sit down."

The news secretary rose and went around the desk to read over Griese's shoulder.

DEAR MR. PRESIDENT:

Except in the sense that the entire nation is ill of

corruption, a contagion of the Vietnam war, the last casualty of that catastrophic adventure is Francis Rowan.

Until now we have failed to secure his freedom through all appeals in the name of justice and fair play, by all legal and constitutional means. Hence, we have been forced into adopting an extravagant and perhaps, to some, repellent instrumentality. In calling on the victim of one war to promote the cause of the victim of another, in enlisting the dead to free the living, we are acting out a dramatic metaphor.

But our purpose is not metaphoric. It is bluntly practical. To put it plainly, we are offering to barter the remains of the Unknown of World War II for the freedom of Francis Rowan.

At midnight tomorrow (Thurs.) we will destroy the remains with high explosives unless the following terms are met:

1. A complete, unequivocal presidential pardon for Francis Rowan.

2. His release from prison immediately thereafter.

3. Assistance in leaving the U.S. for a country of his choice if this is what he wishes.

These are our demands, and they are inflexible. There is no room for negotiation or amendment. All three must be met fully or we will destroy the remains.

As a precaution against any effort on your part to suppress this letter, we have sent copies to several newspapers, which will receive them tomorrow (Thurs.) morning. We trust the networks and other short-order media will overlook the slight.

THE AD HOC COMMITTEE FOR THE
RELEASE OF FRANCIS ROWAN

"Short-order media," Griese said. "That's almost witty."
The phone rang. Griese picked it up and listened.
"The President is in the Oval Office and will see us at once,

gentlemen." He stood up. "Six to five his first words after reading the letter are 'Who the fuck is Francis Rowan?'"

". . . dead man is Sergeant Roger T. Clough, of Pine Bluff, Arkansas. He was shot through the heart at point-blank range."

Raphael groaned. Booth said sharply, "Easy."

The announcer paused; a teletype machine clicked in the background. The station had cut from its musical program to "our newsroom to bring you all the details on this fast-developing story as they develop.

". . . an erroneous report that six were dead. Now it has been learned that five of the sentinels were drugged by an as-yet-unknown drug administered by intravenous injection. The five are at the base hospital at Fort Myer, and they are reported in good condition although still unconscious. The four men, all members of the famous Third Infantry, traditional guards at the Tombs of the Unknowns, are Sergeant Thomas L. Miller, of Laredo, Texas. . . ."

Booth turned the radio down to a low murmur. Raphael said, "They're concentrating on names, so maybe they're still confused about what happened. Maybe there won't be any roadblocks?"

Booth shook his head. "The information is coming out slowly, but they've pieced it together by now. They may even have figured out that we used an Engineers' van."

Raphael looked startled. "Dover. . . ."

"He's clear. He dumped the van an hour ago."

Raphael stepped on the brake abruptly, and a car behind them honked furiously. The driver glared as he shot by them.

"Sorry," Raphael said. "We have a choice. We can either take the Baltimore-Washington Parkway and hook up with Route ninety-five later on, or we can take Route ninety-five directly."

"What's the difference?"

"A little less traffic on the Baltimore-Washington Parkway. Maybe less chance of a roadblock?"

Booth shook his head. "If they've established roadblocks,

they'll have them on all the main roads and at all points of the compass out of Washington."

Raphael chewed his lip. "In that case, Route ninety-five. It's a lot busier, so maybe they'll be less thorough there?"

Booth said, "Pull over, Eddie, and I'll spell you."

"I'm not tired yet."

The focus of an interrogation at a roadblock would be on the driver. "Pull over, please, Eddie."

Raphael said, "I'm not tired," but after a moment stopped the truck. They changed places, and Booth followed the signs to Route 95. Raphael turned up the radio.

". . . the Senator added that quote the sacred and hallowed remains must be recovered at all costs unquote. He said quote that it is beyond the ken of human understanding to fathom the depths of degradation of those who have perpetrated this outrageous, blasphemous, and henious crime unquote."

Booth circled into Route 95 northbound. "Heinous will be the most frequently used, and mispronounced, adjective of the day."

"Well, if you're going to be objective about it, it *is* heinous."

The announcer was reading a thumbnail sketch of Francis Rowan. Raphael squirmed indignantly as he listened. Well, Booth thought, it didn't exactly fit Raphael's specifications for objectivity. Ahead of him, as if in series, red brake lights twinkled.

"What are you doing?" Raphael said.

Booth tapped his brake and came to a stop inches from the bumper of the car in front of him. "The first roadblock, Eddie."

"Maybe it's just a traffic accident or a breakdown." Raphael leaned forward and peered through the windshield.

"Relax," Booth said.

"The *first* roadblock? Christ!"

Booth smiled. "After the first one it'll be easier."

Raphael was not amused. "If they catch us at the first one, there won't *be* any second."

Booth sought for a rationalization that might comfort him. "They've got a limited amount of manpower. They can stop and search only a small fraction of the cars that come through."

A space opened up in front of him. Booth moved up. Far ahead he could see a phalanx of police cruisers and, on foot, troopers of the Maryland State Police.

"That's true," Raphael said. "Mathematically, the odds are in our favor."

"Hold onto that thought," Booth said.

"Who the fuck is Francis Rowan?"

The President sat comfortably in his chair behind the huge desk, which was presently clear of the carefully selected memorabilia with which he dressed it for picture-taking sessions.

He smelled of coffee.

Griese sat beside his desk, the news secretary squarely facing it, the director of the FBI discreetly distant. The news secretary flashed a quick glance at Griese, then answered.

"Sir, he is that Episcopalian minister—"

"Ah," the President said. "He murdered the husband of the choir member he was diddling."

The news secretary, who was clearly in no mood for joking, said, "He was convicted in connection with the murder of Special Agent Arthur D. Solaitis."

"One of my finest men, sir," the director said.

"You weren't director then," Griese said. "He was one of your illustrious predecessor's finest men."

"In a way of speaking," the director said, flushing.

"Let's get on with it, please," the President said. "I'm already running late this morning."

"In, I believe, August of 1972," the news secretary said, "at his farm near Gettysburg, Pennsylvania, Francis Rowan . . ."

The President's memory had already been jogged. But he would continue to hear the news secretary out, wearing that squinting country-lawyer look that in some miraculous way combined shrewdness and openness in a single expression. He was a good listener and a quick study. He could remember anything he wanted to remember in exquisite detail for a

short period of time and afterward clear his mind of it as one
cleared an attic of yesterday's debris.

". . . found guilty by a jury and sentenced to life imprisonment."

"Anything else?" The President was wearing his other expression now—a tight-lipped, narrow-eyed dirt farmer scanning the horizon for cyclones.

"Yes," Griese said. "Another thing is that Francis Rowan is a man of integrity and a fool."

"In what way?"

"He is a martyr, and a martyr is by definition a fool."

The President's face changed back from dirt farmer to country lawyer. Actually, he was neither one nor the other. As a scholarship boy first at Harvard and then at Harvard Law School he had been brilliant against the fiercest competition. The expressions were in one sense cosmetic, to conceal his elitest education, and in another a purely reflexive memory of his humble birth on a farm. His enemies said of him that he was "as honest as Nixon and as smart as Jerry Ford," but the truth was that he was a great deal smarter than Ford and sufficiently more honest than Nixon. He was a man of good intelligence and excruciatingly refined political acumen.

"We are divagating," the President said, "by which I mean that we're waddling up any old cow path. I have already had to push back my luncheon date with the bakhoun of Rashir, and you know how touchy these blacks can be."

"It's the other way around," Griese said. "The rashir of Bakhoun. And he's no blacker than you are."

"All right," the President said. "The question is, how do we proceed?"

"I counsel moving slowly," Griese said. "The whole thing's a giant booby trap. We can save the remains, yes, but at the price of releasing a convicted murderer under extortion by ghouls who have also murdered. It's absolutely essential to know the position before we act."

"But, Em," the President said plaintively, "don't we ever act strictly on principle and be damned to politics?"

He's not a naïve man, Griese thought, so he's speaking for attribution. Is it possible that he's heard about the news secretary's book contract? "I hope not," he said. "I sincerely hope not, sir."

"The deadline is midnight tomorrow," the news secretary said. "That doesn't leave time for dawdling."

"Thirty-six hours," Griese said. "Surely that leaves enough time to heed the outcry of an anguished nation?"

The news secretary gave Griese a look of guarded disgust. He said to the President, "We're going to have to have something from you for the press."

"I deplore it," the President said. "I am stricken by anger and pity at this foulest and most reprehensible of desecrations, and so forth. I, too, had the honor of serving in the great conflict in which the Unknown gave up his life, and who is to say that he is not some comrade at whose side I fought?"

"Someone will say it," Griese said, "who knows that you were a dry-land navy lieutenant jg and never saw a ship in anger."

"He's unknown, isn't he? Maybe he was a dry-land lieutenant, too."

"Yes, well. . . ." Griese dropped the matter; the President was wearing his farmer face. "One last point. I think we ought to reopen the cemetery as quickly as possible. Show we're not paralyzed or intimidated. Also, compassion for the wives and sons and husbands and lovers who have traveled from far corners of the country on their pilgrimage of respect and devotion to their fallen heroes."

The President nodded. "Will you take care of it, Em?" He half rose from his chair. "Thank you very much, gentlemen."

The director, who was first on his feet, said, "Sir, I wish you to know that every available man in the bureau has received orders to make the apprehension of these criminals his instant priority. I am not exaggerating, sir, when I say that we are mounting the biggest manhunt in the history of the nation."

"Good. And now, gentlemen, I must clear the decks for my

luncheon with the bakhoun." He looked sharply at Griese, then smiled and said, "Or the rashir, as the case may be."

Booth switched the radio off. They were about ten cars back from the head of the line.

"It would be perfectly natural to have the radio on," Raphael said. "Why pretend we don't know anything about it?"

"It's a less complicated pretense than sorting out what everybody knows from what only we know. Cuts down on the possibility of a slipup."

Raphael was rigid in his seat; his jaws were clenched. No point urging him to relax—the effort he would have to put out might tighten him even more.

The line of cars split off into two groups, and suddenly they were third in line. The car directly ahead of them was a huge Lincoln, and it would go through fast: The bigger the car, the smaller the interrogation; cops were profound respecters of property.

"All you have to do is seem interested," Booth said. "Being a little nervous is perfectly natural."

Raphael nodded his head jerkily. To the right a VW camper was being pulled out of a line by a watchful trooper who tracked it with his carbine. The driver was a bearded kid with a colorful headband and a rippling fall of blond shoulder-length hair.

"He pulled him out," Raphael whispered.

"VW bus," Booth said, "that's why. They stop them all the time on highways and toss them for drugs."

The Lincoln pulled away, the driver's hand outside the window, waving to the trooper. Booth edged up and stopped in obedience to the trooper's signal.

"Where are you coming from?"

The trooper stood a pace back from the window, holding his carbine with one hand, his finger resting on the trigger. As he bent slightly forward for the answer, there was a creak of leather. His face was red, sunburned, stony.

"Fairfax, Virginia," Booth said.

"Address?" It was snapped out.

"Thirty-four-seventy-six Palm Street."

"Zip number?"

"Two-two-oh-three-oh. Can you tell me what this is all about, officer?" He felt a vibration on the seat as Raphael moved abruptly.

The trooper said, "Where are you going?"

"New York City."

"What's in the truck?"

"Furniture. I'm carrying some furniture up North."

"You're moving up North?"

The questions didn't seem particularly searching, Booth thought, but it was their tempo that mattered: They were meant to solicit immediate and unflustered answers.

He said, "My sister, who lived in Fairfax, has died. She was a widow. I'm taking some of her furniture up North, where I'll keep some of it and sell the rest. We've had a lot of it in the family for years."

The trooper's eyelids flickered, and Booth thought, I've said more than I had to in response to the question. On the other hand, even *they* had to blink once in a while.

"Let me have your license, please." The trooper leaned lower to look past him. "Who are you?"

Raphael gave a fictitious name and address, and Booth, searching through his wallet for the phony license, listened critically to the quality of Raphael's voice. He sounded nervous, but not overly so. Or so it seemed to him. How it seemed to the trooper was another matter.

"You're coming from the same place?"

"Yes."

The trooper shifted his eyes to Booth. "What's he doing here?"

"He's my nephew," Booth said. "The dead woman was his aunt."

The trooper studied the license, then handed it back. "Open up the back, please."

The seat vibrated. Booth said, "Certainly." He switched off the motor and removed the key. The trooper stepped back three paces as he got out of the car, and followed him around to the back, the carbine still pointed toward him. He unlocked the rear doors and swung them open. The packing of the furniture might have been tidier, but the truck looked convincingly full.

Keeping the carbine trained on him, the trooper moved in closer. He reached into the truck, tugged on a chair, tried to peer beyond it along one wall. Booth stood with his hands clasped in front of him and watched. He felt light-headed.

"Close it," the trooper said.

He shut the doors and locked them. As he started toward the front of the truck, the trooper said, "What was the address in Fairfax?"

"Thirty-four-seventy-six Palm Street."

"Move on through, please," the trooper said.

As he sat down in the truck and turned the motor on, Booth became aware that the trooper was watching him. He nodded his head and drove slowly past the roadblock. He heard Raphael's breathing and his own as well. They were out of synch.

"Thank God," Raphael said. The truck picked up speed. "You handled it beautifully." There was a note of elation in his voice.

"Don't get cocky," Booth said. His legs were still trembling.

14

Robbins awoke feeling as if he had been assaulted—which, he reminded himself, had been the case exactly half of the time. He got out of bed with some care, so as not to awaken Foxworth. She was sleeping on her back, her heavy eyebrows—outside of them he found no fault with her looks—drawn together in an imposing scowl, her breasts upright and perky, her black pubic hair matted with the intermingled juices of the night's passage. Desire stirred in him lazily, but he decided to save his ammunition for later, after he had some breakfast, for instance, and his strength was renewed.

He went to the bathroom, on the way pausing in front of the tilted mirror over the dresser to admire himself. Beard, hair, and pubic hair were flaming red and luxuriant, and there was hardly an inch of his body, barring his ass, that wasn't covered with at least a red down. There was a time when he had been ashamed of his body hair—a smooth-skinned contemporary in high school had once told him that he resembled a furbearing animal—but he had long since discovered that chicks didn't object to it; in fact, some of them doted on furbearing animals.

Like Foxworth, for example, sleeping sternly in her bed. She actually turned herself on by rubbing her face in his pelt, nibbling at the fuzz on his shoulders, belly, armpits. It was definitely an asset. He was a glowing carroty aphrodisiac.

From the bathroom he went to the kitchen, where he started a pot of coffee and threw a dozen slices of bacon into a pan. The bacon was crisping and he was stirring eggs in a bowl when he became aware of Foxworth standing in the doorway, dark and beautiful. He stirred again, but some disjunction in her eye deterred him.

He said, "Good morning, Foxworth. Did the delicious smell of frying bacon on the winy morning air awaken you?"

She frowned, sifted his remark for insult, apparently found none and said, "Good morning, Robbins."

"Feel free to kiss me, Foxworth." He shifted into a wedge of sunlight, hoping it would turn his body fuzz into a nimbus and reduce her to a quivering jelly of lustfulness. "Anywhere you please."

She said, "Don't try so fucking hard to be funny."

"I'm not being funny, I'm making overtures. If you don't want me to be aroused, go cover up your gorgeous body."

"Do I ask you to cover yours?"

"And see what's happening to it." He was beginning to rear upward out of his red bush.

"Do you expect me to swoon?"

In the night she had astonished him with tenderness, but now she seemed back on her normal beam. He said, "I'm cooking the eggs and bacon and making the coffee and before long I'm going to start the toast, so you fucking well ought to set the table."

She surprised him by not answering. She went out of the kitchen. When she came back, wearing an old Indian-design bathrobe and looking shiny and fresh, she repaired the omission.

"You're a hundred centuries ahead of us on the proposition," she said. "You can cook breakfast *and* set the table *and* scrub the floor for as long as you live and you'll still be nowhere near to closing the gap."

Nevertheless, she set the table, but with a clatter that said clearly she was doing it only because she wanted to, so don't make anything of it. He put the bacon on paper towels to drain and scrambled the eggs. With his back to her, he grinned. Foxworth was the first Mau Mau libber he had ever slept with, and he enjoyed her. Okay, she was a little too literal-minded about women's rights—if you go on top, then I have to go on top; if I suck you, then you have to suck me—but he liked the toughness of her fiber. These days, when sex was so easy to get, she gave him a sense of accomplishment.

He served the bacon and eggs from behind her, so that his cock brushed her cheek. She gave it a backhand swat, and he doubled up in reflex, laughing.

"Quit that shit," she said. "Put some drawers on so you don't hypnotize yourself with that thing."

He decided for reasons of diplomacy to accept her suggestion. He went back to the bedroom and put his shorts on. He poured coffee for both of them and sat down.

"How are the eggs?" He sounded as if he really cared. Sincerity was the ticket to pave the way for serious talk.

She shrugged.

"Escoffier I'm not—right?"

She shrugged again. He thought, She's got another hundred centuries before she has to stop shrugging. He ate in silence until the eggs and bacon were gone and then sat back and gave her his earnest look.

He said, "What were we talking about last night?"

She reached behind her and switched on the radio. Mozart. And too loud. He made a turning movement with his fingers. She ignored him.

He said, "I think you need to do it to get your morale together."

She said, "We don't need anybody like you to tell us what we need."

"You may not need *me*, but you need *somebody*. Unless you got another explosives expert in your acquaintanceship?"

"What sense does it make dialectically if a man runs it?"

"I didn't say I'd run it. I'd just help out with the details and hook up the explosives, naturally."

"Couldn't you teach us how to do the explosives?"

He grimaced. "We don't need another house blown up by amateurs."

She said, "I'm not all that sold on the idea. The violence doesn't faze me. I just don't see what pertinence it has."

"The pertinence is symbolic. You're not going to blow all the men in New York City to kingdom come or terrify them into some kind of mass surrender. But a bomb is an amplifier, it raises the decibel level of your voice. They'll *hear* you, baby."

"Well, what we were proposing to do was symbolic enough, wasn't it?"

He had to raise his voice to make it heard over the Mozart. "Splattering the walls with horseshit? Kid stuff."

"Not horse. *Human.*"

"Disgusting. That's all anybody will say—disgusting. And afterward they just bring in some poor exploited workers to wash it off and spray perfume all over the place. And then it's business as usual. But you blow the place up and they have to go someplace else until it's fixed, and it costs them money, and most of all, you scare the hell out of them. . . . Then you're *heard,* baby."

She stirred her coffee thoughtfully. He continued to direct his earnest look across the table at her.

"I don't know," she said. "We haven't done anything like it before. Shit is one thing, but a bomb. . . . We don't want to hurt anybody."

"The bang goes off in a deserted location, like the gym at night. Nobody gets hurt."

"Not that I care about them, their death wouldn't diminish the world one fucking bit. But it wouldn't do *us* any good if somebody got hurt."

He said, "Well, look, it's up to you. I don't want to get carried away. It's just that I think it would be a great demonstration of purpose, and I can help you. I mean, it happens to fall into the area of my competence."

She turned the radio down to a normal level. "You think we could pull it off?"

"Yes," he said quietly.

"What makes you so interested? It's not your cause."

He grinned. "If it's a Movement cause, I'm into it. I'm changing the world, baby."

"Bullshit."

"All right." He put his serious look back on. "It's up to you. But if your group is interested and wants to discuss the practical side of it, I'll meet with them and lay out the blueprint."

"We'll see." She stood up. "I'm going to take a shower."

Watching her go out of the kitchen, he thought, "We'll see" means yes; in her negative lexicon anything less than no or a shrug means yes. He thought, It's going to be a beautiful bust; just for the pleasure of thinking about it I'll clean up the dirty dishes and when she comes out of the shower I'll throw her a grateful fuck.

As he started to gather up the eggy plates, his attention was caught by a sudden silence; the Mozart had been cut off. Then a voice said, "We are interrupting our music to bring you up to date on the latest developments in the disinterment of the remains of the Unknown Soldier."

"The *what?*" Robbins said.

He listened with rapt attention for five minutes, and when the announcer had finished and the Mozart returned, he clapped his hands together ecstatically. Then he ran out of the kitchen and stood outside the bathroom and listened to the sound of the shower. He padded back to the kitchen, picked up the wall telephone, and dialed. Waiting, he grinned and slapped his thigh in a form of self-congratulation.

"Yes?" A single pinched syllable, as guarded as a secret.

"Phoebe?" Robbins' voiced trilled beguilingly. "Hello, darling."

"Oh, it's you."

"Must you always mask your passion, darling?" He listened for the little cluck of annoyance and then said crisply, "I want to see you, Phoebe, right away."

"Do you have something to tell me?"

"It certainly isn't for *les beaux yeux.*"

"For *what?*" Then, after a pause, "I'm very busy. What's it about?"

"I can't talk," Robbins said, lowering his voice. "I'm practically within sperm shot of Foxworth. But it's about a matter of the most urgent importance."

"Such as?"

"I told you I can't talk. Believe me, it's not only most urgent, it's most urgent*est.*"

"Are you referring to what I *think* you're referring?"

Christ, Robbins thought, they don't even trust each *other*. But he had caught the quickening of excitement in the voice. "Right. That's what I'm referring to. Can we meet?"

"All right. When?"

"In about an hour. Same place."

"That place? I'd rather not. We've been seen there together too often."

"Okay," Robbins said impatiently. "Do you know the Earthquake on Bleecker Street?"

"What number?"

"I don't know what number. Near Macdougal. They have an awning. You can't miss it."

"All right. At eleven twenty-five."

"I count the minutes. Oh, Earthquake is a gay bar. Better wear your chastity belt, Phoebe darling."

He hung up and stood for a moment rubbing his pelt. He visualized Foxworth soaping herself between her legs and for a moment considered jumping into the shower with her. But then he thought of what he had heard on the radio, and he winked and smiled and clasped his hands over his head like a victorious boxer. He thought, Fox you, Fuckworth, and fox your dirty dishes and fox your dopey little plan to blow up the YMCA. I got much bigger fox to fry.

He went out to the bathroom and pounded on the door and shouted, "You gonna be in there all day? I got to get showered, Chrissake, I got another assignation."

There was no answer. He sensed that Foxworth was shrugging, inflicting another barely perceptible dent on the monolith of a hundred centuries.

Through the window in the Earthquake, Robbins watched Phoebe approach. He was doing everything wrong. Instead of simply walking through the door, he first cased the street up and down, then hitched up his shoulders and took a breath, and finally edged inside like a man sneaking into a porno shop.

He was dressed all wrong, too, as usual. His denims had been bleached to a satisfactory pale blue, to be sure, but they were bone clean. His leather jacket had probably set him

back two hundred dollars at Abercrombie, and his espa-
drilles looked brand new. His hair wasn't nearly long
enough, and he had the overall appearance of a man done
up for a costume ball. Still, it wasn't a bad rig for the Earthquake. He would pass as a square closet queen on an uneasy
excursion into the gay fleshpots.

He stood just inside the doorway, looking helpless. At the
bar three or four denizens began to size him up for a possible
score. Robbins enjoyed his discomfiture. But when a long
skinny fag detached himself from the bar and started sidling
over, he stood up and waved his hand and yelled, "Over this
way, Phoebe."

The waiter was a petite beauty with the blond curly hair
and innocent eyes of a *putto*. Robbins ordered a refill of his
beer and a scotch and soda for Phoebe.

"Where do you find these places?" Phoebe said. His normal voice was clipped and authoritative, like a captain of in-
dustry, but it was a little quavery now.

"It's my life," Robbins said. "I mean, if I didn't know these
places, I wouldn't be any good, would I?"

Phoebe looked at his watch. "This is the worst day of the
year. *Any* year. So let's get on with it."

The little waiter placed their drinks on the table, then ran
his hand over Phoebe's shoulder. Phoebe recoiled.

"What the hell do you want, Kewpie?" Robbins said.

"This buttery leather?" the waiter said. "I would so much
love to own it."

"You don't move to hell out of here, Kewpie, I'm going to
tie your rosy little peepee into knots." Robbins feinted with
his fist and the waiter skittered backward with a graceful
practiced step, as if he were accustomed to threats and had
made an art of retreat. He stuck out his tongue and then disappeared into the gloom near the bar.

Phoebe said, "I think he actually expected me to give him
the jacket."

"He doesn't care about the jacket, he wanted to feel your
silken scapula."

"I'm under the gun today," Phoebe said.

"You mean about the subject F?" Robbins said.

The Talisman

"You know I don't mean that. You implied on the telephone. . . ." He lowered his voice. "Don't you try fucking me around, Robbins."

"Such language." Robbins covered his ears chastely.

Phoebe put his glass down with a clatter. "You're not indispensable, you know. I can cut you off the payroll anytime it pleases me."

Robbins took note of the hardening of Phoebe's classic jawline. Time to get serious. "Okay. The Arlington snatch." Start him off with a zinger. "I know who did it."

Phoebe's reaction was beautiful. His body jerked spasmodically, and he almost knocked his glass over. "Are you trying to tell me that this is one of your. . . .?" He aped speechlessness and glared.

"It's not one of mine," Robbins said with regret, "but it's in my area of competence. Who did it? Movement people. Right?"

"Is *that* what you mean by knowing who did it?" Phoebe looked disgusted, but in the next instant turned suspicious. "Are you holding out on me?"

Robbins shook his head. "I just heard about it on the radio. All that remains is to fill in the blanks. *Which* guys did it. I can find that out."

Phoebe snorted. "You've got an identity crisis. Let me remind you—you're not God, you're just a two-bit paid informant."

"I give up," Robbins said, spreading his hands helplessly. Phoebe started to get up. "No, I don't give up. My country means more to me than my pride. All I want you to do is okay my working on this thing and authorize a few modest expenses."

Phoebe said, "All I want you to do is proceed with your project with the subject F."

Robbins shook his head. "Whether you like it or not I'm going to find the people who knocked off the cemetery and deliver them to you, so you can become the hero of the whole world, and the director of the bureau by acclaim, and maybe someday even President. That's what I'm going to do for you, even if you don't deserve it."

207

The Talisman

"You're off the payroll," Phoebe said.

"Okay. I'm off the payroll. So now I'm going to solve this thing and turn it all over to the cops. No." He smiled sweetly. "I'll give it to one of your colleagues, and then *he'll* be the hero of the world, and the new director of the bureau by acclaim, and—"

"I'm leaving," Phoebe said.

You just blew it, Robbins thought, the presidency of the whole U.S. of fucking A. "I mean it," he said to Phoebe. "The instant I heard it on the radio I told myself, This is made for you, Robbins, tailor-made for your area of competence, you can go out and finger these people. . . ."

He watched Phoebe pick his way through the dark interior toward the door, eyes straight ahead, swerving as he passed Kewpie, who looked at him with covetous eyes. Through the window Robbins saw him start to cross the street, his back rigid, and then he turned abruptly and reentered the Earthquake. He threaded his way back to Robbins' table.

"If you think you can pick up any leads through your contacts with young subversives. . . ."

"I can," Robbins said quietly. "Christ, they might even be people I actually know."

"I'll expect you to report to me anything you learn immediately. Anything, no matter how insignificant it may appear to you. *We'll* evaluate it. Is that understood?"

"Roger wilco," Robbins said solemnly. "Does that mean I'm back on the payroll?"

Phoebe nodded stiffly.

"And that you'll authorize a few modest expenses?"

Phoebe looked at him suspiciously. "We'll see."

He turned and went out again. Robbins didn't bother watching him through the window. He picked up his beer and drained it, then started to work on the remnants of Phoebe's scotch.

Actually, he hated scotch, which meant that he was punishing himself for almost blowing it. When Phoebe had told him he was off the payroll, he had felt a sharp pang of irredeemable loss. Not that he liked Phoebe—how could you like somebody whose asshole was made out of starch?—or the bu-

208

reau, but he liked what they did for his life, which was simply to make it perfect.

When he had been separated out of the army, he had gone native. East Village, beard, the Movement, an infinite variety of babes, popping a few pills now and then, motorcycle, in short, making the scene, the *dolce* fucking *vita*. He loved it, all of it, except the poverty that was a part of it. Because of a fatal flaw in his character, he wouldn't accept money from his old man. That is, he wouldn't accept it because the old bastard expected him to work for it in his sweatshop of a paper-bag factory. He tried welfare for a while, but it wasn't dignified and it was underpaid. He tried panhandling, too, but it was too much like work.

Then, one day, purely by accident, he had lucked into a dream setup. A Phoebe came around to see him because someone had dropped his name in connection with one of the kids who had been blown up in that Eleventh Street house. Actually, he had barely known one of the girls who was involved in the bomb factory, but it was enough for a Phoebe to follow up on. They worked that way—somebody gave them your name, and you gave them somebody else's name, and that somebody gave them another name, and before you knew it they had half the names in the country.

He tossed the Phoebe a few Village names at random, and after that they sat around schmoozing amiably, and for some reason he told the Phoebe that he had been in G-2 in the army (which was true in a very specialized way) and that all his life he had been interested in undercover police work—which was pure bullshit. All he was doing was yarn-spinning, putting the Phoebe on for kicks, but the Phoebe had bought it. A couple of weeks later he got a phone call from another Phoebe—his present one, Anstruther—and they met in a joint and had a long elliptical exploratory talk, in which the Phoebe made no offer and he himself was prepared to be indignant if he did make one, but at the end of which, to all practical purposes, the road was open for him to become an FBI fink. The Phoebe promised to get in touch in a few days, and Robbins spent the time thinking about it. The more he thought about it, the better he liked it. The FBI would subsidize him so he could live exactly the kind of life he enjoyed living, with no more exertion on his part than turning somebody in every once in a while.

The idea of betraying his friends and colleagues created no moral crisis for him. He didn't even think of it as betrayal, but as survival of the fittest. He admitted that he had no principles—except the one about not accepting money from his father—and that was more than enough. In fact, it was so *much* principle that it entitled him to have no others.

At the end of a week he was so hot for the job that he exerted himself a little to get it. He phoned Phoebe and dropped the name of an acidhead who was futzing around with *plastiques* in the cellar of his pad on East Seventh Street, and Phoebe came around and collared him. Robbins told himself that he was doing the acidhead a favor, saving him from blowing himself up. It was the first and last time he sought a justification for informing. Buck fever. After that he was just doing his duty.

A grateful Phoebe put him on the federal payroll.

By now, beyond his appreciating the way being a fink enabled him to sustain his life-style, he had grown to like it. The cops-and-robbers aspect of the work was exciting, and he had a real vocation for it. He was goddamn good at it. Phoebe didn't demand much—information leading to an occasional bust would keep him happy for months, and the salary kept coming in. But the bug had bitten Robbins, and he asked for a promotion to the more elevated and refined position of provocateur. Phoebe at first denied that the bureau ever engaged in such an activity, but suggested that if he had any specific ideas he might get in touch with him. Robbins fell in with a group of wild spades—that's how good he was—who were toying with the idea of kidnapping a Tom on the City Council. They weren't really too serious about it, but Robbins kept nudging them into a corner they couldn't back out of without losing face. "Shit, man, if *I* was a fucking spade, you wouldn't fucking find *me* hesitating about snatching a fucking councilman" kind of thing. He helped them set it up and then passed the word along to the bureau.

A grateful Phoebe gave him the promotion and a raise.

And now, he thought, finishing off Phoebe's scotch, time to go to work. As he stood up, the little waiter appeared out of the gloom.

"Who's your nice friend?"

"Fuck off, Kewpie, he doesn't go that way."

The angelic curls quivered as the waiter shook his head. "I heard you call him Phoebe. So please don't try to tell me which way he goes."

Robbins looked at him admiringly. "I guess you're just too fucking smart for me, Kewpie."

"And if *he* goes that way, and *you* were sitting with *him* . . ."

"Wait here for me, Kewpie," Robbins said.

"Where are you going?"

"I'm going to call up my old lady and tell her to move the hell out of my pad, that you just convinced me, by sheer logic, that I'm gay."

"Serious?" Kewpie lowered his dark lashes in pleasure.

"Then I'll come back and take your little pants down and ball you right on the top of the bar. Okay?"

"O-*kay!*"

15

Marbert Morrison was ready to believe that certain people had willow sticks in their head that dowsed out events. How else could you explain the line of cars that formed at his sentry box at the gate minutes after the cemetery was reopened? The line stretched back as far as he could see and around the bend and maybe was already clogging the Arlington Memorial Bridge and even extended back into the approaches to the bridge in D.C.

They couldn't all have been listening to the news flash on their radio, could they? Yet here they were, and he was passing them in slowly, according to instructions, so that the chief and some FBI's and a few uniformed cops and some Interior Intelligence characters—all of them bunched up at the entrance—could scrutinize them keenly. Before he passed a car through, he waited for a nod from one of the eagle eyes, then he would say in his best servant-of-the-people manner, "All right, sir, pass on through; bear to the right for the parking lot."

Of course, holding them up gave the drivers an opportunity to talk, and a lot of them did. "What's this country coming to?" Or "What kind of rats would do such a thing?" Or "Did they catch them yet—those bastards that stole the Unknown Soldier?" To all questions he either shook his head or nodded, whichever occurred to his neck muscles first, and passed them on through. "All right, sir . . . bear right for the parking lot. . . ."

The Tourmobile buses had gotten the word, too. He had

never seen so many of them, and all full up, whereas on an ordinary day in November there would just be a couple, and half empty, too. The group of brass gave everybody the cold eye and whispered to one another a lot, but they didn't stop anybody, not even one evil-looking character in a wild striped polo shirt and enormous naked biceps who took a pull out of a bottle in a paper bag right in front of them.

Well, they weren't there to collar drunks, but grave robbers—the bit about returning to the scene of the crime, right?—but they must not have seen any, and after a while the chief and the Interior men and the FBI's got in their cars and peeled off into the cemetery, leaving just a few cops behind who were terrific at taking their caps off and running their hand through their hair and then putting the caps on again.

Just before the chief got into his car, he said, "Carry on, Marbert," which wasn't how he talked when there weren't any Interior or FBI men around.

"Can we actually see the grave they took the body from, officer?" A woman with a high beehive haircomb that flattened out against the roof of her car.

"Pass on through, ma'am. Parking inside, bear to the right. . . ."

Instructions were to say only that. No options.

There was no question in P. T. Ronsard's mind but that the whole world had come up here to look at the empty crypt. Except there was nothing much to see. Workmen had carted away the broken slab and swept up the dust and covered the open crypt with a sheet of plywood cut to size. The crowd pressed against the shiny chain that replaced the broken one—he didn't know how many deep—and the ones in back, unless they were seven feet tall, couldn't see anything but the sentinel, doing his thing up near the sarcophagus.

Aside from being the largest crowd by far that he had ever seen at the tombs, it was also the most demonstrative. Every time the sentinel made a turn and stomped they would clap their hands. It shook P. T. Ronsard the first few times he heard it, though he realized that it was some kind of sympa-

thy for the relief commander who had been killed and the
boys who had been drugged. The first time it happened he
saw the sentinel wince, but he didn't do anything, just went
through his routine.

When the new relief commander appeared, walking down
the path from the barracks, there was a little smattering of
applause that became practically an ovation when he started
the changing of the guard. They applauded everything: the
inspection, the snapping and twirling of the rifle, the exchange of orders between the old guard and the new. When
the commander made his little spiel, he was interrupted several times by applause. At the end, he made an impromptu
speech.

"Ladies and gentlemen. . . ." Applause. "Ladies and gentlemen, it is not customary for spectators to applaud here at
the tombs." Applause. "It is not proper and respectful to the
dead to applaud, and I will ask you not to applaud. Thank
you very much."

Applause.

They applauded him all the way back until he went into
the barracks and if he wasn't such a stiff-ass, P. T. Ronsard
thought, he would have come out and taken a bow.

Before the chief left to watch the gates when they reopened, he had warned P. T. Ronsard to keep his eyes
peeled, but he didn't say for what. Right now, eyes peeled, all
he could see was hundreds of people. Well, people and FBI's
and Interior plainclothes cops. There must have been thirty
or forty of them mingling with the crowd, and it wasn't hard
to pick them out because they had these sharp eyes that were
really peeled and kept rolling around the crowd, too. Also,
the FBI's and Interiors kept circulating, moving around,
sliding through the crowd.

When the chief came back from the gate, he shoved his
way through to where P. T. Ronsard was standing near the
north end of the chain.

"Anything, P.T.?" the chief said in a low voice.

"Sir?"

"Any incidents?"

"No, sir."

But at that instant there *was* an incident. The crowd rippled and seemed to be pulling back, a woman screamed, and for a second there was a kind of panic. The chief headed into it, bulling his way through the crowd toward the commotion. Ronsard couldn't see anything, but he heard shouting and then the meaty thwack of a fist, and a few more women screaming.

The chief came back about ten minutes later and told him what had gone on. An FBI agent had had his eye on somebody in the crowd who looked suspicious. He sidled over, leaned on him a little, and felt a sidearm under the suspect's clothes. He pinned the suspect's arm, to keep him from going for his gun, and the suspect had resisted, so he had fetched him a judo chop and felled him.

"Turned out the suspect was an Interior cop," the chief said, trying not to laugh. "We found that out after we hustled him away and went into his pockets and found his identification."

"Be dog," Ronsard said. "A judo chop."

"Pretty good one, too," the chief said. "Broke the fella's collarbone."

"Be dog," Ronsard said. "They say they can bust a two-by-four with one of them chops."

"Kills me," the chief said. He wiped a smile off his face. "Look smart, P. T., the television crews are coming in soon."

"Yes, sir."

"You know any of that judo stuff, P. T.?"

"Afraid not."

"Nothing's ever going to be the same again around here," the chief said. "I could take early retirement, you know."

"Yes, sir."

"Look alive now, P. T.," the chief said as he turned to go. "Keep your eyes peeled."

Bullshit, P. T. Ronsard thought, I don't need no broken collarbone all that bad.

"Turkey sandwich and a glass of cheap Tokay," Em Griese said. "Is that how we feed our important personages in this country?"

The FBI director was standing because he had not yet been asked to sit down.

Griese wafted his hand over the papers on his desk. "But if a choice lies between my going out to a respectable lunch or allowing the nation to fend for itself. . . . Please sit down, Director."

"Thank you."

"Above all," Griese said, "it is a tragedy to squander my valuable time on this ridiculous crime. But I have been charged by my President to oversee it, and so I dine on pressed turkey and Tokay made of urine in Frankfort, Kentucky."

The director said, not in resentment but stating a fact, "I haven't had *any* lunch yet."

"Meanwhile," Griese said, "the President is feasting with the rashir of Bakhoun on hummingbirds' tongues and champagne water. Is that just?"

The director looked impatient.

"But surely, like me, you are too intelligent to expect justice in the conduct of human affairs?" Griese looked challengingly across his desk until he brought a flush to the director's flat high-boned cheeks. But what was the use of baiting a man who would not fight back? "So—you have a report to make?"

"Yes," the director said. He took out a sheet of paper with typed notes on it and put on a pair of steel-rimmed eyeglasses. He wet his lips. "At this point we already know almost everything about this crime except who the criminals are."

"Nobody's perfect," Griese said, saluting the director with his glass.

"I wonder," the director said.

Griese gave him a nod of appreciation. "There may be more to you than meets the eye, Director."

Flushing—whether with pleasure or aghast at his temerity in having attempted to score against Em Griese—the director said, "Three men, in a van stolen from a motor pool at Fort Belvoir, entered the cemetery yesterday evening, probably shortly before it closed. . . ." He paused at a cough from

Griese and glanced up over his glasses. "Yes?"

"How do you know it was three men?"

"From a lab examination of their feces."

"They gave specimens?"

"In the army van, which was discovered in a parking lot in Alexandria, there was a barrel which was used as a latrine. We examined the contents of the barrel in our lab, and it has been determined that the feces therein were the product of three different men."

"The truth in a barrel of shit," Griese said. "Theologies have been based on a great deal less. You deduce there were only three men? Suppose there were another three who didn't use the barrel?"

"Correction," the director said. "I meant to say at *least* three men. We have also deduced, from evidence at the scene and from indications present in the truck, that the marble slab was lifted from the crypt by means of a vacuum device and a winch which was also used to lift the casket into the truck."

"How do you know that the men entered the cemetery last night?"

"Again from analysis of the feces as well as the logic of the situation. We have also determined by direct interrogation of a cemetery security guard that the truck exited the cemetery this morning through the front gate shortly after eight o'clock."

"As simply as that?"

"Human failure. The guard at the gate is not of high caliber. We will look into the possibility that the guard might have been bought off. We will also interrogate the drugged sentinels for collusion when the doctors permit us to. But neither of these seems to be likely."

"You speak policeman's prose expertly," Griese said.

The director nodded stolidly. "Finally, we know where they laid up during the night: A construction site for new graves. Further details: They were disguised in army uniforms, the relief commander was killed by a single shot from an M-sixteen rifle, standard army issue, and analysis of the sentinels' urine reveals that they were administered a fast-acting barbiturate hypodermically. This was expertly done. In fact, in the wrong hands the dosage could easily have been lethal. We are entertaining the thought that a qualified physician might therefore have been involved."

"That is all?"

"To the moment it is all, barring a few unimportant details."

Griese sipped his wine. "Do you know where this wine was made, Director?"

"I believe you said Frankfort, Kentucky."

"I was mistaken. It was made in the bottom of your famous barrel."

They encountered a second roadblock shortly after they entered the New Jersey Turnpike. The troopers were as grim-faced as before, but less thorough. Although Booth was ordered to open the rear of the truck, the trooper barely glanced inside before passing them through.

"That wasn't bad," Raphael said.

"Three hours after the fact they're just going through the motions."

Raphael was silent as the Drivurself picked up speed. Then he said, "What you said earlier—about their manpower being limited and the long odds against our being stopped and searched? Well, your reasoning was faulty. You forgot that they were infinitely more likely to stop a truck or van than a passenger car, since you couldn't fit a casket into a passenger car."

Booth smiled. "I didn't forget, Eddie."

"Oh. I see. You were giving me Dutch courage."

"And myself, too."

"I was a lot calmer at this roadblock." Raphael looked thoughtful. "You know why? Because by now I've half forgotten what we're carrying back there."

Booth nodded. Raphael was defining the process that enabled people to be criminals: They forgot what they were carrying back there. "That's what saves us, the human race, I mean," Booth said. "An infinite capacity for acceptance. If you had given him a week or two, Damocles would have learned to live with a hanging sword."

"I'm starved," Raphael said.

Booth turned in at the next turnpike restaurant. They ate quickly and then drove on. They reached the New Jersey side of the George Washington Bridge at a quarter of three. On the Manhattan end Booth turned off onto Fort Washington Avenue and posted the three remaining letters, addressed to the *Times,* the *Post,* and the *News.* As he started back to the car, Raphael was getting out.

"Paula," Raphael said. "My wife. I almost forgot. I promised I would phone her."

"You can't phone anybody," Booth said.

"I *promised.* It's an article of faith in our family that we keep promises. She'll simply flip out if I don't call. Jason, too."

"You're going to talk to the boy, too?" Booth glared at him. "Get back in the truck."

Raphael said calmly, "Would you prefer it if she put out a missing-persons alarm for me?"

He started walking toward a phone booth on the corner. For an instant, furious, Booth was impelled to lay hands on him, to stop him by force. But Raphael was impervious to his anger. He went into the phone booth. Booth went back to the truck and moved up parallel to the booth. Inside, Raphael was selecting a coin from his palm. He dropped it into the slot and dialed. When he began to speak, he turned his back to Booth.

The major phoned a few minutes after two o'clock. He sounded agitated. "Al, can you come in here a minute?"

Politeness will get you nowhere, Manero thought, and smoked his usual cigarette with his usual deliberateness before going down the hallway. The major invited him to sit down and then lowered his voice to a near whisper.

"I just got a call from S-two. Captain Denniston. He's the Assistant Two. He wants to see you."

"Why did't he call me direct if he wanted to see me? What is this—class consciousness?"

"He said he was being diplomatic for your own welfare. You know, say somebody answers your phone for you, word gets around that Two wants to see you, people start making suppositions that you're a subversive or something. He wanted to spare you that."

"When does this Two want to see me?"

"Right away, Al. Urgent. He wants to see me, too. It's about that van. Christ."

"Are you a subversive, Freddie?"

The major laughed nervously and lit a cigarette. There was a cigarette burning in his ashtray.

"Well, if you're not, don't smoke two cigarettes at the same time. Does he want us both together?"

The major shook his head. "You first, then me. What has subversive got to do with it?" He looked at his wristwatch. "He said right away, Al."

"Let him wait. Make him nervous."

"You know those bastards, Al," the major said. "They got the power to hurt you if they want to."

Manero sighed and stood up. "Okay, I'll go see Denniston. And when *you* go, for Christ sake, remember two things: One, you don't know anything about the van, which happens to be true, and two, you hate all subversives. Is that true, Freddie?"

"Me? Come *on*, Al. I hate the bastards!"

"Hold that thought, Freddie!"

Captain Denniston had a long pale delicate face with very clear eyes and soft black hair. His first question surprised Manero by being direct. "What do you think of people who would be capable of such a monstrous crime, Sergeant?"

"Beats the hell out of me, Captain." Manero knew better than to try to appear sincere; with his sly face it was out of the question. But breezy knowledgeability would be reasonable. "Subversives don't think like you and me, Captain. You got to understand that. So how do you get into their mind?"

"Perhaps," Denniston said vaguely. "Let's discuss the stolen truck for a minute."

"Sonofabitches. I *knew* it was our truck. It *had* to be."

"You had a premonition?"

"I *knew,* Captain. Chrissake, if you were going to pull something off in Virginia and had to have an M-two-ninety-two van, where would you steal it? Belvoir. So, the second I heard we had a van missing I knew whose it was."

Denniston nodded.

"That it was *my* van they used! Captain, for the first time in my life I understood how a Jap could do hara-kiri!"

Indignation was an okay emotion to show—at least in these circumstances. Manero glanced around the room, as if to draw calmness from the cool impersonal quality of the furnishings.

"You know that the van has been found, of course?"

"Certainly. And what I want to know is when the hell I'm going to get it back. If I ever get my hands on the bastards who heisted that van. . . ." Glaring, Manero twisted a neck in his hands.

"You seem more concerned about the van than you do about the remains of the Unknown."

"Look, Captain, it's *everybody's* Unknown. It's *my* van."

Without transition, Denniston said softly, "Has it occurred to you that stealing the van might have been an inside job?"

"Right off. But when I cooled down and thought about it, I didn't believe it. I know my men, Captain, they're great guys."

"I respect your loyalty, Sergeant, but loyalty sometimes blinds us to facts."

"Captain," Manero said solemnly, "I would swear on the rack that not a soul in the outfit. . . ." He paused and caught his breath in sharply, then went on bravely. "Captain, there is nothing like a subversive in the outfit."

"To the best of your knowledge."

"I know those people like I know my own family, Captain. We're a tight-knit outfit and they're great Joes. Even the spades." He paused and then said with conviction, "Even the spades."

"You mean blacks? Tell me about the blacks, Sergeant."

"Nothing to tell. A few of them are like a little militant, you know. But only for black rights, nothing else. They're not what anybody could call subversive."

"How many of these militants are there in the motor pool?"

"Just a few. And they're just *mild* militants. They don't hate whites or anything, they only want a few civil rights."

"Still, you wouldn't mind giving me the names of the militants, would you? Just as a formality?"

"It's a pure waste of time, Captain."

"Nevertheless," Denniston said, "we'll get a list before you leave. Now, a question or two about Major McQuiston."

The change of direction took Manero by surprise. He pretended not to have heard it. "Of course, they all do pot and maybe a few of them snort cocaine every once in a while, but—"

"Who does?" Denniston said, frowning.

"The spades. But only off the post. If I ever caught any of them doing it on—" He did an elaborate double take. "Did you say Major McQuiston, sir? You would suspect an *officer?*"

"I don't suspect him," Denniston said. "In a broad investigation of this sort we cover all angles, however unlikely. Because I'm questioning *you,* Sergeant, doesn't mean I suspect you."

"Me?" Manero stared at Denniston in open astonishment.

"Even though nobody would have a better opportunity than you."

"Me?" Manero said again. "Excuse the language, Captain, but you're out of your fucking mind."

"Perhaps," Denniston said. "Let's come back to Major McQuiston."

"I'll tell you something about myself in confidence, Captain. I happen to be rabid about subversives. I think the bastards should be stood up against a wall and shot and I'd gladly pull the trigger myself. I'm sorry, sir, I have no tolerance for them. Spades—and I'll gladly give you their names later—spades I admit I have a little tolerance for. But subversives?—I hate and despise them."

"Okay. Now, about Major McQuiston."

"A first-rate officer, sir. I mean, I'm an enlisted man, and there's no love lost for officers—okay to be candid, sir?" He waited for a faint smile from Denniston. "But Major McQuiston? A great officer. The men worship him, sir, and so do I."

Manero paused as though searching his mind for anything else the Two might be interested in.

"His family owns Anaconda Copper, Captain."

Denniston blinked. "What is the pertinence of that fact, Sergeant?"

"Well, Captain, if *your* family owned Anaconda Copper and you were going to inherit it, would you be a subversive?"

"I told you before, Sergeant, the major is not under suspicion."

"You know who his idol is? Barry Goldwater."

Denniston looked at his watch. "That's all we have time for, Sergeant. I may call on you again, however."

"Anytime, sir."

"Yes, thank you. Before you go, let me have the names of the militant blacks."

"Yes, sir. There's Spec Three Johnson. . . ."

Major McQuiston was sitting in the anteroom off the captain's office.

"Good afternoon, Major," Manero said. He turned his back to an enlisted man sitting at a desk and talking on a telephone and whispered, "I told him your family owned Anaconda Copper."

"You did? What for?"

"Also that you were in love with Barry Goldwater."

"Christ, Al, my old man *works* for Anaconda."

"He's a vice-president, isn't he? Relax, Freddie, the Two is a dunce."

"I do kind of admire Goldwater," the major said.

"Hold that thought, Freddie!"

16

A police car, cruising slowly north on Fort Washington Avenue, came to a rolling stop, and the driver, lazing back in his seat, pointed to the NO PARKING sign above Booth's head. Booth nodded and pointed to Raphael in the phone booth. The cop nodded back and made a gesture that Booth interpreted as "Okay, but don't be all day," and Booth nodded a strong affirmative that promised obedience. The police car rolled onward.

Raphael was hunched over the phone, his head bobbing when he spoke, rigid when he listened. Booth fidgeted. He didn't relish the idea of the police cruiser returning and finding him still there. He decided to give Raphael two more minutes by his watch and then blow the horn. If that didn't fetch him, he would get out of the truck and drag him out of the booth forcibly.

His hand was raised to the horn when Raphael straightened up and, after a final word, hung up. He got into the truck and Booth drove off before he was fairly settled in the seat. Raphael sat huddled against the window. He looked on the verge of tears.

"Anything wrong?"

Raphael seemed startled, then angry, and Booth realized that he had abruptly fractured his preoccupation with his phone call. Did man ever relive his happy moments with as much passion as he did his unhappy ones? Booth wondered.

"She's worried," Raphael said. "She's very, very concerned."

Booth found an entrance to the Cross Bronx Expressway. "Well, that's natural enough, isn't it?"

The Talisman

"Actually," Raphael said, "the actual word she used to describe her reaction was *aghast*."

"Yes, well, but she knew all about it, didn't she?"

"She didn't know we were going to murder anybody."

"Neither did we," Booth said sharply.

"Neither did Jason," Raphael said. "Nobody did."

Reflexively, Booth stepped on the brake and slowed the car down. "*Jason* knows what we did? You told Jason?"

"I never actually told him, but he saw me working on the vacuum device in the cellar, and when he heard the radio reports today, he put two and two together. He's fairly bright, you know."

"Is Jason aghast, too?"

"Not that you could notice. In fact, he seems to be amused."

Booth's knuckles were white with the pressure of his grip on the wheel. He said, "I imagine Jason has lots of little friends?"

"Practically none," Raphael said. "It's a matter of much concern to Paula and me. He's too bright for his contemporaries and too small for the older kids. . . . Oh, I see what you mean. Jason won't breathe a word."

"You guarantee it?"

"Of course I guarantee it," Raphael said peevishly. "Don't you think I know my own son?"

"Paula, too? Do you guarantee her silence, too?"

"Paula believes wholeheartedly in the Movement. That's your answer. Jason believes in it, too, by the way."

Splendid, Booth thought. The Movement has the full support and understanding of a highly neurotic woman and a five- (or six- if you accepted his theory) year-old boy. Tomorrow the world!

Raphael was turned in his seat, studying his face. "You're upset." Booth turned into the traffic pattern on Interstate 95. "Are you sore because I phoned them?"

"It's done," Booth said. "You didn't also tell them where we're going, did you?"

"Where we're going? Why, no."

225

Had there been a slight hesitation? He couldn't be sure, and there was no point pressing it. If it was done it was done.

Raphael said in a subdued voice, "We've still got five hours ahead of us, and you must be tired. Would you like me to drive awhile?"

Yes, Booth thought, he was tired. He had been up all night. . . . But so had the rest of them, so had Raphael. He started to shake his head, but then said, "Okay, as soon as we find a suitable stopping place we'll change."

"I figure we should make Caro's place by about eight," Raphael said. "Doc and Asbury ought to be there about six or seven. Dover—a little later?"

Booth eased his foot off the accelerator as he saw a turnoff, then suddenly accelerated again. "I'm sort of settled into it," he said. "I'm not tired."

"I'd feel better if you—"

"No." Booth cut him off abruptly, and Raphael retreated to his side of the seat.

I've hurt his feelings, Booth thought, but there's no help for it because I can't tell him the truth. And the truth, he thought bitterly, is that I'm a faster driver than he is, which means that I can lessen the time that Asbury is up there alone with Caro. Of course Doc would also be there, but a wink from Asbury could induce him to take a walk on the beach. . . . He glanced at the dashboard and saw that the speedometer needle was touching seventy. Brilliant. Being caught for speeding was just what they needed.

He eased the accelerator and the needle dropped back to fifty.

Raphael was silent, whether because he was sulking or simply listening to the discordant music of his own torment, Booth couldn't tell. It wasn't until a half hour passed that Raphael finally broke his silence.

"I did."

"What?" Booth said.

"I did." Raphael spoke with slow emphasis, as if annoyed at having to repeat himself. "Did tell Paula that we were going to Caro's parents' place on the Cape."

"Why did you do that, Eddie?"

"I had to," Raphael said. "We tell each other everything. I'm sorry I lied to you before."

And now, Booth thought, if I were to match candor with candor, I would confess to him that I wouldn't let him drive because I was in a sweat to reach the Cape because I had visions of Asbury fucking my girl, wringing ecstatic screams from her, enjoying her ardent and actionful cooperation and the tribute of her fingernails raking thin bloody furrows on his back. . . .

"There's a roadside restaurant up ahead," he said to Raphael. "I'll pull in, and you can drive."

"You must be tired," Raphael said.

"Yes," Booth said.

When Eminence Griese entered the Oval Office, the President was standing beside the west window, lost in reflection. At least that was what a visitor was bound to assume, given the bowed head, the canted eyes, the fingers tweaking the point of the handsome chin. It was the President's favorite position, or pose (if one chose to be cynical, and for Eminence Griese there were no alternate choices), and he assumed it as often as possible.

Although Griese regarded it as a political liability—the electorate's aversion to dreamers or even thinkers—he realized that for the President, at least, it was an improvement over facing a visitor while seated at his ridiculously outsize desk and moistening his lips at the prospect of the drink he denied himself until the sun was over the yardarm.

Griese paused six feet distant from the desk and coughed. The President—predictably—started and turned slowly, as if waking from some beautiful reverie of war outlawed, poverty dismantled, unhappiness as rare as chastity.

"Ah, Em, yes."

"And how was lunch with the rashir?" Griese took his seat beside the President's desk.

"Charming fellow," the President said.

"I don't mean the man," Griese said, "I mean the lunch."

The President sat down. "At the lunch the Vice President came over and volunteered to coordinate what he called 'the recovery of the American military anima.' I thanked him and declined, on the theory that it would interfere with his prayers for my airplane to fall down."

"Very good," Griese said. He meant it as a form of self-congratulation, since he regarded the President's witticism as a paraphrase of his own remark, on an earlier occasion, that the Vice President defined longevity as outliving a sitting President. "Yes, very good."

"It's turning into a terrible pain in the ass, Em. The phone calls never stop."

"I can enumerate them for you," Griese said. "Half a dozen Southern Senators and Congressmen, a Supreme Court justice, the one whose mistress reads his cases to him aloud in bed, the conservative ex-governor from the West, the conservative ex-Senator from the Northeast, the distinguished Washington columnist of the New York *Times*, the other distinguished columnist of the New York *Times*, the member of the Chiefs of Staff with the fascist *Tendenz* and—"

"The what?"

"And your mother."

"But my mother just used it as an excuse to make sure I was doing my back exercises."

Griese said, "I've taken many calls myself. I'm keeping a tally—for release of Rowan, against, mixed feelings, comments that might indicate a disposition to compromise, and so forth. To that, of course, we'll add editorial comment, pressure groups by size and influence, *vox pop* . . . by tomorrow the consensus should be clear."

The President sighed. "I'd like to see the remains saved, if it's at all possible. I wish they hadn't killed that sergeant."

"We'll save them if we can, but only if the sentiment of the electorate sanctions it. It's the American way, you know."

The President pulled his country-lawyer face, which in the circumstances, Griese knew, was the equivalent of a confidential wink.

From the Earthquake, Robbins had gone back to his pad. He turned on the radio to an all-news station. The reports, failing new developments, were repetitious and padded, and after a while he fell asleep in his chair. The phone woke him. It was Ms. Foxworth, breathy and solemn.

"Robbins, we've decided to go ahead with it."

It was a little past three o'clock. The radio was bumbling beside his chair. "Congratulations, Foxworth. It's a watershed decision. You'll never regret it."

"I'd like you to come over here, so we can start organizing it."

"I can't. I have to walk the dog."

"Since when do you have a dog?"

"I'm baby-sitting it for a friend." He held the phone at arm's length and made a yipping sound. "It's just a puppy."

"Don't try to be funny, Robbins."

"I'm *not* trying, it just seems to happen." He heard her tongue cluck in exasperation. "No, listen. The trouble is I have a couple of things to do today. I'll call you later, okay?"

"*What* things?" Her voice was flat, disbelieving.

"I've got to go down to the docks and pick up some contraband and, ah, meet that French sailor. Pierre, the French sailor, he's going to deal me some *plastique*, and there's this other guy, a longshoreman, Rocco, he wants to show me some detonator caps and other stuff."

"Can't you do it later?"

"His ship sails at six o'clock, and the longshoreman, well, he goes home to Brooklyn. This *plastique*, it's beautiful stuff, French Army issue. Grade A stuff, *safe*, it won't blow up in your face, and that's important."

"Well. . . . Will you call me later?"

"Absolutely. When I get back from the docks. Hey, Foxworth, I want to ask you something."

She said suspiciously, "Don't fuck around."

"No. Serious. Why a YMCA?"

"Well, YMCA for Godssake. YMCA. *M* standing for men."

"What I mean, why YMCA. Why *C*? Why not YMHA? Their *M* stands for men, too, doesn't it?"

"What the hell are you bringing sectarianism in for? Religion is irrelevant to the problem."

"You and I know that, but will the world? Suppose they interpret it as anti-*C*, for Christian, instead of anti-*M*, for men? Then you just wasted a lot of good explosives. How about blowing one of each, one YMCA and one YMHA? That way they'll get the message."

She was silent, and he knew she was testing her suspicion that he might be putting her on against the obvious attractions of blowing up two buildings instead of one.

He said, "I gotta rush down to the docks, Foxworth."

"We'd like to do it day after tomorrow."

"Impossible. We have to plan this thing minutely, Chrissake. Also, do you think you rig up explosives in six minutes? You want to blow yourself up? Look, you diddle around for weeks trying to make up your mind, and then all of a sudden it has to be done right now. No go."

"You're fucking me around, Robbins."

"Well, go find yourself another explosives expert," he said, and slammed the phone down.

A moment later he took the phone off the hook. She would think furiously of all the explosives experts she knew and come up with zero. So she would call back and run into a busy signal. Fox you, Fuckworth, you're on the back burner for the time being.

He went out and walked to Second Avenue and bought a *Post.* He brought it home and spread it out on his kitchen table. Under the headline DESECRATION OF THE TOMB, which Robbins thought had a fine biblical ring to it, there was a full-page picture of an empty crypt, with a sentinel off to the right, facing the sarcophagus, and the ampitheater in the background. Inside the paper there were six pages of pictures, equally divided between the past and the instant event. There were shots of the outside of the sentinels' barracks, of the steps leading from the road up to the tombs ("the army truck climbed this steep stairway"), of the entrance to the cemetery, of an army doctor saying the drugged sentinels had awaked refreshed and rested and were in no danger whatsoever, of the chief of cemetery security and a General Dammerling; there were library pictures of the Arc de Triomphe ("beneath which rests a fallen *poilu*"), Westminster Abbey ("last resting place of the British Unknown"), the burial ceremonies attendant on the interment of America's first Unknown, starring Pershing, Foch, and Harding, of Eisenhower and Nixon at the double interment of the World War II and Korean Unknowns, of Ford laying a wreath on the marble slab over the crypt of the Vietnam Unknown. . . .

After looking at the pictures, Robbins read the long running news account, which began on page 3 and ran on in the body of the paper for several more pages, surrounded by half a dozen background pieces. He read the story painstakingly, scribbling an occasional note on a scratch pad. Then he went over his notes, eliminated many of them, and drew up a list.

My Things

Uniforms
Weapons
Army truck
Explosives (?)
Drugs (?)
Lifting machinery (?)

It wasn't much to go on, but it was enough. He picked up his phone and dialed Phoebe.

"Special Agent Anstruther, good afternoon."

"Special Fink Robbins, good afternoon."

There was silence, in which, Robbins guessed, Phoebe was composing an attitude. Since it was always disapproving anyway, Robbins didn't know why he bothered, but that was Phoebe for you, a stick. He tried to visualize Phoebe at his desk, but he didn't know enough about the setup; he had never been allowed to come to the office. Did Phoebe have his own private office, or did he share a bullpen with all the other Phoebes? Did they hang around with their shoulder holsters showing? No, they wouldn't do that; they would have them hidden under their decorous dark jackets with the respectably cut lapels.

The Talisman

"I am extremely busy," Phoebe said finally, "and even if I weren't, I would resent that smart-aleck nonsense of yours. If you have something to report, tell it briefly, please."

Robbins envisioned all his fellow Phoebes, thin mouths pursed, nodding their carefully barbered heads in approval of Phoebe's tone. "Okay. Two things. First, I've got Ms. Foxworth in the bag. They're going to blow up a YMCA. Or HA."

"That's fine," Phoebe said, but his tone was both grudging and abstracted.

"But that isn't what I called you about," Robbins said quickly. "It's about the Unknown heist. I think I have a lead or two."

"That's fine," Phoebe said again, but his voice was still abstracted.

"Have you come up with anything yet?" The silence after Robbins' question was so profound that he knew all the other Phoebes must have joined in *a cappella*. "I mean, you're busy rounding up all kinds of subversives, aren't you?"

"We're not police," Phoebe said coldly. "We don't round people up. We do interrogate them."

Robbins lowered his voice for effect. "The lead I mentioned. I'm going out to Fort Dix tonight to check it out."

"Do you have an actual lead? If so, I want to know it."

"Logic, that's my lead. It figures that the uniforms and the guns, at least, came from Dix. And Dix is my place, right?"

"Why not Fort Myer? After all, that's where the crime was committed."

"Because there are no dissident Nam vets to speak of in Washington. New York is the hot center. New York means Dix. QED, right?"

"Just see to it that if you pick up anything concrete, you inform me of it. Instantly. If I ever find out that you have withheld information from me, even for a minute—"

"I may be a fink," Robbins said, "but I'm an honorable fink. Thanks, Phoebe. Be in touch."

He hung up, laughing, and the phone rang at once. He guessed Foxworth and Foxworth it was.

"We've reconsidered," she said. "We agree to postpone for a reasonable length of time."

"Foxworth, you're a fucking saint. Call you later."

He hung up.

Manero picked up the ringing phone. A hoarse voice said, "Manero, anybody there with you?"

"Who the hell is this?"

"Don't say my name. Johnson. You got any company?"

"Johnson, what the fuck's the matter with you?"

Johnson groaned. "Don't say my *name*. You alone?"

"Wishengrad is here. What's eating your dumb ass?"

"Can't talk. I'm in a phone booth, all crouch down, near the Rec Room. Get rid of Wishengrad and I'll be right around. Manero, I'm in big fucking trouble."

"All right." Manero hung up and said, "Wishengrad, you feel like getting some fresh air?"

The Spec Four barely looked up from his crossword puzzle. "No."

"Well, I'm ordering you to get some fresh air." He watched Wishengrad pencil in a few letters. "Now. On the double."

Wishengrad gave him a sullen look, picked up his puzzle, and went out. Manero lighted a cigarette and waited. In less than a minute Johnson bolted in, showing a lot of white in his eyes. He was wearing OD pants and a fatigue shirt, and he was capless. His skin was ashy and he was sweating. Panting, he ran across the room and dropped into the chair beside Manero's desk.

"Jesus, Johnson," Manero said, "you look like a fucking fugitive."

"If fugitive means somebody is chasing my black ass, that is what I am."

"Calm down, Chrissake. Who's chasing your black ass?"

"The Twos. Four mothers with big forty fives and skinhead haircuts."

"Stop sweating and tell me what happened."

"They busted into the barracks and picked up Telfair and asked where is Jones and Stairwell and Bostwick and me.

Jones and Stairwell and Bostwick are out working. Telfair was goofing off around the barracks, that's why they picked him up. Manero, they are rounding up brothers; it's a fucking pogrom."

"How come they missed you?"

"Telfair told them I was out working. I was in the latrine. But they got my gear. They packed up all the gear of all of us in a couple barracks bags and toted it away. Then they went out and collared Jones and Stairwell and Bostwick."

"Fucking Twos," Manero said. "They can't find a man, they arrest his helmet liner and dubbin instead."

"That ain't all," Johnson said gloomily. "They going to find some grass in among my underwears."

"Much?"

"Just a little."

"How much?"

Johnson made a hopeless gesture. "Maybe forty, fifty sticks. Maybe sixty."

"You stupid bastard," Manero said. Johnson nodded his deflated Afro in agreement. "They're not after you for grass. They're checking you out for pulling that tombs job."

"Man, they are crazy. I didn't have nothing to do. . . ." He stopped and rolled his eyes at Manero. "How you figure that?"

"They had me in this morning. It's because of that M-two-hundred-ninety-two. They had the Old Man in, too. Fuck 'em."

"You can well say fuck 'em. Last time I looked you had that lily-white skin on you. *You* think I was mixed up in that grave robbing?"

Manero shook his head. "No way. You haven't got the brains."

"I know that," Johnson said. "But do the Twos?"

"Where were you last night?"

"Last night?" Johnson smiled. "Shacked up with a fox. Man!"

"Will she give you an alibi?"

"If she don't, she one fucking ungrateful chick."

"What's she like? I mean, what color?"

"Blond all up and down the line." Johnson smiled reminiscently.

"Shit," Manero said.

Johnson's smile disappeared. "Why you say shit? Since when you become a Kluxer?"

"You're my brother, Johnson," Manero said. "But you're not the brother of any of those Twos." He ticked off his fingers. "Forty or fifty or sixty sticks of pot and fucking a white girl. You're in the shit, brother."

"That ain't news. Question is, what do I do?"

"Turn yourself in before the Gestapo shoots you. Then give my name as character witness. I'll stand up for you."

Johnson rose. "Shit on that. I'm splitting."

"If you want to go, I can't stop you." Manero shrugged.

"Better not fucking try," Johnson said. He wheeled around and went through the door.

"Dumb ass," Manero said. He picked up the phone and dialed the Two office.

17

Hyannis Port was the hub of the Cape, its metropolis. It bustled out of season, its shops did a sustaining business all year round, tourists were not uncommon on its undistinguished streets through most of the autumn.

Caroline parked a short distance from the bus terminal and turned the radio on. A Boston news station was quoting an army functionary: "This heinous outrage wreaked upon this sacred symbol of the American fighting man, whose courage and dedication. . . ." Then came a portion of a taped interview with the father of the dead relief commander: " . . . gave his life for his sacred trust . . . . that they will be apprehended and that he shall not have died in vain. . . ." He was making a brave effort to maintain a public face, and the stilted language distanced his sorrow. But the mother was without such resources. Her wail was visceral: "Oh, my poor Roger, oh, God, my poor dear son. . . ."

In the twilight interior of the car Caro whispered, "Oh, Christ . . . oh, Christ," and reached out to turn the radio off, but the mother's voice ended and at once pathos turned to nonsense-as-usual.

"Hey there, boys and girls, have *we* got a bargain for *you*. . ."

Three commercials in a row—one hearty, one folksy, one by a doctor voice on behalf of an anal suppository. Their hype, their promise of a perfect existence deadened the effect of the mother's anguish. What was a mother's agony when the needs and sufferings of an entire world must be catered to? The father was no less pathetic, but easier to bear, intimidated by the microphone, tailoring his emotions to the exigent canons of show biz. Every American was steeped in the convention of the interview, knew what to say when a million people listened in. If he wept, it would be off mike.

The announcer returned and introduced the taped voice of P. T. Ronsard, the cemetery security guard who had made the first discovery of the defilement. Prompted by a newsman, P. T. Ronsard described the scene:

". . . seeing the crypt gaping open, the marble slab like just tossed aside, you know, and broke up, too. . . ."

Through the windshield, in the distance, Caro saw two figures walking toward the car. She recognized the long dominating stride of Asbury, and Doc beside him, half his size or seemingly so.

". . . how I felt? Like . . . like a soul of something had been busted up. You know what I mean? Like a soul was laying there in pieces."

"Yes. Can you be a little more specific?"

P. T. Ronsard spoke in poetry, and the newsman urged him to transmute it to baser metal. As Ronsard spattered "likes" and "you knows," thrown off his stride and made to feel that he had failed his public trust to the great unseen audience, Caro switched the radio off. She thought of Booth, of what his reaction must be to the death of the relief commander. It would change him, in ways that she—and perhaps he, too—could not define. He would need her more than ever now, and that was too bad, because she was already beyond his reach. She had not ordered it so, it was simply the way it was.

A blond head poked through the car window, teeth gleaming. Asbury found her lips, and his tongue slid into her mouth. She responded for a moment—tongue to tongue—and then pushed his face away.

"Get in the car," she said furiously. "Get in!"

Was it asking too much of a presumably responsible tongue, she wondered, to not respond like a tropism to any tongue that broached it? Thinking of Booth, she said to herself despairingly, Don't mourn me, you're better off out of it.

She started the car and pulled away before Asbury and
Doc were fairly seated, and heading toward the streaming
lights of the main road.

Robbins spent the afternoon pub-crawling in his East Village neighborhood. The barflies he spoke to expressed
mindless approval of the heist ("Oh, wow . . . crazy . . .
heavy. . . . "), but none offered any intelligent clues. He
hadn't expected any. He was convinced that the answers
were to be found at Dix.

At the last of the joints he pumped a motorcycle freak on
the off chance, however unlikely, that a bike gang might have
been involved. But the freak was barely coherent and mainly
interested in peddling eight handsome joints he swore had
just arrived from Morocco. Eventually, zonked out by whatever pills he was popping, he put his head down on the table
and began to snore. Robbins pocketed the toothpick box containing the joints and split. He returned to his pad and
turned on the TV set.

The six o'clock news had already begun. On screen an
army colonel wearing the caduceus insignia was speaking to a
mob of reporters in a hospital corridor.

". . . five sentinels are in a satisfactory condition. The barbiturate was professionally administered, in my opinion, not
only as to technique but in terms of dosage. Too little and
unconsciousness would not be instantaneous, too much and
the subjects might have died."

The anchorman: "We take you now to the steps of the Justice Department, where, this afternoon, the director of the
Federal Bureau of Investigation. . . ."

Robbins saluted the image of the director. "You are my
true and only leader."

". . . the bureau, in conjunction with other governmental
agencies and the police, is engaged in a supreme effort to ap-
prehend. . . ."

Robbins yawned.

The director was replaced by the head of the Senate
Armed Services Committee, who hid a cigar inefficiently behind his back and bumbled into a thicket of microphones. He

was followed by the commander of a veterans organization, a man in his late seventies with a leathery lined face under an overseas cap.

". . . our patriotic anger at this most sacrilegious of crimes. . . ."

Robbins yawned again and shut his eyes wearily.

". . . offering a reward of fifty thousand dollars."

Robbins snapped his eyes open. The old face faded out, and the anchorman, reading from a sheet of paper, said, "This offer brings the total up to more than one hundred thousand dollars, and several veterans and other interested organizations have yet to be heard from. A modest estimate of the eventual total in reward money would place it at. . . ."

"A quarter of a million," Robbins yelled at the screen. Maybe half a million. Robbins, you can be a rich man! He shook his fist at the screen. "Get it up, you chintzy bastards! A lousy quarter or half a million for this great hero of the nation? Shame on you! Get it up!"

He rolled over on his back and kicked his legs at the ceiling in high exhilaration.

After fixing himself a bite to eat, Robbins dressed with careful attention to detail in army fatigue trousers, a fireman's dress coat, a butternut Confederate cavalry hat, and a yellow silk scarf to match the braid on the hat. He walked crosstown—unlike the bike freaks on his street, who trundled their machines up the steps and parked them beside their beds, he kept his motorcycle in a garage—and roared seventy-five miles south and west through New Jersey to Wrightstown, adjoining the camp limits of Fort Dix and McGuire Air Force Base. It took him an hour and fifteen minutes, and it was slightly after nine thirty when he walked into the Left Flank.

Unless by accident—which was to say, in ignorance—straight soldiers never went to the Left Flank. And on those occasions they soon left. Not so much because the pot haze was too much for their respiratory apparatus to cope with or even because the talk was so often disconcertingly off the main subject—pussy—but because the pussy itself bewil-

dered them. The girls were all Movement groupies, and they
flushed out the straights in about six seconds and began
proselytizing them; and then, if they didn't get anywhere, in-
sulting them. Fortunately, accidental drop-ins were at a minimum, since the Left Flank was a block or two off the main
stem, where there were lots of joints happy to welcome the
square Dix soldier with some bread in his pocket and plenty
of apolitical whores and aspiring amateurs to go around.

Robbins paused for a few minutes inside the entrance of
the Left Flank, accustoming his lungs to the rich mixture of
pot and alcohol fumes. Meanwhile, peering through the
haze, he picked out some familiar faces, including one or two
that might be specifically helpful.

He started toward the bar to pay his respects to Joe Brock,
the owner, pausing now and then to acknowledge a greeting,
to slap an outstretched hand, to deposit a chaste kiss on the
pale brow of a groupie. He admired Brock, whom he considered to be a man in his own image. Brock combined counter-
culture sympathies with entrepreneurial shrewdness. He
served the Movement and at the same time profited from it.
And Robbins regarded the exquisite thinking that had gone
into naming the joint as something approaching genius. It
resonated the three guiding motifs of the clientele: political
(Left), sexual (Flank), and military (Left Flank). Also, if you
wanted to push the point, it had an international flavor in its
homophonic echo of Left Bank.

"Robby, baby," Brock said, reaching across the bar for a
hand slap. "How they hanging?"

Brock was bald on top, but long limp hair like Spanish
moss hung down over his ears and collar. According to rumor, he had shot an ARVN general accidentally-by-mistake.
He had beaten the rap at his court-martial and been thrown
out of the army with a less-than-honorable.

"Straight out and up and like a periscope, man, scanning
the waters for pussy."

"Ho," Brock said. "Dig the snatching of the Unknown Soldier stiff?"

"Beautiful," Robbins said.

He moved off to the far side of the room and joined a

group in a booth. There were five of them, including a groupie who looked like a recent runaway, a pale thin creature who was sixteen at the very outside. He sat beside her and slapped hands around the table.

They were having a war-story-fest, movement style: The fascistic captain and platoon sergeant who had been greased during a firefight by their own men, using a captured Kalashnikov AK-47 assault rifle to deflect suspicion to the innocent NVA. The squad that had gone off on a night patrol near Phuoc Long and taken two slant whores with them and spent the whole night balling them a couple of hundred yards away from base, returning at dawn convincingly exhausted. The grunt who blew pot in the colonel's face. The company that declined to make a suicidal attack on an enemy entrenched on high ground, and the spade "epiphanist" of the occasion, who had told the CO, "Sheet, man, they want a fucking fight, tell them to come on down *here!*" The gung-ho major whose bed had been boobied with a land mine. Examples of the bravery of the tough little Congs. . . .

Robbins shook his head or laughed uproariously as the occasion demanded, and waited patiently. Sooner or later the talk would get around to the instant subject. No great hurry. He had all night.

Here and there, after they turned left off Route 6, there were lighted houses and once, as they passed a church—small, in need of paint, dimly lit inside, as though to proclaim sanctity through parsimony—they saw a cluster of cars (a meeting of vestrymen, Booth thought, gathering to discuss money or the indifference of youth). But as they approached the bay, the darkness and silence was complete. The road overlooking the murmurous water was lined with the dim hulks of summer houses.

There was a faint seepage of light at the edges of the drawn blinds of the house at the end of the street facing the water, but the darkness quickly consumed it. Booth drove down the sloping gravel driveway, past Caro's car, drawn up on the brown scrubby grass, and pulled up before the shut door of the garage. He turned off the headlights.

He said to Raphael, "Let them know we're here."

He watched Raphael walk around to the porch. He rolled down his window and listened to the sound of the wavelets below, edging softly into the shore. After a moment a patch of light fanned out from the porch steps and around the corner of the house. Asbury, carrying a glass, was in the lead, long-legged, dashing, then Doc, smiling, and at last, after a long moment in which his mind leaped to wild conclusions of disaster, Caro. Raphael shambled down behind her.

Asbury shouted, "Welcome, main ghoul!"

Booth got out of the car and submitted wearily to handshakes, thumps on the shoulder. Caro stood a little apart, but when he turned to her, she came to him and lifted her head. He kissed her and tasted tears on her face. Her lids were lowered, he couldn't see her eyes. He moved away from her.

"Somebody open the door. Let's start unloading."

On the still air, against the tireless whisper of the water, his voice was harsh. He recognized in it the sound of a man in pain.

There were two entrances to the basement: a direct one through a sloping wooden casement that opened on a short flight of concrete steps leading down, and another through a zinc-lined door from the garage. Booth backed the Drivurself into the garage. He opened its doors and they began to unload, passing the articles of furniture from the truck through the zinc-lined door into the cellar in a form of bucket brigade.

When they had finished with the furniture, they began to remove Raphael's gear, which, for some reason, moved everyone to laughter. Raphael became "the perfesser," "Mr. Rube Goldberg," as if he had been an eccentric failure, or if a success, a comic one. Raphael didn't seem to mind. He was concerned and anxious to see that his gear was removed intact. It was to be buried underwater eventually—Booth reminded him of this, somewhat tartly—but Raphael was stubborn.

"Well, until it's disposed of, I don't want to see it mishandled. I designed it myself, you know, and. . . ."

He trailed off, but Asbury and Doc, in unison, finished up for him—"and it has feelings!" Even Caro joined in the laughter.

Finally only the casket was left. With four of them working, they tilted its weight, and Caro slid the dolly beneath it. At the edge of the truck they removed the dolly, placed it on the garage floor, and, groaning with the effort, lifted the casket down. Then, each holding a handle, they pushed the loaded dolly through the door in the cellar.

Doc intoned the melody of the *Marche Funèbre*, and Asbury joined in. The spirit was satirical, and yet, Booth thought, their pace was that of a funeral cortege, disciplined by the weight of the casket and even, for some of them, the illimitable presence of the corpse. Caro followed behind them, her step as measured as theirs, a solemn follower who might have been the wife, the mother, of the fallen hero.

They eased the casket to the concrete floor. It settled heavily in a little flurry of dust. It sat by itself in a clearing, isolated, surrounded by the furniture, by Raphael's gear, by some striped deck chairs and umbrellas and a large dismantled redwood outdoor table. In the poor light of the single bulb hanging from the raftered ceiling, the bronze was dulled down, almost black. Only the handles gleamed, burnished by the oil and warmth of their own hands.

"For I am the resurrection and the life. . . ." Asbury chanting, his hands folded in piety under his chin. "Dust unto dust, shit unto shit. . . ."

"Let's go," Booth said.

They started up the steps leading to the living quarters, Asbury swinging an imaginary censer, mumbling fake Latin.

Before he stepped into the kitchen, Booth looked back at the casket, huge, somber, enigmatic.

18

Robbins was beginning to feel worried. He table-hopped energetically, but the pickings were sparse. There was lots of talk about the snatching of the Unknown, but none of it was enlightening. And the subject had a tendency to get pushed aside. Although they were Movement soldiers, they were soldiers first, and parochial; a "prick of a first sergeant" weighed more heavily on their minds than matters of broader latitude. The army was a narrow world, and it whittled its personnel down to fit its special dimensions, whether they were aware of it or not.

"Hey, Red."

Robbins turned to the sound of the voice and saw Garrison sitting alone. He must have slipped into the Left Flank in the last few minutes, but he looked as if he had been stoking himself up for hours. He was spaced out, his eyes half shut, his smile blurred and rubbery.

Robbins sat down. "The rip-off of the Unknown?"

"Byooful," Garrison said.

"Beautiful."

Garrison was one of the gurus of the Movement at Fort Dix. He was a twenty-year man who had a mysterious racket going for him with the PX and the commissary. He did a thriving business selling everything from a candy bar to an entire steer. He was also reputed to work with weapons as a sideline.

"Power out of the muzzle of a gun," Garrison said. He had one empty highball glass in front of him and two full ones.

His speech was slurred; his eyes were glazed. "Show power you got power. Right?"

"Right on."

"You know who they are?"

That's what I hoped *you* would know, Robbins thought, and said confidently, "They're local fellas, from the New York area. No doubt they got outfitted right here at Dix."

"How you figure that?"

Robbins carefully assessed Garrison's tone for suspicion or hostility and judged it to be innocent. "I figure it because it figures. Myer is a VIP base full of chickenshit soldiers. Maybe some militancy in a few spades, but that's all."

"Shoot a white one," Garrison said. "That's a militant spade's idea of militancy. Shoot a white one and rip off his wallet. No idealism."

Garrison was the color of bittersweet chocolate, but he didn't think of himself as a black man, possibly because he didn't sound like one.

"So like I said," Robbins said, "they're local Nam vets, and they got outfitted right here by some friendly, idealistic supply sergeant or armorer."

"Wasn't me," Garrison said. He smiled slackly. "More's the pity."

"You could have been like the middleman? Between those fellas and your friendly, idealistic supply sergeant or armorer? Beautiful."

"Wasn't," Garrison said. He lifted one of his drinks and slurped up whiskey noisily.

"But you reckon it was some dude here at good old Dixie?"

"Wished it was me," Garrison said. "Combining cash and deep-down idealism."

"Make a guess who?"

Garrison eyed him, and for a moment Robbins thought he might have blown it, but Garrison, one eyelid drooping, lower lip pendulous, was simply trying to do some heavy thinking. He was having trouble with his head. It kept inclining toward the tabletop even though he was supporting it on his hands.

"You gotta think who was the connection," Robbins said. "Use that beautiful brain."

"What for?"

"So I can shake his fucking hand and say, 'Man, you are one fucking hero.'"

"One fucking hero."

"And whoever gave them those rifles and uniforms, he's a hero, too. Some unknown, unsung, obscure supply sergeant is the real hero. *Salud*, unknown supply sergeant!" He picked up one of Garrison's glasses and drank.

Garrison's hand folded back, and without support his head drooped to the tabletop. Robbins looked at him in disgust and frustration. The trouble with Garrison was that, clear-headed, he wouldn't give anything away, and stoned, couldn't.

He punched Garrison's shoulder, waited, then punched again, harder. Garrison's head rose slowly from the table, his lips trailing a thin shiny strand of spittle.

"Garrison," Robbins said, "who are the Movement doctors on the post?"

Garrison brushed away the filament of spittle and moved his hand to a pocket of his safari jacket. He fumbled maddeningly and finally produced a ratty roach less than an inch long. He placed it on the table and stared at it.

"Movement doctor," Robbins said. "Garrison, you know everything, don't you? Who's a Movement doctor on the post?"

"Know everything," Garrison said. "Captain Feinstein, right?"

"Right. Old Feinstein a pretty good boy with a needle?"

Garrison stared at him without comprehension.

"A needle," Robbins said. "You know. Give injections and like that. Feinstein handle a needle pretty good?"

"Feinstein a fucking shrink. Couldn't find his own asshole with a compass."

"There's gotta be more than one friendly doctor on the post. An ace with a needle?"

A sudden gleam of intelligence flashed in Garrison's murky eyes, and Robbins thought, He's got it, he knows and

246

I just planted it in his stupid head. So if I gave it to him, he has to share it with me.

Garrison was focusing on him across the table. "Why you ask so many fucking questions?"

"Why are you giving me so many fucking answers?"

Garrison looked stunned. As clearly as if his skull were made of glass, Robbins saw his sodden mind try to cope with the question and give up in confusion.

"I'll tell you why," Robbins said. "Because we're fucking buddies, and we got the same fucking cause, and we're going to blow those fucking fat cats off the face of the fucking earth. And the dudes who pulled this Unknown job belong in the fucking Hall of Fame. Right?"

Gratefully, his problem solved, Garrison said, "Right."

"And get the fucking Nobel Peace Prize. Right?"

"Right."

"And that's why I trust you," Robbins said sternly, "even if you do give a lot of fucking answers." He snapped his fingers peremptorily. "Name of the ace needle man, Garrison."

"Yeah," Garrison said. "Name is Doc."

"That's no name, dunce."

"Doc is his name."

Garrison stared over the table earnestly and raised his hand, palm outward, in the attitude of a man taking an oath. The effort exhausted him, and his head sank slowly down until it touched the table. Robbins grabbed him by the hair and pulled his head upright. The roach was stuck to his damp forehead.

"Doctor what, Garrison?"

"Doc, God damn it." Garrison's mood changed; he glowered suspiciously. "You don't know little Doc is no fucking doctor, you don't know *nothing.*

Robbins' memory suddenly made a connection. His heartbeat revved up. "Doc. Little runt who used to be a medic. Of course I know him. Does a little dealing around here? I'll tell you something, Garrison, I'm personally nominating that little dude for the Nobel Prize."

"Second the motion."

Robbins took out the toothpick box with the eight joints

that he had lifted from the bike freak. He opened it, peeked in, then shut it secretively. He repeated the process until he had Garrison's attention. Then he opened the box and shoved it under Garrison's nose.

"Cast your greedy eyes on the contents. Premium grass. Fresh in from Morocco, specially grown for the viceroy of Mexico."

"Beautiful." Garrison reached out with a shaky hand.

Robbins withdrew the box. "Not here. Fucking animals get a sniff of this rare aroma, they'll be all over us. Some things it's a sin to share. Right?"

"Sin," Garrison said. "Give."

Robbins shook his head. "Got your car parked outside?"

Garrison nodded. "Sin."

"Sin. So we'll go outside to your car and smoke up all by ourselves."

Helping Garrison through the door of the Left Flank, Robbins thought, If I can't tease it out of the sonofabitch, I'll beat it out of him, but one way or another I'll get it.

Caro drove to Hyannis Port for a second time, to pick up Dover, arriving on the eleven o'clock bus. Booth had insisted on accompanying her, and they were both uneasily silent for the whole of the ride. It occurred to her that it resembled the aftermath of an unresolved lovers' quarrel, except that there had been no quarrel, nor were they, except in the most technical of terms, lovers any longer.

Dover was waiting at the prearranged corner; his bus had arrived ten minutes ahead of schedule. He greeted them with a nod of his head and got into the backseat.

As they started to move off, he said, "Everything go okay?" His voice struck her as being strained.

"Fine," Booth said.

"That's wonderful." The young voice, out of its depth in reaching for sarcasm, succeeded only in sounding bitter. Booth shifted in his seat to look back at Dover.

"Anything the matter, Bobby?"

"Hell, no, just one little minor thing wrong—I wish we had never dreamed up this whole damn thing."

They edged out of town and the traffic dwindled. Booth paused for a long time before answering, and Caro sensed that he was straining to be patient. But his tone, as if rebelling against his intention, was testy.

"Well, it's a little late to be wishing. We did dream it up. And did it, too,"

"I still wish we didn't. Okay?"

Booth faced front again. In the dimness he looked grim and exhausted, and Caro felt a surge of anger on his behalf. He was the leader—the elected one and the natural one—and he carried it all on his own shoulders, all the various and conflicting temperaments, Asbury, Raphael, Doc, and now Dover, who was usually the least troublesome of any of them. He allowed himself an occasional testiness, but even that would not last. She knew that he would go to work on Dover, that he would bring him around, that he accepted that role and did not feel sorry for himself on its account, but she felt sorry for him nevertheless. For everything.

He said, "We didn't do it because we thought it was nice, Bobby, but because we thought it would be effective."

"It's effective, all right," Dover said. "You should hear what they're calling us and saying about us. On the bus, for instance, they were comparing us to the soldiers who killed Christ!"

She sensed impatience in Booth again and intervened. "Well, we're not like that," she said quietly. "We simply took a box full of dust."

He was polite, as he had been taught to be at home in his dealings with women, but nevertheless firm. No, it wasn't just dust. If it had been just dust and of no value, they wouldn't have taken it. Ideas were even less solid than dust, and yet people respected ideas, followed them, even deified them and died for them. Christ was really just an idea. And what was Christ himself now but dust?

His eloquence took them by surprise, and they said nothing, listening to the echo of his voice. He was breathing hard, almost panting, as if the effort of speaking in abstractions had been as difficult for him as running up a hill.

After a moment Booth said softly, "He might have been in

my division, you know, maybe my company. Maybe I screamed at him to keep his idiot head down and he didn't and got killed." Booth's tone became even more muted. "So I cursed him and wept for him and then put him out of mind because we had to move on. He might have been some rifleman in my company, Bobby."

"That ought to make it even worse." Dover was sullenly triumphant.

"It doesn't," Booth said. "I wouldn't think any more of him, or less, than all the others who died. What makes him so different from any other kid who raised his head above the skyline?"

"He's different."

"Dead people are equal to one another. Great men and villains and babies and whores and especially soldiers. One simple fact ties them all together—they don't exist. That's all of it."

"What the Unknown stands for makes him different." Dover was no longer eloquent, merely obstinate.

Caro came into Orleans, at the crook of the Cape's elbow. The streets were dark. The movie house was just letting out its audience.

"The way he died was not different," Booth said. "He lifted his head and a bullet smashed into his brains. He knew better, too. But maybe he couldn't stand hugging the ground anymore. Maybe he just followed an impulse to take a deep breath without inhaling ants or dust."

"We violated *him*," Dover said stubbornly, "not all the others."

The darkened houses and motels slid by. Caro glanced at Booth. He was shaking his head. He looked exhausted.

"Bobby," he said, "you're going to have to find the answers all by yourself." He might have gone on, might have succeeded in manipulating the boy, but he would not try, perhaps because it no longer mattered.

"Well. . . ." Dover's voice was gloomy, hopeless. "Maybe I found them. But it's too late."

When they reached the house, they discovered that Asbury had planted loaded M-16 rifles at several windows in the living room.

"Those are our defensive strong points," he said in answer to Booth's questioning stare.

Booth was too tired to argue with him.

Zooming back to the city on his motorcycle, his fireman's coat filled with air and ballooning out behind him, his yellow scarf flapping with a sound like firecrackers, Robbins was in a state of euphoria. His luck had been spectacular. Not that he had gotten so much information from Garrison in terms of quantity, but everything he had gotten was pure gold.

He bared his teeth to the chill wind as he recalled the scene in the parking lot. He had teased Garrison with the joints and had him drooling. He lit one and blew the smoke in his face. Garrison tried to grab the joint, but he held him off easily. With the windows in the car shut, the pot smell was overpowering.

"You promised, you fucker," Garrison moaned, and reached out again for the joint. Using the flat of his hand, Robbins shoved Garrison back against the window.

"First you got to tell me where Doc's pad is."

Garrison mumbled, and his chin sank down on his chest. He wasn't going to last too much longer. Robbins pushed his head upright.

"Where is Doc's pad? So I can give him the Nobel in person."

"Someplace." Garrison's head started to lower, then suddenly straightened. "Jackson Heights."

"Garrison, you're lying, old buddy. You got to have square corners to live in Jackson Heights."

Garrison nodded solemnly. "But his shack-up lives there. He moved in."

"What's the shack-up's name?"

"Give over that joint, give it over."

Robbins held him off. "The shack-up's name."

"That nurse, God damn it. Agnes."

"Agnes what?" Robbins' pulse was jumping. Nurse: drugs.

It fit. It was beautiful. "I'm about to lay the joint on you, Garrison. The rest of her name. Agnes what?"

"O'Reilly, you miserable fucker." Garrison lunged. Robbins let him take the joint.

He watched Garrison fumble the joint between his slack lips. He sucked deeply, and the glow lit up his face. He looked terrible.

He exhaled and fell forward against the steering wheel.

"Sit up straight, you dumb bastard."

But Garrison was out cold. Robbins tried slapping him awake, but he was far under, tucked in for the night. He pried the joint from between Garrison's fingers, pinched the coal out, and put the joint back in the toothpick box. He got out of the car and crossed the parking lot to his bike. Suppose Garrison had passed out two minutes earlier. He raised his eyes piously to the dark sky. The God of Finks was watching over him.

He raced northward to the Jersey Turnpike and came out of the Manhattan end of the Lincoln Tunnel at five minutes past one. He whipped through the city streets to the Queensboro Bridge, took the ramp, and had clear sailing up Northern Boulevard. He pulled in at an all-night diner and leafed through a telephone book looking for Agnes O'Riley. He found one in Flushing and another in Sunnyside. He cursed Garrison out in a fury, then had an idea. He leafed backward in the phone book, and there she was: O'Reilly Agnes T . . . Jk Hts, and practically around the corner from the diner.

He went into the phone booth, breathing another heartfelt prayer of thanks to the God of Finks, and dialed. The phone was answered on the third ring.

"Agnes? Hi. This is Robin Robbins."

"Who?"

"Robin Robbins. We met once. Remember me? Gee, I hope I didn't wake you up."

"I was about to go to sleep. Robbins?" She had a tiny baby-sweet voice.

"Yeah, we met at . . . oh, a party, I forget where. I was

with that tall blond girl? Well, it doesn't matter. Doc there, Agnes?"

"He's not here. Fact, he's out of town."

Beautiful. He gave his heartbeat a couple of seconds to calm down, then moaned and said, "Oh, Jesus. Out of town? Oh, hell, that's bad."

"What's the matter?"

"I got this. . . ." He lowered his voice to a whisper. "I got this certain package for him. Gee, what am I gonna do?"

"Well, he'll be back in a couple of days."

"Yeah, but I can't hold it. It's, you know, an *important* package." Silence hummed over the wire. He reduced his voice to a barely audible breathiness. "Agnes, can I trust you?"

After a moment's hesitation her child's voice said, "I guess so."

"Well, it's hash. Hashish?"

"Oh. Well, Doc's out of town, but if you just hold onto it for a few days. . . ."

"That's just it, I can't. I'm up against the gun. My wife and I—you know, the blond girl I was with the night we met?— we're spending the night with her brother out on the Island, and I can't take a chance. He's smoke."

"Smoke?"

"A cop. I can't take a chance. He's a suspicious character, and he hates my guts, and he's just as likely to go through my clothes as not. God, what am I gonna do, Agnes?"

"Maybe he won't search your clothes."

"He's done it before. I'll have to get rid of the package. I'll have to throw it down a sewer. All that money, Doc's money. Look, Agnes, I hate to ask this, do you think. . . ?"

"Well, I guess you can bring it here if you want to."

"Ah, gee, Agnes, you're beautiful. You just saved my life. Doc's, too."

"Will you be long? I was just about to go to sleep—"

"I can be there almost before you finish hanging up. I'll just hand it over and split, and five minutes from now you can be fast asleep."

"Ring the downstairs buzzer and I'll let you in."

"Thanks, Agnes, you're a saint. I mean it. Sunday I'm going to burn a candle for you."

Robbins, he told himself exultantly as he hung up and hurried out to his bike, Robbins, you're cut out for this business, you're a fucking genius.

19

The street was lined with medium-size apartment houses of Tudor persuasion. Robbins found a space for his bike nearby. In the outer foyer he pressed the button marked A T O'REILLY and waited for a voice to come through the grille of the intercom. But instead a buzzer sounded. He leaped for the heavy door to the inner lobby and pushed it open. Agnes was very trusting.

He took the elevator up to the third floor. At the end of the hallway a woman stood in an open doorway. She had red hair purer than his, which was really on the orangy side, and very white skin. He was surprised, considering her voice, to see that she was about thirty-five. She was wearing an emerald-green robe and beneath it a floor-length pink nightgown.

"Hi, Agnes. Remember me now?"

He put out his hand and, before she could respond, placed his palm flat against her chest and shoved. She flew backward into a foyer and he followed quickly, backhanding the door shut behind him. He clapped his hand over her mouth, turned her around, and half pushed, half bumped her into the living room.

He whirled her around to face him, reversing his palm to keep her mouth covered. Her eyes were agape, not so much in fear as surprise. They were very blue eyes, which, Robbins thought, along with her red hair and white skin, made a very patriotic color scheme.

"Agnes," he said, "admit it—you're one dumb broad."

She didn't struggle, but hung limply under the circle of his

255

arm around her waist, pulling her in tightly against his body. But when she felt him rise against her belly, she tried arching away from him, and her eyes showed fear for the first time.

"Don't worry, baby," Robbins said. "That's just the reflex action of the healthy American male. All I'm going to do is ask you a few questions. Dig? Nod your pretty Irish head if you comprehend."

She nodded, but her eyes remained in a fixed uplooking focus.

"Okay. Now I'm going to take my hand away from your mouth. But if you try to scream, I'm going to punch you right in the face and maybe break your nose and knock some teeth out. Are you going to scream or not going to scream? Indicate one or the other by the appropriate movement of your head."

Beneath his hand her head shook minimally from side to side. Watchfully he removed his hand from her mouth. Her lipstick was smeared.

"Okay? No noise?"

"No." Her baby voice sounded calm enough.

"I apologize for calling you a dumb broad. You're a smart broad. Go sit down over there on the sofa."

She must have been glad enough to put distance between them, but her movements were unhurried. A cool chick. Maybe she was an operating-room nurse, accustomed to keeping her emotions under control. He sat down beside her. She shifted away from him slightly.

"Who are you?" The tiny voice was firm.

"I'm a cop."

"Bull. You're no cop. Cops don't have all that hair or dress like that."

He touched his fireman's jacket. "Plainclothes cop, baby."

"You call that plain?"

Her delivery was deadpan, but there was no question she meant to be funny. Cool chick, he thought again, and with that Irish wit. He began to see what Doc might see in her.

Down to business. "Agnes, where is Doc?"

"He's out of town. I told you so."

"I believe you. *Where* out of town?"

"He didn't *tell* me where."

"When did he leave?"

"Tuesday morning."

"And exactly where is he?"

"I told you—he didn't tell me."

"Didn't you even ask him where he was going?"

"I did that."

"Well?"

"He said to mind my own fucking business."

Robbins lowered his pale lashes and shook his head sympathetically. "That's a rotten thing to say to your old lady. Weren't your feelings hurt?"

"They were that." There was a flash of temper in her blue eyes. "I told him so. He apologized and said—" Something else showed in the eyes, which she tried to conceal by lowering lashes that were as pale as Robbins'. "He apologized."

"And he said what?" Robbins smiled encouragingly.

"I don't remember. Nothing important."

Robbins slid his hand between the folds of her green robe and captured her breast. Still smiling, he began to squeeze. Agnes gasped and clawed at his hand, but he held fast. He squeezed harder and she slid down on the couch, squirming, whimpering, her eyes filling with tears. He gave her breast a final terrible squeeze and then abruptly withdrew his hand. She bowed her head and covered her breast tenderly with her hands.

"What did Doc tell you, Agnes?"

"That was a filthy mean thing to do." Her little girl's voice was pinched and tinny with pain.

He feinted toward her and she shrank away from him. "Agnes, that was just a little sample. If you keep lying, I'm going to twist it clear off your chest. And then I'll do the other one, and you won't have any tits left at all."

Her clear blue eyes stared, assessing him. Presently she nodded her head, as if to confirm, at least to herself, that she took him at his word. In Nam he had seen that same belief take hold in the eyes of captives he had worked over when he had been a G-2 interrogator—never mind that bullshit about the inscrutable Oriental—but it hadn't always been the prelude to success. Although people told the truth out of fear, they also lied for the same reason.

"So, Agnes," he said, "one more time—what did Doc tell you?"

"He said it was better if I didn't know where he was going, that what I didn't know couldn't hurt me."

"That's what I thought he said. Why didn't you say so before and save me the trouble of hurting you?"

"I didn't know before what a rotten mean bastard you were."

"But you know now?"

"I do that."

"So, now that you know what a bastard I am, where did he go?"

She covered her breasts protectively and looked at him in despair. "I'm telling the truth."

"Maybe."

"I'm telling the truth." There was a firm stubborn Irish set to her jaw now. "No matter how much you hurt me again, I can't tell you what I don't know."

He was convinced that she wasn't lying. And if that was the case, then Doc was out of reach and he had reached a dead end. He couldn't guess whether or not she knew what Doc was involved in, but there was no point in bringing it up. Whatever degree of patriotism she might have, it doubtless wouldn't outweigh her loyalty to Doc and might even toughen her determination to shield him. He moved closer to her. She didn't shrink away, but watched him warily, her hands cupped over her breasts.

"Agnes, do you know any of Doc's friends?"

She shook her head. "Not many."

"A few?"

"Not many. I don't like his friends too much. Come to think of it, most of them look like you."

"You remember any of their names?"

"I don't think so."

He frowned. "You want me to start hurting you again?"

She shook her head, and he savored the touch of fear that darkened the color of her eyes.

"Didn't you ever double-date with Doc and his friends?"

"Mostly, when we double-date, it's with people at the hospital. I'm a nurse."

"Agnes, you're pissing me off again. I want you to think very hard and remember any of Doc's friends—not yours—that you had a social evening with. Okay, Agnes?"

"Okay." She tilted her head up to the ceiling, concentrating. Then she looked down, almost with surprise, and said, "We had dinner once . . ." and broke off.

He placed his hands on top of hers, cupped around both of her breasts. He squeezed her hands, and she flattened them, trying to protect her breasts. He said harshly, "Don't fuck me around, Agnes, or I'll hurt you so bad you'll dream about it the rest of your life."

She studied him for a moment. "I believe you would. We had dinner at their house one night. It was out on the Island. He was a nice fellow, and his wife, too. He didn't look like you. I was surprised."

He had a sinking feeling that she was talking about a straight friend of Doc's. "What did you talk about that night? I mean, did you talk about Vietnam, the war, radical things?"

She nodded. "All night long. That stuff bores me. I mean, Doc is in the right about it and all, but. . . ."

"What was the friend's name?"

"I can't remember." She shied away as his hands tightened. "Wait, they lived in Elmont, out on the Island."

"His name, you twit."

"Oh, dear god. . . ." She tilted her head to the ceiling. "Ed. . . ." She shook her head helplessly. "His name is Ed."

He doubled up his fist and placed it against her face, letting her feel the hard bone of his knuckles. "Ed *what?*" He drew his fist back and held it poised. "Ed *what*, Agnes, or I'm going to shatter your fucking cheekbone."

"Ed Raphael."

It was almost three when Robbins put his bike away in the garage and walked home, brushing off white-booted whores and snarling at drunks and indecisive muggers. It had been a long and productive day, and, like Garrison, Agnes O'Reilly had provided information of high quality. She hadn't re-membered any other names, although he had hurt her a lit-tle to jog her memory, but in Ed Raphael she had given him premium value. He found that out as he was ready to leave.

"What does this Raphael do for a living, Agnes?"

Weary, her baby voice faded almost to a whisper, she said, "He's some kind of an engineer or something."

Doc for the injections, Raphael for lifting up the slab—the team was beginning to shape up. Gently he withdrew her hands from her chest, drew her robe apart, and tenderly kissed her bruised breast. To his surprise, her nipple rose to the touch of his lips. But almost immediately she smacked him hard on the forehead with her open palm. He laughed and got up and left.

He opened his door—police lock, dead-bolt Segal, house lock—and went inside and undressed. He got into bed, took up the telephone, and dialed a number. It was picked up on the fourth or fifth ring. The answering voice was muzzy and depressed.

"Phoebe?" His voice was a whisper. "It's me. The fink."

"Christ!"

"I woke you up," Robbins said. "Gosh, I'm no end sorry."

Phoebe coughed rackingly. "Why are you calling me at this hour?"

In an aggrieved tone Robbins said, "You instructed me to, you warned me if I didn't—"

"Yes, yes. Make your report."

"What's the reward money up to? Hit half a million yet?"

"Is that what you phoned me about?" Incredulity and in-dignation ran Phoebe's voice a full octave up the register.

"Well, I just want you to know that if I get the reward money, I don't forget my friends. I split with you right down the middle."

"You idiot! Don't you know law-enforcement officials are ineligible to receive rewards?"

"Then I'll have to slip you your share under the table."

"And neither are you." Phoebe roused himself to project a note of malice. "You're on the federal payroll."

"Phoebe," Robbins said, "this is a hell of an hour to be making bad jokes."

"It's the law. Now tell me why you called, and be very quick about it."

Robbins closed his eyes and watched a tall, neat stack of green bills, hundreds of thousands of dollars, peeling off one by one and blowing away out of sight in a mindless wind.

"Okay, Phoebe, I'll make it snappy. I called to tell you that you're nothing but a stuffed-up toilet and that I have learned through unimpeachable sources that you suck your poodle's cock."

He paused. No reaction from Phoebe. Maybe stunned? He went on.

"Also, you fuck your mother in dark hallways, you sell your sister's services to bad women, you've got a wooden prick, and you read *Quotations from Chairman Mao* before you go to bed. With your poodle."

Phoebe exploded with a burst of uncharacteristic vulgarity. "You fuck! You fucking fuck!" He hung up.

Robbins waited for a moment, then dialed again. The phone was picked up on the first ring. He said, "I'm going to report you to the special agent in charge for using foul and abusive language to an employee of the bureau."

Phoebe laughed harshly. "You're a *former* employee, you miserable bastard. You're off the payroll!"

"As of when?"

"As of this instant!"

"I protest," Robbins said. "I'll demand a departmental trial—"

Phoebe hung up with a bang. Robbins listened to the hum of the dead circuit, then replaced the phone. The stack of lovely green bills reassembled itself like a movie being run in reverse. With a satisfied smile, he fell back on his pillow and went to sleep.

Booth woke to a feeling of deprivation, but without any memory of the dream that induced it. The loss persisted into consciousness, a weight of unshed tears behind his lids. He opened his eyes and traced the stretch of his left arm curving across emptiness. No Caro.

His heart thumped hollowly, his fingers twitched. He lay still for a moment, focusing mindlessly on the low ceiling, and then threw off the blankets and got out of bed. Shivering a little, he rummaged in the darkness and found his jacket. He went out into the living room. It was empty. A glint of starlight pierced the drawn blinds and struck a reflection from a mirror. He paused with his hand on the knob of the door leading to the porch. What will I do if I find Caro and Asbury outside, squirming on the sand—kill him, kill both of them, kick sand at them, break his prick off? He didn't smile at the absurdity of his thought.

He turned the knob. Caro was sitting at the edge of the porch, smoking, wrapped in a heavy old-fashioned bathrobe that had carried her through some serious sickness of her teens and that she still regarded with affection. She turned and watched him make his way across the porch. He felt no relief, only that same hollow thump of the heart. He sat down beside her, drawing the jacket around him against the night air. The breeze ruffled the small hairs on his bare legs.

He said, "Can't sleep. Overtired or something."

"You went out like a light."

She had drawn his head to her breast, and on its warmth he had fallen asleep immediately. She expelled a puff of smoke; it drifted upward into the darkness.

He said, "Are you all right?" But of course it was he who was not all right, who had corrupted himself by suspicion.

She said, "I was thinking of my father."

He nodded, staring at her mouth, the lips slightly parted to show a gleam of teeth. Her breath was warm, tinged with a smell of tobacco.

"What he would say if he knew what lay in his cellar, what we were using his house for."

"I can imagine," he said, and thought, I will weep for her mouth, for the duskiness of her skin, for her cries in the night.

"No." She shook her head. "He was a radical in his youth. He marched in May Day parades, he picketed factories and fought American Nazis in the street, he had his scalp opened up by a cop's billy. He believed in the violent overthrow of the government and the ultimate triumph of the workers' paradise in the Soviet Union."

"He did all this and practiced dentistry at the same time?"

She had occasionally mentioned her father, but only peripherally, sketching the broad impersonal outlines of a successful life: He had operated three chairs, worked like a dervish, avoided a coronary, amassed a fortune, and chucked it all up at the age of fifty-five. Now, with his wife, he spent six months of the year on the Cape, fishing and tanning, and the other six months traveling from one *grand luxe* hotel to another: Dorchester to George Cinq, to Excelsior, to Gritti Palace.

"Just in his student days and before he had built up a practice. Then he stopped being, well, what we call an activist nowadays. But philosophically he remained true to his cause. He attended rallies, contributed money, supported their press, voted for their candidates. . . ."

Booth listened to her voice, strangely harmonious with the tireless soughing of the wavelets below the bluff, and although he could not interest himself in her remote and shadowy father, he was content that she talked and that he could pay heed sufficiently to untrack him from that terrible question that he could not ask aloud, only poison himself with: Caro, have you slept with Asbury?

"My father? The radical in him never quite died out. These days it doesn't have much outlet outside of upsetting the help at elegant hotels by being overfriendly. Right at this moment he's probably exchanging confidences with the bootblack at the Alfonso Thirteenth in Seville." She smiled. "If he knew about this? It would thrill him, all except the violence; that would horrify him."

"He believed in violent revolution when he was a young man.

"As a theory, but not for him personally. He was one of your mild Irishmen." She was leaning forward, frowning slightly. "It was a different breed of radical in those days."

It occurred to him that he was much closer chronologically

to her father's generation than to her own (and Doc's and Asbury's). Suddenly he was wary. Out over the bay the sky gave
the illusion of being brighter, and he thought he could pick
up the shadowy shape of the target ship. Caro placed her
cheek against his. Her skin was cool, slightly moist; the round
of her cheek was a blessing.

He said, "I'm not like your father."

"No." Her cheek moved against his. "You're much different."

He picked on a nuance. "But not entirely?"

She backed off so that she could look at him. "My father
clung to his dream of the workers' utopia long after Russia
had become just another nationalistic superpower. He was a
man who hated to see something end."

He understood the father better than she did, Booth
thought. At their age every ending was a little death.

She said, "After this, after Rowan is freed, it *will* be the
end, the ugly war will be finally over. There's nothing more."

He said, "There's always something else," and if she had
had an analogy with their own relationship in mind, so had
he. *It needn't end, Caro, it needn't end.*

"Nothing more," she said firmly. "Fighting gets to be a
habit, but if there's no opponent, then you're just shadow-
boxing."

"There are other causes." But wasn't he close to saying that
the cause itself mattered less than having one? "Worthy
causes."

She nodded, not agreeing but dropping the argument,
and lit another cigarette. The sky had brightened perceptibly. Over a mile of water the target ship was beginning to
take shape.

"Do you hear that?" Caro tilted her chin to the sky.

It was distinct from the sound of the waves. A drone. He
looked upward, but the sky was a gray blank.

"The Dawn Patrol or something," Caro said. "They're
about to give the *James Longstreet* its first clobbering of the
day."

The drone became louder. He searched the sky, but the
first he knew that the plane was there was when he heard a

dull echoing thump and saw a puff of smoke rise amidships. I have a kinship with that superannuated hulk out there in the bay, he thought. We are both relics of past wars.

The plane, black and stubby, swooped upward in a fast-climbing arc. Beneath it, with the dust of the hit settling, the target ship sat stolidly, unmoving, impregnable. Well, there was some comfort there, he thought, it's unsinkable.

"Might as well get some sleep," Caro said.

They stood up, feeling the chilliness of the air. Caro put her arm around his waist and held him very tightly.

Booth opened his eyes into a dazzling streak of sun slanting through the canted blind. The bed beside him was empty. He brought his wristwatch up to his eyes and blinked at it. A quarter past nine. He smelled coffee. Caro had let him sleep late. He felt a twinge of guilt; the puritan impulse was never very far beneath his surface.

As he started to get out of bed, he heard the sound of a car. He tensed, but the sound stopped or dwindled. He relaxed and began to dress. He was feeling for his shoes beside the bed when the door opened and Dover appeared.

"A police car." Dover was breathless. "Stopped in front of the house. Cop getting out."

Raphael and Doc had crowded back from the living room into the jogged corridor that would conceal them from the door. Raphael was pale. Doc was trying to look unconcerned. He motioned them back and inched forward so that he could peer around the jog into the living room. Caro was moving toward the door. He watched her touch the knob, and then, as he was pulling his head back, he caught a glimpse of Asbury. He was crouched behind a chair, an M-16 fitted to shoulder and cheek, trained on the door.

Part III

20

When the news secretary entered his office, Eminence Griese, with ostentatious furtiveness, covered the yellow legal-size pad on his desk with his palms.

Without so much as a good morning, the news secretary said, "I've got to have something to tell them at the press briefing. It's topic A, you know."

"Apprise them of the President's nationwide telecast this evening—"

"His *what?*"

"— on a nonpartisan subject in the national interest. I wish you to set up such a telecast for, oh, shall we say eight o'clock?"

"You don't *set up*," the news secretary said, "you *request*."

"These grubby details are of no interest to me. We will require approximately ten or fifteen minutes."

"Forgive me for asking, but does the President know about this?"

"Do you imagine that I make such major decisions unilaterally?" Griese smiled. "You are correct. I will acquaint the President with the situation presently."

The news secretary hunched his shoulders and then dropped them, in a gesture combining protest and hopelessness. "They will want to know the subject of this address in the national interest. I presume I am at liberty to tell them?"

"The rubric 'a matter of grave national interest' will suffice."

"It won't satisfy them. Damn it, why do we have to have secrecy when there's no point to it?"

"Simply because it is my wish," Griese said. Watching the news secretary's face darken, he thought, I'm already cast as the villain of his unreadable book anyway—so why not give him fresh ammunition?

The news secretary shifted ground. "I enjoy an excellent relationship with the networks, and I wouldn't want to jeopardize it. If it's all the same to you, I'd prefer waiting until the President agrees before I approach them."

Griese sighed. "Did you ever know him to refuse a television appearance?"

"There's always a first time," the news secretary said stubbornly.

"There is *not* always a first time," Griese said sharply, "and I'll thank you to spare me your superstitious notions. Have you ever thought of writing a novel?"

The news secretary was taken aback. "No. Why do you ask that?"

"Because contrary to widespread belief, there is no correlation between the writing of skillful, even superb fiction and intelligence."

The news secretary brought his left arm forward in an abrupt, violent motion, and Griese thought incredulously, He's going to hit me. But the news secretary was merely shooting his cuff to uncover his wristwatch. But maybe he *will* hit me one of these days, Griese thought. Hopefully, after his trashy book is published and he has become a rich man, so that I can profitably sue him.

Curiosity prevailed over the news secretary's resentment. "I'm late for the briefing. But I *would* like to know what's going on. Are we going to spring Rowan?"

"The answer is in these charts." Griese lifted his palms from the yellow pad and quickly covered it again. "They are a recording of the sentiments of the nation—the press, various organizations, churchmen, politicians, and, of course, the ordinary citizen, who is our sovereign."

The news secretary rolled his eyes toward the ceiling.

The Talisman

"I have been up all night compiling this—shall I call it heartbeat of the nation?—and shall continue to do so until a verdict is reached."

Actually it was not he who had been up all night, but his staff—known popularly as "Griese's graduate students." They were not graduate students but young professionals, bright, ardent, Griese-worshiping, who were unrelenting in the performance of any duty he asked of them and who, like graduate students, expected no public credit and little reward beyond the satisfaction of serving their master.

"Thank you so much for putting me in the picture," the news secretary said. "And now, not to take up too much of your invaluable time, I'll run along to my briefing."

"I would suggest that one of your assistants might handle the briefing," Griese said blandly, "so that you can devote all of your energies to arranging the telecast. I'm much obliged for your heartfelt cooperation."

The news secretary gave him a look of naked loathing and stalked out of the office on stiff legs. How ridiculously easy he is to provoke, Griese thought, and turned to more important matters.

The light blue tunic and the brown stetson conferred an immediate sternness upon him, but his smile was a sunburst. Behind him his cruiser was drawn up on the road.

"Good morning, Caroline."

She filled the space between the door edge and the jamb, but he was tall enough to look past her head into the living room if he wanted to.

"Doing the routine door-rattling inspection," Perry said, "and thought I'd just drop by and say hello."

She smiled and wedged herself into the door opening.

"Old house is holding up pretty good." He cast an assessive eye upward at the angles of the façade.

"When my father built it, the local experts all said it wouldn't stand up to a single Cape Cod winter."

Perry grinned. "If he had asked me, I'd have said the same thing." His eyes lowered, and she realized that her bathrobe

271

had opened and he was eyeing a curve of her breast. With one hand—she was clamping the door against her haunch with the other—she folded the bathrobe under her chin.

"Feeling better this morning? I mean, away from the city and its problems?"

"Oh, yes, it works wonders."

She didn't know what was going on behind her. Doc, Raphael, and Dover had retreated, but she had seen Asbury leap for a rifle. Nervously her hand slipped down from her robe, and the folds slid apart. She closed it again. He raised his eyes slowly, and she thought, Christ, he's going to think it's a tease.

He was sniffing the air. "Having your breakfast? I'm sorry if I—"

"No, it's okay, Perry, I'm finished."

"Coffee smells good." He gave her the dazzling smile that had unshipped a thousand pairs of panties.

"Perry. . . ." It had to be done diplomatically, and so she paused for a smile, realizing a second too late that it might seem a form of coquetry.

"Yes?"

He turned up the candlepower of his smile, and she thought bitterly, Damn it, why don't you sleep with your wife instead of catting around? It wasn't really all that marvelous seven years ago, though we thought it was, or at least I did, arched beneath you in untutored passion on the nighttime beach. . . .

She said abruptly, "Perry, if you're bucking for an invitation, forget it."

It obliterated his smile, and he flushed and said, "Look, Caroline, all I was angling for was a cup of coffee. If you thought it was anything else. . . ."

The smile was gone, perhaps for the rest of the day, the rest of the week. Caro, she thought, you're such a clumsy bitch. "Look, Perry." She softened her voice and smiled—not provocatively, she hoped, but gamely. "I'd ask you in for coffee, but I can't. I'm, well, not here by myself."

"Oh?"

"My old man is here with me." Better translate. "My boyfriend. I'm sorry I didn't tell you yesterday, but, you know. . . ."

She saw with relief that she had hit on the right approach. Now he could retreat with dignity, his manhood restored. He almost smiled, but not quite; that would still take some time.

"Hell, Caroline, I'm a big boy. You could have told me." He was eyeing her breasts again. Goddamn robe. . . .

"It's all right, anyway," she said. "We're going to be married."

"Married?" He brightened and she read his mind: Hell, *I* didn't have to marry her to screw her. "Well, that's great, Caroline. Congratulations."

"Thanks, Perry."

"Just great. Lucky man." A small smile appeared on his face—not the great blockbuster yet—and then it disappeared, and he was frowning, peering over her shoulder. "Is that a rifle I see in there?"

"A rifle?" One of Asbury's "defensive points." She turned inward to the house so that he would not see the terror on her face, her mind racing through dizzy premonitions of disaster. But her father rescued her: the summer he had bought a rifle and popped away at tin cans on the beach. "Oh, the target rifle. My beau was shooting at tin cans."

His frown turned admonitory. "Well, be careful, Caro, we don't want any accidents."

"Don't worry, Perry, my beau is a fanatic about safety."

"Okay. See you."

He tapped the brim of his spotless hat to her and went down the path to his car, handsome in his blue tunic and tan pants with the check vertical stripe, his gleaming boots, his wine-red leather holster. She waved to him as he gunned his cruiser showily and drove off. She was trembling.

Each page of Em Griese's yellow pad was trisected on a horizontal axis by ruled lines. The three segments were headed PAY UP NOT ONE PENNY FOR TRIBUTE and SHEER NONSENSE Whenever he received a phone call or an advice from his graduate students, Griese evaluated it and then methodically entered it in synoptic form—or in paraphrase—under the appropriate heading. Column one was overwhelmingly the longest.

At the beginning he had taken all comments at face value and assigned them accordingly. But as he went on, he realized that considerations of policy frequently camouflaged actual intent, and so he began to make value judgments. Thus, he had first listed all the veterans organizations under NOT ONE PENNY FOR TRIBUTE but presently relocated them to the PAY UP column. Without exception, the veterans groups—American Legion, Amvets, Veterans of Foreign Wars, Disabled American Veterans, and the "specialty" groups, that is, those organized along the lines of race, creed, or color—had reacted almost identically, both as to sentiment and prose style.

"The most heinous and impious crime since the killing of Christ . . . the work of Communist storm troopers . . . if we bow to the outrageous demand of these bestial extortionists, then our honor will be eternally besmirched . . . this Rowan, a man of the cloth who brought shame upon God, stands with Judas as a paradigm of villainy . . . no price is too high to pay for the safe return of this Holy Relic except the one these murdering monsters demand. . . ."

Nevertheless, he had moved the veterans groups to column one. They would blow and bluster (and increase the amount of their rewards), but in the end they would grudgingly support the President for pardoning Rowan because the alternative, destruction of the remains, was unacceptable in their theology.

The fewest entries were in the NOT ONE PENNY FOR TRIBUTE column. Notable among them were the depositions of the Ku Klux Klan and the Nazi Party of Amerika. Griese's notes for the Klan read: "We revere the IDEA of an Unknown, but the ACTUALITY is open to question. . . . Who can say, in the absence of hard evidence, that the remains are not NIGGER, JEW, or CATHOLIC remains? Unacceptable! We stand unequivocally opposed to meeting the ransom terms."

The Nazi Party of Amerika was brief and to the point: "On the 10 or 15 percent chance that the remains are the remains of a Jew, we stand 100 percent against the ransom. We are not 85 percent or 90 percent for racial purity, but 100 percent for racial purity. Heil Hitler!"

Griese had long since ceased to enter capsule records of newspaper editorial comment after discovering that most of it could be divided into what he categorized as the New York *Times* approach and the New York *Daily News* approach.

The *Times*: ". . . this distasteful deed of misguided and insensible persons . . . fanatic act that has nauseated the civilized world. . . . Although the remains are without substantive value, they are a metaphor for brave men who died for their country and whose avatar is being exploited basely for political purpose. . . . No cause can prosper, however profoundly its adherents believe in it, when it is built on so base and revolting a fundament . . . nevertheless, we hope that the President will issue the pardon, distasteful as this decision may be. . . ."

The *News*: ". . . far more reprehensible than the Crucifixion, because these miserable rats know what they do. . . . This act is the supreme horror in the context of a once-great and still-beloved country whose permissiveness has brought it to low estate in the estimation of all right-thinking Americans. . . . These unspeakable punks deserve to be torn limb from limb, drawn and quartered, broken on the rack. . . . With heavy heart, faced with a Hobson's choice, we must opt for the return of the remains even at the intolerable cost of pardoning the unpardonable, that miscreant, revolting so-called man of the cloth. . . ."

Left and Right in the political spectrum, riding different lines, arrived at the same destination. Liberal: "Rowan, though perhaps unwise, was a martyr to the cause of sanity, peace, justice. . . . Therefore we wish to see him pardoned, although we hold no brief for the militaristic fetishism represented by idol worship of these pathetic remains. . . ." Conservative: "Rowan is a tin-penny subversive, a corrupter of the highest ideals of American patriotism. . . . However reluctantly, we would set a thousand Rowans free to recover the remains of one who represents the ultimate in heroism, sacrifice. . . ."

Both in the PAY UP column.

Unions, which tended to be rightist in most matters other than those which concerned their own economic self-interest, echoed the conservatives. An exception was the Brotherhood of Gravediggers, which declared that if the Unknown had been interred by highly skilled professionals instead of all-thumbs soldiers, the remains would undoubtedly still be intact in the tomb.

The Weathermen: "Burn down these cemeteries of moldering carcasses that are monuments to Militarism. We spit on the remains of the Unknown Dupe. The back of the hand to military corpses, the helping hand to the living, loving poor and oppressed."

All religious denominations, while they condemned the disinterment as blasphemy of the highest order and expressed contempt for the recusant Francis Rowan, felt that the recovery of the remains outweighed other considerations. Several equated the crime with a falling off of youthful attendance at church (and synagogue and mosque).

A spiritualist church said that the remains themselves were of no consequence. His spirit, however, had been heard wailing piteously at innumerable seances.

After some thought, Griese placed the spiritualist entry in the PAY UP column.

The American Civil Liberties Union was foursquare for the pardon and release of Francis Rowan, whose civil rights had been grievously abridged, and was initiating a study into the question of whether or not the civil rights of the remains had been violated.

An old-line black organization invoked the name of God at frequent intervals in pleading for the return to rest of the "soul" of the Unknown. A militant black organization predicted that Rowan—a motherfucker who was not noted for holding any strong opinions in favor of racial equality—would be released because of the color of his skin.

Puerto Rican Independistas: You waste time on this matter, which is of absolutely no importance, while the people of the Island groan under the yoke of mainland oppressors. "Free Puerto Rico now!"

All branches of the military establishment, with heavy heart, declared for the return, at whatever price, of their Very Own.

Many special-interest groups, with what could be only minuscule followings, lost track of the main issue to advance their own causes. Griese had listed some of these on a separate sheet of paper headed MEMORABLE QUOTES:

"Legalize marriage between consenting adult males."

"Free tuition, books, pencils, ball-point pens, and loose-leaf paper for all students in the New York colleges."

"Euthanasia as the Fifth Freedom."

"A federal law requiring dog owners to carry a cleanup kit in the streets."

"Limit the height of all new housing to two stories."

"Lower the voting age to twelve."

What it was boiling down to, clearly, was that (with the exception of extremist groups at both ends of the spectrum) while few people were rabid about saving the remains, practically nobody wanted to see them destroyed. A hurry-up Gallup poll, brought in by one of the graduate students, confirmed him:

For paying the ransom and getting back the remains: 74 percent

For not paying the ransom at the cost of losing the remains: 12 percent

No opinion: 12 percent

Have never heard of the Unknown Warrior: 2 percent

Special Agent Anstruther (Phoebe) and Special Agent Burdis picked a finicky path between trucks, handcarts and shouting men with bare muscular arms exposed to the chill of the morning. At least five times per block they were compelled to walk into the gutter, looping around a truck backed up onto the sidewalk or a chute down which slid bulky packages fastened with baling wire and boldly marked with addresses (everything, Anstruther noted with bafflement, seemed to be headed for one destination or another in North Carolina).

Special Agent Burdis said in surprise (and perhaps reproof), "You're covered with dandruff."

Anstruther didn't look at himself but at Burdis, whose dark topcoat and hat were covered with a powdering of motes. The air itself was swarming with motes.

"It seems to be dust," Anstruther said.

They walked on, brushing vigorously at their coats, fanning their hats in the air. The dust was easily dislodged, but soon settled again.

Anstruther noted the number on a building. "Should be the next block."

They crossed a street that was more like an alley and that, astonishingly, was a thoroughfare for trucks that appeared too wide for it. Their number was the third building along. A man in a leather vest, squat and powerful, his shoulders covered with a mass of hair like epaulets, was braced in the doorway.

"Good morning," Anstruther said.

The man said, "So?"

"My name is Anstruther. This is Mr. Burdis."

The man's response was drowned out by a voice inside the storefront shouting on the telephone. The man raised his voice and yelled, "You lost or something?"

"May I ask you your name, sir?"

"Sid." He turned as the phone slammed into its cradle, and the man who had been shouting came up behind him. He looked like a twin—squat, muscular, hairy epaulets, leather vest. "This is Julie," Sid said. He pointed to the peeling gilt lettering on the window. "Julie and Sid. Express."

"Julie and Sid what?" Burdis said.

"Just Julie and Sid," Julie said. "What are you—the fucking FBI?"

"Yes."

"Yes what?" Julie said.

"Don't holler, Julie," Sid said.

"Yes," Anstruther said. "We are special agents of the Federal Bureau of Investigation."

"Whattya know?" Sid said.

"They're bullshitting us," Julie said. "They're fucking fire department inspectors. Tell them we're paid up till the first of the month."

Burdis said to Anstruther, "I don't think we've gotten very far so far."

"Make them show their crededentials," Julie said.

Anstruther flipped open his wallet and held it under Julie's gaze. Julie ignored it. "What's their crededentials say, Sid?"

"Federal Bureau of Investigation. I'll be a fuck. They ain't fire inspectors, Julie. They're FBI."

"Tell them what do they want," Julie said.

"We'd like to speak to you, sir, if it's convenient."

"Convenient? You're out of your fucking mind," Julie snorted.

"It's the busy season," Sid said. "We're going crazy."

"We'd appreciate your cooperation," Anstruther said. "We believe you may be able to help us in a criminal investigation."

"Oh, certainly," Sid said. "In that case."

Julie said, "The kid is too goddamn nice to strangers. A bum comes around, he gives him a shilling. A guy says lemme have halfa your sandwich, he gives him halfa his sandwich. I'll tell you something. Our old man—should rest in peace—always said Sid was too bighearted for his own good. You can't be bighearted in business, or they eat you up. Right? Ain't it the same in your business?"

The phone rang. Julie whirled inside, snatched up the phone, and began to shout. Sid unblocked the doorway and shouted, "Come on inside."

Anstruther and Burdis followed him in. The office was furnished with two yellow oak desks, two filing cabinets stacked to the ceiling with papers—yellow, pink, blue, and white—a pair of chrome chairs, and at least a dozen calendars. The ocher walls, there they were not covered with calendars, were scribbled over with hundreds of notations: names, phone numbers, addresses, some of them enclosed by doodled hearts.

". . . fucking bill of lading up your ass," Julie was shouting. "Fuck you and your fucking bill of lading. Go fuck yourself with your bill of lading."

"Have a seat," Sid said.

Anstruther and Burdis eyed the chairs, which were covered with a half-inch accretion of dust, and Anstruther said politely, "It's all right, we don't mind standing."

"Okay, Rocco," Julie was shouting. "But don't come on no more with that fucking bill-of-lading shit. Know what I mean? Or I'll shove the bill of lading up your fat Sicilian ass. Know what I mean? How's the little woman, Rocco?"

Julie paused for a reply, grunted, and then hurled the phone back into its cradle.

"Who let these two guys in? Sid, the old man was right about you. Busiest time of the whole year."

"We'll try to make it as quick as we can," Anstruther said. "We have information to the effect that these premises served as headquarters for the Committee for Justice and Human Reparations."

Sid and Julie looked at each other blankly, and Anstruther thought, Either they're terrific actors, or the bureau's Intelligence has got something screwed up.

"Headquarters is right," Julie said. "Headquarters for Sid and Julie's Express. See the sign on the window?"

Sid, gazing up at the mottled tin ceiling, lowered his eyes and plucked at Julie's arm. Julie ducked his head, and Sid whispered in his ear. But it was a whisper only in the relative terms of a perpetual shouter, and Anstruther was able to hear every word.

"He must mean them kooks over there." Sid gestured with one of his huge sloping shoulders toward a partition.

"That was a *committee?*" Julie said. "I seen plenty committees in my life, and they never looked like *that.*"

"Do you mind if we take a look?"

Burdis was already turning the corner of the partition. Anstruther followed. There were two desks in the room, a decrepit club chair, and a half-dozen slatted wooden camp chairs of a type Anstruther hadn't seen in twenty years. The room was gloomy, its dimness relieved only by a weak spread of light coming through a clear margin in the black-painted window front. The walls showed light areas where pictures or papers had been removed. The desks and chairs were covered with the indigenous dust of the area, settled, undisturbed, of a measurable thickness. Burdis was tossing the desks, pulling out drawers, checking the cavities before replacing them. Anstruther dumped the contents of a wire wastebasket on the floor and combed through it. Nothing but crumpled Kleenex, not even a scrap of paper.

Burdis said, "Nothing in the drawers, nothing stuck between them. Clean. They must have expected us."

"Flown the coop," Anstruther said, kicking the Kleenex back into the wastebasket. "From the amount of dust, it must have been weeks."

"You can't tell anything from the dust," Burdis said. "You've got almost a quarter of an inch on your hat right now." He checked the wall. "They didn't write anything down here. They were at least that smart."

They walked back over the undulant rotted floor to the other side of the partition.

"They're gone," Anstruther said. "You could have told us that. When did you see them last?"

Sid shrugged. "Four, five weeks ago? Six? They could have been gone weeks without I knew it."

"Didn't they say they were going? Didn't they say good-bye?"

"Who says good-bye?" Julie said.

Burdis said, "Are you aware that you have been harboring subversives?"

"What kind of subversives?" Julie said. "They were against the Vietnam War."

"The war has been over for some time."

"So? So the war was over but they kept the committee. Like when there was no more infantile paralysis, they kept the March of Dimes, didn't they?"

Anstruther said, "The war was long over when they *came*

here." Sid and Julie looked at each other in bafflement. Anstruther didn't doubt that they were innocent bystanders. Nevertheless, he said sternly, "You guys better come clean. You know we're federal officers and empowered to arrest—"

"Don't threaten," Julie said.

Sid said, "Don't get aggravated, Julie. It's like the fire inspectors. If we made a couple of violations, we made a couple of violations. So now we have to find out how much these guys get."

"Sure," Julie said. "All we got to do is shmeer the whole fucking world."

Burdis said, "Let's get organized here. When did they first show up?"

Sid and Julie shrugged. Sid said, "Maybe eight, nine months ago?"

"And they asked to rent the space?"

"They asked if they could have it free. It was just standing here empty, so we said okay."

"*You* said okay," Julie said. "Fucking Santa Claus."

Burdis said, "Who asked for the space? What were the circumstances?"

"I guess it was the little guy," Sid said. "The circumstances were he walked in off the street and asked could he have the space."

"What is the little guy's name?"

Sid shrugged and looked at Julie, who shrugged.

"Can you describe him?"

"A little guy with long hair on him."

The phone rang. Julie turned away and picked up the phone and began to bellow.

"How many of them were there?"

"Six or eight or ten, I guess. Chrissake—" Sid showed a touch of Julie-like impatience. "You think we paid any *attention* to them kooks?"

"Can you describe *any* of them?"

"Young guys with hair. Some was taller and some was shorter."

"But you saw them coming or going frequently, didn't you?" Burdis was shouting to make himself heard.

"They came and they went. Who looked at them?"

"Maybe you didn't look at them," Anstruther said, "but only a thin partition separated you. Surely you must have heard some of their conversation. . . ." He stopped short. He was screaming to make himself heard over the competition from Julie's voice and from the din outside. "Names. Did you ever hear them address each other by name?"

"Never," Sid said. "Except maybe the old guy."

"Old guy?" Anstruther exchanged alert glances with Burdis. "What sort of old guy? What did he look like?"

"Like an older fella."

"How old?"

Julie finished his phone call. Sid said to him, "How old was' the old guy?"

"You mean Boot'?"

"Boot?" Anstruther looked at him sharply. "Was that his name?" Bureau Intelligence would be sure to have him somewhere in the files.

"Boot'. That was his name."

Burdis had his notebook and tiny silver pen in his hand. "Boot? Spelled like what you wear on your feet?"

"Nah," Julie said. "What I wear on my feet is spelled S-H-O-E."

He winked at Sid, who, after a momentary uncertainty, shook the walls with his laughter.

21

Eminence Griese ran his finger down the log of the President's schedule of appointments for the remainder of the morning: ten minutes with the minority leader, twenty with the Secretary of the Treasury, the rims of whose eyeglasses were square to match his economic theories, photographs with the Hemophiliac of the Year to kick off a fund-raising drive, fifteen minutes with the Speaker of the House to discuss his business relationship with his brother, an oil magnate under grand jury indictment, ten minutes with a dozen members of the House and Senate to witness (with photographs) the vetoing of a pork-barrel bill which would probably be overridden, a session with the Soviet ambassador, who would press for a little police brutality directed against demonstrating anti-Soviet Jews. . . . Best bet, Griese thought, would be to try to squeeze in between the Secretary of the Treasury and the Hemophiliac of the Year.

As it happened, the Secretary used only twelve minutes of his time, and Griese edged into the Oval Office smoothly before the Hemophiliac of the Year, a pale, sinfully handsome boy, and his press agents could stir.

"Em?"

"You're going on the tube tonight."

The President fingered the right side of his face. "Tell them to stay away from tight close-ups. I've got this damn hickey."

"It's just a tiny spot. Pancake makeup will hide it."

"Am I going to pardon him?"

"That's your decision, sir," Griese said solemnly, "to make

in that solitude of heart and mind where none but you can enter."

"Yes," the President said with his country-lawyer look. "What is the consensus?"

"The returns are still coming in, but it looks like a landslide for the pardon."

The President grimaced. "It's a loser whichever way you look at it. When is the nationwide—I assume—address to take place?"

"Eight o'clock, prime time. About fifteen minutes tops. Maybe you ought to cancel the luncheon with the women reporters."

"They'll be pissed off, they've all turned women's lib in their old age."

"Can't be helped. National emergency. I'll send a couple of speech writers in when I leave here."

"I don't want Rossi, he uses too many big words. I'm thinking of firing him or trading him off to the Vice President."

"You handle them very well."

"Oh, I can handle them all right, I just don't *like* doing them. My constituency would feel better if I fumbled them, but somehow, no matter how hard I try, I can't seem to botch them up. I'm a literate man, Em, it's a curse."

"The speech," Griese said. "Something on the order of: In this melancholy hour, when the heart of the entire nation beats to a sombre cadence, blah-blah, the most difficult decision I have ever faced. . . . On the one hand, these despicable blah-blahs, on the other, these honored remains typifying the most glorious tradition, blah-blah. I have had the high honor of serving in two wars myself. . . . And so I have turned, as I always do in times of great stress, to the wisdom of the great American people. And so, blah-blah, I have instructed lawyers of the Justice Department to prepare a full pardon—"

"Jesus, Em, they're murderers, too."

"We'll get that in the speech someplace and deplore it. Finally, looking right into the camera, tight close-up—"

"I said no tight close-ups."

"We won't let them go any lower than the eyes. Okay—an

apostrophe to the villains. We are keeping our part of the bargain. I cannot appeal to your honor, since you have none, but I warn you—if any harm comes to those beloved remains, I promise you, with all the authority of this great office, that we shall pursue you with all the resources and fury, blah-blah, unto the end of time. Then you address the remains themselves: Old Comrade, I promise you in the name of the American people that ere long you shall be returned, blah-blah."

The President shook his head. "Too much. I'll gag on it." The President put on his farmer face. "You're sure about the consensus? I mean, you'd better be damn sure about it."

"How often have I been wrong?"

"In this case, once would be once too many." The President looked at his watch. "Thank you for your help. I'd better get to my next appointment."

Hemophiliacs must vote right, Griese thought. He stood up. "I'll brief the speech writers and have them come by with a rough draft at lunchtime."

Griese went back to his office. His secretary was awaiting him with an anxious look and the telephone cradled between her breasts.

"The director of the FBI, Mr. Griese. He says it is of the urgentest."

"He would," Griese said, and, reaching very carefully between his secretary's breasts, took the telephone. "What is it, Director? I hope you understand that my time is at a premium?"

"I believe the subject is important enough to warrant your personal attention," the director said stiffly.

"Proceed, Director."

"I have just received a phone call from the warden of Lewisburg Prison. Rowan is raising hell. He is demanding an interview with the warden—"

"He is supposed to have been placed in solitary confinement."

"Somehow, apparently by prison grapevine, he has learned everything that is going on."

"Do we know he didn't know about everything before-hand? Never mind. Continue."

". . . interview with the warden and insisting on being allowed to make a statement to the press. According to the warden's description, he has gone berserk. The entire population is upset and is turning ugly. The warden fears an outbreak."

"Mr. Rowan is under no circumstances to be allowed to speak to anyone, especially the press."

"The warden stresses that the prison is being besieged by reporters. He has not allowed them inside, but they are getting unruly. Apparently it's quite cold up there—"

"Neither the warden nor Mr. Rowan is to be allowed to discuss this matter with anyone in any shape or form. Is that understood?"

"By me, certainly. But the warden strikes me as being highly distraught."

"Do you know where Lewisburg Prison is, Director?"

"Certainly."

"I wish you to leave for there at once. Your brief is twofold. First, to take over from the warden. Second, to speak to Mr. Rowan, *in camera,* and calm him. Inform him that the President will address the nation at eight tonight. You are at liberty to advise him unofficially that. . . . No, strike that. Simply reassure him that he will be kept abreast of events and that he will be allowed to make a statement to the media later tonight. If none of this is effective, have the prison doctor knock him out."

"Have the prison doctor *what?*"

"You will kindly leave for Lewisburg at once. If there are any unusual problems, phone me. Good-bye."

He replaced the phone between his secretary's breasts and went into his office. He sat down behind his desk and called the chief of his graduate students.

"I want a complete dossier in our own inimitable manner on Francis Rowan, as soon as possible."

"Roger, Em. Will do. Soonest."

What barbaric diction for the holder of three master's and

two PhD's, Griese thought. He hung up the phone with a sigh.

Em Griese spent the hour between one and two, less taxi time back and forth, in the Massachusetts Avenue apartment of Bullets Beall.

Once his arrival had been announced—"a certain government person, madam," the discreet and well-greased doorman had said—Bullets had unlocked the door and then stretched out on the sofa, partially for seductiveness, partially because she was five and three-quarters inches taller than Griese and thought that she looked like a freak when she stooped.

In fact, her solicitude was misplaced. Tall girls with long legs were almost a fetish with Griese. It was not like him to delude himself consciously in anything concerning himself, nor did he do so in this matter. As a young man he had been rejected often by most girls and always by tall girls. Now, as a personage, girls of all sizes vied for his favors. Aware that he was motivated by the deprivations of his youth, he had been heard to say, "Psychologically, I am a Jack the Ripper, but a benign one."

"Darling, darling Em," Bullets Beall said as he entered, and by artful accident exposed one incredibly long leg to the hip.

"I am neglecting affairs of state to be here," Griese said. "I have exactly one half hour to spend with you."

"Oh, Em, what a marvelous tribute to me." Bullets sat up and gracefully bared the small projectile breasts that had earned her her nickname. "Come to my bazoom, darling."

Griese regarded the room with distaste. Bullets Beall's apartment was underwritten by Senator Domertz of Michigan, and his taste was literally Grand Rapids. Griese—who owned a buhl cabinet and a Biedermeier breakfront and a Pleyel piano—had complained bitterly about it, and Bullets, in deference to his sensibilities, had attempted to persuade Senator Domertz to refurnish. But the Senator had refused flatly—not out of miserliness or even lack of taste, but from

The Talisman

loyalty to the city that each six years delivered a thumping majority of its votes.

"I have no time for anything," Griese said. "I am here solely to replenish my soul by feasting my eyes on you."

"Feast!" Bullets said. She stood up and threw off her negligee—six feet two inches of glowing flesh. "Replenish!"

"Please don't do that," Griese said, and, with his fingers crossed, added, "I'm only human."

"Take your clothes off," Bullets said, "or I'll rip them offen you." It was a line from one of her pre-Senator Domertz porno films, and she had found it as effective in real life as in the cinema. "Fuck me," she continued, "or I'll burn up to a shrivel!"

Griese, who had seen the film, rather liked the line. "I could shrivel up myself, Bullets. But there's no time."

"My flesh insists upon you!" Bullets crossed the room and threw herself into his arms. Griese clasped her and tilted back to gaze at her face, with its million-dollar bone structure.

"Don't torture yourself, my dear Bullets."

Bullets improvised. "What's my little torture compared to your torture?" She slid her hand down between his legs. "How can you attend to the affairs of state in this magnificent condition?"

"I'm not indispensable, or at least so some people say." He placed his hand on the top of her head and forced her downward, gently but firmly.

She sank to her knees in front of him, thinking, as she did, that if it was possible to lose one's hair from having one's head pushed downward, one would have been bald ages ago. So unnecessary, since all anybody had to do was ask her straight out for a blowjob and she would oblige pronto. But men, at least politicians, were very delicate about such things.

"I'll bet you're handling that business of the Unknown Soldier." She unzipped his fly and probed for him inside his underpants.

"Correct."

She held him in her hands and cooed rapturously.

"In addition to everything else," he said. "But if you run a major country—"

"Don't talk, my darling, not at this sublime moment."

"Don't *you* talk," Griese said.

At three Griese put a stop to his poll. The list was already cumbersomely long and massively weighted—never mind the face-saving qualifications—for buying back the Unknown by pardoning Francis Rowan. He lay back in his chair to reminisce on his brief but satisfying encounter with Bullets Beall, but was presently interrupted by the entrance of one of his graduate students, who had just gotten wind of a distressing incident. It seemed that at a luncheon of members of a subcommittee of the House Foreign Affairs Committee with a delegation of Frenchmen from the Ministry of Finance, a serious breach of protocol had occurred. Discussing the stealing of the Unknown's remains, a Congressman had become incensed by a Frenchman's apparent indifference and had shouted, so that everyone at the luncheon table could hear, "One more fucking Gallic shrug out of you, and I'll flatten you!"

"Foreign affairs," Griese said, dismissing his aide. "Not my table."

He returned to contemplation of Bullets Beall, lazily tumescent, but was interrupted again, this time by the appearance of the junior Senator from Iowa, towing a middle-sized, elderly, atrociously dressed lady with lovely blue eyes and an utterly beguiling smile.

"You must forgive this invasion, Em," the junior Senator said. He stood out in front of the lady and rolled his eyes up to the ceiling in open appeal. "I know how busy you are. . . ."

Griese controlled his irritation. The junior Senator was vice-chairman of the Agriculture Committee and the key to passage of the President's pet farm bill. And so he waved the Senator and the lady to chairs. The lady smiled at him. Griese, without knowing why, smiled back at her.

"You are always welcome in this office, Senator," he said. "And your charming constituents, as well."

"Oh, more than a constituent," the junior Senator said.
"Permit me to introduce Mrs. ah. . . ."

"Jane Worley," the lady said. "Of Waterloo, Iowa."

"Mrs. Worley." the junior Senator paused and said with
great distinctness, "Mrs. Worley is a district co-leader in my
bailiwick and one of our very finest workers."

A mitigating circumstance, Griese thought. The Senator
was up for reelection next year.

"Mrs. Worley flew in from Waterloo today to tell me her
story," the junior Senator said, "and asked to see the President. It is a most, ah, interesting story, and I felt that as the
President's surrogate you should hear it." The junior Senator tugged at his collar. "Mrs. Worley agreed to allow you to
stand in for the President."

"How gracious of you, Mrs. Worley. Pray tell me your
problem."

"Oh, it isn't *my* problem, sir, but *yours,* that is to say, the
President's. I believe I may be able to comfort him in his
hour of travail."

"That is very kind of you indeed," Griese said. If we must
suffer fools, he thought, then let them be fools with well-
modulated voices.

Sweating visibly, the junior Senator said, "Mrs. Worley has
reason to believe that the Unknown Soldier of World War
One is her father. Is that correct, Mrs. Worley?"

The lady nodded. "He is Corporal Thomas T. Worley, of
Waterloo, Iowa, my father. And while it is true that I *do* know
that he is the Unknown Soldier of World War One, it is my
mother who told me so. The credit belongs to Mother."

Griese stared at the junior Senator, who averted his gaze
and said, "Perhaps you should get to the point. Mr. Griese is
a very busy man."

"Sir," Mrs. Worley said, "I wish the President to know, on
behalf of my father, that we support him in whatever decision he elects to make, in his hour of travail."

"I am most grateful, madam," Griese said, "and I shall con-
vey to the President your good wishes and pledge of support."

"Mine do not count for so much," Mrs. Worley said, "since

I am an ordinary person. But I believe that my father, as the person closest in spirit to them, speaks for all the other unknowns as well as for himself. I hope this will be of comfort to the President."

The junior Senator rose and nodded to Mrs. Worley, who also stood up. "Thank you very much, Em, most kind of you."

"Oh, no," Griese said, ushering his visitors to the door, "the kindness is yours, for bringing Mrs. Worley to me. And to Mrs. Worley, of course. And above all to Corporal Thomas T. Worley, for his sympathy in the President's hour of travail."

He shook the junior Senator's trembling hand and touched his lips to Mrs. Worley's delicate gloved one. She gave him her lovely smile.

He returned to his desk and, under column one, PAY UP, wrote the names of Mrs. Jane Worley and Corporal Thomas T. Worley. Then he squared the papers away and took them to the Oval Office.

Against all odds in a town of its size, there were three Ed Raphaels in the Elmont phone book. Robbins, his skin tone darkening, as it did when he was frustrated, began to feel haunted. Since his triumph of last night with Garrison and Agnes O'Reilly, everything had turned sour. His stinking alarm clock had failed to go off and he had slept through until noon. Then, when he got to his garage, his bike was hemmed in against a wall by three cars, and no one was around to extricate it. He routed the attendant out of a coffeee shop up the street and dragged him back to the garage by the neck. The attendant, muttering darkly about somebody's head running into a tire iron one dark night, moved the cars. Robbins rolled the bike out and discovered that the rear tire was flat. It took another half hour, after he chased the attendant out into the street in a rage, to dismount it and roll it a half-dozen blocks to a puncture shop.

But at last he was on his way. He whizzed out to Elmont doing a steady seventy and, when he wasn't stopped by a traffic cop, took that as an omen that his luck had swung back again. But then, after parking and thumbing through the phone book, he had to turn up three fucking Raphaels. He stared angrily through the glass of the phone booth and hated what he saw: a post-office substation, a five-and-dime, a pork store (what kind of stupid specialization was that?), a crummy department store, a Middle America-type street with a handful of women shoppers, all of them in pants, some dragging whining kids. . . . He turned back to the phone book: Raphael Edward, Raphael Ed, Raphael Edgar A.P. But then he noticed that Raphael Ed and Raphael Edgar A.P. lived at the same address on Forest Avenue, and—the Robbins God was in his heaven, after all—following Raphael Ed was the notation "eng." The number for both Forest Avenue entries was the same.

He dialed the number, with his left hand poised to disconnect if anyone answered. He listened to the ringing phone and looked idly at the substation, a storefront with a counter and a back room where a couple of civil-service types were busy doing nothing. He was about to hang up, cursing the return of bad luck, when the phone was lifted and a breathless voice said, "Hello."

The PO substation gave him an idea, and he didn't disconnect. Instead he said, "Residence of Mrs. Edgar Raphael?"

"Yes?"

"Ah, this is the post office. You Mrs. Raphael?"

"Yes, this is Mrs. Raphael."

The voice still breathy, but with an underlay of excitement or apprehension. "We have, ah, special-delivery letter for Mrs. Raphael. Tried to deliver it but nobody home."

"Oh? Yes, I was out picking up my child at school." Then, after a pause, "Does it say who it's from?"

"Ah, well, reason I'm calling, got another trip out your way. If you're staying home, I can make delivery. Okay?"

"Yes. Thank you. I appreciate it. It's very nice of the post office."

"Right. About ten minutes."

He hung up. *Robbins, no matter how many times you've heard it, I have to tell you again: You're a fucking genius.* He slid out of the phone booth. Partway down the street a meter maid, nattily dressed in a navy jacket and skirt, white boots and white cap, was tagging a Volkswagon at an expired meter. He asked her the way to Forest Avenue. She gave him explicit directions. He thanked her boyishly and she smiled. Busty woman in her early forties. Did housewives become meter maids to sublimate sex drive unsatisfied by busy husbands? Find out some other time. Make her keep her hat and boots on and hold a parking ticket in her teeth. Kinky. He went back to his bike and drove out to Forest Avenue.

It was a broad development street, lined with houses of three or four basic types, each plot garnished with struggling bushes and trees. Every driveway contained a small car, a tricycle, a plastic bat, a football, an uncoiled green hose, a slanted basketball net over the garage door. The Raphael house was at the end of the street, where Forest Avenue looped around and came back on itself. The driveway contained a car, a plastic bat, a tricycle. . . .

Robbins parked his bike beside the car, a faded blue Toyota. He walked up a flagstone path that curved over the lawn to the front door. He scuffed his feet on the doormat and rang the bell. Up the street three women stood in a driveway chatting; at the house next door a child was pedaling a tricycle with manic energy through an open garage door.

A woman wearing an expectant smile opened the door. Robbins lowered his shoulder and butted her back into the house. He followed, slamming the door shut behind him. She was still staggering backward, fighting for her balance, but she tripped on the edge of a carpet and fell. He took a couple of steps forward and dropped down on top of her. A small boy sitting in an armchair looked on with wide sober eyes.

Robbins raised himself on his palms like a man doing push-ups. He had knocked the wind out of her and she was gasping. She had nice skin, delicate and transparent. Her eyes were shut, and she was rolling her head from side to side as if to convince herself by repeated denial that nothing had happened.

"Open up your eyes," Robbins said.

She opened her eyes to slits, but directed her glance at a point past his shoulder.

"Look at me," Robbins said.

She gave him a quick frightened glance. "Please," she said weakly.

"You ever see anything scarier in your life? Well, I'm even worse than I look."

"Please. You can take anything you want, but please don't hurt us."

"What's your name?"

"Mrs. Raphael. Please don't—"

"I mean your first name."

"Paula."

His arms were beginning to tire under his weight. He lowered himself onto her. Her body shook with a sudden spasm.

"I won't resist. You won't have to hurt me." She rolled her eyes toward the boy in the chair. "Jason, don't look. Hide your eyes."

The boy looked at her expressionlessly. He didn't move.

"Please, may I send Jason out of the room? I don't want him to witness. . . ."

Robbins shifted to an elbow, relieving her of some of his weight. "You think I'm going to rape you?"

"You're not?" Her eyes filled with tears. "Oh, thank you."

"No rape and no robbery," Robbins said. "Just a little bit of info."

"Won't you let me send Jason out of the room?" She looked at him in bafflement. "Then what *do* you want?"

"I want you to tell me where Edgar Allan Poe is." She went rigid under him. "And if you don't tell me, Paula, I'll do such horrible things to you that they'll make Jason into a raving maniac for life."

"He isn't home. Honestly, Eddie isn't home."

"I know that, Paula. Where is he?"

"I don't know. Please believe me. I really don't know."

He read the lie in her eyes; it was easy for an expert. "Paula, I'm getting mad. I'm giving you fair warning, I'm a fucking animal."

"I don't know where Eddie is. I swear." She tried to convince him with her eyes; they were still lying. "Why do you want to know? Who are you?"

"I'm going to rape you after all," Robbins said. "Turn over on your stomach."

"Oh, no, no, not rectally. I beg of you, not rectally."

"It's the only way I'll rape anybody," Robbins said. "I've got this enormous—"

"I would tell you, honestly, I would tell you if I knew." She struggled and came up on her elbows. "Jason, go out of the room. Mother wishes you to leave the room. At once. Go upstairs and read a book."

Jason's eyes flickered for a moment in his immobile face, but he made no attempt to get up.

"Who's Eddie with?" Robbins said. "Doc?"

The fear in her eyes turned to despair. About five minutes more should do it, Robbins thought. He dropped down on her heavily.

"Oh, Jason, Jason darling. . . ."

I can do it in less than five, Robbins thought. He pushed up lightly onto his feet and crossed to the armchair. He lifted Jason out of the chair, then sat down with the boy on his lap. Paula Raphael screamed.

"One more peep out of you," Robbins said, "and I'll kill this boy."

She clapped her hand over her mouth and stretched her hand out to him imploringly. She began to sob. Her complexion was no longer flawless, but blotched. Robbins put his hand around the boy's neck. It was long and slender and felt as fragile as glass. The boy was looking directly at him. He tightened his fingers slightly and the boy gagged. Paula Raphael scrambled across the floor toward them on hands and knees.

"Let him alone. I'll tell you anything."

She was swaying in front of him, her hands clasped under her chin in an attitude of prayer. He gave Jason's neck a squeeze. The boy's eyes filled with tears, and he made a hoarse choking sound. It went on even after he had relaxed his grip, then turned into a paroxysm of coughing.

"Keep quiet," Robbins said. "You're not being choked now."

The boy cleared his throat with effort and spoke for the first time. "I'm not coughing because I'm being choked, but as a consequence of being choked."

He looked down, and Robbins thought with astonishment, He doesn't want me to read in his eyes that he thinks I'm dumb. Paula was clawing at his arms. He pushed her off.

"Paula, that's enough fooling around. I'm going to break Jason's neck if you don't quit stalling and deliver."

Her eyes were agape with terror. "I'll deliver, I'll deliver." She fell forward and began to kiss Jason's bare knee. He drew his knee up and away from her.

"Where is Ed?" Robbins put a slight pressure on Jason's neck. The boy's tongue came out and he gagged.

"I'll tell you. He's on the Cape. Cape Cod." She reached out for Jason. Robbins held her off.

He gave Jason's neck a token squeeze. "Where on the Cape?"

"Near the town of Orleans."

"Never mind *near*. Tell me exactly."

"Between Orleans and Eastham, or North Eastham, I'm not sure. The house . . . it belongs to Caroline, to her father, his name is Dr. Meade, he's a dentist. I don't know the address, it's directly on the water, they've been there for years, anybody will know the house, Dr. Meade. . . ."

He slowed her down and made her repeat everything. She wasn't lying now; she had given over entirely to her terror for the boy's safety. Edgar Allan Poe Raphael was now the forgotten man.

"Who's there with him?"

"Doc and Booth and Asbury and the young fellow, I forget his name." She was trying to kiss the boy's knee again.

"How many of them altogether?"

"Four or five, I think, and Caroline, she's Ken Booth's girl-friend."

Robbins smiled at the boy. "Thank you for your cooperation, Jason."

"I didn't cooperate," Jason said. "I was passive. *She* cooperated."

He stood up, with Jason in his arms, and gave the boy to his mother. She enveloped him, engulfed him.

"Have they got a telephone?"

"Yes, no. . . . I mean, there's a telephone, but it's disconnected."

Robbins smiled. "Much obliged, Paula. You, too, Jason."

"Don't thank me," Jason said. "I didn't cooperate. She did."

He turned a look of cold hatred on his mother, and Robbins thought, He's pissed off, he despises her for spilling the beans. Maybe a little disappointed, too, he may have wanted her to be raped, maybe not rectally, but who knows, maybe *especially* rectally.

At the door he paused and said, "Do you know what your Eddie is into, Paula?"

She shook her head vigorously. She was lying, but it didn't matter now.

"Please don't hurt Eddie, he's a wonderful person. Who are you?" Her voice rose on a note of incipient hysteria. "Who *are* you?"

"I am called Ishmael," Robbins said in a sepulchral voice.

"That's from *Moby Dick*," Jason said. "In choking, the cause of death is asphyxiation. Did you know that?"

Asphyxiation, that's your fate, sonny, Robbins thought as he opened the door and went out, but at least *I* would have done it quickly. He crossed the lawn to his bike and zoomed around the loop. He looked at his watch as the almost identical houses of Forest Road slid by him. A little past four. He would have to stop for gas and to pick up a map, and then it would be about four and a half or five hours out to the Cape. The deadline wasn't until midnight. Enough time for a fast shooter on a lucky roll.

22

From the morning onward their collective mood had shifted through the scale of emotions like a wildly fluctuating fever chart, with two significant peaks: the visit of the cop and,
much later, the radio announcement of the President's tele-
vised address at eight o'clock.

After Caro had turned the cop away at the door, Booth's
interest in her account had been curiously detached. Listening, half listening, he had stared at the curve of her breast
and felt a compulsive urge to reach out and draw the folds of
her robe together. But Caro had become conscious of it herself and closed the flannel about her neck. Asbury, carrying
the M-16 parallel to the ground, holding it with one hand at
the balance, was tense and grim, and Booth had thought,
He's unfulfilled, he didn't get the chance to shoot anybody.

Doc needled him. "Asbury may *look* frustrated," Doc said
blandly, "but he didn't really want to shoot the cop, that's
why he left the safety on."

Asbury's eyes dropped to the rifle, and his hand moved toward the safety. It was off. Doc laughed.

Asbury's eyes showed the white of anger, but Caro calmed
him. "Let's all relax. He won't come back. I saw to it."

Asbury's mood shifted. Smiling, he said, "You told him no
soap, right?"

"Yes, I told him no soap." Her voice was level. She paused
and then said, "There has never been any soap, either."

She's said too much, Booth thought as Asbury snorted. So
there had been soap, sometime in the distant past. It's not
any of Asbury's damn business. Nor mine, either.

Asbury said, "My guess is there *was* soap—night after night after night under the stars with the sand scratching your back."

He had scored, Booth thought, watching Caro color. She started to answer him but was drowned out by a sudden deafening blare of the radio. Asbury turned his wrath on Raphael, who looked around in confusion and apology and turned the radio down.

"Fucking technical genius doesn't even know how to turn a radio on!"

Doc laughed, and Asbury, after glaring at Raphael for another few seconds, joined in. Inadvertently, Raphael had saved the day; the tension was eased. But for how long?

". . . at eight o'clock this evening."

A loud roar drowned out the radio announcer's voice. Booth signaled for silence and after a moment they quieted down.

". . .White House will not confirm that the subject of the President's brief address will be a response to the ransom demands, but the news secretary, in answer to a direct question, would not deny it. . . ."

There was another outburst, this time derisive. Only Raphael expressed anxiety. "But if that's what it's about, why wouldn't they say so?"

Even Dover joined the laughter. Booth said, "They're creating a little suspense to build up the audience. If the subject hasn't been announced, he could be confessing to an infidelity or announcing the end of the world."

"Or," Doc said, "that's he's going to diddle his wife coast to coast to set an example for the country in healthy marital relations."

"Yes," Raphael said, "but even if he does talk about it, how can we be sure he's going to meet our terms?"

"Because he doesn't want us to blow the shit out of his Unknown," Asbury said.

"Because he has no choice," Booth said, and saw Raphael relax. The Old Man has spoken, he thought. We're going to blow them right off that hilltop, men. . . . But the Old Man was merely being inspirational. He didn't really know that they wouldn't all die on the slope of the hill.

After the announcement about the President's address they had all subsided into something resembling a coma of boredom. They looked, Booth thought, like the dregs of a defeated army, played out and with no resources left for coping with their captivity. And, confined to the house, they were indeed prisoners. The radio, tuned to a Boston news station, bumbled on mindlessly, chewing its desiccated cud of repetition.

Only Caro and Dover seemed profitably occupied, and he knew that even that was more apparent than real. They were playing chess, but Dover was no match for her. Caro's face was fixed in an impatient set as she moved her pieces abruptly and decisively. Dover studied the board intently before each move and kept exclaiming in surprise or dismay as his pieces were captured or enticed into deadly traps.

Raphael had been rummaging for a half hour in the shelves for a book that might please him. The books were an accumulation of fifteen or twenty years of aimless summer reading: paperbacks which simply piled up because Caro's father was too lazy to dispose of them. Doc had brought along his own reading, which Agnes O'Reilly had stolen for him from the hospital library: *Cleft Palate: Surgical Procedures.* "You never know," Doc had told Dover soberly, "when some guy might need an emergency cleft-palate operation." But Doc was turning the pages idly and studying the grotesque plates with indifference.

Asbury, stretched out on the floor, said, "If I don't get out of this fucking place, I'm going to go ape. I feel like a fucking caged bird."

The radio, near the end of its half-hour cycle of news, was marking time with fillers before it started over again with the major events of the day. Booth listened idly. An investigative reporter was scoring the venality of a food company that filled its huge package with more air than cereal. A woman with a brittle confident voice told the inside, "exclusive-with-me" story of a Hollywood marriage that had foundered. A weatherman droned on about a two-feet-deep snowstorm in Idaho. A voice simulating a dog's barked out a message for a home burglar alarm. A man reunited with his sister after a separation of sixty years relayed his joy in a voice cracked by age and wonder.

Raphael, in an ill-tempered outburst, said, "How could your father stand reading all this junk? There isn't even a popular book on science."

"He isn't a scientist," Caro said. "He's a dentist."

Asbury, speaking to the ceiling, said wearily, "Raphael, why don't you shut up?"

"Right," Doc said. "Asbury is right. You haven't got any resources for passing the time. Be like Asbury."

"What's *he* doing?" Raphael said indignantly.

"He may seem to be just lying there and doing nothing, but he's actually growing his hair."

Dover's chair scraped back suddenly and he leaped to his feet, rattling the chessboard. Caro reached out reflexively and steadied the board. Dover was trembling, his face intense but abstracted, as if his action had taken him by surprise and must now double back on its tracks to find a motivation. Then his arm shot out at a downward angle, and a finger came out of his fist and pointed fiercely at the floor.

"How am I supposed to concentrate with *that* down there?" His voice was high, angry. "Not a one of you gives a goddamn about it!"

Caro, straightening the fallen chessman, said, "You had a promising game there, Bobby. Sit down and finish it."

"We all know it's there, Bobby," Booth said. "We just don't talk about it."

"It's a *person* down there!" Dover's eyes welled with angry tears.

Booth shook his head. "It's a dead soldier who was killed a long time ago. You know what a dead soldier counts for, Bobby. In fact you've killed a few of them yourself."

"Everybody has his hang-up," Doc said. "Shut up, Bobby, and sit down and lose your chess game."

"You go to hell," Dover said.

The Talisman

Booth forced patience upon himself. "The less we think and talk about it, the better. Everything has been done, Bobby, nothing can change. Don't think about it."

Caro was watching him with her head tilted quizically. She's reading my mind again, Booth thought, she knows that I'm rationalizing as much for myself as for Dover.

"There's nothing wrong with thinking about it," Dover said. But his anger had expended itself. "Nothing wrong."

Caro said, "I've got the board set up again, Bobby. It's your move."

Dover hesitated, his gaze drawn to the board, perhaps struck by something he saw there, and Caro beckoned to him. She'll throw the game, Booth thought. Dover made a hopeless throwaway gesture, as if dispossessing his feelings, then sat down. Another crisis averted, Booth thought wearily.

Asbury was standing at the door to the porch, his hand reaching out for the knob.

Booth could not have said later how he had managed to get between Asbury and the door unless he had jostled him, which might have been the case because Asbury's eyes were fired up. Even less could he understand the cold pleasure he took in the prospect of imminent violence.

Asbury had moved or been pushed back a step, but he closed the distance at once. Their faces were an inch or two apart, and their chests were actually touching.

"Move out of there," Asbury said.

There was a steeliness to his voice that was pure performance and yet, at the same time, was deadly serious. It occurred to Booth that for Asbury the two were identical: When he was serious he was acting, when he was acting he was serious.

"No," Booth said. He heard the tremor in his voice and knew that Asbury, being Asbury, would misread anger as fear.

"Last chance," Asbury said. "Step aside, Colonel."

Asbury wouldn't make his move until he had fulfilled the dramatic potential of the scene, and he would telegraph his

303

intention. Booth focused on Asbury's moist gleaming teeth and thought with vicious satisfaction, I'm going to hit him squarely in the mouth and bloody his smile.

"Okay, Mr. Booth. . . ."

The flicker he was waiting for appeared in Asbury's eye, and he saw, as if in slow motion, the dropping shoulder. . . .

"It's all right. I'll go with him."

Caro had pushed between them, and her hand weighed on Asbury's right arm. His fist was still clenched, but it seemed already to be forgotten. A slow smile was wiping away the calculated ferocity of his expression.

"I told Perry I wasn't alone," Caro said. "There's no harm if anybody spots us walking on the beach together."

Asbury opened his fist and turned his smile toward Booth, mocking and victorious. I should have hit him when I had the chance, Booth thought, but simply nodded his head in acceptance of Caro's reasoning.

He stepped aside. Caro linked her arm through Asbury's, and they went out. In Spain, Booth thought, they deployed cows to soothe fighting bulls who might otherwise kill each other. Caro was pacifying Asbury—and him—as she had done with Dover a few minutes earlier. But, in Spain, were the other bulls sick with doubt and jealousy?

Griese ignored the flashing phone as long as he could, then snatched it up in irritation.

"I am not to be disturbed when I am in session with the party fund raisers for anything less than an atomic explosion. Were those not your explicit instructions?"

"Yes, sir," his secretary said.

Griese smiled flatteringly at the fund raisers. "Well, then," he said, "has there been an atomic explosion?"

"I don't know if it's atomic," the secretary said. "I can ask him."

"Ask *who?*"

"The director of the FBI. He is phoning from Lewisburg Prison. He says there has been a bombshell and must speak to you at once. Shall I ask him if it is atomic?"

"I'll ask him myself. Put him through." He turned to the fund raisers. "Sorry, gentlemen." The fund raisers, who were all bald in much the same way, nodded their shiny heads understandingly.

The phone clicked, and the FBI director said, "Sir, I'm afraid I have a bombshell."

"Atomic?" Griese winked at the fund raisers. "Please report, and with a little less literary color."

"Francis Rowan categorically declines a presidential pardon."

Smiling for the benefit of the fund raisers, who were feigning lack of interest, Griese thought, For once I was not all-knowing, all-seeing. It must not happen again.

"As I'm sure you know, Mr. Griese," the director said, "acceptance of a pardon is discretionary upon the part of the pardonee."

"Does he know that?"

"He is aware of his rights in the matter. I advised him, however—"

"Hold it." Griese covered the phone and said to the fund raisers, "An emergency of the gravest national concern, gentlemen. You will forgive me."

When they had filed out sullenly, he returned to the phone.

"You advised him, however, of what, Director?"

"I advised him that we could avail ourselves of a perfectly legal way of circumventing his declination. Technically, an inmate of a federal prison has been remanded to the custody of the U.S. Attorney General. Thus, the Attorney General, at his pleasure, may simply release the prisoner."

"And what did he say to that?"

"Nothing. He merely smiled."

And he could well afford to smile, Griese thought. He would refuse to leave the prison, maneuver the warden into throwing him out by force, directly in front of a large group of reporters hungry for news. . . .

"Do you have new instructions for me?" the director said.

"Yes. Return to Washington."

"But, sir—"

"At once." He hung up and buzzed his secretary. "Ask the news secretary to come to my office."

"Yes, sir. Sir, was it atomic?"

"That is classified information."

He called one of his assistants and instructed him to arrange for immediate helicopter transportation and told a second to contact the warden of Lewisburg and apprise him of his coming. He phoned Bullets Beall himself to postpone his dinner date.

"Oh, Emmy darling, I thought we would eat in tonight. I've bought a huge steak and that Tokay wine you like so much, and. . ."

"It was unwise of you to form a liaison with the most important man in the United States."

". . . and I'm so horny, Emmy darling."

"I'll get back to you as soon as possible. Maintain the status quo."

The President, with his television coach hovering over him, was practicing his speech in front of a mirror propped up on his desk. It was an old scratched glass set in an ornamental gilt frame that he had brought from his boyhood home. He called it his lucky mirror.

"The eyes straight ahead," the TV adviser was saying as Griese entered with the news secretary. "Remember the way Nixon's eyes used to shift furtively? We don't want that. If you must alter the head-on stare at the camera, move your whole head. You've got the profile for it. Left profile is slightly better, however."

"Leave us," Griese said to the television adviser.

The TV coach looked outraged. "I take my orders from the President of the United States."

"Now, Em," the President said. "An occasional hint of courtesy wouldn't hurt you."

"It would cramp my style. However. . . ." Griese smiled graciously at the coach. "I have business of the most sensitive nature to discuss with the President. If you have top-security

The Talisman

clearance, you may remain. However, since I know you do not, you are required to leave."

"Sir?" The coach turned to the President.

"I'm sorry," the President said. "Hang around in the staff room and I'll call you back in a little while."

When the coach had departed, Griese said, "Rowan will refuse to accept a pardon." He paused politely for the President's exclamation of astonishment and then went on. "We can evict him legally, but then he'll denounce us, and the remains will be destroyed. I'll go to the prison myself and try to persuade him to change his mind. I'm leaving in a few minutes."

The President shook his head. "I don't get it."

"What about the eight o'clock address?" the news secretary said.

"Yes," the President said. "I don't want to have to learn the damn thing if I'm not going to give it."

"The speech is on unless you hear from me to the contrary," Griese said. "I'll try to phone before seven thirty."

The news secretary looked aghast. "They've all rearranged their programming. I can't call them at seven thirty—"

"What the hell has this Rowan got in mind?" the President said.

"A deal of some sort," Griese said. "He's either smarter than any of us thought, or much stupider."

The news secretary said, "Look, it's five thirty already. If I give them notice right now—"

"*You* look," the President said in his farmer's voice. "If the President of the United States can learn a speech he might never give, your fine television friends can afford to be slightly discommoded, too."

"May I leave now, Mr. President?" Griese said.

"Straighten that fella out, Em," the President said, "or we're all going to die in the fallout."

"Don't even leave your office to pee," Griese said to the news secretary. "You'll hear from me."

"It's a rotten job," the President said.

"I thrive on rotten jobs, sir," Griese said.

307

"I meant mine," the President said.

"Mine, too," the news secretary said under his breath.

Griese paused at the doorway. "Not a word of this must leak. If it does, good-bye Unknown. Shall I send the television cockroach back in?"

In a helicopter bearing him northward (the army's newest and fastest) Griese studied the voluminous material his undergraduates had put together on Francis Rowan. In addition to providing him with information which might be tangentially valuable to him, it also helped divert him from the possibilities of aerial disaster, a factor one could not ignore, given the whip hand natural forces held over a presumptuous construction of metal, wood, and alloys. Beyond that he relied on his belief in the essential sobriety of a dimly perceived Providence, which would see no humor in destroying one of its finest human assets in a commonplace accident. He was aware that sooner or later he would go the way of Machiavelli, Talleyrand, Metternich, but only in a remote and as yet threatless future.

He first refreshed his memory with the facts leading up to Francis Rowan's imprisonment: Three young antiwar bombers of a building on a Midwest campus, during the hot years of university rebellion, had driven cross-country and asked for refuge in his farmhouse near Gettysburg. Granted. "Three of God's creatures, who had perhaps overreached in their pursuit of an ideal, sought a place to rest their heads and contemplate their actions. As two thousand years ago I would not have turned away the Holy Family, so I could not refuse these brave but confused young men. I do not suggest that these three young men are the Trinity of this century, merely that, as with the Holy Family, they were sorely pressed and in need of charity. Was that not enough for me to open my house to them?"

A pompous ass? Worse, Griese thought, he is that most impenetrable of humans, the True Believer.

He skimmed the accounts that followed: huge force of troopers and federal agents, tipped off by some young Judas (also one of God's creatures?), surround the farm, call for surrender, are met by gunfire. More appeals, more gunfire. A special appeal, to Rowan himself, by a bishop of his own (recent) faith rushed to the scene. Bishop calls upon him as a recent man of the cloth to avoid bloodshed in the name of God, to surrender his young apostles. More gunfire, and the bishop, who has exposed himself in his zeal, is thrown roughly to the ground for his own safety and, comedy touch, falls on bullhorn and breaks a rib painfully. More gunfire. Special Agent Solaitis is killed by a ricochet.

Consultations. Rush the farmhouse? Kill its occupants in a hail of bullets? No. Compromise of a sort. Tear-gas launchers lob canisters through the windows. The door opens, and a figure appears, choking, streaming tears. Put out of his misery by an overeager trooper. The other two youths and finally Francis Rowan stumble out into the daylight. No further shooting; they are captured intact.

Rowan is charged with a variety of crimes, the worst of which is murder. Bad enough. But then rumors begin rising: He had exhorted the boys to resist, to become martyrs; he had reloaded guns, like a pioneer's wife under siege by hostile Indians. He had actually taken his place on the firing line and pumped bullets out in the direction of the lawmen. All of this, in the event, sworn to by one of the surviving two young men, repentant and, perhaps, offered a deal by the prosecutor.

The grand jury indicted. The trial was held with much fanfare. The apostate youth swore that Rowan had fired. The other denied it, claiming that Rowan had in fact beseeched them to surrender without violence. But under cross-examination he had been forced to admit that he had not kept Rowan under observation the whole time. Rowan himself on the stand: denied he had fired. Dignified, passionate, impressive. But, goaded by the prosecutor, he aired his political views. Fatal. Alienated the jury. Guilty. Off to prison, claiming he had been framed, which, in Griese's estimation, was most likely true, a neat collaboration between the apostate youth and the ambitious prosecution. And so a thorn was plucked from the paw of the Establishment.

And the thorn remained imprisoned through the inter-

vening years as the war ebbed and flowed, corrupting whatever it touched, impoverishing a nation physically and eth-
ically; remained in prison as the war ended, as it faded from
the scene, abiding only as a persistent virus poisoning the national memory; remained in prison while all about him were
being freed: a little amnesty, a little more, then unconditional amnesty. But he was not a veteran, had neither resisted the
draft nor deserted, and so remained in prison, not quite forgotten, an occasional rallying point rather than a real issue.
Until now, when he had been suddenly thrust back into the
limelight by a crime perhaps more subtle and satirical than
its perpetrators knew.

With a sigh Griese turned to other documents: police and
FBI reports, abominably written; profiles in the newsweekly
magazines; articles *contra* the man in conservative media (humorless, painting him black as the devil) and *pro* in liberal
media (humorless, painting him with "understanding") and
radical media (humorless, painting him as a martyr).

In his vibrating crate, shuddering through the air over
Pennsylvania farmland, Griese turned the pages rapidly,
hoping to extract some detail that might help him in his coming negotiations. Only son, handsome boy, pampered by parents and two horse-faced sisters. Said to be descendant of
Henri, Duc de Rohan, noted Huguenot leader of early sev-
enteenth century. Lawrenceville, brightest boy in the school.
Class picture: round-cheeked and beautiful with wavy blond
hair. Yale, football, prize philosophy student, and new look:
cheeks flat, high bone surrounding now far-gazing eyes, still
extremely handsome in more adult mode. Divinity school.
Period as missionary in Africa, captured by backward tribe
and almost eaten. Rescued by intrepid British policeman said
to be model for Scobie in Graham Greene's *Heart of the Matter,* but not by Greene or by the policeman, so take with grain
of salt.

A needless stricture, Griese thought. It is the doctrine I
live by.

Back to Francis Rowan. After return from Africa, owing to
glamour of having nearly been eaten, quickly advances, gets
desirable post as second banana in most fashionable church

in New York. Then, like Leonard Bernstein for Koussevitzky, steps into the pulpit to substitute on short notice for top banana, who comes down with laryngitis. Reads such a fiery sermon that he makes the newspapers, shakes up the fashionable parishioners, whose wives, dazzled by that masculine, high-fashion, handsomely boned face, proselytize ardently for removal of top banana. They succeed. Rowan does not disappoint them. Accepts promotion.

So far a somewhat unorthodox but not unstable career. Then the turn. Takes leave of his church for six months to wander through India, Asia, Asia Minor, Africa again. Photographed frequently in long floppy shorts and bare chest (handsomer than ever, more romantic, eyes sinking ever deeper into bone, full speed ahead toward the fanatic look) among paupers, beggars, lepers, children with distended bellies, men and women with limbs missing or half devoured by appalling tropical diseases. Two expressions on his face as he passes among these *misérables*: tender and caring in repose, unbelievably sweet in the smile. Bucking for saintdom, a *nouveau* Schweitzer. Ah, yes, he meets Schweitzer, who, perhaps sensing competition, is brusque. Still, Schweitzer gives grudging praise: "He speaks knowledgeably of Bach."

Return to New York and the pulpit. First sermon after his return, a full house. Eyes burning, he informs them, right off the mark, that they are all scum: the men financial bandits, the women whores. Gasping, the ladies wonder if he will name names. The men, immured in their aura of wealth and expensive body cologne, listen expressionlessly and agree tacitly that their fancy preacher is finished.

Rowan beats them to the punch. Farewell, this is farewell, he says, slowly taking off his robes (an ecclesiastical striptease—will he remove the dark trousers as well?), he is resigning his post, this citadel of the rich, the pampered, the useless.He has failed to save their mortal souls, but places no blame upon them for *he* is the miscreant. The fault is not in our flock, but in ourself. Unworthy though you may be, I am unworthy of you.

He leaves the pulpit, head bowed atop the athlete's shoulders, a beam of light striking the sun-streaked hair to gold....

Next stop, predictably, Appalachia, where, as he tells the press, "the bodies are wasted, the spirits shrunken by poverty and the inexorable certainty of a hopeless tomorrow...." Three years in Appalachia, performing emergency midwifery, binding up running sores with the tail ripped from his own spotless shirt, rocking dying phthisics in his arms as they take their final agonized breaths, tilting valiantly and vainly against the indifference of governmental agencies.

Came the Vietnam War, and Rowan found his great cause. Carrying picket signs in front of the Pentagon, chaining himself to the White House fence, riding in crowded patrol wagons, spending the night in various jails among bearded pot-smoking antiwar youths, serving as master of ceremonies at draft-card-burning parties, throwing plastic bags filled with animal blood at prowar Senators, defacing the walls of police stations, making speeches at rallies, marching in demonstrations, marching, marching, marching....

Fifteen minutes from takeoff Griese closed the dossier on Francis Rowan. Through the Plexiglas window, risking a look below, he saw in the near distance the squat buildings of the prison, resembling a sand castle built by some painstaking but unimaginative child on a nightmare beach.

Creaking, bucking drafts, the helicopter dropped down toward the prison.

23

Directly below, in front of the main gate, a small crowd of people was congregated. Demonstrators? No, Griese thought, any demonstrators worthy of the name would have shaken their fists at the craft and called upon it to crash. It was the news reporters, of course. The helicopter floated over the prison wall, past the guards in the towers, and set down gently in the center of the prison yard. A man in a black suit waited prudently until the spinning rotors came to rest, then came forward. Griese took his extended hand and allowed himself to be helped down.

"Welcome, sir, I am Warden Raupp. Welcome to Lewisburg."

Griese looked at the colorless stone and uncompromisingly blocky lines of the buildings. "Nice place you have here," he said.

The warden, who looked like a high school disciplinarian, eyed him suspiciously for satirical intent, but appeared to have determined that he could not in any case challenge this Very Important Person. "Thank you, sir," he said.

"I don't wish to rush you, Warden, but I'm running on an extremely tight schedule. I must see Francis Rowan at once."

They hurried across the yard to the nearest of the buildings. "The prisoner has been brought up, sir," the warden said, "and is awaiting your arrival." He paused at the entrance to a barred gate and looked behind him. "Your pilot will remain with the airship, I trust? It bothers me to see anything come over those walls so easily."

The Talisman

"He is armed to the teeth," Griese said. "Those news people—you have not spoken to them or allowed them entry?"

"Certainly not. Nobody gets into this prison who I don't want to get in."

A guard opened the gate for them and they went inside. A few feet farther on there was another gate. It opened for them and clanged shut behind them. They were in a form of reception hall. Two more gates led into the prison proper. Above them rose tiers of cells, a mass of steel cages that chilled Griese. Three convicts gazed down at them over a railing. They were talking to one another, smiling secretly, and Griese read their thoughts: Now if we had *him* as a hostage.... He was relieved when they hurried through another gate to a bare corridor. Still another gate, and at last, they stopped before a heavy wooden door guarded by a turnkey armed with a carbine.

"This is Officer Roger Donovan," the warden said. "He will stand guard inside the room during the interview."

"I must be alone in the room with the prisoner," Griese said.

"This man is a dangerous criminal, sir."

"I am a karate expert of black-belt class," Griese said blandly. "Open the door."

The guard unlocked the door, which opened inward.

"Nevertheless," the warden said, "I will instruct Officer Donovan to enter at the first suspicious sound."

Griese went inside the room, and the door swung shut behind him. Rowan sat at one side of a wide table with his back turned. Griese walked around the table, and Rowan watched him as he sat down.

"Good afternoon, Mr. Rowan," Griese said.

"Who are you, sir?"

Griese read Rowan's *curriculum vitae* in his confident, well-modulated voice. He was wearing prison twill, the shirt open at the throat. He was well tanned but unshaven, and there were circles under his eyes. Studying his handsome features and sunken eyes, Griese could understand how women would love him and disciples follow him. He was a Savonarola who had—at least thus far—escaped the consuming flames.

Smiling, Griese said, "I thought perhaps you might recognize me. I am Emerson Griese."

"Yes, of course." Rowan gave him a fleeting smile of apology, and Griese thought, Good manners, encouraging, people with good manners hate to say no. "Well, then, sir." Rowan's eyes glowed with a dark light. "Since you are Emerson Griese and have a reputation for omniscience, perhaps you can tell me why I have spent the better part of two days in the hole?"

"You have been in the hole? A man of your stature?"

"I have been there before, for verifiable infractions of the rules. That is one thing. This time I was put there without cause."

"I do not have an explanation, sir. But I *shall* have one, from the warden, and if it does not satisfy me, I will have the man removed from his post."

"You can do *that?*"

For the first time Rowan seemed impressed. Bear in mind the correlatives, Griese told himself. In this kingdom of the blind, the warden is king.

"I can do anything," he said. "I wish you to understand that, please, Mr. Rowan. I can do anything."

Rowan nodded his head, then took Griese by surprise. "I thank you. It is the first time in five years that I have been called mister."

Another clue, Griese thought. Even a martyr can regard imprisonment, or at least its humiliations, as *infra dig.*

"I do not hold you to be my inferior. In some ways, in fact. . . ." He produced a disarming smile. "But no, I can't say it, it would damage my reputation if it ever got out."

"I had not expected you to be so"—Rowan paused, searching for a word, and Griese thought, Say "charming," so that the next time I visit my late father's grave, I can throw it in his face—"quite so candid."

Still smiling, Griese said, "I find candor to be a useful weapon in argument with very intelligent people. They can't resist it. I exploit this particular weakness."

Rowan's lids lowered over his intense eyes. "I have *many* weaknesses, Mr. Griese."

Humility, Griese thought, the eighth deadly sin. He said, "You mustn't flagellate yourself." Was this the kind of advice to offer a flagellant? He struck off in a new direction. "Although I have not been an admirer of your cause, I must tell you that it pains me to see a man of your abilities confined here in this place, with these, well, with these *common* felons."

"These common felons are my peers, as in Africa, in Asia the tribesmen were my peers." He looked reflectively at the brushed concrete ceiling. "Certainly confinement is onerous. Yet I have few complaints. The food in this place . . . yes, I would say that the food is an outrage. You may be interested to know that we have formed a Committee of Ten to deal with the warden directly."

"Indeed?" The man was a born committeeman.

"But you didn't come here to discuss these aimless matters. Shall we, perhaps, arrive at the gravamen of your visit?"

Griese nodded. "It is my understanding that you refuse to accept a presidential pardon. No reason given."

"One doesn't explain one's motives to the fascist director of the fascist FBI."

"He also informed you that we could release you despite your declination of the pardon?" He paused to take in Rowan's secret smile. "But such an action could be catastrophic to our purpose, so we will say no more about it." He paused again and watched Rowan's smile broaden. "Surely, Mr. Rowan, you must yearn for freedom?"

"Yes. And I shall have it." Rowan stared at him. "I have heard you spoken of as Machiavellian, Mr. Griese."

"Flattery. I serve my prince as best I can, with what wits I have, but Machiavelli was a theoretician of power. I have no theories. I am merely an improviser."

"As of today, sir, I too am a Machiavelli. I have learned guile."

The worst of all possible worlds, Griese thought, the lamb attempting to play the fox. He said politely, "Would you explain yourself, sir?"

"Until today," Rowan said with an almost mocking smile,

"I have been the hero of the antiwar left. After today I shall be the hero of the entire country."

"I don't quite take your point." But, oh, dear, I believe I do.

"It's quite simple. I refuse the pardon. I refuse to gain my freedom by means of criminal extortion. You see?" His smile turned sly. "By taking a stand on principle, for decency, I turn the public's sentiment around toward me three hundred and sixty degrees. I do not *need* your pardon. The nation will *clamor* for my release."

Suspicion confirmed. "Perhaps we might have some refreshment." Griese rose and circled the table to the door. "And then I will point out the fallacy of your reasoning." He pounded his fist on the door. "Trickiness isn't as easy as it looks, you know. One can't simply become Machiavelli overnight. It takes long years of practice and, if I may be personal, a certain warped brilliance."

The door opened, and the guard, holding his carbine at the ready, said, "All finished, sir?"

"Bring us coffee and perhaps something to munch on."

"You'll detest the coffee," Rowan said. "It's high on the list of complaints of the Committee of Ten."

Functioning like Raphael's vacuum pump, Asbury's departure had evacuated the tension in the room, but left Booth in despair. Jealousy. There was no other way to characterize it, and the word itself, defining lush melodramatic passion and the hot unfinished ardors of youth, stood as a rebuke, an accusation that mocked his fifty years, his experience, whatever knowledge of himself—and of others—he had painfully acquired through those years.

Caro had asked to go with Asbury to relieve a dangerous situation. But had she also wanted to be alone with him? His mind rode the ambivalence like a seesaw, ending always where he had begun. And it did no good to remind himself that he had no valid claims on her.

Raphael had at last selected a novel from the shelves, but he was not enjoying it. He seemed puzzled as he turned the pages, as if he were reading in some dark science that he could not understand and hence disapproved of. Doc had returned to his textbook on cleft-palate surgery. Dover was playing against himself at the chessboard and, from the look on his face, still losing.

Lying on the sofa, Booth stared at the blind drawn over the window facing the bay. Beyond that window, past the porch and the patch of tough brown grass, down the abrupt drop of the bluff, lay the beach. And somewhere on the beach, at the base of the bluff, hidden from the blind houses above. . . . The urge to rush outside and down the steps to the beach became intolerable. He pressed himself deeply into the sofa, as if to increase his body's density, to collaborate with gravity so that it was impossible for him to get up.

Yet when the *crump* sounded outside, he was on his feet at once and moving swiftly toward the window. He pushed the metal slats of the blind apart. Above the rippling water a plane was climbing, and another was coming in. A splash as the second plane missed the target ship and started climbing.

"It's all right," Booth said over his shoulder. "They're plastering the target ship again."

He lingered a moment at the window, searching for Caro and Asbury. Searching where, since the beach was not visible: on the water, in the curving sky? With a gesture of self-revulsion, he let the slats snap back into place. He circled around the sofa—he could not lie there again staring at the blinds—and turned up the volume of the radio.

". . . Emerson Griese, who has flown to Lewisburg Prison, where Francis Rowan is incarcerated."

The silence in the room was suddenly intense. The announcer went on: Chief Presidential Adviser Griese, in a high-speed helicopter, had flown dramatically over the prison walls. A sharp-eyed reporter outside the walls had spotted him in the descending helicopter. Griese's office at the White House would neither confirm nor deny speculation that Griese's visit could be interpreted as indicating that the President had decided to pardon Rowan, with Griese making the arrangements. . . . The announcer concluded the report with a reminder that his station would carry the President's address at eight o'clock.

Booth lowered the volume of the radio. Dover said, "Griese. *That* guy. I don't like it."

Booth said, "The rumor makes sense. Arrangements do have to be made. . . ."

Doc smiled and said quietly, "We've got a winner, gentlemen."

Raphael was shaking his head. "Why send Griese? He's so damn tricky."

Dover addressed a question to Booth, who didn't hear it. He was listening to footsteps on the porch. He faced the door, rigid. It opened and Caro came in. She looked cold. Asbury followed. Booth avoided looking at Asbury. If there was so much as a smile on his face he would smash him, kill him. Asbury moved past him, and he could not help glancing at his face. Surly, the mouth turned down. Caro was taking off her jacket. Their eyes met, and although he tried to mask his feeling of relief, he knew that she read him clearly, as she always did. He looked for resentment, but all he could see in her eyes was pity.

"No, really," Griese said. "Please have them yourself."

The hand that held the plate of cupcakes—nestled in fluted papers, topped with chocolate icing—shook with fear and avarice, and for the first time Griese fully sensed the deprivation that prison meant. The hand continued to offer the plate, a triumph of breeding over base desires.

"I'm on a low-cholesterol diet," Griese said, "and I may not have them." Still the plate was extended. "And low sugar and salt-free as well."

The plate was withdrawn and set down on the table. Rowan's hand captured a cupcake and brought it with sensuous slowness toward his mouth. He bit down and chewed with restraint—a thirsty man must sip water, not gulp it—and a froth of crumbs appeared on his lips. He cleaned them up with his tongue, then popped the remainder of the cupcake into his mouth. His eyes rolled upward orgiastically. Griese pretended not to notice and poured coffee into their mugs.

"I give you fair warning about the coffee, Mr. Griese."

Griese sipped. "But it's quite good."

Rowan snatched up his mug and sniffed at it suspiciously before tasting. He slammed his mug down on the table. "It's the warden's own coffee, don't you see?" He looked around him angrily.

"Do have another of those cakes, Mr. Rowan."

Rowan raised a cupcake to the threshold of his trembling lips. "I'm sorry to go on like this. Although our concerns in here may seem insignificant to you, to us they are large and passionate matters. Shall we return to the subject?"

Griese nodded, but waited for Rowan to start munching. *Let him tranquilize himself.* "I have a question. Do you know the people who perpetrated this crime on your behalf?"

Rowan shook his head. "You disappoint me, sir. Would you expect me to say so, even assuming that I knew?"

"You misunderstand me. I mean—do you know their character?"

"I could sing paeans to it, Mr. Griese."

I can do without your songs, Griese thought. "Knowing their mettle, do you believe they will destroy the remains of the Unknown if their conditions are not fully met?"

Rowan sipped the warden's coffee appreciatively. "Allow me to give you a little lesson in revolutionary guerrilla activity, Mr. Griese. A threat must never be made unless it is to be carried out. Otherwise our terrorist tactics would become useless. Yes, sir, they will destroy the Unknown."

"They will feel no qualms?"

"No qualms."

"It is, after all, harmless dust," Griese said. "To be sure, I understand better than most that harmlessness is no protection against serious purpose." He shrugged. "But I am, after all, a famous cynic. What of yourself, Mr. Rowan—a churchman, a fighter for selfless causes, a man of compassion. . . ?"

His teeth stained with chocolate icing, Rowan smiled pityingly. "I am no longer a churchman but a revolutionary. Are you asking me to be sentimental about a poor soul who died in the service of an imperialist war? You surprise me, sir, with the poverty of your argument."

"Oh," Griese said softly, "it is not at all my argument. Like you, I shed no tears for the dust in the coffin. I am simply establishing a basis for demonstrating that you have taken a stand on a false premise. Sir, you will not become the idol of the nation by rejecting a pardon, but the blackest scoundrel of all time."

Still smiling, still chewing, Rowan cocked his handsome head skeptically.

Like most noble men, he is simple, Griese thought, and said patiently, "For you and for me, for the grave robbers, the remains are a pawn, a nothing. But for the public, for all those tens of millions who do not enjoy our advantages of clear-mindedness and insusceptibility, they are everything. If such were not the case, I would not be here. If such were not the case, the remains would never have been stolen."

Rowan said, "Those are obvious points." But he seemed bewildered, at sea.

"The power to save the remains is no longer ours," Griese said. "That power has passed over to you."

"Of course."

"But with the power, responsibility has also shifted from us to you. And with responsibility the burden of blame."

"Will you come to the point, sir?"

Griese suppressed a sigh. "Mr. Rowan, please follow me closely. If the blame for the destruction of the remains falls upon *you*, will the populace, who fervently do not wish to see the remains destroyed, will the populace then clamor for your release?"

Rowan's expression froze. The chocolate cupcake into which he had just bitten seemed to have lost all flavor.

By sheer speed and boldness the news secretary cut off a Cabinet member who was slow in rising from his chair, and slipped into the Oval Office.

"I'm sorry, Mr. President, to break in this way, but I must have a minute of your time."

"You look terrible," the President said.

"Sir, we have to do something about the eight o'clock speech. It's almost seven thirty."

"Well, the speech isn't till eight, is it?"

They had the notion that networks were toys, the news

secretary thought. "I can't wait to the last minute. They need time to inform their affiliates, to reschedule their programming. . . . It's very complicated."

"Yes, well," the President said a little impatiently, "everything is complicated. They have no monopoly on that, do they?"

"They're already setting their equipment up. I simply must give them some decent notice."

"You don't want to offend them, is that it?"

"I can't afford to, sir. You see, they think they're important, too."

"They have no monopoly on that, either," the President said. "Well, what do you want to do?"

"I can't wait to hear from Griese. I'd like your permission to phone him at the prison."

"Okay. Call him."

Griese experienced an uncharacteristic feeling of pity for Rowan and even contrived a charitable explanation for his confusion. Captivity had dulled his senses, scaled them down to an animal-survival level. Nevertheless, he would finish him off.

"So you see," he said, "you really have no bargaining position at all. In fact, it was a delusion to think you ever had one."

Rowan's fingers crept along the splintered wooden table and felt blindly for the plate. There were no cakes left, only a few tiny crumbs. Get him some more? No, I may be able to make an advantage of his need for a fix.

Rowan passed a hand across his brow. "I may have misjudged the situation, but. . . ." Some focus returned to his eyes. "An aspect of this is eluding me. I take your point, but I believe there must be an alternative." He paused before saying grimly, "I mustn't let you win."

"No rush," Griese said agreeably. "Winning doesn't mean that much to me, but I recognize a checkmate when I see one."

Rowan's furrowed brow suddenly smoothed, and his face lit up. "No, not checkmate. Stalemate."

Griese looked at him warily. What new idiocy had he concocted to throw the orderly game into disarray?

"Stalemate," Rowan said. "Agreed that if I decline a pardon and as a result the remains are destroyed, I will be branded a scoundrel."

"Even your fellow prisoners will loathe you."

"But I am already established as a scoundrel. It can only become a degree or two worse. But you"—he smiled with satisfaction—"now you, too, will become a scoundrel."

"Hardly. The world will know I tried to persuade you to accept a pardon."

"We will both share the blame." His confidence seemed restored. "But while blame can do little to worsen my lot, it can hurt you grievously. You haven't come here because of concern for me but for yourself, which is to say your President, your administration. Will you admit that?"

"I admit it. You're correct in theorizing that if the remains are destroyed we both become abominations. But there is no profit in that for anyone. Don't you see that by accepting the pardon we can both become heroes?"

"Ah, yes, but that *does* put it up to *me*, doesn't it? You are helpless to make us both heroes. Only I can do that." His triumph was open. "Which means that I hold the trump card."

"I am not a prisoner," Griese said. "You are. Your freedom is at stake."

"You are a prisoner, too. Otherwise you would get up and walk out. You are my prisoner. You must barter with me for your freedom."

He wasn't this shrewd earlier on, Griese thought. Can it be that his intellect has found sustenance by touching on mine, as Antaeus renewed his strength in contact with the earth? "Very well," he said with a sigh. "What are your terms?" Never attempt to defend an indefensible position.

Rowan stared at him blankly across the table.

There was a knock at the door. The guard entered, carbine first. "Phone call for you from Washington."

24

Coldly, Griese said, "You have interrupted me at a critical juncture in my negotiations."

He sat at a large desk in the warden's office. It held some papers and a coffee-making machine. A barred window—narrowing the difference between warden and prisoners—looked down on the yard.

"I'm sorry, Em," the news secretary said, "but I had no choice. I've simply got to tell the network people whether the speech will go on or not."

"There is *your* timetable and there is *mine*. Mine is not attuned to the concerns of the networks but of the nation."

"I'm going to tell them we can't go on at eight."

"Do as you wish. Nothing is settled here."

"If you could give me a definite time, I can try to have it rescheduled."

"I can't guarantee anything where sensitive negotiations are concerned."

"It is my function to be loved by all," the news secretary said gloomily, "or at least hated by no one. I wish you would try to help me, Em. I haven't even thought of a reasonable excuse to give them for the eight o'clock cancellation."

"Anything will do, so long as it isn't the truth. You know how to lie at least as well as I do. Say the President has suffered a sudden indisposition. Make it a common-touch illness. Diarrhea? No, too undignified. What about a crisis in the Middle East? Call in some Arab minister or other; he'll love the attention."

The Talisman

"I'll do that," the news secretary said. "There's always a crisis there. But what about rescheduling the speech?"

"Make it for ten thirty," Griese said testily.

"Yes, but if we're still not ready for them—" The news secretary groaned.

"Your technical problems bore me," Griese said, and hung up. Through the barred window the yard below was empty except for the helicopter. In the cockpit the pilot appeared to be asleep. Griese shrugged and left the warden's office.

The warden was reading a magazine in the anteroom. "It's almost time for me to go home. But if you wish, I'll be glad to stay on duty."

"Stick around," Griese said. "And send some more coffee up. No cupcakes."

When Griese reentered the room, Rowan was wearing a casual look that in no way—to the practiced eye—concealed his tension. He had little capacity for deception, Griese thought. Of course, he didn't need it. He held the trump card.

"Forgive me," Griese said as he took his seat. "A call from Washington on an entirely unrelated matter."

"Of course. I'm sure this is merely one of the lesser problems you deal with in an average day."

"I will be candid with you," Griese said. When your position was known to the enemy, nothing was lost by telling him what he already knew. "On this day nothing is more important to me or to the nation than yourself. You are A-Number-One Top Priority, Mr. Rowan."

The guard entered with his carbine and a pot of fresh coffee. He placed the pot on the table and left. Rowan looked disappointed.

"They've run out of pastries," Griese said. "I'm terribly sorry." He filled both mugs with coffee. "Now, where were we?"

"You were trying to convince me that we could both be national heroes."

Griese shook his head. "We had gone beyond that point. I

325

had asked you for terms. I am ready to meet any reasonable request."

Rowan sipped his coffee and smacked his lips with enjoyment, whether because of the coffee or the strength of his position Griese couldn't judge.

"While I was gone from the room," Griese said, "you had ample time for thought, and unless I'm mistaken, you have formulated your demands."

"You are aware that I could simply walk out of this room and leave you high and dry, Mr. Griese?"

Griese shrugged. "You won't. We are by now old enough adversaries to have come to rely on each other's behavior."

"It won't do to take me for granted." Rowan looked grimly defiant. "Now, sir, I must ask you—please don't be offended—what is the extent of your authority in dealing with me?"

"On my own, Mr. Rowan, I am a very powerful man. In this case my power is enhanced to the ultimate degree. I speak for, and with the voice of, the President himself."

Rowan nodded. "And now I must ask you, risking offense again, whether your word is to be trusted."

"Yes, sir. Not because my word is my bond, for it is not, but because our interests parallel each other. I could not hurt you without hurting myself, and I have never been known to do that."

"Very well. My first condition: No inkling of what has gone between us must ever be revealed. Do I have your word for it?"

"Better than my word—my vanity. I have been bested."

"Next, I wish to be permitted to leave the country."

"Agreed."

"Tonight. Immediately upon my release."

"Certainly. I will arrange for the issuance of a passport."

"You see," Rowan said, "contrary to your assurances, I will *not* be regarded as a hero."

Griese's protest was cut short by a decisive gesture of Rowan's hand.

"The point is not worth arguing, because, sir, I do not wish to remain here. I no longer respect this country. Much more to the point, I no longer wish to help this country in its predicament."

"As you wish. Where do you want to go?"

"I realize that I will not be welcome everywhere. I will expect you to make extraordinary efforts on my behalf if it is necessary."

"Agreed." *And it would be nice if you chose Siberia.*

"I wish to go to Africa."

"*All* of Africa?"

"The period I spent in Africa was, perhaps, the happiest of my life. I was *useful*, Mr. Griese. No man can or should aspire to anything more than to be useful."

"In what way may I help?"

"I am not a private person. I am a convict. I have had a highly unfavorable press. I suspect that my entry to an African country may have to be negotiated on a high level. Are you prepared to undertake this?"

"To the best of my ability. Which country do you have in mind?"

"It doesn't matter, providing it is one of the underdeveloped countries."

"There are many such. I may have to consult with the State Department in order to—" He interrupted himself. "Wait. Do you know Gabon, on the west coast of Africa?"

"I have passed through it. I met old Schweitzer there."

"They'll love you in Gabon. A splendid little nation, but very poor, even benighted. It offers glorious opportunities for a man like you. And, as it happens, I know the Prime Minister personally."

"Gabon. I think it may be suitable."

"Perfect. A country sorely in need of, ah, what you have to offer it. I will phone the Prime Minister at once. And perhaps, if it is handled skillfully, there might be something in the government . . . perhaps not *in* the government, but a consultancy?"

"As to Gabon, yes. As to the consultancy, no. I wish to go to the people, to be among them and of them."

Griese started to rise. "I'll put in a call to the Prime Minister at once."

"Not yet, sir. There are still other conditions."

Griese frowned. "You aren't overdoing?"

"It is my wish to be put on a plane tonight, immediately after my release."

"Done. I will have my office make the arrangements. We will be happy to pay your fare. First class."

Rowan nodded. "I accept because I have no funds of my own. Now, the final condition. I wish to speak to the American people."

Griese slumped in his chair. "I can deliver everything else, Mr. Rowan, but I cannot deliver the American people."

"I will make a short speech, a sort of valedictory address, at the airport, perhaps. I ask that the press and the television people be present."

Griese spread his hands. "I don't control the media."

"All you need do is announce the time and place of my departure. I assure you that the media will be there."

"What will you say? How can I sponsor you, in view of the things you are likely to say?"

"I will say nothing that is pleasing to you, granted," Rowan said, "but there is something in it for you nevertheless. It will be proof to the people who have the remains that you are acting in good faith. They don't exactly trust you, you know. But if they hear me and see me board the plane. . . ."

"Will you give me some idea of what you intend to say?"

"I will speak my mind, sir."

"About me, about the administration?"

Rowan shook his head. "About this country. I will deliver some home truths."

Griese sighed. "Very well, sir, you have a deal. I will go now to phone my friend in Gabon."

A disembodied hand slid in and out of the picture, leaving something on the anchorman's desk. The anchorman finished his sentence and picked up a yellow sheet torn from a teletype machine. He scanned it rapidly and faced the cameras again.

"We have just received word"—he offered the sheet of paper in evidence—"that the President's address, slated to be delivered at eight o'clock this evening, has been canceled."

He cocked his head at the paper.

"This information comes from the White House and is complete at this time." He raised his brows to someone off camera as if to say, "Is that *really* all?" and shrugged his shoulders. The screen went blank, then came alive again on a slow-motion commercial featuring a girl depilating her leg.

Asbury was the first to speak. "They're fucking us around! They're not going to deliver!"

"What does it mean?" Dover's innocent eyes were pleading. How did the Old Man interpret it? What move would the Old Man recommend? Well, the Old Man couldn't figure it, either. And his counsel? Heads down, don't panic.

"Keep it down." Booth pointed at the TV screen, where the girl, her long legs dehaired, strode confidently down a street filled with strong-jawed, admiring male models. "Let's see if anything else comes through."

Doc said, "Asbury, you're gorgeous and strong and brave as a lion, but you think with your asshole."

Unexpectedly Raphael came to Asbury's defense. "I think he's right. They're trying to pull something."

Asbury's eyes were wild. "I'm going to wire up—"

"Shut up," Booth said. On the screen the anchorman had returned. He held another sheet of paper in his hand.

"A crisis in the Middle East"—the anchorman allowed himself a skeptical tilt of the head—"is given as the reason for the postponement of the President's address. No, as of now postponement is not the right word. Cancellation." He waved the paper at the camera. "The announcement comes from the White House news secretary. It does not elaborate on the Mideast crisis other than to say that the President will see Ali Aqbar, the Syrian ambassador. As you know, the President was expected to speak on the question of a pardon for Francis Rowan. If the situation changes, we will of course break in. . . ." He introduced the sports announcer.

Booth, shaking his head, avoiding Dover's trustful eyes, said, "It's peculiar and I don't pretend to understand—"

From a corner of his eye he saw Asbury striding purposefully toward the kitchen. "Asbury, where are you going?"

Asbury paused and said with elaborate courtesy, "Sir, I'm going to the cellar. Colonel's permission?"

"What for?"

"Because I'm fed up with you silly bastards and I want to be by myself. Any objection?"

He was squared full around now, his chin outthrust in defiance, and Booth thought, We're in pointless confrontation again. Caro was staring at him. He shook his head. Asbury turned abruptly and went into the kitchen. The door slammed, and Booth heard the sprung steps singing under his descending weight.

Doc stood up. "I better go down after him."

"What for?"

"Because the—"

Raphael cut him off with a shout. He was pointing at the TV screen, where the anchorman, holding still another teletype sheet in his hand, was saying, ". . . informed that the President's address to the nation has been rescheduled for ten thirty this evening. We will bring you the address at that time."

"—because if I know Asbury," Doc said, "he's going to start fooling around with explosives." Booth sprang up. "Stay where you are," Doc said, "unless you think you can handle him better than I can?"

Booth returned to his seat.

Griese dispossessed the warden from his office and phoned the chief of his undergraduates.

"Yes, Eminence?"

"I must talk to the Prime Minister of Gabon at once. Gabon is a republic in West Africa, on the Atlantic Coast, just below the indentation in the outline of the continent. Formerly in French Equatorial Africa. Call State and have them initiate the call immediately—orders of the President."

He paused to allow his assistant's pen to catch up. An unwritten law: When Eminence spoke, verbatim notes were to be taken.

"If the Prime Minister is not in his office, which seems likely, since it is roughly one o'clock in the morning in Gabon, try his residence. If he is not there, he must be tracked down. He is then to be put through to me here." He read off the warden's number. "Do you have all that?"

"Yes, Eminence." A hesitation. "But suppose the Prime Minister cannot be located."

"He is to be found at all costs. Don't take any crap from State. Tell them this is an emergency of the first order. They are to use all their red-alert mumbo jumbo to effect the call. Gabon won't have much of a phone system, but it probably works where the Prime Minister is concerned or the operators get their hands chopped off. Maybe State has a hot line or a lukewarm line. At any rate, they know how to cut telephone red tape when there's an emergency. I will expect the Prime Minister's call in no more than twenty minutes."

He rang off, with some apprehension. It would need some luck. He had been rash in promising Rowan immediate action without allowing for the technical problems. Still, State had its tricks, it could move quickly when it had to.

He leaned back in the warden's chair and shut his eyes. For the moment the matter was beyond the reach of his active mind, and he would not tax his energies with things he could not control nor even understand, such as electronic impulses or whatever it was that made telephones work. He emptied his mind and, although he did not quite fall asleep, achieved a state of perfect relaxation.

The phone rang. He picked it up. "Emerson Griese here." Less than fifteen minutes since he had spoken to his assistant.

"Warden, a convict in Tier Five here has a swole-up belly and keeps hollering he needs a midwife—"

"Hang up," Griese said. He slammed the phone down and ran out to the anteroom, where the warden was doing a crossword puzzle. "You have a pregnant convict in Tier Five. Call there, but don't use this extension."

He went back into the office and shut the door. Half past eight. One thirty in Libreville. He shut his eyes and emptied his mind. The phone rang at twenty minutes of nine.

"Emerson Griese."

"Sir, we are waiting with your call to Libreville, Gabon."
An American voice, calm and well modulated, a superopera-
tor.

"Put it through."

Clicks, heavy intercontinental breathing, more clicks, and
then, tinny but clear, a man's voice: *"C'est M. Griese?"*

"Oui."

"Bien. M'sieu, voici son excellence, M. le Premier."

At once a deep voice spoke rapidly and unintelligibly in
what could only be an African dialect. Griese waited patiently
and, when the voice paused, said, "Your Excellency, forgive
me, but may I request that you speak in English?"

*"Pourquoi doit-on parler en anglais? Ce n'est pas ma langue. Je
préférerais parler en gabonnais."*

"Je suis désolé," Griese said, and switched to English. "I
wanted in the worst way to take a course in Gabonese at college, but to my astonishment they had none. It goes to show
that Harvard is much overrated."

A violent explosion turned out to be laughter, and then
the Prime Minister said in English, "Ah, Charlie, you kill me.
All right, I will conduct the conversation in the language of
colonial imperialism."

"Thank you, Prime Minister. I appreciate the courtesy and
I apologize a thousand times for waking you."

"You didn't waken me. I'm in a cathouse. Why are you calling, Charlie?"

For some doubtless unprofound reason, the Prime Minister had started calling him Charlie when they were class-
mates some fifteen years ago. In those days the future Prime
Minister had been a rapscallion princeling, heir of a ruling
chieftain in what was then a French colonial possession. He
had been bright but dissolute, a drinker and a womanizer
with a scandalous allowance. When he flunked out of Harvard, he had been ordered home by his father. Equatorial
Africa was not his idea of paradise, and he had vowed that he
would soon escape to Paris, where he would spend the rest of
his life in the pursuit of pleasure. Griese had in fact gotten a
card from him from Paris shortly thereafter. But with his father's death he returned to his own country, where he un-

derwent a remarkable sea change. He turned serious overnight, began agitating against French rule, led the fight for
independence from France, which became a fact in 1960,
helped draft the constitution of the new republic, and now,
at the age of thirty-eight, and for the past two years, was
Prime Minister.

"I am calling to ask a favor, Prime Minister. I pray you will
forgive me for presuming on an old friendship."

"Favors are tigers that stalk the forest and devour the teth-
ered goats of friendship," the Prime Minister said. "That is
not an old Gabonese proverb, Charlie. I just made it up."

"I realize I am at risk of helping the tigers eat up our
friendship. Nevertheless—"

"Come to the point, Charlie. Ask your favor, and I'll see
what I can do. For old times' sake, hey?"

"Thank you, Prime Minister. I wish to intervene on behalf
of a certain citizen of this country who seeks admittance to
your country."

"For what reason?"

"He wants to do good works."

"Oh, dear."

"He is a cleric, a former cleric, that is, a man of the highest
character. Several years ago he spent some time in Africa,
doing these good works, and now desires to return and carry
on where he left off."

"Why didn't he simply apply as an immigrant through the
regular channels?"

"Well, Your Excellency, we both know regular channels,
don't we?"

"I smell a rat, Charlie."

"He will be an asset to your country. Perhaps another
Schweitzer."

"God forbid! Don't tell me this joker also plays the organ?"

"He plays no instruments whatsoever, to the best of my
knowledge."

"Is he a physician?"

"No."

"Charlie, what is this bloke's name?"

"Oh, you've never heard of him. It's Francis Rowan."

The Talisman

A burst of Gabonese clattered over the phone. "Same old Charlie. Charlie, don't you think I read the news? That's the character who stole your Unknown Soldier. And you're trying to palm him off on poor emerging Gabon? Oh, Charlie, you kill me."

"You see, I have no capacity for guile. Prime Minister—can we make a deal?"

The Prime Minister chuckled. "Now we're speaking the *lingua franca* of diplomacy in earnest."

"What does Gabon need, Prime Minister?"

"Everything."

"Be reasonable, Prime Minister."

"Our most pressing need at the moment—you'll laugh, Charlie—is for cold cash."

"Impossible. Our cash position is killing us."

After a pause the Prime Minister said coldly, "Your move, Charlie."

"Airplanes? I know where I can lay my hands on some absolutely super, slightly used fighter jets."

"Cream puffs, eh? Piloted by little old lady schoolteachers?" The Prime Minister's laughter erupted. "Come again, Charlie."

"Ah, I have it. I'll lay on a state visit, twenty-one-gun salute, a White House reception, a cruise on the presidential yacht. Think of what it will do for your prestige in Africa."

"Charlie, you're sadly out of touch. You fellas are *vieux jeu.* Arabs, Charlie, it's all Arabs these days."

"Farm implements?"

"Let's get back to cash."

Griese sighed. "Name a figure, Prime Minister."

"Say one hundred million dollars?"

Griese shook his head and said nothing.

"Fifty million?"

"Five. And it means tapping discretionary funds. We simply can't tackle Congress with this kind of request."

"Under the table, eh, Charlie? Make it ten."

"You've got a deal, Prime Minister."

* * *

334

As Doc descended the springy steps into the cellar, Asbury glanced up without expression. He was leaning against the casket, pulling objects from an old-fashioned musette bag between his feet: three bright red sticks of TNT, several blasting caps, a kitchen timer, and a coil of slow-burning orange fuse. He set them down on the casket.

Doc moved closer as Asbury picked up the timer and peered at the electrical terminals. "It figures," Doc said. "You didn't score with Caro so you're going to do the next best thing—blow us all up."

Asbury didn't react. He took up one of the TNT sticks, weighed it in his hand, and then put it down again—with a reasonable amount of caution, Doc noted. Asbury was in one of his moods—his other moods—a sullen broodiness that was the underside of his normal bravado. Doc picked up one of the sticks of TNT. He weighed it in his palm for a second, then tossed it up in front of him and caught it.

"Christ!" Asbury said.

Doc laughed. "No interest in suicide, right?"

Asbury took the stick and replaced it carefully on the lid of the casket. His brows were drawn together, his lips pressed in a tight line.

"Me neither," Doc said. "So if you try to wire that thing up, I'm going to get a needle and put you out of your misery."

Asbury said listlessly, "I can put it together in five minutes."

"You don't have to. Word just came through. The speech goes on at ten thirty."

"It smells bad. What are they trying to pull?"

"How do I know? Maybe build up the suspense. We've got until midnight; there's plenty of time."

"Don't think you can talk me out of it. If they cross us, I'm going to blow this fucking thing sky high."

"I'm with you," Doc said.

"Booth isn't."

"Booth has problems. We'll blow it up—you've got my word for it."

"He's a fucking pantywaist."

Doc shook his head. "Booth is okay. Trouble is his heart bleeds in too many directions. He's a terrorist with a conscience."

"Stuff his conscience. I'll blow it over his dead body if I have to."

"That's the old Asbury I know and love. Let's put this shit away and go have a drink."

Asbury shook his head. "I'm going to prepare it. Suppose somebody finds us here. I want it all hooked up and ready."

"Nobody's going to find us here, you dumb bastard."

"What about that shitkicker cop?"

"Nothing. Caro handled him, and he went away."

"Maybe. I'm going to rig it up and put it into the casket."

"You'll blow us all up."

Asbury shook his blond head stubbornly. "It's like posting pickets. You hope nobody will come, but if they do, you're ready for them."

He took his gear from the casket item by item carefully and placed them on the floor at his feet. "I need a hand with this." He tapped the lid of the casket.

"What's going to prevent it from going off?"

"I won't attach the timer. There's no danger."

Asbury faced the casket with his fingers curled under the lip of the lid. He gestured to Doc to do the same.

"Maybe it's sealed," Doc said.

"No seal. All it takes is muscle. Grab hold."

"There could be a stink; it might knock you out."

"Ready?"

Doc fitted his fingers to the lip.

"Go," Asbury said, and strained upward. The lid lifted an inch or two and dropped back. "You sonofabitch, you weren't lifting."

"You feel something, Asbury? I mean, you grasp the solemnity of the occasion, or anything like that?"

"I don't feel shit."

"Booth's comrade-in-arms," Doc said, "died in the last good war. And you don't feel shit?"

Asbury's eyes flashed. "Shut up and help."

"Alley-oop," Doc said.

They both strained together, knees flexed, backs bent. The casket lid began to come up slowly. Doc caught a whiff of something, not powerful, but it was there. The smell of dissolution? The incense of heroism? He shifted his hands to the underside of the lid, grunting, laboring. The lid went up and back, balanced upright, and held.

"Jesus." Asbury was staring down into the open casket.

Doc was not prepared for what he saw. It was a mummy, or something partially mummified—a skeleton in a leather-like skin. Bone showed where the integumental covering had been eaten away by bacteria. It was nothing like a medical-school skeleton, clean, gleaming white bone. There was some hair, a lifeless dusty growth. There were a few shreds of cloth.

Asbury had withdrawn to a corner of the cellar. Doc heard him retching. He grinned. Great big hero. He rested his hands on the edge of the casket and inspected the remains. He frowned and peered closer, then straightened up and backed off slightly for perspective. He bent close again, his nostrils pinched against the faint odor of decay. He shook his head slowly from side to side. Softly, under his breath, in a tone in which awe and astonishment met midway, he said, "I'll be fucked!"

25

At Fall River, a town of huge brick many-windowed textile mills that resembled a set for a grim musical about industrial exploitation at the turn of the century, Robbins wheeled his motorcycle off the highway for something to eat. It was close to eight thirty, and he had been riding for over four hours. The early part of the trip had been slow and frustrating, and just before clearing New Haven on the Connecticut Turnpike, he had been pulled over by a motorcycle trooper.

"I could swear I wasn't speeding, Officer."

"So could I," the trooper said. "Who could speed in this congestion?" The trooper was standard: booted, goggled, tanned, shaved to a quarter inch below the skin line. "You were weaving in and out like a maniac and imperiling life and limb."

A talker. Maybe he could be handled. "Well, you know, Officer, I have this bike, and all these gigantic cars clogging up the road, so when I see an opening I slip gently into it. Same as you do."

"I'm a police officer."

"Very true, sir," Robbins said, conceding the point with a gracious nod of his head.

"You longhairs think you're above the laws of the road. Well, you're wrong."

Careful, Robbins thought, one of those hair-hating fascists. It might mean being tossed for dope. Thank God he was clean. Not that the bastard was above planting something on him if he took the fancy. "I guess it's true, Officer. I guess I really was weaving a little too much."

The Talisman

"A *lot* too much."

"Split the difference, sir? Say *medium* too much?"

He relaxed slightly when a flash of white teeth appeared in the trooper's tan. Not exactly a lovable smile, but better than the great-stone-face number.

"See your papers," the trooper said.

He handed over his license and registration.

The cop tilted his goggles up to read them. "Robin Robbins? Be damned."

"My mother," Robbins said. "She was wild about Robin Hood. But it could have been worse. Suppose she named me after Friar Tuck?" The trooper laughed again, this time with genuine amusement. Robbins pushed on. "Or if she was a feminist, I could have ended up Maid Marian Robbins."

The trooper made his smile disappear and said sternly, "You're a menace, Robin." He pushed his goggles down over his eyes. "If I let you go, what do you do?"

"I start riding like Maid Marian, sir."

The trooper scowled, but Robbins judged that he was just giving the screw a playful turn. Robbins maintained a look mixing sincerity and anxiety. The trooper handed back his papers.

"Okay, Robin Hood. But from here on you go straight like an arrow. Got it?"

Robbins smiled admiringly at the arrow joke. The trooper firmed himself on the seat of his bike and prepared to push off.

"After you, sir," Robbin said.

The trooper went with a roar. Robbins waved at him cheerily and, under cover of the noise, shouted, "Fuck you, Cossack."

The fate of a nation in his hands, he thought in a rage, and they were making him run an obstacle course. But he had held his speed down even after he reached open road with relatively little traffic. He found a Portuguese restaurant in the center of Fall River, drank a beer with his meal, and washed up. A helpful waiter who had lived in Provincetown gave him precise directions to his destination. He took off again, refreshed, his spirits revived. He crossed the Saga-

339

more Bridge and scooted at high speed toward the lower Cape.

Except in the broadest way, he hadn't planned ahead to a conclusion. Thought was the enemy of action, and he had unlimited confidence in his genius for improvisation. It hadn't failed him so far, had it? One thing at a time. Play it by ear and by instinct. First item: Scout the Meade house to make sure they were there. Not that he had any serious doubts about it, but it would also help him get the lie of the land.

After that? The local cops, and play it by ear again. Not the FBI. FBI was out because his connection with them might compromise his position with respect to the reward money. Boston cops? More sophisticated than the locals, but he would never be able to convince them over the phone, and besides, they couldn't get here in time. Not much over two hours before the midnight deadline. Local cops—they weren't allowed to accept rewards, either.

Which raised a vexing point. What were the specific conditions of the reward? For *recovery* of the remains? For information *leading to* the recovery of the remains? He hadn't paid much attention to it. Best to work fast and try to save the remains if he could.

Past Orleans he wheeled around a traffic circle and zoomed northward. A few minutes later, around a sweeping turn in the dark road, he saw the traffic blinker he had been told to watch for. *Blinker, here I come, the great improviser, the fierce avenger, screaming into the wind, great white teeth bared, whipping my iron steed on to a rendezvous with destiny. Who needs Phoebe? Phuck you, Phoebe!* But he would borrow from the FBI technique—only crank it up to high speed—by interrogating a local storekeeper, who would tell him where the girl lived. He would show that phucking Phoebe! Show his phucking phather, too!

He gunned his bike toward the blinker.

There was a group of two or three stores just off the road on the left, but they were dark, and so was a gas station except for a night light in the office. On his right was a cluster

of larger buildings and, just beyond the blinker, a small
structure with a spotlight shining down on a police cruiser.
The local police headquarters.

Robbins moved on slowly under the blinker, which was
strung across the road and swaying slightly in the wind. Redheaded asshole! Counting on stores being open at night in a
hole-in-the-wall country crossing!

He eased up and braked to a crawl. Okay, immediate
change of plans. O-kay. Broach the local cops right away. But
just to ask the way to the Meade house. Nothing more than
that or he might scare them. A simple stranger asking directions. Some advantage in that—it would establish prior contact and acceptance so that he wouldn't be a stranger anymore when he came back from the Meade house and broke
the big news. *See, Robbins, luck is working for you again.* The
closed stores could turn out to be a blessing in disguise.

He made a sudden sweeping U-turn, then a sharp left turn
into the police parking lot. He pulled up beside the cruiser.
A golden eagle was perched over the lintel of the headquarters door. Inside, a young cop in a uniform like a state trooper's was sitting at a desk with his hands clasped behind his
head. When he heard Robbins at the door, he straightened
up in his chair. Robbins shut the door behind him.

"Good evening, Officer."

The cop gave him a head-to-toe scrutiny before saying
"Good evening" in a grudging voice. Fucking cops were all
the same. This one was young, with longish golden hair—
long for a cop, that is, Robbins thought, *I've got more hair
than that in my goddamn crotch.* He was cleanly shaved and
tanned *(sonofabitches must all use the same razor and sunlamp),*
well built and good-looking. He wore a .38-caliber cop gun in
a wine-colored holster.

"I'm trying to locate a certain party in town, Sergeant,"
Robbins said. "Can you help me?"

The cop gave a shrug that was a minimal form of assent
and gave him the head-to-toe treatment again. *Shitkicker
cop—if I was wearing a jacket and tie, he would be tugging at his
fucking forelock.*

"They gave me these explicit directions," Robbins said with

a smile, "and would you believe it, a few miles down the road I took them out to read them, and damn if the wind didn't grab them out of my hand and blow them away."

The cop swiveled in his chair and grunted. He hasn't had so much fun, Robbins thought, since he threw his last drunk in the slam or busted some crummy high school kid for doing pot. But he continued to smile; he needed the sonofabitch.

"I was finished until, thank God, I saw your light."

"Name of the party?"

"Meade."

The cop tilted his head in an odd way and said, "Did you say Meade?"

"Yeah, Dr. Meade."

The cop's face had lost its stolidity. It showed a set of emotions Robbins couldn't interpret, except that it signified a sudden change in the climate. From regulation suspicion to a particularized one?

"So you want to see Dr. Meade, eh?"

A casualness in the voice. Prick wasn't all that hard to read. *Trying to trap me.* "Look, I want the location of Dr. Meade's *house*, right?"

"Yeah," the cop said, and now his expression had turned resentful. "Look, we're not any information booth. Somebody, a stranger, drops in at ten o'clock at night, we don't hand out information just like that. We're here to *protect* those houses."

Robbins was baffled. Something was eating the cop's ass, and it wasn't just hair and a motorcycle. Be sincere, Robbins. "Let's start all over again please, Officer. I'm a stranger in these parts and lost. Could you kindly direct me to Dr. Meade's house?"

"Don't try to crap me," the cop said. "You want to see Caro."

Caro—for Caroline, as Paula Raphael had called her. Light beginning to dawn. He leered and said, "Hell no, man, I'm here for a root-canal job."

The cop's face had turned an angry shade of red. "It figures that she would go for your kind of a type."

342

Full daylight, Robbins thought, shitkicker tipped his hand. Onetime boy friend of Caro's, still has a big hard-on for her. But I shouldn't have needled him.

"Hey, wait one little minute." The cop was suddenly alert and suspicious. "I thought you were *there*. When I was out that way this morning, she said you were there."

A new complication? "How could I? I'm *here*, Chrissake, and trying to *get* there."

"How many boyfriends has she *got*, Godssake?"

Robbins shot his finger out. "Just watch it, Sergeant, that uniform doesn't give you the right to cast aspersions about my fiancée, so just watch it." *In defense of my girl's virtue. Versimilitude—right?*

"*You* better watch it." The cop leaned forward in his chair. "Just watch your goddamn mouth."

So much for verisimilitude. It was the obstacle course again, dunces throwing themselves in his path. He felt his temper fraying and fought to control it.

"Okay, Sergeant, let's cool it, all right?"

"Don't you tell me what to do, buster. I don't like your attitude." The cop got to his feet. "So I'm fucking well not going to tell you anything."

Robbins experienced a graphic cartoon flash of money and glory (money a wad of cash the size of a baseball bat, glory a naked fat woman with a long-stemmed rose in her teeth) zooming off into infinity, and found himself clutching a bunched-up portion of the cop's tan shirt in his hand and screaming into his face.

The cop wrenched himself away, backpedaled a couple of paces, and whipped his .38 out of its holster. He held it up in front of his face with two hands, squinting through the sight at Robbins' chest.

"Freeze," the cop said.

"I'm frozen," Robbins said. "Don't get nervous."

"Don't give me orders. I'm the man behind the gun."

"Okay," Robbin said, "you're the man behind the gun and I respect you. Now what?"

"Now you're going to get tossed into a cell until morning."

Mother of God, is this the end of Robin Robbins? "You can't! What's the charge?"

"Assaulting an officer." The cop smoothed out his wrinkled shirt.

"Well, I'll tell you something, Officer—I'd sooner you blasted me."

The cop took one hand off his gun and scratched his face. "I'm putting you in a cell."

"Great," Robbins said. "And the balloon goes up at midnight. Tomorrow morning you're going to be one sorry sonofabitch."

The cop placed his free hand back on the gun. No swearing, Robbins told himself. It makes him nervous.

"I don't know what the hell you're talking about, and I don't care. I want you to move past into the inner room, and don't pull anything or I'll blast you, so help me."

"You're actually gonna put me in a cell?"

"Bet your ass." The cop moved to one side and motioned with the gun for Robbins to advance.

He means it, Robbins thought on a note of hysteria. The crazy shitkicker is going to end everything. Jump him? No, he's scared, he'll pull the fucking trigger. But you can't let him lock you up. Think, you redheaded cocksucker!

"You hear me? Move along."

Robbins sighed, held up his hands for a moment, and then let them drop helplessly. "Okay, no choice. I got to blow my cover."

"Your *what?* What kind of jive is that?"

"You got a tie-in line with the FBI?" Robbins spoke crisply. "Get moving."

"Please," Robbins said. "The masquerade is over. I'd like you to contact Special Agent Anstruther at the bureau office in New York and inform him that you have Robin Robbins in custody."

"You trying to con me that *you're* an FBI agent?"

"I am advising you to make the call," Robbins said with dignity. "There is little time to waste."

The cop narrowed his eyes. "Impersonating a federal agent—now that's a *real* charge."

With patient weariness Robbins said, "If you do not contact Special Agent Anstruther, Sergeant—and I'm not
threatening you, I'm simply stating a fact—then it's your ass,
for sure."

The cop seemed uncertain. "You got credentials?"

"I don't carry credentials. I'm assigned to the FBI and I'm
on the bureau payroll, but I don't carry credentials."

The cop smiled. "You're full of shit, right?"

"I'm a paid informant, and we do not carry credentials.
Will you please get in touch with Special Agent Anstruther.
If you don't have a tie line, I'll give you his office number and
his home phone as well."

The cop seemed impressed or, at least, uncertain again.
"But you're not on duty now, and you assaulted an offi
cer—"

"I'm very much on duty," Robbins said. "I'm here on
official business of the very highest priority."

The cop snorted. "You're Caro Meade's boyfriend. You
call that—"

"I've never seen her before in my life," Robbins said, and
the cop brightened. Asshole, Robbins thought, all he cares
about is that I'm not going to screw his ex-girlfriend.

"I don't get this. I don't get this one little bit, except that
you're trying to fuck me around in some way."

Robbins shook his head in despair. He was getting no
place. If the shitkicker did phone Phoebe, it might get him
off the hook, but it might also mean blowing the reward.

"All right," he said, "how would you like to make a lot of
money?"

The cop's face hardened. "Are you offering me a bribe?"

"I'm taking you into partnership. You want to listen?"

"I ought to punch your goddamn head in."

Robbins appraised the cop's indignation and found it
wanting. "A basketful of money, say a hundred grand."

"You're going into that goddamn cell," the cop said. But
his gesture with his gun was unconvincing.

"A hundred grand, and you'll be the most famous cop in
America, to boot."

"And this has something to do with Caro Meade? Bullshit."

He stopped abruptly. His eyes became inward-looking, then suddenly widened, as if acknowledging a revelation.

"Yes," Robbins said. "It has everything to do with Caro Meade."

"Bullshit," the cop said, but without force now. "Who's going to pay out this so-called hundred grand, and for what?"

Got him reeling, Robbins thought, now poleax him. "For recovering the remains of the Unknown Soldier."

Speechless, Robbin thought, sonofabitch can't even encompass it, it's so tremendous. He's stunned, speechless.

"The balloon goes up at midnight, right? So we haven't got much time. You want to listen?"

"Central calling car one-one-two."

Perry was seated at the radio console trying to raise Joe Bates, who was handling traffic at the high school, where the basketball game would just about be over. Robbins was standing beside him.

He was quite a character, Perry thought. Five minutes ago he had been staring into the hole of a .38, and here he was practically calling the shots. Not that he had seemed the least bit scared—or even respectful, Chrissake—when he had been up against the gun. If anybody was scared, Perry thought, it was me. There was one little minute there when he was positive Robbins was going to rush him, that his finger had tightened on the trigger. A hairbreadth more of pressure. . . .

"Come in, car one-one-two."

Robbins started pacing, then disappeared into the captain's office. Perry thought of the weapons in there and half rose. But he held the keys to the racks.

"Central to car one-one-two. . . ."

With the game over, Joe Bates would be out of his car and on the main road, directing cars out of the high school grounds. Still, he was supposed to stay within earshot of his radio. Of course, he could just lock up and leave the station untended until Joe got back, but he was reluctant to get started. Scared, really, if he had to call it by its right name. The biggest manhunt in history, Robbins had called it, and that was probably true. Maybe the *only* part that was true. For the rest, he was going on the unsupported word of a big New York hippie who *claimed* to be connected with the FBI. Except for one thing—that rifle he had seen at Caro's house.

Although it had barely registered on him at the time, what he had glimpsed was an automatic army-type rifle. But when it *had* registered, a couple of minutes ago, then, at once what Robbins had been saying suddenly began to seem possible. Who shot at tin cans with that kind of weapon?

Robbins came out of the captain's office with a thoughtful look on his face.

"Calling car one-one-two. Central to car one-one-two."

Caro? Christ, he had known Caro since she was fifteen years old, and she was rich folks in the context of their little town. But that didn't mean anything. Radical girls were almost always upper middle class, and when it came to terrorist activity, they were, if anything, more reckless than men. Caro had been a radical for a long time, as far back as when they had been making it together. Against the Vietnam War, against wealth, against the military. Her radical talk had always irritated him, but he had rarely argued with her. She was too goddamn clever for him, she knew all the answers.

"Calling car one-one-two."

Mostly he had ignored it, let it sail right by him. And when it got too annoying, he knew a surefire way of turning it off. Just slip his hand up between her legs, and Karl Marx took a walk.

"Central to Joe Bates. . . ." His voice was husky with the memory of Caro.

Robbins was back in the doorway of the captain's office. "That's quite an arsenal you got in here."

Perry was struck by a sudden thought that made him color angrily. "Hey, you bullshitter. A cop can't accept a reward."

"Of course not," Robbins said impatiently. "I'm giving it to you out of my pocket. Under the table, so you don't even have to pay taxes."

"So you say. But what's to stop you from shutting me out after you collect?"

"Nothing. But whatever else I might be, FBI fink or whatever, I'm a man of my word. Besides, look at it this way, even if I screwed you out of the money—which I won't, swear on my mother's grave—I still can't screw you out of the glory. You'll be a big man all over the whole goddamn country."

It was true, Perry thought, he would be on every front page in America. He could have the captain's job for the asking when the old man retired, or even better than that. He didn't believe for a second what Robbins said about sharing the money, but the glory . . . there was no way he could be screwed out of the glory. God, it would be beautiful. He would be back in the limelight again, the way it was when he was all-state and the recruiters all flocked down to talk to him. Only bigger, a hundred times bigger.

Robbins said, "Come here a second," and disappeared into the captain's office. Perry got up from the console. Robbins waved his hand at the weapons rack—rifles, shotguns, Mace, the tear-gas-grenade launcher. "Maybe we ought to take some of this stuff along."

"What for? We're just going to—what you said—reconnoiter."

"That's one way. Peek into a window, then phone up the FBI so they can try to get an army down before they blow the fucking thing up and split. The other way is to take them ourselves."

"You're kidding. How big of a hero do we have to be?"

Robbins shrugged. "We can do it all on the telephone—if that's what your idea of police work is."

I knew he would try to sell this, Perry thought, I knew it all along. And I wanted him to. Perry Knorr going for the big yardage, right? He said casually, "How many of them are there—if they're there at all?"

"They're there. I told you I got it from the *wife* of one of them. There's three or four, according to all the reports."

"They'll be armed," Perry said.

Robbins waved at the weapons racks. "They're armed, but they can't have anything like this stuff."

"Yeah," Perry said. His excitement was growing, and it was hard trying to keep sounding cool. "Tell me—you have any combat experience?"

"I had a company of fucking grunts in Nam. Rank of captain."

"We haven't really got the authority," Perry said, "and if we botch it up. . . ."

"We got all the authority we need. You're a fucking cop, aren't you?"

"Sure, but. . . ." I'm ready, Perry thought, give me one more little push. . . .

"In that house," Robbins said, "they're sitting ducks. But if you're chicken, we'll just reconnoiter and make our phone call to the FBI and let them take all the fucking credit. We'll still have the cash, anyway."

"I *could* get the off-duty men," Perry said. "Don't call me chicken, buster. I mean, I don't care who the fuck you are, don't ever call me chicken."

"I'm sorry," Robbins said. "I really and truly am."

"That's okay," Perry said. He stroked his chin. "That's assuming the off-duty men are at home."

"They'll be at home," Robbins said, "waiting to hear the President's talk. Look, move it, will you, Perry?"

The Oval Office resembled a television studio mock-up of the Oval Office: cameras, lights, cables, smooth network types. The President sat behind his desk, a bib around his neck, being made up by a large woman in a smock. Griese entered the room and the news secretary went to meet him.

"Thanks, Em. I really appreciate your phoning me. The networks bitched a little, but—"

Griese walked by him. The President glanced up from his speech. "Eminence!" He extended his hand. Griese leaned across the desk and took it. "Congratulations!"

"Thank you, sir." Griese mustered up a look of modesty.

"Nobody but you could have swung it. I'm citing you in the speech."

"I'd prefer you didn't, sir." He made a gesture of surrender. "But I cannot pursue an argument with the commander in chief."

The makeup woman held a mirror in front of the President. He turned his head right and left, upward and downward. "You've hidden the hickey very nicely, but"—he touched the right side of his face near his nose—"the mole is barely visible."

"It's just that you know it's there, sir. The camera won't pick it up."

"Exactly." The President smiled. "I want it to show."

"But, sir, it's an unsightly wen, it mars your—"

"Did it spoil Lincoln's appearance? Uncover it, please."

As the President watched studiously in the mirror, the woman dabbed at his face with a towel.

"Is it all right now, sir?"

"Continue," Griese said. "The President will say wen."

The President's acting coach appeared, looking harried. "Ten minutes, sir. Shall we run through it once more, quickly?"

"No."

The President waved the coach and the makeup woman away with a single inclusive gesture. The news secretary approached, circled the desk, and whispered into the President's ear. Griese leaned over to catch what he was saying.

"Two of the three networks are putting on panel discussions after the speech."

The President shrugged. "Screw 'em. I've got the people."

Griese drew the news secretary off to the side. "Airport arrangements all laid on?"

"All set."

"Exactly as I instructed?"

"Yes."

"Nobody knows?"

"Nobody. The first the media will know about it is when they hear it in the President's speech. They'll still have ample time to rush out to the airport."

"If any single detail of our arrangement goes wrong," Griese said, "I shall hold you personally responsible, and I promise you that I'll hound you out of your job. And I never go back on a threat."

The news secretary waited for a technician to pass, then whispered, "I've never said this before, because I don't hold with invective. But there are limits. Sir, you are a prick."

Griese smiled. "Try telling that to a grateful nation."

26

A moment after Perry had made the last of his calls to the off-duty men, Joe Bates came in on the radio. "Car one-one-two to Central."

"Where the hell have you been? I want you right back here fast as you can make it. K."

"There was a fight, Sarge, and one kid pulled a knife. I'm bringing the kid with the knife in. K."

Robbins, scowling, said, "Ditch the kid."

"Ditch the kid," Perry said. "Get your ass right in here. We've got a flash emergency."

"He cut the other kid on the arm, not too bad, but the knife is a foot long. Emergency?"

"You're the fucking sergeant," Robbins whispered.

"God damn it, Bates, I'm giving you an order. Turn on your siren and burn up the road."

"Okay, okay, Sarge. K."

"I'm not calling the captain," Perry said offhandedly to Robbins. "He's too old to do any good in an operation like this, and besides. . . ." He shrugged.

"And besides," Robbins said, grinning, "he might want to hog the glory."

"And besides," Perry said as if he hadn't heard Robbins, "he's probably fast asleep."

Joe Bates arrived before any of the others, skidding his cruiser into the parking lot on two wheels. He was twenty-one and the most gung-ho cop on the force. He stared at Robbins.

"Who's this dude?"

"This is Robbins. He's with the FBI."

"FBI? Christ, what's cooking, Sarge?"

"We're making a raid."

"A raid? On *what?*"

"I'm only going through it once," Perry said, "when the rest of them get here."

"What rest?"

"The whole force." Perry started into the captain's office. "Don't just stand there, lend me a hand with the weapons."

As he was unlocking the weapons rack, Bates, his eyes wide, said, "Captain coming, Sarge?"

"Captain don't answer his phone," he said. Robbins smiled and patted him on the shoulder. He started handing down the shotguns.

They left the headquarters building on the dot of ten thirty, which Perry regarded as a good omen. Even though it was pure coincidence, it lent the enterprise an air of military precision. They traveled in three cars: Perry and Robbins in car one-one-one, Joe Bates with Stanfield and Parks in car one-one-two, and the other three—Foss, MacNee, and Stahrman—in Stahrman's Mustang. The backseats of all three cars were piled with shotguns, boxes of extra shells, and tear-gas canisters.

Perry's feeling of excitement, which had tailed off while they were waiting for the off-duty cops to show up—not that it had taken any of them more than ten minutes from phone call to arrival—was beginning to rekindle. Admittedly they didn't exactly give the impression of people about to go off on a history-making bust. Only two of the off-duty men were in uniform—Foss and Stahrman, who were due to take the midnight-to-eight shift. The others were wearing jackets and slacks, and didn't look too much like cops, though they had at least all remembered to tote their revolvers.

Perry signaled a turn and took the road leading toward the public beach. They hadn't passed a single car. There would be little enough traffic ordinarily, but with the President due to speak—he had probably begun already—the roads were deserted.

He checked the other two cars swinging in behind him, then glanced at Robbins. He was half reclining in his seat, his beard and hair aglow in the minimal light from the dashboard. He was a real cool cat, Perry thought, and wished enviously that he was like that himself. He had had some experience of violence since joining the force, but it was penny-ante stuff. As for shooting, he had fired his gun only one time aside from target practice. That had taken place a few years ago, when he had chased some stoned kids who had tried running him down after he pulled them over. He had fired twice out of the window of the cruiser, left-handed. He hadn't hit anything, of course, but he had been damn well trying to, and the kids apparently realized that, too, because they pulled off the road and waited for him to catch up with them.

"At the end of this road we make a right turn," Perry said, "and then we run along on Hubbard, parallel to the beach, and at the end of that street is the Meade place."

"Stop just before the right turn and we'll get out," Robbins said. Suddenly he laughed. "The whole fucking police force, all three shifts, right?"

"They're good men," Perry said stiffly.

He wasn't so sure that was true. A few of them—say Joe Bates and Foss and maybe Stanfield—could be depended on, but they were the young ones. The others were fifty or better—and MacNee was coming up to sixty-five and fat as a beer barrel—and not exactly fire-eaters. Still, they could be counted on to handle a gun if they had to; they were all hunters and knew one end of a shotgun from the other.

He remembered how they had looked when he broke the news to them. Some blanched faces, some nervous glances and lip biting, but mostly pure amazement. MacNee had brought up the matter of the captain, and Perry had simply repeated that he hadn't been able to raise him on the phone. Then he had added, mostly for Robbins' approval, "That means I'm in charge, and I give the orders. Understood?"

It was a pretty informal police department, but the gravity of the situation must have hit them, because nobody made any jokes, and a couple of them said, "Right, Sarge," and they even stood a little more erect and dressed up their line. He had warned them that it *might* be a false alarm, but they were to act at all times as if it were the real thing.

He had still been searching for some final, perhaps inspirational word, when Robbins had broken in: "Okay, Perry, let's do the number."

He stopped just short of the right turn into Hubbard Road and braked to a stop.

"Get them all out," Robbins said. "We're walking the rest of the way. Lights off."

They stood in a small huddle, hunched up against the wind and other, invisible chills.

"Okay, men," Robbins said. He looked very serious, and Perry thought, He knows how to command. "We walk the rest of the way, and we don't make a sound. Noise carries like crazy in the nighttime."

"Right," Stanfield said. "One time, in Korea this was, we were out on patrol, and just a couple of coins clinked in this guy's pocket, and suddenly the whole Chink army was shooting at us."

"Each man with a shotgun," Robbins said, "and load up your pockets with extra shells. Perry, you take the launcher. I'll take the tear-gas grenades. Move ass, boys!"

They stepped out smartly and Perry felt a pang of envy, but just for a moment. True, Robbins took over as if he owned the police force, but if he was to admit the truth, the initiative had long ago passed over to Robbins. Well, he had had a company in Vietnam, so it was all right.

They walked briskly along the dark windy street, lined on both sides with boarded-up summer houses. They went in files of two, himself and Robbins leading, with a yard or two between ranks. There was no sound except for their footsteps, but the wind, cutting toward them, would carry it away.

"That's it," Perry whispered.

It was the last house in the line, fronting the water, and in the bright starlight they could make out its erratic outlines, in sharp contrast to the standard saltboxes. Robbins held up his hand, and they stopped.

"No lights," Perry said. But then he concentrated on the house, squinting. "No, I see some light at the windows. They must have the blinds drawn."

But it looked placid and innocent, and suddenly Perry was convinced that it was a big false alarm. God, he was going to look like the stupidest sonofabitch, and when the captain found out about it. . . .

Robbins was chuckling. "Who draws blinds when there's nobody within a mile of them?"

The blinds had been drawn this morning, too! Who did that on the Cape when there was sunshine and clear light to let in? Suddenly Perry started shivering, and not from the chill wind. It was about to start!

"Here's where we separate," Robbins whispered. "We go as teams of two each, each team with a walkie-talkie. Perry and I are going to skin out between those two houses and edge along parallel to the water, and we'll cover the house from the front. You two dudes. . . ."

"Ladies and gentlemen, the President of the United States."

Our letter is about to be answered, Booth thought. They were sitting on chairs or on the floor in a rough semicircle surrounding the television set, which Caro had painstakingly tuned to reasonably good reception. No one spoke.

The camera focused on the President at his desk in the Oval Room. "My good friends. . . ."

The President paused, his eyes narrowing, as if in search of his audience. Dover sighed, and his head lolled. He had drunk too much wine with his dinner, Booth thought. If he allowed his eyes to close, he might miss the big moment altogether.

"Early on Tuesday morning this nation learned of a crime that sickened it to the heart. A crime so repellent and inhuman that it defies all efforts of the imagination to envision the sort of people who might commit it. Certainly they cannot be

The Talisman

described in any of the terms normally reserved for civilized discourse."

Asbury laughed. Dover stifled a yawn. Doc said, "Your speech writers are copping out, Prez."

Caro said, "Shut up, please," without looking away from the screen.

"I shall not elaborate, my good friends, on the utter revulsion I feel at the abominable and heartless defilement of a national shrine. I know that these feelings are shared by all of you."

"*Basta*," Doc said. "Enough intro. Let's get down to facts."

"Of the misguided persons who perpetrated this ultimately self-degrading act, I shall not say that I despise them, but instead that I pity them because they are so utterly devoid of humanity and decency. Recriminations are pointless at this stage of the game. It is now our task, our sacred duty, to recover, and restore to its honored place, the revered relic of American heroism."

As the President looked out levelly at his audience, the camera came in on a tight close-up, and his face filled the screen.

"He has a pimple near his mouth," Raphael said.

"We have been asked a price for the return of the beloved remains of the Unknown Warrior. That price is the pardon and deportation of a convicted murderer."

"Whose shoes you aren't fit to shine," Asbury yelled.

". . . or they will wantonly destroy the remains."

The President paused and turned a page. Get on with it, Booth said to himself. Get on with it.

"It has been said that we live in an era much changed from the one in which the Unknown of World War Two gave up his life. An era that in its sophistication, its hardheadedness, its cynicism, its disillusionment with certain age-old assumptions has eschewed patriotism, has eschewed religion—for respect for the dead is indeed a form of nonsectarian religion. Before this week began, I would have been hard pressed to deny that this was true."

"Hurry up, damn it," Doc said, "you're putting Bobby to sleep." Dover's head jerked upright and he blushed.

". . . since Tuesday morning, my good friends, the out-pouring of grief and lamentation has been overwhelming, immeasurable. As if with one voice, the people said, 'We love and cherish our dead hero, and there is no shame in saying so.' Now, my friends. . . ."

Raphael said, "It's coming now. He's going to do it. We've won."

"It is to this voice, to *your* voice, fellow Americans, that I am responsible."

Everyone shouted, drowning out the President. Doc gave a rebel yell. Asbury pounded the floor with his fists. Booth, raising his voice, said, "Keep it down. Let's get the rest of it." He was trembling.

The din subsided gradually. Grimly the President was saying, ". . . pardon signed. He has been released from prison. Passage has been booked for him on a plane for Paris, departing at eleven fifteen tonight. From there he will go on to the small African country of Gabon, where, according to his wishes, he will work among the poor and needy. I hope that in this work he will succeed and that this will be his penance and his salvation."

The President paused for a long moment, looking down at his hands. He raised his head slowly.

"I hardly need tell you, my good friends, how painful it is to submit to blackmail by murderers and ghouls. But I have arrived at a balance of accounts, and it has given me some peace of mind. Perhaps it will do the same for you, my good friends. In releasing Francis Rowan, a convicted murderer, I have rid the nation of that which it despises. In regaining the Unknown Warrior I am recovering that which the nation worships. I say to you that to recover our Unknown Hero I would gladly give up a thousand, no, a million of such as Francis Rowan."

It was the hard arithmetic of politics, Booth thought, and if the vote had gone the other way, so would his equation.

". . . swear to you, and above all to those grieving parents of the fine young man who died there in Arlington Cemetery in the brave and selfless performance of his duty, I swear that he will be avenged." The camera closed in on his eyes, fiercely resolute. "He will be avenged. This is a solemn promise."

"Prez," Doc said, "you never kept a promise in your life."

". . . and the television cameras will be present as he boards the plane, so they can see for themselves that we have kept our word. We expect them to do the same, to release the casket containing the remains of the Unknown with all dispatch.

"Ladies and gentlemen, I said before that I pitied these men. This is the truth. They are the last casualties of the Vietnam War, the last squeezed-out bitter fruits of hate and anger. Let us hope we hear no more of that tragic episode in our nation's history."

It was true, Booth thought. Out of that slick studied mouth had come the plain truth. *They,* and not Rowan, were the last casualties of the war. And now the hideous book could at last be closed. It was over, over and done. And now, he thought, what will I do? Caro was staring at him, reading his mind. It's over, Caro, ten long years of my life. Now there is none of it left to hate, to fight for or against, *and what shall I do with the rest of my life?*

". . . nation joins me in solemn prayer. . . ."

"ATTENTION IN THERE! YOUR ATTENTION! LET ME HAVE YOUR ATTENTION!"

Later Booth was to remember that he had grasped nothing, even though Asbury was already scrambling toward one of his firing points and the others were turning to him with stricken faces. That disembodied iron voice seemed to come from some indefinable place, and his first thought was that the planes had returned for an attack on the target ship and were haranguing each other across the sky.

There was a tinkle of glass as Asbury, at the front of the house, rammed his M-16 through the blind and the window, and then the room clattered with sound as he emptied his clip into the darkness.

The burst of fire from the house went far to their left and high over their heads. Perry dropped behind the embankment and brought Robbins down with him. They both dug in against the loose brush to keep from sliding farther. A few seconds after the rifle fire they heard pistol shots from outside the house; four or five rounds from the right, then two shots each from the front and left side.

Laughing, Robbins said, "You know what that means? We're famous."

"Jesus, that was close." Perry's face, turned toward him, was pale in the starshine. Perry moved his hand in a scything motion close to his face. "This near, I swear, right past my head."

"He wasn't within fifty feet," Robbins said. "Get yourself together, man. Hit the walkie-talkie and tell your troops not to fire until they're told to. As ordered, right?"

"Christ," Perry said, "they've got a goddamn machine gun."

"Relax. It's an M-sixteen and he shot the whole clip off in a single burst. Do what I said—get on that walkie-talkie."

Robbins edged his way back up the incline and rested the bullhorn on the level ground. Perry started jabbering on his walkie-talkie. Ahead, the house was silent. By focusing on the spot where he had seen muzzle flash, Robbins thought he could make out a bulge in the blind where the barrel of the M-sixteen might have poked through.

He spoke into the bullhorn: "THIS IS SPECIAL AGENT ROBBINS OF THE FEDERAL BUREAU OF INVESTIGATION. YOU ARE COMPLETELY SURROUNDED AND OUTNUMBERED BY A COMBINED FORCE OF POLICE AND FBI AGENTS. I ORDER YOU TO THROW OUT YOUR WEAPONS AND LEAVE THE HOUSE. THROW OUT YOUR WEAPONS FIRST AND THEN COME OUT, SINGLE FILE AND HANDS ON YOUR HEAD."

In the house somebody screamed, "Fuck you!" followed by another burst of rifle fire. Without moving, Robbins watched the muzzle flash. Perry cowered. There was a single pistol shot from the darkness to the right —probably that gung-ho fucking Bates again—and then silence.

"They're going to put up a stiff fight," Perry whispered from below. "We ought to get reinforcements."

"Bullshit," Robbins said harshly. "We'll do it all by ourselves." He put his mouth to the bullhorn.

"They won't come out," Perry said.

"They'll come out, or we'll blast the sonofabitches out." He spoke through the bullhorn: "IN THE HOUSE. IN THE HOUSE. NOW HEAR THIS, COCKSUCKERS. . . ."

Asbury, lying on his side beneath the sill and fitting a fresh clip into his rifle, screamed, "Man those firing points."

Nobody moved.

They were still partially stunned, Booth thought, except for Asbury, who functioned on a plane where action preceded thought or even replaced it altogether with reflex. There had been no warning, no foreshadowing, and their minds were lagging behind their senses. Perhaps they would never catch up; perhaps they would be dead or wounded to death and still be struggling to overtake reality.

Asbury was pouring out abuse, exhortation, urging them to be men, to prove their mettle, strange idioms out of a romantic past, which was where Asbury really belonged and where he might be soon enough. They were all lying on the floor, and Booth remembered now that at the first pistol shot from outside, he had yelled, "Hit the deck!"—an atavism from *his* distant past.

He sought out Caro. She was lying prone, with her head raised, and seemed to be staring at a blind at a side window that had been torn by a bullet. There was a vague almost-smile on her face, and in a flash of insight that turned the tables on her mind reading of his thoughts, he knew that she had been struck by an absurdity: *How will I ever explain that hole to my father?*

"My God! How, how, how?" Raphael's voice was constricted, his face had fallen in on itself.

Raphael told his wife . . . no. If they were betrayed, it was not by Raphael's wife. If we have been betrayed, Booth thought, I am the betrayer, through oversight or faulty planning or simply because I got them all into it.

The bullhorn voice filled the room: "THIS IS SPECIAL

AGENT ROBBINS OF THE FEDERAL BUREAU OF IN-
VESTIGATION."
The television set was still flickering. A panel of newsmen
"analyzing" the President's speech, telling the public what it
had just heard.
"TOSS YOUR WEAPONS OUT AND THEN WALK
OUT, SINGLE FILE AND HANDS ON YOUR HEAD."
Asbury rolled to the window, screamed, "Fuck you!" and,
the rifle jumping, spewed another entire clip into the darkness beyond the porch. Then there was a moment of rever-
berant silence, followed by a single shot from the side of the
house. Booth heard it strike the house, but it didn't pene-
trate. Asbury was crawling away from the window in standard infantry fashion, rifle cradled in his arms, using his
shoes and elbows and knees, hugging the ground.
"God damn you!" His face was furious. "Let's fight those
bastards. Man those fucking guns!"
"IN THE HOUSE. IN THE FUCKING HOUSE. NOW
HEAR THIS, COCKSUCKERS!"
"Raunchy talker," Doc said. "I didn't know FBI agents
knew such words, let alone used them."
Doc had rolled over on his back. His head was cradled on
his arms, and he was smiling upward at the ceiling. Doc had
recovered, Booth thought, he had caught up with reality. He
might still die, but he would at least know it was happening.
"You. . . ." Asbury was head to head with him. "You're
the leader, aren't you? Let's see you fucking lead!"
Yes, Booth thought, and look where I've led you to so far:
to a dead-end surrender. Except for Doc, who was still directing his secret smile at the ceiling, they were all looking at
him. Hoping, expectant. Not for deliverance, perhaps, but
for the guidance he owed them. Yes, he thought, I'm the
leader and therefore must lead—the Old Man—and must
counsel.
Asbury was screaming again, exhorting everyone to start
shooting.
Dover started to roll over—the habit of obedience died
hard in Dover—but Booth stopped him.

"Wait. There's no sense shooting if you can't see what you're shooting at."

Asbury was up on his haunches, glaring, his eyes blazing. This was the true betrayal for Asbury, Booth thought, the refusal to die mindlessly, by instinct.

He ignored Asbury and said calmly, "We have only two choices. Give up or die. It's as simple as that."

In the silence that fell, he caught a phrase from the television set, almost an echo of his own words: ". . . President had very few options, and—"

". . . no fucking guts." Asbury, his voice contemptuous, his lip curled. "You want to throw in the sponge, old man."

Lowercase, Booth thought, not the leader but a man who had gone old. He looked at the others. Raphael held his head in his hands. Caro was expressionless. Dover . . . to Dover, at least, he was still the Old Man.

"I can't make the decision for you. It's nothing to do with tactics. It's to do with whether you want to live or die."

"Die like men," Asbury shouted, "or spend the rest of your lives in prison!"

Booth nodded. "Those are the alternatives."

"But we want to know what you *think,*" Dover said.

"We're sitting ducks. It's hopeless. But that isn't to say we can't put up some sort of fight if we don't mind dying."

"Hopeless," Asbury said. "Is that what you told your troops in that ancient war, old man?"

"This is a different kind of army. We map strategy by consensus."

"Maybe we could make a deal with them," Raphael said. But his voice was listless, he seemed to have withdrawn into some deep privacy, and Booth thought, He's counting regrets.

Caro said, "Even if we could somehow fight our way out, we're marked, they know us. We'll be fugitives, and eventually we would be run down." Her voice darkened, and her eyes filled with tears. "I don't want to see anybody killed."

"Maybe we could get out of the country," Raphael said.

Doc said, "I know a spade who gets fugitives out of the

country through some kind of underground pipeline. Well, he gets *spade* fugitives out."

Asbury said, "You sicken me. The whole lot of you. I swear, you sicken me."

"ATTENTION IN THE HOUSE! YOU HAVE TWO MINUTES BEFORE WE BLAST YOU OUT. START COUNTING, GHOULS. . . ."

Doc, with sudden decisiveness, said, "Try dickering with them. See if you can make a deal."

"What do I bargain with?"

"The remains. Our freedom or we blow up the casket."

"Do you want to blow it up?"

Doc shrugged. "I don't care particularly, one way or another."

Asbury, in a sudden fury, threw an ashtray at him. Doc ignored it as it went hurtling by his head.

"I'd like to be sure they keep their word about Rowan." Caro nodded toward the television set. "We'll know in fifteen minutes. Try to buy that much time, at least."

"Do a deal," Doc said. "If Rowan gets off on the plane, we'll give the remains back."

Booth gazed around the circle of faces. Four nods. Nothing from Asbury, whose blond head was bent, hidden between his knees.

"Better go now," Raphael said. "The two minutes is almost up."

Booth rolled over on his hands and knees and started crawling toward the front window.

27

"There's somebody at the window trying to talk to us," Perry said.

Robbins listened for a moment, focusing on the window where he had spotted the M-16. He heard the voice, but what it was saying was borne back by the offshore breeze.

Through the bullhorn he said, "SPEAK UP, GHOUL."

The voice called out more strongly, and the words became distinct. "We'd like to talk to you."

"NO TALK. ALL WE WANT TO HEAR IS THAT YOU'RE COMING OUT OF THERE."

"I'll come out alone," the voice said calmly. "Unarmed and with my hands on my head."

"See what he wants," Perry whispered. "Nothing to lose."

"WE DON'T NEGOTIATE WITH GRAVE ROBBERS."

"Let him talk," Perry said. "Maybe they want to surrender."

"THE ONLY THING WE'LL DISCUSS IS YOUR UN-CONDITIONAL SURRENDER."

After a pause the voice said, "Do you want the remains back?"

"They can blow it up," Perry said with an edge of hysteria. "Talk to him."

It might jeopardize the reward money if the remains were destroyed. He spoke into the bullhorn.

"OKAY. COME OUT SLOWLY, NO WEAPONS, HANDS ON HEAD."

"I'm coming out."

"Christ," Perry said in a whisper.

"LEAVE THE DOOR OPEN. WE WANT TO SEE YOU."
Robbins put the bullhorn down and picked up the shotgun
and trained it on the doorway. The door opened and a man
stepped out. He left the door slightly ajar. His hands were
clasped on his head.

"Open up the door wide," Robbins yelled.

The man shook his head, his elbows moving from side to
side with the motion of his head, like a man doing a simple
calisthenic.

"I want that door wide open," Robbins yelled.

"You can see me, and I can't see you," the man said.

It didn't matter, Robbins thought. He had the man squarely in his sights, zeroed in on the broad chest, and thanks for
the white shirt, buddy. It was an easy shot. With the spread
of the gun he couldn't miss. "I can blow him right off that
fucking porch," he said softly.

"No, for Godssake," Perry said. "Find out what he wants."

Robbins yelled, "What's on your mind, ghoul? Make it
fast."

"Do you want the remains of the Unknown back intact?"

Robbins shouted, "You harm those remains, you bastard. . . ." In the dim light he saw the man's shoulders move
in a shrug. He had already threatened to kill them, Robbins
thought, so there was no further threat left, and the man on
the porch knew it. "Let's stop wasting time. Get the rest of
those bums out here."

"There's a high-explosive charge in the casket," the man
said. "We can touch it off instantaneously."

"No deals," Robbins yelled. He shook Perry's hand off his
arm. "Your blackmailing days are over. Unconditional surrender, that's the only deal we'll make." He rested the stock
of the shotgun up against his cheek. "I'm going to blow a
hole in his chest."

"Don't, for Godssake." Perry put his hand on the barrel of
the shotgun and pressed it down. "Let's listen to what he has
to say."

Robbins wrenched the gun free and tucked it into his
shoulder.

Perry called out to the man, "We're not about to let you go, if that's what you got in mind."

"Who am I talking to now?"

"Sergeant Perry Knorr of the town police. Speak up and make it fast."

"I want you to know that we're serious about destroying the remains."

"Then blow them and fuck yourself," Robbins yelled.

"Sergeant Knorr, is that your view, too?"

"Bet your ass it is," Robbins yelled.

Perry's tone was firm and decisive. "Yes. We're not letting you walk out of here, and that's final. Blow them if you want to."

Good for Perry, Robbins thought, and called out, "And that's the last fucking word on the subject. The interview is over."

He saw the man hesitate, then turn and look through the opening in the door into the house. He seemed to be saying something. He faced front. "All right. We'll give up."

Robbins heard a howl from inside the house and a medley of indistinct voices. The man on the porch looked back for an instant, turning only the upper half of his body so that, once again, he looked like a man performing calisthenics.

"All right. Will you tell me what time it is?"

Robbins laughed. "You want the weather report, too?"

"I'll explain myself in a moment. Will you tell me the time?"

Perry looked at his watch. "It's one minute past eleven."

The man nodded his head. "If you'll give us approximately fifteen minutes, we'll walk out of here and surrender and turn the remains over to you, too."

"What are you going to do in fifteen minutes that you can't do right now?" Perry yelled.

Robbins saw a white glimmer come and go. A smile. "Look at the television."

Perry muttered, "He's nuts."

"What are you, a comedian?" Robbins said. "I can put a bullet right through your laugher, ghoul."

The man called out, "Francis Rowan's plane leaves at eleven fifteen, and it will be covered on television. As soon as he boards the plane—"

"What the fuck are you talking about?" Robbins yelled.

The man was silent for a moment. "Did you hear the President's speech?"

"No," Robbins said, "we were too busy tracking down some ghouls."

"All right," the man said. "He has pardoned Rowan, who is boarding a plane for Paris at eleven fifteen. There's television coverage. As soon as we see him board the plane, we'll come out."

"How do we know you're not bullshitting us?"

"I'm not," the man said.

"Fifteen minutes," Robbins said. "So you can wire up that corpse?"

"It's been wired up for two days."

"I believe him," Perry said. "Let him have fifteen minutes. It's worth it to get the Unknown back."

"Fucking ghoul." But there was really nothing to lose; they couldn't get away. And if recovering the remains meant the difference between getting all the reward money or just part of it, why blow it? He spoke to the man. "Okay, you've got fifteen minutes. After that you come out like little lambs. Okay?"

"Yes. Thanks." The man turned and slipped inside the house.

"Get on the walkie-talkie," Robbins said. "Explain the situation, but tell them to stay on the alert. Got it?"

I sure have got a new boss, Perry thought, but he nodded and began to speak on the walkie-talkie.

It was a measure of their despair, Booth thought, that they barely acknowledged his return. They remained seated, facing the flickering TV set, their faces pale and somber in the darkened room, only fitfully visible, the bluish light seeking out the facial prominences: noses, cheekbones, and foreheads. Caro, in the wing chair, nodded her head neutrally. Doc gave a careless twitch of his narrow shoulders. Dover looked at him doggishly, but no longer with hope that the

Old Man would pull them out. Raphael sat with his head bowed, perhaps wondering whether it was Paula—under what unimaginable stress—who had betrayed them.

On the TV screen the panel was still dissecting the President's speech, but by now they must be down to the bare bones, vamping until the cameras were ready for the big show at the airport.

Booth sat down beside Doc. "Where's Asbury?"

Doc shrugged. "In the cellar. Sulking, and also rigging up the explosive to the casket."

"He won't get nervous and blow us all up, will he?"

"Asbury is a shit, but he knows explosives. He has two fields of expertise, explosives and dames."

"The funny thing. . . ." Raphael's voice rose over the bumble of the TV set, melancholy but heightened, as if he had stumbled on a major insight. "Arithmetically, it's a joke. We're getting one man out of prison and putting six in."

Snatches of response flashed into Booth's mind: Yes, but he's worth the six of us. As a symbol he represents more than mere numbers can define. But he could not bring himself to articulate them. He thought of Rowan in his prison denims, the sheer theatricality of his martyr's eyes and strong cheekbones, his pitiful preoccupation with the prison food. He had no real answer for Raphael. Maybe, in time—and there would be plenty of it in his cell—he would recognize the absurdity of the arithmetic. It remained to be seen. He had never tested himself against a martyrdom of his own or, he reminded himself, expiation for the guilt of ruining five other lives.

A strip of letters was sliding silently across the bottom of the screen: WE WILL BE GOING SHORTLY TO THE AIRPORT FOR THE ANNOUNCED DEPARTURE OF FRANCIS ROWAN. . . .

He said to Doc, "What's taking Asbury so long?"

"You worry too much about your old buddy in the coffin. It's just old bones. When I was down in the cellar with Asbury before, I took a look at them. Medical curiosity."

Booth said nothing. But he felt a wave of revulsion, as if at a trust—no, an intimacy—breached.

"Don't look so pained," Doc said. "You think there's a great sanctified hero in that box?"

"Maybe not to begin with, but he was beatified, he was *made* into a hero."

"By lottery. He was one of twenty or so candidates they dug up, right? They chose one of them to become the Unknown, and the other nineteen were shoved back into the ground to become anonymous again."

"They were all heroes, all young men who were killed before their time."

Doc smiled. "Well, let me tell you how I reconstruct your hero's death." He glanced around the room and lowered his voice. "It happened in Italy, right?"

"It could have happened anyplace in the ETO. Or the Pacific."

"Okay, but I'm telling the story, and I pick Italy. A fuck-up PFC, okay? He has bagged a *signorina* with a couple of chocolate bars and pulled her into a barn, and he's balling the hell out of her. A big-tit, broad-assed, garlic-smelling Sicilian chick. Okay?"

On the TV screen the scene had shifted to a shot of the airport. "We take you now to. . . ."

The camera swept the field in a panoramic shot, then closed in on a plane sitting on a runway. It read the letters on the silver body: AIR FRANCE. It shifted to the stairway leading up to the open door. Spreading backward from the foot of the stairs, forming an aisle to the approach, was a large group of people. A stewardess stood at the top of the stairs. The camera came closer to the aisle of people: reporters, some with microphones and backpacks, some with cameras; others with the alert, guarded look of law officers. The area behind the plane was clear.

"A few more minutes," Booth said, "and we'll know."

"Yes," Doc said. "Let's come back to that barn in Sicily and the infantry grunt."

"We didn't call them that."

"GI—okay? He's on a pile of hay or loose manure, bobbing away on top of the *siciliana*. She's putting on an opera for

him, squirming, eyes rolling, hollering, 'Fuck me faster, Joe.'
Beautiful. So now we shift the scene. A few miles away a Ger-
man battery hidden under camouflage. A recon plane radios
down: 'Suspicious structure behind their lines.' Terrific, the
Kraut artillery officer says, I'll knock it for a loop. You know
artillery, Ken, if they see something standing, they take it as a
personal insult."

On the airfield a series of bright lights lit up like suddenly
opening flowers.

". . . asks for the coordinates, lines up his gun, and gets
off a shell. He misses, but his second shot is closer. The GI
hears it, knows they're zeroing in, but he's not about to stop
what he's doing just for a couple of H/E shells. He jabs away
like a maniac, and just as he starts to make it, the third round
comes in and makes a direct hit."

There was an air of expectancy on the airfield; even the reporters had stopped moving about restlessly. All heads were
turned toward a door giving onto the field from one of the
airport buildings. The camera focused on it, held. A guard
or two standing there, nothing else.

Doc said, "Graves-registration people. All day long they go
around picking up stiffs. They toss them in bags and tag 'em,
and later they dump them into GI pine field coffins. Sounds
gruesome, but they say it's not a bad deal as army jobs go."

"Asbury is taking an awfully long time," Booth said.

The camera was probing the building doorway, but it was
blank.

"You know what a skeleton looks like? Not a med-school
skeleton, nice and white and shiny, with all the skin and flesh
carefully boiled away. A skeleton that has lain in a grave for
thirty-odd years. It's a kind of badly preserved mummy—"

"Here he comes," Booth said.

The building door was flung open, and a group of a dozen
men shoved through and began to move in a tight body
across the field, hurrying, almost running. A camera placed
on a high point somewhere kept pace, and Booth picked out
Rowan in the center of the mass. He was wearing a dark suit
and a white shirt open at the throat, and he was carrying a
plump flight bag.

"ATTENTION IN THE HOUSE. SEND THE GIRL OUT.".

Caro looked up in surprise, then slowly shook her head in refusal.

"CARO, THIS IS PERRY. COME OUT SO THAT I CAN TALK TO YOU, CARO."

Rowan was almost to the foot of the stairs, still in the center of the hurrying, jostling mass. The reporters surged forward, microphones held high, but they recorded only the effortful grunts of Rowan's escort as they hustled him to the stairs. There all but two of them fell away. The two took his arms and half carried him up the stairs. He seemed to be protesting. At the top of the stairs the stewardess smiled dazzlingly. For her, Booth thought, a passenger was a passenger. *Bienvenue. Welcome to Air France, sir. We hope you will enjoy your flight.* . . .

"TIME IS UP. LAST CHANCE TO SEND CARO OUT."

The two guards relinquished Rowan's arms. He faced outward. He raised his hand, as if for silence, and opened his mouth to speak. At that instant the jet engines of the Air France plane roared into life. Rowan continued speaking, but all that could be heard was the roar of the engines, and he seemed merely to be pantomiming speech. Suddenly the two guards took his arms, turned him, and, lifting him off his feet, carried him into the plane. The stewardess followed. The camera held on the empty doorway while the announcer babbled. The two guards appeared and started down the stairway. The door closed.

"INSIDE THE HOUSE. YOUR TIME IS UP."

"All right," Booth said. "They can have their remains back."

And then, by reflex, before his mind knew what he was doing, he was on his feet and running toward the cellar door.

Robbins felt his impatience mounting. Silence and waiting were diluting the drama. There had been enough delays all day long, and it had to be resolved before he lost his cool. Damn it, you didn't charge up to a climax and then postpone it.

They were still lying in the same position, their heads and shoulders on the level ground, their bodies slanting down the slope, resting on sand and bracken. He said, "How much time left?"

Perry's watch had an illuminated dial. "About three minutes. Listen, I'd like to get Caro out of there."

"What for? You want to fuck her once more before she goes into the slam?"

"Cut it out. I just don't want to see her get hurt."

"Nobody gets hurt if they walk out the way they're supposed to."

"I've known her since she was a kid. I mean, you know, I was her first. She's always been a *little* radical, but not to this extent. I think she's just a dupe."

And you're a dope, Robbins thought. The female of the radical species made a lot of the men seem like pussycats.

"I'd like to see if we can get her out." Perry's voice was hung up between stubbornness and pleading.

"Forget it. She won't do it."

"I'm going to try." Perry picked up the bullhorn.

Robbins started to take the horn away from him but stopped. Let him try. She wouldn't come out and might even tell him to go fuck himself. Let him learn the facts of life at first hand.

"With the engines going," Bullets Beall said, "you couldn't hear a word he said."

"It sometimes happens that way," Griese said. "An accident of timing."

Bullets pressed the remote-control button, and the television screen blanked out. "They didn't even mention your name once."

"I shun the limelight," Griese said. "The only reward I seek is to serve my country."

Bullets suppressed a giggle and offered her projectile breasts to Griese's lips.

"You laugh, my dear Bullets?"

"Only because I am so supremely joyous when you are fucking me. Bite them, please." He kept his lips closed. She straddled him and bent low to strike him sharp blows on the sides of his face with her breasts. "The whole civilized world will know who the hero of the affair is. I will tell the world myself."

"I told you it's of no importance to me."

Bullets giggled again and said, "Won't you please bite little Bullets' bullets?"

She forced a breast between his lips. He spat it out. "You must never forget that I am Eminence Griese," he said coldly. "Never forget who I am."

"Oh, Em darling, I never forget it for a moment."

He glanced up between her breasts, searching the vacuous face for irony. For an instant he thought he saw a remnant glint of laughter in her eyes, but then it was gone.

"I wish you had three peenies," Bullets said, "so that I could make love to all three of them at the same time."

A sentence from her porno hit. She was waiting for him to deliver the next line. "Each one in a different place," he said.

"Not place, orifice," Bullets said. "But seriously, I'm terribly proud of you."

"Well, if we're to be serious," Griese said, "so am I."

In the army Booth had had the reputation of being a hunch player. He had accepted that characterization until, one day, he had figured out that what seemed like a hunch was an instinctively triggered action that came out of almost unconscious observation. He simply got a head start on his intellect.

And so, as he ran down the springy cellar steps, he knew that he had been troubled by the length of Asbury's absence, and what had made him act was knowing that Asbury was unaware that Rowan had gotten off on the plane and, in fact, might not care anyway.

Asbury was not there. Booth's eyes widened in surprise, as if at a magician's trick, and for a single confused moment he thought that Asbury had somehow, and for some unfathomable reason, hidden in the casket. His eyes turned toward it and he saw a length of fuse and the kitchen timer dangling from under the lid. The timer was ticking. As he started toward the casket, the garage door was kicked open and Asbury burst into the cellar. Before the door had time to slam shut behind him he was already running. A dozen soft-drink bottles hung from a cord tied around his waist. The bottles were filled with a colorless liquid and wicks stuck out of their necks. Firebombs. There was a length of fuse in his mouth, the ends glowing, drooping down at both sides of his chin like a mandarin mustache.

"Asbury!"

He braced himself, but Asbury had the advantage of momentum. His lowered shoulder caught Booth in the chest and bowled him over. He broke his fall with his hands but still landed jarringly. Asbury ran by him and took the steps two at a time.

Booth got to his feet and was already running toward the stairs when he remembered the ticking. He turned and ran toward the casket, then stopped and looked at it blankly. The timer ticked loudly. The sound guided him in his ignorance. He curled his hand around the timer and jerked. It came free in his hand and something dropped with a thud inside the casket. He winced and hunched his shoulders. Nothing happened. The timer stopped ticking. It was at rest on zero.

He threw the timer away and ran for the stairs. He burst through the kitchen into the living room. Asbury was at the rear door, touching the wick of one of his firebombs to an end of the lit fuse in his mouth. He started running toward Asbury but he was too late. The door opened and the firebomb was already flying through the air. It struck and burst into flame, and in its light, and an instant before Asbury slammed the door shut, he heard a scream and saw a man jump up, his hair on fire. An incredibly lucky hit.

Almost before the fusillade of shotgun fire began, Booth shouted, "Down!" and threw himself on the floor, burying his head in his arms. He heard a tearing, splintering sound as slugs penetrated the wooden walls or ripped through windows and blinds, showering the room with bits of glass and fragments of plastic.

"Cover me!" Asbury screamed.

Booth rose to his knees as Asbury, a firebomb in his hand, loped toward the front door. He was graceful even with his burden of bottles. Booth saw Dover leap up and run crouching to the M-16 rifle at the front window, and he was already ripping shots off into the night as Asbury whipped the door open, took a long stride forward, and threw his firebomb. He remained poised there for a moment, his long arm still moving forward in a graceful follow-through, his legs braced apart, and Booth thought, He has an authentic star quality, he's a performer with style, and it's too bad that he must die to prove it.

The shotgun blast struck him in the chest and slammed him back against the doorjamb. He bounced off it, came upright for a moment, his back bloody where the slugs had torn an exit, and then pitched forward onto the porch.

If Robbins had not been rounding on Perry, screaming at him to order fire over the walkie-talkie, even though the others had already begun shooting, he might have hit the man in the doorway sooner. As it was, he saw the man's arm come forward and something bright streaking toward them by the time he was in position, the stock against his cheek, the figure in the doorway in the sights. He pulled the trigger and yelled as the figure slammed back against the doorjamb. There was an explosion behind them. Perry whimpered.

The blast surged back toward him and he felt the ground tremble, but the firebomb had sailed over their heads and exploded down the slope, where it burned brightly now. When he turned back, he saw that the door had been shut again. He fired at it with his second barrel and heard his slugs rip into it.

Perry yelled, "I'm hit."

A tiny fragment of glass glittered in Perry's bloody cheek. Robbins pinched it between his fingers and pulled it out.

He rolled back on his stomach, reloaded, and discharged both barrels at the window on the porch where an M-16 was firing. The loose blind sagged inward, then bellied out again with a jagged hole in it. Behind him the brush was burning,

throwing up a bright flickering curtain of light. The rifle fire
coming from the front window was low and close to them.
The shotgun fire continued from the other three sides of the
house.

"They're tearing the house apart," Perry yelled.

"Fuck this shit," Robbins said, "with that light behind us
we're giving that M-sixteen something to shoot at. I'm going
to lob some tear gas in there. Hand me the launcher."

"Launcher? Oh, Jesus, I must have left it back in the
car."

Robbins clenched his fist, and Perry ducked his bloody
face. Robbins said, "Listen to me, you dumb bastard, I'm going to try to drop a canister through that hole in the window.
I want you to cover me. Shoot at the muzzle flash in the window, and don't stop. Barrel at a time and reload as fast as you
can."

Perry ducked as a rifle bullet sped over his head. "He's
coming awful close."

"Then try to stop him, you stupid fuck."

He pulled himself up to level ground, drew the pin from
the tear-gas grenade, and with his fingers curled tightly
around the lever, began to run in a crouch toward the right-
hand end of the porch. He heard Perry firing. A rifle bullet
passed close by him, and he knew that the man at the window
had seen him. He dug in, pushing himself forward against
the hard spring of the ground. He put on a burst of speed
and reached the porch.

He paused for a second, then threw his leg over the porch
railing and pulled himself up. The rifle at the window had
stopped firing. He edged toward the window, hugging the
wall. He stopped just short of the window and released the
lever on the canister. He counted to four and then reached
over and flipped the canister through the hole in the blind.
He heard it go off inside the house, and almost at once the
choking stink of tear gas was pricking at his nose and throat.
He vaulted over the porch railing and streaked across the
dead lawn toward the embankment. He threw himself down
beside Perry and grabbed up his shotgun.

"Get ready. When the sonofabitches start coming through the door, we'll blast the shit out of them."

Almost with detachment, Booth had watched Dover roll away from the window, stretch out his foot, and kick the door shut, then roll smoothly back to the window, where he began to fire again. Asbury's death must have shocked him, but it hadn't impaired his efficiency.

He roused himself and started to climb to his feet—to what end he never knew—when he saw Dover rock back from the window, blood and hair flying from his ruined head.

He shouted Dover's name, although he knew he was dead, and started toward him in a crouch. Something came rocketing through the window. It rolled past him, and in the instant before it exploded, he knew that it was a tear-gas canister. The cloudy whitish smoke poured out into the room. Almost at once his eyes began to sting and nausea welled up in him.

He had been teargassed several times at demonstrations, and he knew how effective it could be even in the open. Here in the room it would be intolerable. He began to choke, and the coughs of the others were like an echo of his own. He staggered to his feet, groping for Caro, but his eyes were pouring tears and he couldn't find her. Somebody was pushing him toward the door, and he stumbled forward, choking, with the acid of vomit rising in his throat. Gulping, gasping, he knew that no matter what lay on the other side of the door—mutilation, death, the end to everything—he couldn't remain inside.

He didn't know, then or later, whether it was he or Doc who opened the door, only that both of them were crowding through it to the sweet promise of untainted air, and then his legs were taken away from him and he was falling.

28

Manero was listening to the Flotsams doing their big hit, "Tears Are Turning to Icicles," when the announcer broke in.

"We interrupt our program for a bulletin."

He turned on his pillow and faced the radio with a frown of annoyance that he hoped would kill the announcer on the spot.

"The casket of the Unknown Warrior of World War Two has been recovered. The entire gang of perpetrators has been apprehended. That is the entire story to this moment. Stay tuned for further developments. To repeat. . . ."

Manero looked up at the ceiling and sighed. There were a million Maneros, and it would take time, of course, but eventually they would trace his relationship to his *cugino*. Not the Twos, not those dumb bastards. But the FBI. They were slow, and not all that fucking smart, but they were thorough. There were a million Maneros, but only one whose motor pool had had a missing M-292 van.

He waited until "Tears Are Turning to Icicles" ended, hoping for another announcement. But instead a new record started.

Doc wouldn't say anything, assuming he was still alive, but the family relationship was bound to come out.

Manero spoke to the ceiling: "So how many motor-pool sergeants do *you* know who have a numbered account in a Swiss bank? And a validated passport? And two thousand dollars in mad money under the mattress?"

It was a pity to leave the best job he had ever had in his life, the most rewarding in terms of money, power, and laughs. *Bless you, my army, you have been a good provider.*

Surely there must be a way. Call the Twos and pin it on the major? Wake up the duty officer and lay it on him: Been wrestling with my conscience all day, sir. The major. I respect the rank, sir, but such a heinous crime! Sir, it is my very own major, a subversive from the word go, who supplied that van. . . . Fucking Two would pop a gland, call out some skinheads, rout the poor major out of the sack. . . .

No way. Doc is my *cugino.*

Brazil was antipodean, right? This was November, which meant that it was spring there. Couldn't take everything, so dress for the weather, right?

Manero got out of bed. Leisurely, without haste, folding his clothes with finicky care, he began to pack his bags.

People came and went and returned, more or less aimlessly, or perhaps in curiosity that couldn't be sated by a single visit. Sometimes they came singly, but more frequently in pairs, chatting tonelessly, callously objective, like doctors making rounds in a charity ward. They would talk about what had happened or would happen and then move off, but almost always they left something behind, some clue that enabled Booth to piece together a pattern of events.

The first one who acknowledged their sentience, who spoke to them directly, was a giant hairy man—red beard and curls—who squatted beside them, grinning.

"You two studs have made me rich and famous." To Booth's astonishment the voice of this raffish figure was the voice on the bullhorn that had identified itself as an FBI agent. "I just want you to know that I'm much obliged."

They were lying at the edge of the level ground, above the beach. Booth could remember being hauled down off the porch and across the scrubby lawn, his legs dragging, the pain excruciating. The voices then had been loud, ragged, almost hysterical, filled with rage and pride, the euphoria of victory. They went back for Doc and pulled him across the grass, too, and let him flop like a rag doll.

Booth had vomited in great upheavals that emptied him,

torturing his spine and chest, racking his shattered legs with incredible pain. He didn't try to look at his legs because he saw no purpose in confirming brutalized flesh and splintered bone and bloody skin. But it did occur to him, with detachment, that he was alive only because someone, whether through errant aim or a form of mercy, had fired low and, instead of cutting him in half, had merely ruined his legs.

The memory of other tear gassings had instructed him on what he could do about the agony of his eyes. He had raised up on his elbows and faced the dark waters, where the chill wind whipped in and blew away the gas, at least moderating the burning pain.

He had helped Doc into a sitting position and faced him into the wind, forcing down bile when his hands sank into a shifting, jellied mass of blood and lacerated flesh and mucus. Doc had murmured in protest and perhaps passed out, because his eyes had shut. He had painstakingly pried them open so that the breeze could cleanse them. Booth let him down gently, and Doc lay still.

He was groping for his pulse when Doc opened his eyes and said, "Let me take a look at your wounds."

"I'm fine," Booth said. "Can I do something for you?"

"Who's the doctor around here?"

Two men drifted over, for once silent, just staring down at them from above. Maybe they were simple blood freaks, Booth thought.

Doc said, "Where is everybody?"

Booth said, "Can you get a blanket for my friend? It's cold and he's shivering."

The two men said nothing, but, as if aggrieved, moved off abruptly.

"What about the others?" Doc asked.

"You passed out for a while," Booth said.

"Nature's own remedy. I feel great now, well rested."

"Asbury is dead," Booth said.

"I saw that."

"Dover was killed at the window, just before the tear gas came in."

"I know. It took his head right off his body."

"Raphael and Caro ran out the back door. Raphael is dead."

"Caro," Doc said.

"Caro is all right. They didn't fire at her."

Doc chuckled. "That's the advantage of dealing with squares. They still think woman is a weaker vessel. I'm glad, Ken."

"Yes," Booth said. "She's out near the road in a police car. They won't let her talk to us."

"What's to say?" Doc gave one of his minimal shrugs.

"They've put in a call for an ambulance. It should be here soon."

Two policemen—tan trousers with a vertical baby-blue stripe—came across the lawn and stood over them with folded arms. Before they turned away, one of them said, "That's her boyfriend?"

"Yeah, the old guy."

"I'd like to speak to Caroline Meade," Booth said. "Please?"

Without reply the two men moved off.

A moment later they heard a motor racketing down the road. Booth told Doc to hold on, that the ambulance was coming. But it was a photographer, a grossly fat kid in his early twenties, who began shooting pictures gluttonously. He stood, sat, lay prone, bent into their faces, their wounds, blinding them with his flash. Finally he went off, but they caught a reflection of his flash, so he was still shooting: the other bodies, perhaps Caro huddled in the back of the police car, perhaps the cop whose hair had been burned off by Asbury's first firebomb. Exclusive photos by local photographer, Booth thought. Another one we will have made rich and famous.

Three men in windbreakers loomed up.

"Where's the ambulance?" Booth said.

One of the men said, "You dirty bastards, you were going to blow up those blessed bones."

"Can you bring us a blanket?"

"Thank God we were in time, you fucking Antichrists."

The man who had spoken hawked up phlegm. Booth

braced himself, but the man thought better of it. He kept his mouthful of phlegm, and he and his silent companions went away.

"Thank God we were in time." Doc was trying to laugh, and Booth became alarmed. He was too sick to laugh; everything might tumble out of the gaping hole in his body. "Blessed bones. Oh, boy."

Booth forced himself to think about what had happened. The operation was a success—Rowan was free—but a number of the patients had died. How many? He started to count: Asbury, Raphael, Dover, don't forget the relief commander . . . but he lost interest. It was too remote from his world, which consisted of the piece of ground he lay on, and Doc beside him, and the wind off the dark waters, and his shattered legs, and the tall figures that kept coming and going. It was a small world, but it was all that mattered.

A lone man was standing over them. He wore the police uniform, he had blond hair, there was dried blood on one side of his face.

"Which one is Booth?"

Booth raised his hand, palm out, as if responding to a roll call.

"You're Caro's friend?"

"Yes."

"You are? I'm Perry Knorr."

Yes, Caro's old boyfriend. We have a kinship, Booth thought, we're brothers of sorts, we both loved Caro Meade. Perhaps Knorr felt the bond, too. His voice was gentle.

"Caro is all right. She isn't hurt."

"I'd like to speak to her."

"I'm sorry, I can't allow that." He paused, awkward. "But if you want me to tell her anything. . . ."

You couldn't ask a former lover to serve as the messenger for a declaration of love. "I'm sorry. Just tell her I'm sorry."

Perry nodded. "About the ambulance. There was a road accident. But it should be here pretty soon."

He hesitated, as if he might say more, but turned away and went back toward the house over the bristly lawn.

Doc spoke up abruptly, as if he had been waiting impatiently for Perry to leave. "Back in the house—remember?—I was telling you about the remains when we were rudely interrupted."

"The ambulance should be here soon," Booth said.

"The blessed bones." Doc's voice was weak but persistent. "Gray bones and leathery skin, an arm twisted half off by the blast, the hand missing, blown away at the wrist. The skull crushed and split, the spine bent out of shape. But enough left for the trained eye to analyze. You following me?"

"Yes," Booth said soothingly. "You're the doctor."

"Nothing left of the face, the genitals, other organs that the bacteria had gotten at. But old Doc Manero checked the width of the shoulders, the size of the bones, the shape of the pelvis. . . ." Doc chuckled. "It's a reasonable assumption that if you're tearing off a quickie in a barn in the middle of a war, you don't get fancy. You do the old missionary position, with the man on top. Correct?"

Booth was scarcely listening. He looked out over the water and thought that in the distance, dimly, he could make out the battered, unsinkable target ship. He remembered how he had identified with it last night, when he had sat on the porch with Caro, the breeze ruffling the hairs on his bare legs. Well, he had overrated himself. The ship was still afloat, but he had sunk.

"If the grunt—excuse me, GI—was in the superior position, his body protected her. It's possible, right? Along come the graves-registration doggies—doggies okay for your war, Ken?—and they sift through what's left of the barn. They find a stiff and toss it into the bag—"

Booth heard a siren in the near distance. "The ambulance is coming." Suddenly he caught the drift of Doc's words. He whipped his head around.

"They picked up the wrong pieces," Doc said. "It's a girl."